THE
ESCAPEMENT

By K. J. Parker

THE FENCER TRILOGY
Colours in the Steel
The Belly of the Bow
The Proof House

THE SCAVENGER TRILOGY
Shadow
Pattern
Memory

THE ENGINEER TRILOGY
Devices and Desires
Evil for Evil
The Escapement

THE
ESCAPEMENT

The Engineer Trilogy
Book Three

K. J. PARKER

www.orbitbooks.net

ORBIT

First published in Great Britain in 2007 by Orbit

A CIP catalogue record for this book
is available from the British Library.

ISBN 978-1-84149-279-7

Typeset in Horley by M Rules
Printed and bound in Great Britain by
Clays Ltd, St Ives plc

Orbit
An imprint of
Little, Brown Book Group
100 Victoria Embankment
London EC4Y 0DY

For Melanie Ann, Ashley Kate, Polly Esther and their
sister, whatsername;

And for Gabby Nemeth, who's been forced to
read practically everything I've written

Chapter One

"The quickest way to a man's heart," the instructor said, "is proverbially through his stomach, but if you want to get into his brain, I recommend the eye socket."

He reached out with the tip of the rapier and tapped it against the signet ring he'd hung by a strand of cotton from the arm of the ornate gilt lamp bracket. The ring began to sway slowly backwards and forwards, like a pendulum. He took a step back, then raised the sword again, and slid his front foot smoothly across the tiles as he lunged. The point of the rapier tinkled against the ring as it passed through its centre.

"That's very good," Psellus said. "I don't think I'll be able to do that."

The instructor nodded. "Not to begin with," he said. "You've got to work up to it. But try it anyway."

Psellus frowned, then nodded. "You never know," he said. He closed his hand around the grip of his rapier. ('That's it. Imagine you're holding a mouse; tight enough to stop it escaping, but don't crush its ribs.") He felt a stabbing pain in the overworked tendons of his elbow as he raised his hand into the third guard, and knew he'd regret all this later. Twenty years holding nothing heavier than a pen, and now he would insist on learning to fence.

"Just look at the ring," the instructor said. "Forget about the sword, just the ring."

Psellus felt his muscles tense, which was quite wrong, of course.

He'd been told about that, and it had made sense and he'd under-stood, but for some reason he couldn't stop himself doing it. That was what came of fifty years of imagining what it'd be like to fence with a real sword.

"When you're ready," the instructor sighed.

That meant, *get on with it*, freely translated from the diplomatic; so he snatched a half-mouthful of breath, fixed all his attention on the tip of the sword and prodded desperately at the ring. The rapier point missed it by a handspan, glanced off the base of the bracket and gouged a small chip of plaster out of the wall.

"Not quite there yet," the instructor said, in a very calm voice. "You'd have taken a chunk out of his ear, but that'd probably just make him hate you. Now then."

Psellus lowered the sword until the tip rested on the tiles. It was hopeless, he reckoned. For one thing, they'd given him a sword that was far too heavy. You couldn't expect to be able to do fine work with a great big heavy thing, it'd be like trying to write with a scaffolding pole. He'd mentioned this several times but the instructor had politely ignored him.

"It's basically the same idea as everything else we've covered so far," the instructor was saying. "You start off slow and easy, just leaning gently forward and *putting* the point in the ring; and when you've done that a thousand times or so, you can gradually pick up speed and force until it's right. So, as slow as you like, lift the sword and just point at the ring, like you're pointing with your finger."

Ten times (which meant only nine hundred and ninety to go), and then Psellus said, "I'm sorry, I think I'll have to stop now, my elbow's hurting rather a lot. Perhaps we can try again tomorrow, if that would be convenient for you."

"Of course." The instructor reached out and tugged the ring off the cotton, which dangled like a strand of dusty cobweb. "If you can possibly make time to practise before then, I think you'll find it very useful."

He put his rapier back in its case, buckled up the strap, bowed ever so politely and left. When he'd gone, Psellus walked slowly back to his desk and sat in his chair for a while, unable to think about anything much apart from the pain in his elbow. So much for fencing. It would have been nice to be able to do it; and now that he was the chairman of Necessary Evil, in effect the supreme ruler of the City, he'd assumed that the ability would somehow have come to him, as part of the package. Rulers, princes could do that sort of thing; they could fence and ride and shoot and dance minuets and fly hawks and sing serenades while accompanying themselves on the rebec or psaltery, because those sorts of thing were what princes did; you never heard or read about a prince who couldn't hunt or swordfight, so obviously there was some kind of basic connection between the job and the ability. But maybe it didn't apply to chairmen, or maybe there was rather more to it than that. Still, at least he was trying; and perhaps nine hundred and ninety more tentative jabs with the very heavy sword would turn him into what everybody seemed to think he was these days. Or maybe not.

The truth is, he thought as he reached across his desk and uncapped his inkwell, I seek to make myself ridiculous, because I know I shouldn't be here. A pretender (the perfect word; ever since it had occurred to him, he'd been hugging it to himself like a child's toy) ought to have ridiculous pretensions, such as fencing, riding, archery, dance, falconry, all of which he's hopeless at, and that's how the people come to realise he's not the true prince. Tomorrow, if there's time, I must find someone to teach me how to dance. It's practically my duty.

If there's time. He looked down at his desk. If he was really a prince, someone else would be reading all these reports for him, and he'd have all the time in the world. He'd have a chancellor or a grand vizier, either bald and enormously fat or long, dark and saturnine, discreetly running the empire while His Imperial Highness rode to hounds or recited poetry to beautiful, empty-headed young women.

He lifted his head to look out of the window, and thought about his enemy. Duke Valens was reckoned to be the finest huntsman in the world, so clearly he was a proper prince. It should have followed, therefore, that Valens was a pinhead, the natural quarry of clever, austere predators like himself. But maybe Valens wasn't a proper prince either; too intelligent, or else how had it come about that he was bearing down on the City at the head of an army of a million savages, while the ruler of the Perpetual Republic flounced and panted up and down a chalk line, trying to master the rudiments of the low guard?

Perhaps, he thought, that's why I want to be able to fence and dance and hunt and compose pastoral eclogues in trochaic pentameters;

because I secretly believe that these accomplishments will turn me into someone who can also command armies and fight battles, and save my city from the million savages. Quite possibly there's a grain of sense in that, except that I've left it far too late to start learning all that stuff now. Somewhere he'd read that in order to fight your enemy, you had to understand him; more than that, you had to *become* him. It had struck him as extremely profound at the time, although something a little less inspirational and a little more practical would've been even better; how to run an efficient commissariat, for example, or the basics of fortifying against artillery.

That was, of course, the problem. The Perpetual Republic had a complete monopoly of all skills, trades, sciences and crafts, except one; it had no idea how to fight a war. There hadn't been any need; not until now, when mercenaries refused to sign up for fear of the Cure Hardy and the murderous field artillery designed and built by the defector Ziani Vaatzes. So, quite unexpectedly, and far too late in life, the citizens of the Republic were straining themselves trying to learn to be soldiers, as improbable and ill-fated an enterprise as Lucao Psellus learning the smallsword, the stock and the case of rapiers. Hopeless, of course; the sheer helplessness of the situation was apparent from the fact that Guild politics had practically ground to a halt. Suddenly, nobody wanted to run or be in charge of anything, there was no opposition, no factions; just a blind, desperate consensus of goodwill, support and pitiful enthusiasm, led by the unwilling ignorant under the supreme authority of a jumped-up clerk.

A million savages under arms; well, that was what everybody was saying. The intelligence reports put the figure at a mere eight hundred thousand, including the Vadani cavalry and the Eremians. Psellus closed his eyes and tried to imagine eight hundred thousand of anything, but he couldn't. How many bees were there in a hive, or leaves in a forest? He believed in big numbers, that there could exist a million silver thalers, in the context of a budget deficit, or eight hundred thousand rivets, packed in barrels COD at Lonazep. But men, human beings, with weapons, on their way here to burn down the City . . . What strategic advantage did eight hundred thousand have to offer over, say, six hundred thousand? Or were numbers of that order of magnitude as much a liability as an asset? He didn't know, of course, but he knew that there were answers to that kind of question, and without that knowledge he'd soon be presiding over the fall of the Republic and the annihilation of its people.

He opened the door and said, "Hello?"

Immediately (he couldn't get used to it; like an echo, only faster) a clerk materialised, like a genie out of a bottle. Psellus took a moment to look at him, because it was like looking in a mirror. The clerk was in his fifties, bald, with wispy grey clouds over his ears, soft-chinned and stout, like a pig being fattened for bacon. It was always my ambition, Psellus reflected, to be a senior clerk in the administration office. Instead . . .

"Go to the library," he said, "and get out all the books you can find about military logistics."

Silent pause, long enough to count up to two. "Military . . ."

"Logistics." Psellus scrambled for words, gave up. "Anything called *The Art of War* or *The Soldier's Mirror* or anything with war or soldiers in the title."

The clerk looked at him as though he was mad. But Psellus was getting used to that. "And then," he went on, "I want you to read them."

The clerk said nothing. It was the sort of silence you could have built houses on.

"You may want to get someone to help you with that," Psellus continued. "Anyway, read them, and I want you to make an epitome with references, anything to do with supplying an army – food and hay and boots and so on – how much of everything you need per day, and how much it costs, and how you get it to the soldiers in the field; carts and roads and changes of draught horses – I'm sure you've got the idea. On my desk by tomorrow evening, please."

The clerk gave him a horrified stare, as though he'd just been ordered to eat his grandfather. Psellus knew that look, too. He'd worn it often enough himself. "Get as many people on it as you need," he added, because he knew the clerk would like that. Being allowed to order his fellow clerks around would go some way towards making up for the bizarre and unnatural nature of the assignment. Which reminded him. "I'm sorry," he said. "I don't think I know your name."

The clerk hesitated, then said, "Catorzes. Simuo Catorzes."

Psellus nodded, as if to signify that that was indeed the answer he'd been looking for. "I'm appointing you as my research assistant. My *chief* research assistant. Do you think you'll be up to the job?"

Catorzes hesitated again, then nodded grimly. "Of course," he said; then, almost reluctantly, "Thank you. I'll, um, do my best."

"I'm sure you will."

There, he thought, as he sat down again at his desk, I've done something. Quite possibly something useful, although that remains to be seen. Have we actually got any books about fighting wars? Yes, we must have, because the Copyists' Guild copies and binds all the books in the known world for export, though we never actually read them ourselves, and I'm sure we must keep copies, if only out of habit. Of course, there's no guarantee that any of the books is any good; probably they're just collections of bits copied out of other books copied out of other books by men who've never been in a battle in their lives. But real princes buy them from us, so they must have something in them, if only . . .

He looked down at his hands; ten soft brown worms attached to two flat cakes of putty. I *must* cope, he told himself. I must find a way of coping, because there's nobody else but me. I know I'm not fit to be in charge of a war, I know I'm hopelessly ignorant and not particularly clever. But unless I find a way of coping, a million savages will come and break open the city like a crabshell and pick us all out like shreds of meat; and war can't be all that difficult if a lot of bone-headed princes can do it, surely.

He glanced up at the opposite wall, where the clock stood. It was a Pattern Fifty-Seven, the best specification of all, guaranteed accurate to within an hour a year if properly sited and maintained. If the City fell, of course, there would be no more clocks, because nobody else in the whole wide world knew how to make them. How long, he wondered, would it take for the clock to be reinvented, and how long after that before anybody was skilled enough to build a clock up to the standards of a Pattern Fifty-Seven? A thousand years, possibly; or never. If we die, everything dies with us . . .

No, he reflected, not quite. If Valens and the savages come and the walls are breached and we're slaughtered like ants in a crack between flagstones, there'll still be one of us left. Ziani Vaatzes could build a clock, if he wanted to and he set his mind to it. Ziani Vaatzes, the abominator, our greatest enemy and civilisation's only hope.

He thought about Vaatzes; studying him so intensely for so long, finally meeting him in the empty streets of Civitas Vadanis. To the best of his knowledge, Psellus had never been in love; but if he had to imagine what love must be like, his nearest reference would be how he felt about Ziani Vaatzes, the supreme enemy. Which was strange, and more than a little disturbing, since Vaatzes was to blame for everything. He'd brought the war here, like a man carrying the plague – infected, a victim and also a predator, a weapon, an enemy. Under other circumstances, Psellus liked to believe, they'd have been friends, good friends (which was, of course, absurd, since a ranking Guild official would never condescend to mix with manual workers, outside of circumstances that in themselves precluded any possibility of friendship). Perhaps it's because I'm so isolated from ordinary people that the only one I ever bothered to try and understand fascinates me so. In which case, I'm even more pathetic than I ever imagined.

Be that as it may; the clock told him it was a few minutes to noon, at which time he was due to meet with the Strategy and Tactics Committee to discuss the progress of the war . . .

"I can't help thinking," he told them, and they just looked at him, as they always did, "that we might as well be logs meeting in the grate to discuss the fire." He paused. They were waiting for him to say something – *anything* – they could possibly construe as coherent. "Siano, you're in charge of intelligence. Where are they now?"

Siano Bossas, Drapers' Guild; a closed box of a man, with the biggest feet Psellus had ever seen in his life. "According to our contacts in Jasca, they crossed the Redwater two days ago, which puts them somewhere between Lopa and Boc Polizan." He paused, well aware that Psellus didn't have a clue where the Redwater, Lopa or Boc Polizan were. Neither, Psellus suspected, did Siano Bossas.

Psellus nodded gravely. "Could somebody please go out to the front office and fetch in the map? I had one drawn," he explained. "There didn't seem to be one that showed all the places you've been telling me about, I suppose they hadn't been built yet when the specifications for the maps were drawn up, so they couldn't officially exist. Strictly speaking, I suppose that means I've committed an abomination, but never mind. We really ought to know where all these places are, don't you think?"

It wasn't a very good map, by Guild standards. The calligraphy was poor, and it wasn't even coloured in. But it did show Lopa, Boc Polizan and the Redwater, and if it was drawn to anything like scale . . .

"Nine days," Psellus said, after he'd put down his dividers. "In theory," he added. "But I don't suppose they'll actually be here in nine days, because of lines of supply and things like that. It'd help," he added mildly, "if we knew where they were getting their food and forage from." He bent his head and looked at the map. "Does anybody know anything about this countryside here? I mean, is it farmland or moor or heath or what?" He waited for a moment or so, then added, "Someone must know, surely."

Apparently, nobody did. Psellus straightened his back and looked round at the empty faces surrounding him. "Fine," he said. "Now, I've ordered a study of military logistics, which I hope will tell us what we need to know about how armies are fed and supplied. What I'd like you to do for me is find out everything you can about the country between *there*" – he prodded at the map –" and the City. I want to know whether they can feed themselves with what they can find and steal as they go along, or whether they need to carry their supplies in carts from somewhere else. Also, it'd be helpful to know something about the roads, that sort of thing. Also, it's really no good at all relying on little bits and pieces of news we get from carters and carriers. We need proper scouts to observe their movements and report back. Can someone see to that, please?" No volunteers; he looked round and chose someone at random. "Feria, that can be your job. Now then, what else?"

Slowly and painfully, like a snail climbing a wall, he led and dragged them through food reserves, materiel procurement, finance, the condition of the City walls, recruitment and basic training; things he'd heard about, mostly, without really knowing what they meant, so that he had to reconstruct them from first principles as he went along. It was like trying to read and understand a book whose pages had all been lost, so that all he had to go on was the list of contents.

"Arms and munitions production," he said at last, and he could sense the relief, since finally they'd reached a subject they all understood. "I'd like one of you to be my permanent liaison with the ordnance factory; Galeazo, you know the setup there as well as anybody. Do you think you could get me copies of the production schedules, so we can be sure they're making the right quantities of the right things. Wall-mounted artillery's an obvious priority, but we're also going to have to kit out a large number of infantry in a hurry, as soon as Lanuo here has recruited them for us. You'll need to talk to the Tailors and Clothiers as well, boots and helmet linings and padded jackets – what's the word, gambesons; those things you wear under your armour to cushion the blows. I know we used to make them for export, it's just a matter of getting everything up together so every helmet we issue's got a lining to go with it. Just common sense, really."

As he spoke, he thought: this is hopeless. We don't know what we're doing, and they're all desperate to leave it up to me; only because they're afraid, but that doesn't really make it any better. The fact is, we can't, *I* can't fight a war against eight hundred thousand men, any more than I can build a Fifty-Seven clock or a water-mill. We don't have a specification for a war, and there isn't enough time to write one.

The meeting ended and they left, as quickly as possible without being ostentatiously anxious to escape. When they'd gone, Psellus sat for a long time, staring out of the window. He had the best view in the Guildhall: the grounds, with the formal gardens in the middle, surrounded by the cloister gardens, each with its own fountain and arbor. It wasn't beautiful, in any meaningful sense, but there again, it wasn't supposed to be.

Very well, then, he decided. I don't know about war and I can't fight eight hundred thousand men. But I know Ziani Vaatzes and I can fight one man, and maybe that's all I need to do.

Simuo Catorzes handed in his summary on time. It covered both sides of twelve sheets of charter paper, was copiously annotated with references to the source material, and would probably have been exactly what Psellus wanted if the handwriting had been legible.

"Excellent," he said. "Now, could you please take it away and get someone else to copy it out again?"

Psellus spent an hour reading a report he didn't understand about proposed reforms of fiscal policy, then left his office, walked down three flights of stairs and several hundred yards of corridor, and eventually found the library.

He'd never been in there before, of course. No need. Ever since he'd passed the professional examinations and qualified for the clerical grade, he'd spent his life reading, but could still count on his fingers the number of actual books he'd had occasion to open in the course of his work. He stood in the doorway for a moment and stared, like a man on a cloudless night looking up at the stars.

He'd checked the regulations. Every book acquired by the Copyists for the purposes of publication reverted to the Guildhall library after they'd finished with it. The room – if it was laid down to grass, it would easily graze two milking cows and their calves for a week – was lined with shelves that reached up from floor to ceiling, and every shelf was full. In accordance with Guild policy, every book was the same height, and identically bound, with the title written in tiny lettering at the base of the spine. The only thing like it that Psellus had ever seen was the review of troops, just before the army left for Eremia.

At the far end, under a long, thin window, was a desk, behind which a small man sat on a tall backless stool. The sunlight glowed on his bald head.

"Excuse me," Psellus asked him. "Are you the librarian?"

The bald man looked at him. "Have you got an appointment?"

"My name is Lucao Psellus."

The librarian's eyes widened a little. "How can I help you?"

"I'm looking for . . ." *A book*, he nearly said. "I need to see everything you've got on the fortification of cities against artillery."

The librarian breathed out slowly through his nose. "I'll have to look in the general catalogue," he said. "If you'll bear with me for a moment."

He hopped down off his stool like a sparrow and walked quickly to a table on which rested a single enormous book; each page as wide as an arm, as tall as a leg. "There was a clerk in here a day or so ago," the librarian said. "He was looking for military books." Something in his tone of voice suggested that military books ranked about equal in his estimation with pornography. "With any luck – ah yes. Case 104, shelf twelve. If you'd care to follow me."

Psellus found the click his heels made on the wooden floor embarrassing, and he tried walking on the sides of his feet. It helped, a little. "Case 104," the librarian announced proudly, like an explorer on a mountaintop. "Shelf twelve." He looked up, counting under his breath, then put his foot on the bottom shelf, reached up and started to climb, each shelf a rung. The bookcase trembled under his weight.

"Fortification," he said, and hung for a moment by his left hand as he picked a book off a shelf, clamped it between his teeth and clambered down backwards. He wiped a drop of spittle off the cover with his sleeve before handing it over.

"Thank you," Psellus said. "Is that all?"

The librarian looked at him as though he didn't understand the question. "Was there something else you wanted?" he asked.

Psellus shook his head. "Is it all right if I take this with me?" he said. "I may need to hold on to it for quite some time."

The librarian took a moment or so to reply. "Of course," he said, in a rather tight voice. "I'll make a note."

For some reason, Psellus couldn't bring himself to open the book or even look at the spine until he was back in his office; even there, he had to resist an urge to wedge a chair against the door. He cleared space on his desk, then peered at the writing on the white pasted-on label:

Varus Paterculus

Psellus frowned. A Vadani name. The book creaked loudly as he opened it and turned to the title page, where he could find the date when it was acquired and copied. A little mental arithmetic. The book was two hundred and seven years old.

Well, he thought. On the other hand, we have nothing else. He turned to the first page: a dedication, in Mannerist dactylic pentameters. He skipped all that.

Of the various kinds of artillery; in particular, the various types of engine used by the Perpetual Republic of Mezentia.

Psellus smiled. Ah, he thought, Specification. Military technology was the one exception to the Republic's most inflexible rule. Even so, the siege engines (drawn to scale in meticulous detail, with numbered parts) were essentially the same as the ones he'd seen on the walls a week ago, when he'd made a rather self-conscious tour of inspection. Whoever Varus Paterculus was, he had an excellent eye. After scanning a couple of pages, Psellus reluctantly skipped the rest of the chapter, and moved on to:

Of the various devices whereby a city may be defended from the said engines.

He tried to read on, but he couldn't. The diagrams, he assumed, were supposed to represent fortified cities, seen from the air; but they made no sense. On each page was a shape; abstract, symmetrical, perfect. The simplest were like ornate, many-pointed stars. Others were like gears from some extraordinarily sophisticated machine, or blades for a circular saw designed to cut through some desperately resilient material, or frost patterns on a pane of glass. After staring at a dozen or so, Psellus leafed forward until he found text.

The explanation helped, though not much. The basic theory was that a city under siege needed to be protected against siege engines and sappers. A plain, straight wall meant that the defenders' engines and archers had a very limited arc in which they could shoot down at the enemy, who would be safe in any event once they reached the foot of the wall. To give the defenders a better field of fire, it was desirable to build projections at regular intervals. The simplest ones were triangular, like the teeth of a saw. These offered opportunities to shoot straight ahead, and also sideways, at attackers venturing into the V-shaped gaps between the projections. Faced with these, however, the attacker would inevitably react by digging trenches, zigzagging across the open ground in front of the city like a mountain path, so that his army could approach the walls in safety. This could be countered by making the shape of the projections more elaborate. Instead of a simple V offering only three directions to shoot in, the defender's mantlets and ravelins (the terms weren't explained) should be pentagonal or hexagonal, multifaceted as a jewel, so that wherever the enemy led his trench, one face of the defensive works should always be in line with it and able to shoot down into it. Furthermore, since a determined attacker with plentiful manpower would sooner or later over-run or undermine even the best defence, there should be two, three, or even four concentric rings of fortification, banked up on mantlets and toothed with ravelins so that the inner rings could harass any assault on the outer rings by shooting over the lower defenders' heads. The best material for building such works was not stone, which shattered under the impact of heavy missiles, but sand and soft earth turfed over and retained inside simple shells of treble-skinned brick; such defences being capable of withstanding intense bombardment without shattering, and also frustrating the sapper, since an attempt at undermining would simply result in a fall of earth that would stop up and smother the sap . . .

Psellus closed the book. Sooner or later – sooner, he was very much afraid – he'd have to open it again, and try and wrap his feeble mind around it. But not now. More than anybody else in Mezentia, he flattered himself, he knew his own limitations. If he tried to read any more, the tremendous weight of information would cave in on him and bury him, like the wretched sappers . . . Well, he said to himself, I asked a question. I can't really complain about getting an answer, even if it's so huge it'd take a hundred men a lifetime to understand it. He remembered a story he'd heard when he was a boy, about a tiny doorway in the side of a mountain that led into another world; vast plains and mountains under unlimited skies, all contained inside a little door. Closed, the book was just a flat brown thing; you could put a couple of reports on top of it and bury it completely, so you wouldn't know it was there. Open, it led to something monstrous and huge; reading it, he thought, would be an undertaking on a par with invading a large and hostile country, and once you ventured inside, there was more than a chance you'd never get out again.

He stood up, opened his door and called, "Hello."

Simuo Catorzes appeared from just out of sight. "What can I . . . ?"

"Come in here," Psellus said. "On the desk, look."

Catorzes looked sideways at the spine of the closed book, and said nothing.

"Did you read that one?"

No words, just a nod. Then: "I didn't include it in the epitome."

"Oh." Psellus frowned. "Why not?"

A slight pause before Catorzes answered. "It's very old," he said. "Out of date."

"I don't think so," Psellus replied mildly. "I think it looks very useful."

There was resentment in Catorzes' eyes, working itself up into hatred. "If you say so," he said. "I'll add it to the—"

Psellus sighed. "No, don't bother," he said. "You've got enough to do, I'll look at it myself. But I want you to search through the books of maps; I seem to remember seeing plans of towns and cities – quite old, some of them. I want to know if anybody's ever actually built a city with all those sticking-out bits."

Catorzes smiled; just a hint of malice. "Ravelins," he said.

"Exactly, yes. What I'm getting at is, was all this stuff ever *real*, or is it just a lot of ideas and complicated drawings? That's the trouble with books," he added bitterly. "There's no way of knowing whether what's in them is valuable practical advice or just someone's flight of fancy." He stopped, as a strange thought struck him. "Two hundred years ago," he said. "Do you know much history?"

"Me?" Catorzes scowled, as though he'd just been accused of a particularly disgusting crime. "Well, yes, I suppose so. As much as anybody else does."

"Ah." Psellus smiled. "Probably about as much as I do, then. And it's just occurred to me that I know hardly anything about what things were like two hundred years ago. Maybe there were cities built like the ones in that book, only we don't know about them because they aren't there any more. I have an idea that the Republic fought a great many wars a few centuries ago, mopping up the little city states that used to exist hereabouts, until only Eremia and the Vadani and the Cure Doce were left. It may well be that they fortified their cities against our artillery – that's why there's pictures of our engines in the book, and details of how they work and what damage they can do." He thought for a moment, then went on: "In which case it stands to reason that either they didn't do what it says in the book, or they didn't do it well enough, or the book's just plain wrong. I guess you'd have to go out with a sextant and a ream of drawing paper and find the shapes in the grass where the old cities used to be. But we haven't got time for that, obviously." He looked up and saw that Catorzes was fidgeting. It's embarrassing, listening to your superiors talking drivel. "See if you can find those maps," he said. "And ask the Architects' if they can send me someone who knows about building walls."

A look of panic flickered in Catorzes' eyes, and Psellus felt a pang of sympathy. How would he have liked it, when he'd been a clerk, if his master had given him an order like that? "Excuse me," Catorzes said slowly, "but they'll want a bit more than that. I mean, building walls is what they all do, surely . . ."

"Building walls *quickly*."

He could sense the relief, verging on joy, that the clerk felt as he finally escaped. He envied it. More than anything in the world, he wanted to change places with him. Perhaps he could trick him – lure him into the office, slam the door, lock it and run away, leaving poor Catorzes to rule the Republic. That wouldn't work, of course.

Nine days.

The Cure Doce ambassador was a small, wiry man with short white hair, enormous hands and a nose like a wedge. As soon as Psellus walked into the room he jumped up, as though the door was a sear that tripped the catch that held him in his seat. He spoke in snips, like a man cutting foil.

"Thank you for seeing me on such short notice," he said. "Time, obviously . . ."

Psellus nodded vaguely. "Quite," he said. "They tell me – please, sit down – they tell me the savages are nine days' ride from here. Time is therefore very much on my mind at the moment." He sat down and wondered, as he always did when he had to conduct meetings with important people, what the hell he was supposed to do with his hands. He could fold them in front of him on the table, but that implied a level of briskness that he didn't really feel capable of. And the only alternative was just to let them hang from his wrists, like coats in a cupboard. "If you have any suggestions to make, I'd be delighted to hear them."

The ambassador nodded, and folded his hands on the table. "My understanding," he said, "is that at the moment you have no effective field army. Is that correct?"

Psellus smiled. "Yes."

Perhaps the ambassador hadn't been expecting a one-word answer. He flinched, as though Psellus had just said something rude. "We can offer you twelve thousand archers, eight thousand men-at-arms and eleven hundred heavy cavalry," he said. "We've already taken the precaution of mustering them at Liancor . . ."

"Where's that?"

Another rude word, apparently. The ambassador took a moment to recover, then said, "It's the closest point on our side to the road the savages are likely to take. We've mobilised simply as a precaution, to discourage them from trespassing on our territory." He smiled. "We have no quarrel of our own with either the Vadani or the savages. However . . ." He snatched a little breath, and Psellus thought: Ah. He's about to lie to me. "However, we feel that it would be impossible, ethically speaking, for us to stand idly by and watch while the savages over-run and destroy a great city crammed with helpless civilians, women and children. We are prepared to help you . . ."

"Thank you."

The ambassador looked like a man trying to wrestle with an opponent made entirely out of water; there was nothing to get hold of, and it kept slipping away unexpectedly. "Provided," he went on, "that you in turn recognise the nature of the commitment we're making to you, and undertake to bear it in mind when the post-war balance of power comes to be reassessed. For a long time now, we've been actively seeking a closer relationship with the Republic, a relationship which you have hitherto seemed less than eager to pursue. We feel—"

"Excuse me." Psellus held up his hand (nice to find a use for it at last). "I'm very new at this, and I'm afraid I don't speak the language very well. You've probably heard I didn't want the job, I'm really not capable of doing it, by any stretch of the imagination, and I still don't quite understand how I came to be given it. One minute they were going to execute me, the next . . . well, here I am." He shook his head sadly. "But there we are, it's done and can't be helped, and now it's all on my shoulders, whether I like it or not." He looked up. "You don't mind me telling you all that, do you?"

The ambassador was staring at him. "No, of course not. Your frankness is—"

"The thing is," Psellus went on, looking over the ambassador's shoulder at a mark on the wall, "I really do have to find a way of saving the City, because nobody else is willing or able, and so if I don't do it – well, it's not something that bears thinking about. So, I've got to manage it somehow, but I don't know the first thing about diplomacy, so I'm not even going to try. I'm going to ask you to bear with me while I do the best I can. Is that all right?"

The ambassador nodded. He seemed to be having trouble finding any words.

"Thank you," Psellus said. "This is how I think matters stand, and perhaps you'll be kind enough to tell me if I've got it all disastrously wrong. Now then. Like me, you can't really bring yourself to believe that the savages will be able to take the City, even though there's a quite ridiculously huge number of them, and they've got the abominator Vaatzes helping them, which means if they haven't already built siege engines as good as the ones we make, they'll do so pretty soon. No; you look at our walls and the City gates, and you think – just as I used to do – there's no power on earth that could ever crack that particular nut, engines or no engines." He paused to draw breath, then went on, "But you know that we haven't got any proper soldiers any more; we have no army of our own, and so many mercenaries got killed fighting the Eremians and the Vadani that they simply don't want to work for us any more, especially now the savages have found a way of crossing the desert and have joined up with our enemies. You believe – quite rightly, of course – that we're terrified, feeling helpless, we don't know what to do, and so we'd be willing to pay anything and make any concessions you'd care to name in return for the loan of your army, just to make us feel a little bit safer until we've had a chance to pull ourselves together and figure out how we're going to defend our city." He paused again, smiled meekly and asked, "Is that about right, or have I misunderstood you entirely?"

"That's about right," the ambassador said.

"Splendid, I'm glad about that. It's so important that people tell me when I make mistakes, or how will I ever learn? Anyway; I'm sure you know much more about fighting wars than any of us do, so you must've assessed the position and decided that the advantages – the concessions you can screw out of us while we're on our knees like this – outweigh the rather dreadful risk you're running, picking a fight with a million savages. Oh, did you know that, by the way? Actually, it's closer to eight hundred thousand, when you leave out the carters and drovers and all the people in the army who don't actually fight, but that's still an awful lot. You do know; excellent. Well, of course you do, now I come to think of it; I imagine it was you who gave us the figures in the first place, because we haven't got any scouts, and who else would be out there counting?" Psellus smiled again, and continued: "Now I'm the last person to tell you that you've made a bad decision, and it's very encouraging to know you've got so much faith in us, since you know so much more about these things than we do. I still can't help thinking that in your shoes, the last thing I'd want to do is let myself get dragged into a war that's none of my business, fighting against a vast army of savages who'll wipe me off the face of the earth if they win. Still, if that's a risk you're happy to take, far be it from me to argue with you. We need you desperately, and in return you can have anything you want."

There was a long, dead silence. "Anything?"

Psellus nodded vigorously. "You name it. Money, land – you can have Eremia if we win, it's no use to us, or the Vadani silver mines if you'd prefer, it's entirely up to you. Just say what you want and I'll have a treaty drawn up. And in return, you'll lend us your army. Well?"

The ambassador took a moment to clear his throat. "Agreed," he said.

"Splendid." Psellus beamed at him. "There, we've made an alliance, and it was so much easier than I thought it'd be. When Boioannes was in charge, it used to take weeks to hammer out a treaty, and he knew a lot about diplomacy, unlike me. Now, how soon can your soldiers get here? Or . . ." Psellus frowned. "Here's where it gets difficult again. I don't know whether we need them here at the City, or whether they'd be more useful hindering the savages and making it hard for them to reach us. You're the expert. What do you think?"

Nothing in the ambassador's long and varied experience had prepared him for a question like that. "It's a complicated decision," he said. "On the one hand . . ."

"The way I see it," Psellus went on, "an army of a million people is obviously a great advantage in a battle, no doubt about it, but until you actually get to the battlefield, it's also a tremendous problem. Must be. Food and so forth, hay for the horses, clean water. Now, we've done a little research – dreadful, really, it's taken something like this to make us realise just how woefully ignorant we are about everything other than making things and selling them – and we can't see how the enemy can keep themselves fed and watered just from what they can find in the fields and villages, which means they must be having to bring in their food and so on from somewhere else. God only knows where," Psellus added with a grin. "I mean to say, you increase the population of the mountain duchies by a million, the Eremians and the Vadani could only just about feed themselves at the best of times, so it's not like there can be any huge granaries bursting at the seams with stockpiled sacks of flour. Probably some of your merchants have been trading with them – it's perfectly all right, I quite understand – but from the little I know about your people, I don't suppose that can have made much difference. No, the only source of supply I can think of is the savages' own herds of cattle – they're nomads, as I'm sure you know, that's how they live, and they must have managed to bring their cattle with them across the desert when they came. Which is fine, of course, from their point of view, except that there can't be all that much pasture in the mountains for all those hundreds of thousands of animals; and when the grass has all been eaten, and any hay that our men overlooked while they were there, they'll have to slaughter most of them before they starve; and yes, they can salt down the carcasses, but even that won't last for ever. Time, you see. They're almost as short of it as we are." Psellus stopped talking for a moment, as if thinking about something, then added, "Of course, all this stuff is just what's occurred to me while I've been thinking about it, and like I've told you already, I'm hopelessly ignorant about military matters, so I may have got it all completely wrong. But if I'm right – and if I'm not, do please say so – it seems to me that the best use we can make of your army is messing about with their lines of supply. Would you agree?"

The ambassador hesitated, as though trying to translate what he'd heard into a language he could understand. "Of course," he said. "It's the only logical—"

"Though obviously," Psellus went on, "there's a bit more to it than that. The last thing we want to do is make them come here before we've done what we can to get ready for them. If your soldiers were to drive off all their cattle, it could force them to attack us straight away, simply because the only reserve of food large enough to feed them and close enough to be any use is what we've got here – though I think you ought to know, we're not exactly well provided for in that department ourselves. Of course, I've made arrangements for every ship we can buy or hire to bring in as much food as possible from across the sea – the old country won't send us soldiers any more, but they're still happy to sell us wheat, thank goodness – but it's all got to come in through Lonazep, and I understand it's absolute chaos there at the moment. Still, they probably don't know that, and if they do, it's not as though they'd have a choice, if we somehow contrived to run off all their livestock. So, we don't want to leave them starving. We just want to slow them right down, so we've got time to build up our walls and get in as much food as we can for a long siege. That's our best chance, I reckon. If it's a matter of who starves first, I think we can win. If it comes to fighting, we might as well not bother." Psellus breathed out (he still wasn't used to talking uninterrupted for so long), then added, "Do you think I'm on the right lines here, or have I got it all wrong? Really, I'd value your opinion. It's been such a worry, trying to learn all this very difficult stuff in such a tearing hurry. It'd be a relief if an expert like yourself can reassure me I haven't made a dreadful mess of it all."

The ambassador looked at him warily for a while, then said, "Can I ask you what you did before all this?"

"I was a clerk."

"A . . ."

Psellus nodded. "I was a records clerk for nine years, after I'd finished my apprenticeship. Then I got my transfer from the executive to the administrative grade; I was a junior secretary in the Compliance directorate for six years, and then general secretary for five years after that. And then," he added sadly, "Ziani Vaatzes came along, and now look at me. Lord of all I survey. I met him once, did you know that? Vaatzes. He's the key to it all, of course." Psellus shook his head. "I'm terribly sorry, I'm rambling, and you're a busy man. Now then, about this army of yours."

Later, in the ten minutes or so between appointments (he had his beautiful clock to thank for such an indecent degree of precision; he still loved it for its beauty, but it nagged him like a wife), he wrote down the minutes of his meeting with the ambassador and compared them with the plan he'd prepared beforehand. Well, he thought, now at least we have a few soldiers, thanks to the incredible stupidity of the Cure Doce. He still couldn't quite believe it. But then they'd been brought up to believe the Republic was invincible; invincible and gullible. Two mistakes, and they'd probably cost the Cure Doce their existence. Not that it mattered, if they could buy him time to turn the City into one of those extraordinary star shapes he'd seen in the book.

He put the sheet of minutes on the pile of papers to be filed, and spent his last few moments of solitary peace going over his plan for the meeting with the architects. He would never be able to understand the book, but they might.

Suddenly, he smiled. Wouldn't it be a superb piece of irony, he thought, if we actually contrived to get away with it? A million enemies, and we beat them because there's too many of them to take the City. The sheer perversity of it appealed to him enormously. They lose, because they sent a million men to do the job of fifty thousand; I beat a million men by fighting just one.

Which reminded him. He pulled a fresh sheet of paper from the pile, inked his pen and wrote, wastefully, in the middle of the page:

His wife.

Chapter Two

He was cold, hungry, and still damp, though it had stopped raining through the hole in the roof. He could feel drops of water trickling down his forehead from his sodden cap, and smell the stench of drying wool.

I might be late, he remembered her saying. *It's hard for me to get away in the evenings.* Well, of course it was. She had a husband to look after, and right now he'd be the busiest man in the City; rushed off his feet, frustrated by his inferiors, yelled at by his masters for not working miracles, painfully aware that nothing was under his control, but everything was his fault. So, naturally, when he finally got home from work, he'd expect a hot meal on the table and everything just so. That didn't alter the fact that she had other responsibilities, and no excuse for not performing them efficiently.

He had to have a new coat. This one was worn out, useless. She'd have to steal one from her husband – shouldn't be a problem, she could say that she was sick to death of seeing him in that tatty old thing, so she'd thrown it out, given it to a beggar . . .

(He grinned angrily. That'd be no less than the truth.)

The straw he lay on was filthy, too. Of course, straw was a problem, a luxury the Republic couldn't afford, now that all the carts were being used to carry grain and flour for the coming siege. That didn't alter the fact that it stank and was starting to go black, because of the damp. It was all intolerable, every wretched detail. She'd have to find him somewhere else.

Worst of all, needless to say, was not knowing what was going on. All he knew was what he could figure out from what he'd seen in the streets, when he'd felt brave enough to venture outside. Constant traffic, of course, all the grain carts blocking every thoroughfare in the City – that was the fault of the highways superintendent at the prefecture. He tried to remember the man's name, but he couldn't, though he could dimly picture a short, plump man with a big moustache. Whoever he was, he wasn't doing his job very well. In any event, the gridlocked traffic told him that they were still getting in supplies; so the enemy hadn't taken Lonazep (it would have been the first thing he'd have done) or cut the road to the coast. Since they weren't fools, or at any rate the Vadani duke was no fool, he didn't know enough about the leaders of the savages to form an opinion, the logical inference was that they hadn't taken steps to cut the City's supply lines because they weren't in a position to do so. And that, of course, could mean any one of many things. That aside, all the factories had moved from four to three shifts. He couldn't approve of that. Lengthening shifts was all very well, but it was a proven fact that working men too hard always led to a slump in productivity. So, whoever had ordered the shifts to be cut either didn't understand simple management, or else needed to give the impression he was doing something, even if he knew it'd be counterproductive. Since that was the more likely explanation, it suggested that things weren't going well for the new regime. He smiled at that, but it worried him. Even though they were his enemies, he was relying on them to save the City, just as everybody else was. Didn't the morons realise they simply couldn't afford to make mistakes?

He heard footsteps, and felt his stomach twist with instinctive terror; but it was only her, finally.

"You're late," he grumbled. "I thought you weren't coming."

She was wearing a scarf over her hair; it was drenched, so presumably it had started raining again. She had the child with her. "I thought I told you—"

"I told him I had to take Moritsa to the doctor," she snapped. "It was the only way I could get out of the house at this time of night."

He scowled at her; stupid woman. Talking like that in front of the child, bringing it here. Didn't she realise that the child now knew where he was? Naturally she'd have made it promise not to tell anybody, but children couldn't be relied on to keep secrets. They told their friends at school: I know a secret, my mummy's taking food to a strange man in a stable; and then the friend told its father, who happened to be a corporal in the Watch. Still, he couldn't very well say anything, since he'd already made the point several times. The last thing he could afford was for her to take offence and stop coming.

"You did bring the food, didn't you?" he said.

She took a basket from the little girl's hand and gave it to him. He snatched off the cloth that covered it. "Is this all?"

"It's not easy," she replied defensively. "You wouldn't believe how much prices have gone up lately, and we aren't made of money. I'm just surprised he hasn't noticed we're feeding four instead of three. Usually he goes over the household accounts at least once a week. Just as well he's so busy at work. When he gets home, he's too tired to do anything except flop in a chair."

He wasn't listening. A loaf (a small loaf, and distinctly stale); a knob of cheap yellow cheese; some rather slimy cold chicken, with splodges of cold brown gravy – scraped off her husband's plate after he'd finished, presumably. I'm reduced to eating table scraps, like a dog or a pig. Marvellous. Two soft, waxy store apples; three raw carrots; half a dozen flat scones, blackened round the edges . . .

"I burned them on purpose," she pointed out, "so I could throw them away. He told me off for being careless and wasting flour and eggs. You can hardly get eggs any more. Some fool's ordered all the chickens in the City slaughtered, because they reckon we can't spare the grain."

He rolled his eyes. Small, stupid, petty things like that were a sure way to ruin morale. "Did you bring anything to drink?" he asked hopefully. "I'm sick to death of rainwater out of dirty barrels."

She handed him a small jug stopped with screwed-up cloth. He sniffed it and pulled a face.

"I can't drink that," he said. "It's gone stale."

"If it wasn't stale, he wouldn't have let me chuck it out," she snapped back at him. "Malt's half a dollar a pound, and that's if you can get it. Pretty soon all we'll have is water."

My heart bleeds, he thought. "It'll have to do, then," he replied sullenly. "Will you come again tomorrow? You can say the kid's still off colour."

She was looking at him, and he didn't need his lifetime of expertise in handling women to interpret that particular expression. *She doesn't love me any more, oh well, never mind. At least she's got enough common sense to realise she's stuck with me.*

"I'll try," she said. "It's lucky he hardly notices me these days, so long as his food's on the table and the laundry gets done."

The little girl was bored. She was playing with the buckles of her shoes, undoing them and doing them up again. It was annoying to watch, but he decided against saying anything. Idly, he wondered about her; whose daughter she was, not that it mattered very much. He couldn't bring himself to feel anything about her at all; just another pointless complication. But she'd been married to Vaatzes all those years and there'd been no children, then all this had started, and suddenly there was one. Only natural to wonder, though he'd never had the slightest interest in breeding offspring.

"Did you find out about the war, like I asked you?"

She sighed. "He's rushed off his feet building siege engines, that's all I know," she said. "He doesn't like talking about work when he gets home. My friend whose husband works in the paymaster's office said something about some new alliance, but she didn't know any details."

He frowned. "Did she say anything about the Cure Doce?"

"Who?"

He shook his head. "Try and find out more if you can," he said, doing his best not to let his impatience show. "It's vitally important I keep up to date, if I'm ever going to get out of this mess. And then," he added awkwardly, "we can finally be together."

She nodded. It was a curious gesture in the circumstances, like a servant accepting orders without forming any judgement of whether they were good or bad.

"I need another coat," he said. "This one's useless."

"I'll see what I can do," she said.

He took a moment to look at her, something he hadn't done properly in a while. The changes were only very slight, almost too slight to notice or describe: a little thinner around the face, tighter around the mouth and eyes. She looked dried, like stored fruit; the sap drained out in the interests of endurance. But she'd put on a little weight, just enough to spoil the curves and radii of her figure. Her waist had thickened up, her arms were starting to turn podgy where once they'd been rounded and soft. He realised, with the sense of someone noticing he'd forgotten something that used to be important, that they hadn't had sex for – how long was it now, six months? Since Psellus

went to Civitas Vadanis – now how could those two facts be at all connected, though clearly they were, somehow. He thought about that.
They'd had the opportunity, all these clandestine meetings in dark,
secret places, and he had no doubt that she'd have agreed to it if he'd
suggested it, because she'd never refused him anything. Did he want
to? Not, he decided, in the slightest. Even if he'd still wanted her,
found her even remotely attractive, it would be frivolous, a ridiculous
indulgence for someone in his position, like a starving man spending
his last three quarters on candy floss.

He looked away, feeling disgusted and betrayed. For her sake,
he'd risked and lost everything. In that sense, she was to blame; the
astonishingly fierce desire he'd felt for her at first, which had made
everything else seem trivial, couldn't reasonably be called his fault,
since he'd had no control over it, none whatsoever. Now it had gone,
evaporated as the heat of the consequences burned through his life,
and here they were, stuck with each other, like an old couple resent-
fully celebrating sixty years of an arranged marriage. It was hard to
believe that either of them were the same people they'd been then, of
course. But at least she still had enough to eat, and slept in a bed,
under a roof that didn't leak. And as for the scale of losses incurred,
there was no possible comparison. What had she lost? Nothing at all.
She'd traded one unsatisfactory husband for another, but the two
men were practically interchangeable in any event, they even did the
same job, so that couldn't possibly count as a loss. He, on the other
hand – well, that didn't bear thinking about.

"I'd better go," she said awkwardly. "I'll try and come tomorrow."

"You've got to find me somewhere better than this," he said
angrily. "I can't live here. At least find me somewhere I can have a
fire. I've been wet through to the skin for days now."

"I'll try."

But that was always her answer: she'd try, she'd do her best. "I'm
sure you will," he replied, knowing that she wouldn't hear the irony –
because naturally she did try, she did do her best, but it wasn't
enough. "Maybe it's time I got out of the City for a while," he said.

"No." She almost barked the word at him, and he could see panic
in her face. "No, you mustn't do that. How am I supposed to bring
you food and stuff if you're . . . ?"

"You wouldn't have to," he replied reasonably. "If you bring me
some things I can sell – just ordinary household junk, they'll buy

anything City-made in the villages. It'd be better than sleeping in a godawful hole like this, and I wouldn't be scared to death every time a watchman looked at me."

"But what about the savages?" she said, and he knew that what she really meant was *what about me?* At least she had the instinctive good sense to realise what a poor argument that was these days. "People are saying they'll be here any day now."

"Are they? How soon?"

She frowned. "I don't know, it's hard to know what to believe. Some people say ten days, some people say five, they're just guessing."

"Then there's nothing to worry about, is there?"

The panic glowed brighter in her eyes; at last, some sign of life. She looked better for it. "But the savages really are coming, everybody knows that," she said. "And suppose they shut the gates, and you can't get back in? And what happens when you run out of money? You can't go, it'd be dangerous." She'd wanted to use another word. He wondered: is this love? Or just a habit, unwanted but now unbreakable; a dependency, which is what love always becomes. Like alcohol, or smoking hemp; the need increases as the pleasure fades into pain. Better to be abstemious, to indulge only occasionally, socially, among friends.

"Fine," he said, making a show of resentful concession. "I'll stay here, then, if you're that worried. But you've got to find me another place."

"All right."

All right, not I'll try. "And a new coat."

She nodded. "There's his old winter coat he never wears any more. There's a hole, but I can darn it. If he misses it, I'll say the moths got at it. He'll be angry at me for not looking after it, but . . ." She realised he wasn't listening, and added, "I love you, Maris."

"I love you too." She turned to leave. The child was playing with the remains of a rotten sack, pulling threads out of a frayed hole; she grabbed it by the hand and it stood up. "Don't forget the coat," he added, because women never heard anything unless they were told at least three times.

She left him and walked quickly up the narrow alley until she reached Chairmakers' Street. Moritsa was tugging at her hand.

"Are we going to see the doctor now?" she asked.

"No."

"Oh. I thought. . ."

"It's all right. You don't have to see the doctor."

"Oh. Does that mean I'm better?"

"Yes."

That seemed to make sense to her, and they walked in silence for a while. Then she asked, "Mummy, who was that man?"

"Just a friend." She frowned, and went on, "He's been very unlucky and lost his home and all his money, so we're looking after him until things get better for him."

"I see. He sounded very unhappy."

"Yes. But you mustn't tell anybody about him, do you understand? It's very important. There are bad people looking for him, and if they find him they'll hurt him, and we don't want that to happen, do we?"

"No." A pause, then: "Did he do something wrong?"

"No. Just remember, not a word to anybody. All right?"

At the top of Chairmakers' Street, left into Spangate. A fine drizzle, just enough to be annoying. She'd been longer than she'd expected to be, but she could explain that by saying she'd had to wait for the doctor. With luck, he wouldn't have noticed anyway. Most likely he'd be asleep in his chair, like an old man. She found the thought of him mildly disgusting, and considered whether she could get away with taking one of his shirts as well as the coat. She decided she probably could, if she let it get burnt while it was drying in front of the fire. Stealing from him pleased her; it was like winning, like achieving something positive.

He wasn't asleep when she got home; but he was sitting at the table with a pile of papers and his counting-board, and he didn't look up as she closed the door behind her. She sent Moritsa straight off to bed, then stood over him until he looked up.

"The doctor says she's fine," she told him. "Just a tummy bug, it'll clear up in a day or two."

He frowned, then said, "That's good."

She didn't move. "You could at least make it sound like you cared."

She saw him wince. It meant he didn't want to fight, couldn't face the aggravation that would follow if he answered her back. "Of course I care," he said. "But you said yourself it wasn't anything serious. I just—"

"It's all right," she snapped. "But I'll need six quarters to pay the doctor."

He nodded, felt in his pocket for the coins. That'd buy a shirt; a cheap new one, or a good one second hand. He never begrudged her money so long as she said what it was for. Somehow, she tended to see that as a fault rather than a virtue.

"Are you going to be long?"

He nodded. "I've got to get these costings finished by tomorrow, and you know what I'm like with figures. I keep asking them to give me a clerk, but . . ." He stopped; that I-know-I'm-boring-you gesture of the head and shoulders. "I don't know how long I'll be. You'd better go on to bed."

"It's all right," she said wearily. "You know the light keeps me awake."

That pleased her, too; another tiny wound inflicted, another pinprick of guilt. Sometimes she imagined him as a piece of knitting, and she was unpicking him a stitch at a time. Very occasionally, it occurred to her to wonder why, but when she did, she never liked the answer very much. Besides, he'd brought it on himself. Any man who'd betray his friend just to get his wife deserved to end up with the sort of woman who'd cheat on her husband with his best friend. To pass the time, she took the old winter coat down from behind the door and started darning the hole.

After she'd done five rows, she asked, "Have you heard anything new about how the war's going?"

She pitched it just right; as though she was making conversation as a way of showing she'd forgiven him. He paused, two brass counters held between his fingers. "The latest is, we've made an alliance with the Cure Doce."

"Who?"

"Quite." He put the counters carefully down on a square, shifted another from the bottom to the top. "They live out east, on the Vadani border. Little better than savages, really, but they're sending troops, and we're in no position to be fussy."

"That's good, then."

He shrugged. "Can't see there's enough of them to make any difference," he said. "All I know is, we're sending them eighteen thousand suits of three-quarter-length mail and sixteen thousand helmets, which is rather more than we've got in stock. Which is why

I'm having to sit up doing these bloody costings instead of getting some sleep." He sighed. "It seems to me that any soldiers who haven't got their own equipment already can't be much good. I mean, you can't just turn a man into a soldier by sticking an iron hat on his head, or else we wouldn't need the Cure Doce. But if they want to go out and get killed on our behalf, let them. I suppose it'll keep the savages off our backs for a little while longer."

She waited for a moment or so, then said: "Is that all we're doing, then? Hiring these . . ."

"Cure Doce. No." He wrote something down. "I get the impression they're planning something a bit more positive than that."

"Go on, then."

He sat back in his chair. He had his back to her, but she could see the weariness. "They've told me I've got to find seventy thousand twelve-inch billets of hardening steel, out of what we've got in stock," he said. "And when I asked what for, they told me spades and shovels, pickaxes, sledgehammers, that sort of thing. Sounds like they're getting ready to start building up the fortifications. And they must have something pretty big in mind, because I know for a fact we've got close on a million shovels sat in the warehouse; I was after some of them myself, for the steel, to make into arrowheads. So, if they've already got a million shovels and they want seventy thousand more, they must be planning on moving a lot of dirt, though who they're going to get to use all these tools I have no idea. Still, at least it looks like someone's trying to do something."

He paused, then frowned. "Of course, you know who we've got to thank for that," he added. "Your old friend Lucao Psellus."

The name hurt her. "Him," she said.

"I know. But you can't deny it, he's doing a good job, in the circumstances."

"He's horrible. I should know. And think of all the difficulties he made for us over our wedding."

"Yes, sure. All I'm saying is, he's doing *something* about the war. God only knows what sort of a state we'd be in if we still had that arsehole Boioannes running things."

In that moment, she realised, she'd never hated him so much in all the time they'd been together. "Like your opinion matters," she said. "You don't know anything about it."

He turned and looked at her, and she thought: one of these days,

I'll go just a little bit too far, and then I'll lose him. But not today. "Fine," he said, "let's not talk about it. I'll just get on and finish these figures."

She turned her back on him, picked up the coat and sewed for a while, although there wasn't really enough light; he'd taken the good lamp to read his papers by, and the other lamp needed a new wick. She didn't want to do sloppy work on a coat she was going to give to *him*; not that he'd notice, but she'd know, and feel ashamed. She'd have to get up early and take it over to the window, to catch the first light. "I'm going to bed now," she announced. "You'll have to get your own lunch tomorrow, I haven't had time to make anything."

"Mphm." He didn't look at her. "I can get something from a market stall on my way in."

For some reason, she was offended by that; he'd made it sound as if she was so unimportant that even a gross dereliction of duty on her part couldn't possibly matter. But of course, that wasn't what he'd meant, he was just trying to be considerate. On balance, though, she preferred to take offence. "Fine," she snapped, as she crossed the room to the bed and dragged the curtain across so savagely she nearly pulled it off the wall.

Falier waited until he heard her snore, then put down his pen and carefully swept the counters off the board into his cupped hand, making sure they didn't clink together. It had been a dreadful, hateful evening. He had no idea why, but it seemed like there didn't have to be a reason any more. Ever since . . . He stopped what he was doing and concentrated, trying to pin down the moment with all due precision. Ever since the Vadani duke had evacuated his capital city, not long before the savages got involved. He thought about it some more, trying to correlate the vast events of the war with the most significant turning-points in their marriage. The correlation gave him a coherent chronology and verified his conclusion, but offered no explanation. Perhaps, he thought, it's like astrology; the movements of stars and planets bearing on the tiny lives of men and women. Perhaps the war's got so huge and heavy now that it's pulling our lives along with it, the same way the moon draws the tides. There were other explanations, of course. Since the war got so busy – ever since Vaatzes betrayed the Eremians; he'd been directly involved in that – he'd had so much work on, been so wrapped up in production targets and productivity ratings, felt so tired in the evenings when he finally got home . . . Obviously he'd been neglecting her, and wouldn't any woman resent that? He felt properly guilty about it, of course, but unfortunately there was nothing he could do to set it right. He couldn't even resign, they wouldn't let him, and as for delegating, that'd only make things worse; they'd make a mess of everything, and he'd have to work even longer and harder trying to get it all straight again. To begin with he'd hoped she'd understand, because of the national emergency and the threat to the City, but apparently not. He couldn't blame her for that. *Just because the savages are coming, why should that mean you don't love me any more?* She didn't need to say it out loud, and he could tell her it wasn't true until they were both sick of the sound of his voice. She'd never believe him.

And for this, he thought, I betrayed my friend. It really shouldn't have turned out this way. If you're going to do some unspeakably evil thing to gain your heart's desire, you should at least have the basic good manners to take proper care of your heart's desire once you've got it, instead of leaving it lying around neglected, like a spoilt child's toys.

But that was far too easy to rationalise. The crime contains its own punishment; wasn't that a quotation, or a proverb or something? His betrayal had led directly to Ziani escaping and defecting to the Eremians; that in turn led to the war, which was ruining their marriage. In other words, he could never have won her without making losing her inevitable; not to mention bringing destruction down on the entire Republic, like someone carrying home the plague in a shipment of tainted grain. To bring the world to ruin, for love; put like that it sounded wonderfully romantic – be mine, and let the whole world burn; another quotation, most likely. But he couldn't twist his mind far enough round to see it in that light, somehow. Rather, he'd done it because he really had no choice in the matter. He had to have her, and it had been the only way to make it happen; the consequences were irrelevant, regardless of how many strangers died because of it. It wasn't his fault; love was nobody's fault, just like nobody was to blame for hurricanes, or lightning setting fire to the thatch. It's not the apple's fault that it falls from the tree, because it has no choice, if the branch can't hold it any longer. He'd had no choice, because there had been no other way.

Even so . . . He looked at the calculations he'd just finished making, so much hardening steel, apportioned between shovel blades and arrowheads. Arrows to kill men with, shovels to bury them with; add together the inventory of arrowheads already in stock and the requisition for arrowheads ordered to be made, and then imagine them, ten million arrows, each one cutting through flesh, into bone. A mercenary captain he'd talked to in Eremia had told him that in an average battle, one arrow in twenty hits something. He didn't need his counters to do the calculation. Half a million hits; say a fifth of those manage to pierce armour and reach the flesh inside. Fifty thousand wounds (think of how much a splinter in your finger can hurt; think of an arrow as a huge barbed splinter). He shook his head, remembering the stacks of dead men he'd seen at Civitas Eremiae; stared at them in blank horror, and never even realised that what he was looking at was the true meaning of love.

He was desperately tired, but he couldn't get into bed, not with her there. He leaned back in his chair, lifted the mantle off the lamp and crushed the flame to death between thumb and forefinger.

They said that the Vadani duke had married the widow of the Eremian duke, who he'd had killed on some flimsy pretext. You didn't need to be a politician or a diplomat to figure that one out. It's love that makes the world go round, they said; also, that the Vadani duke had only brought his duchy into the war for her sake. And then he'd married a princess of the savages, and when she'd been killed by the Republic's cavalry in some skirmish, that meant the savages were in the war too, and now the City needed a million shovels double quick, to dig a hole to hide in.

(I did all that, he thought. For love.)

He closed his eyes. He'd be asleep in no time; and then he'd wake up with a crick in his neck from sleeping all night in a chair, because he couldn't bring himself to share a bed with the woman he loved.

They said Ziani Vaatzes must be mad, to have done all those dreadful things and brought disaster down on the City. Well; they were quite right, for once. And it never rains but it pours, and it's always darkest before dawn, and every cloud has a silver lining, and sooner or later everybody falls in love with the foreman's daughter. All perfectly true.

So he closed his eyes, but it was a while before he fell asleep; his mind was still crowded with numbers and sums, bits of random information, facts he preferred not to face, things he wished he didn't know. Just before the confusion in his head exhausted itself and faded into sleep, a question formed; one that he hadn't ever considered before, and yet unless it was answered, nothing in the whole wide world could ever possibly make sense again. It flared up like the last ember of a sleepy fire, burned itself out and faded, and then he slept . . .

Why did Ziani make the thing in the first place?

She wasn't there when he woke up. Bright grey light filtered through the window. His neck hurt.

There was the end of a greyish loaf, some white butter, and a thumb's-length of water in the jug. He changed his shirt, put on his coat and left for work.

You could tell the time in the City by the smell. They'd already lit the furnace fires, but the smell was woodsmoke, not the foul, clinging taste of coal, so the kindling hadn't burnt through yet. That meant he was a little bit late, but not enough to feel guilty about. The pavement was sprinkled with black snow, yesterday's soot settled overnight and not yet trodden in. He stopped at the one-eyed man's stall and bought a barley cake and half a dry sausage. The streets were still quiet; the day-shift workers weren't expected to show up until the fires had had a chance to heat up, caking over the forges and bringing the water in the boilers to the simmer.

The factory porter opened the wicket gate for him, and he stepped out of a narrow street into the cloister that led to the main shop.

It wasn't possible, of course; but Falier had always fancied that the roof of the main shop was higher than the sky outside. The City sky always seemed low and cramped, even in the summer heat; now, when the grey clouds crowded in, like stoppers on the bottles whose necks were the City's drop towers and chimneys, you could make yourself believe that if you stood on tiptoe you could reach up and touch it, though you'd want to wipe your hands on something afterwards. Inside, though, it was different. To see the factory roof you had to lean your head right back, your eye drawn upwards along the line of the great wrought-iron pillars, close, straight and tall as pine trees in a forest. Outside, light seeped down through the cloud and the constant blanket of smoke like blood through a bandage. Inside it came in sideways, through the regularly spaced series of tall, narrow windows, so that during the day there were practically no shadows anywhere, and at night the whole place filled up with an orange glow so thick it was practically a liquid.

There was always an hour's break between shifts; enough time for the previous shift's fire to burn off the last of its fuel and die down without letting the brickwork and the tue-irons cool to the point where they'd start to crack. During that hour, the only activity was dragging out the clinker, sweeping up the drifts of scale flakes, oiling and greasing the bearings of the trip-hammers; quiet, careful work, acts of recovery, almost of tenderness. Men hauled buckets of water to fill up the slakes, refilled the coal bins, greased the bellows leathers, generally made good before the destructive effort of the new shift. It was the time of day when the factory was pleasantly warm instead of uncomfortably hot; warm as the bed you leave when you get up to go to work, assuming you didn't spend the night in a chair.

The floor smelt of coal, oily water, wet rust and the unmistakable aroma shared by blood and freshly cut steel. On the toolroom side of the shop they were scrambling about on ladders, greasing the overhead shafts and dusting the long loops of drive belt with chalk, for grip. Two old men who'd been old as long as Falier could remember were walking slowly up and down the ranks of machines, filling the oilers from tall copper jugs. At the end of one row a sudden shower of orange sparks blossomed as someone trued up a grinding wheel, adding the scents of carborundum and burnt steel to the mixture. Falier had seen gardens, he'd even been in the grand formal garden in the inner courtyard of the Guildhall, but he'd never found them convincing. Somehow they'd always struck him as pointless attempts to copy the main shop, using trees and shrubs to represent wrought and cast iron.

The superintendent's office was on the eighth level of the galleries that encircled the main shop like the banks of seats in a theatre. Falier climbed the iron spiral staircase, pausing at each level to look down. With a practised eye you could take in the health of the factory at a glance from here, in mid-shift, when the men scurrying about below dwindled out of individuality into flowing shapes of movement. Between shifts, the factory looked like its own schematic, a reduction intended to convey the workings of the machine. Ziani Vaatzes had told him that once he'd been in here when it was completely empty, apart from himself; there had been some reason for it, a total closedown while everything cooled, maybe the only time in its history when it had been entirely still. As he paused on the seventh level, Falier tried to imagine what that must've been like; to be the only living soul in the factory, nothing moving, no sound at all.

He reached his office. It had no door; it'd be pointless, since it'd be open all the time. He dropped the sheaf of costings on his desk, glanced down at the notes left for him overnight. Cracks in the lining of number six furnace; that was bad, since cooling off number six meant damping down five and seven as well. Two of the big capstan lathes in the fifth aisle had shot their bearings and would need stripping right down to rebuild, out of action for two shifts and part of a third. Too much work, Falier told himself; too many shifts and not enough maintenance, and it'll only get worse as the pressure grows. A strong superintendent wouldn't stand for it, no matter what the politicians said. But was he going to tell Necessary Evil that they couldn't have their ten per cent productivity rise? Of course he wasn't. So the machines would wear out and seize, the firebricks would start to crack, output would fall when it should be rising and it'd all be his fault. But not today. And maybe it'd all be academic anyway. Maybe the savages would come and smash the factory to rubble with their home-made trebuchets before the authorities noticed the production slump. You've got to look on the bright side, haven't you?

He sat down in his chair (a Pattern Twenty-Nine, so it was perfectly joined, fitted and finished to within the exacting tolerances of its specification, but that still didn't mean it was comfortable) and tried to twist his mind round to charcoal reserves, but it had seized like a rusty bolt; too much force trying to shift it and it'd shear. He was my friend, he thought. And yes, I betrayed him, for love, but I always thought I knew him well. So why did he make the stupid thing?

A mechanical toy; to be precise, a quarter-size model of an old tramp, with a performing monkey on his shoulder. Turn the key twelve times widdershins, turn up the catch and the monkey danced an awkward, crabbed little dance, while the man's hand lifted up and down, holding a hat to catch coins in. The pattern number was sixty-seven; they were produced mainly for export to the old country, where real monkeys were commonplace and the people were, apparently, easily amused. He thought about that. Ziani would have made all the internal parts himself, but it didn't seem likely that he'd have gone to the trouble of making the castings for the heads, hands and so forth. He'd have had to start off by carving wooden patterns – highly dangerous as well as time-consuming and pointless, since the slightest difference would've marked the thing as an abomination, so clearly that anybody who'd seen the real thing would have noticed. Of course, he could have borrowed authentic castings and taken impressions of them to make his mould. But Ziani had never built a foundry at his home, had he? Surely not. It would have taken up far too much space, and the neighbours would've given him hell because of the smoke. Besides, there had been no mention of aberrant castings in the indictment at his trial.

It followed, therefore, that he'd got hold of genuine castings from someone in the Toymakers'. That on its own should have aroused suspicion; what would an ordnance foreman want with toy components? But supposing he had someone who owed him a favour . . .

Correction. The shaped outside parts weren't solid castings, they were hollow and pressed out of thin brass sheet on a screw-mill. That made a bit more sense. No bother for someone in the Toymakers' shop to slip a few extra blanks into the mill when nobody was looking, so it wouldn't have to be a very big favour he'd been owed, as would be the case if the parts had been cast.

Falier smiled. When the war started to get serious, the Toymakers' had closed down their pressing and spinning shop. The heavy plant had been moved here, to the sheet-working section of the ordnance factory, and their operators reassigned; now they pressed elbow cops, greaves and tassets out of armour plate, and spun shield bosses and helmet crowns. In which case, the man who'd given Ziani the doll pressings must work here now, under the direction of Superintendent Falier . . .

An office runner appeared in the doorway, waiting to take the costings up to the Guildhall. Falier handed them over, and said, "And when you've done that . . ."

(The boy's face fell.)

"I want you to fetch me the record cards on all the tin-bashers who came over from Toymakers' when they closed down the pressings shop. I expect they'll be in the personnel archive. East tower, fourth level. Get someone to help you if you can't understand the filing system."

The boy nodded miserably and slouched away. All right, Falier said to himself, as his eye skipped off the charcoal dockets for the fifth time, maybe I can trace whoever got Ziani the pressings. So what? What do you want them for? Oh, I'm building a Sixty-Seven for my kid; she'd set her heart on one, and you know how much they cost. No, of course I won't mention your name if the shit hits the flywheel.

(Whoever the unknown donor was, he must've been wetting himself ever since Ziani was arrested. Aiding and abetting an abominator – well, he might get off that, if he pleaded ignorance of what Ziani was planning to do, and if he had good friends in the chapel hierarchy. But theft of Guild property, unauthorised supply, breach of trust; enough there to get a man ten years on the treadmills. It'd have to have been a very substantial favour, or else Ziani had known where a body was buried.)

All that for a stupid doll; but if the kid really had set her heart on one, and if she was highly skilled at nagging and Ziani was soft enough, you could just about fool yourself into believing it. But he knew Moritsa. She'd never shown any interest in mechanical toys. Far more likely that she'd think something like a Sixty-Seven was sinister and scary, and burst into tears at the sight of one, rather than persecute her father until he made one for her. Put like that, it simply didn't make sense.

Faced with the impenetrability of that conclusion, he turned away like a horse refusing a jump, and applied himself to charcoal reserves. What charcoal reserves? They were, he realised once he'd unscrewed the figures, desperately short of the stuff, and it was essential. The only alternative was coal, a substance he knew very little about. It was scavenged off the beaches of some province of the old country, shipped across sporadically in huge barges; for three months after a barge convoy had docked, it was cheap and plentiful. Then it disappeared. Charcoal, on the other hand, came in once a month from some huge forest out the other side of the Cure Doce country. The supply was so reliable and the price so stable that nobody ever thought about it. The deliveries still came – an endless line of high, gaunt carts drawn by thin horses, always reaching the City in the early hours of the morning, so they could unload and go away before the streets clogged with traffic; so discreet and invisible, you could easily believe in the Charcoal Fairy – and the quantities and price were exactly the same as ever. That was the problem, since demand had doubled. They needed twice as much of the stuff, preferably at half the price.

He paused, and tried to think clearly. Surely there were other forests, or could you only make it out of certain kinds of tree, or in certain places? Unlikely, but he didn't *know*. Besides, it wasn't his place to seek out new sources of supply. That was Exchequer's job, or Foreign Affairs (he had no idea whose responsibility it was, assuming it was anybody's; more likely, the charcoal people simply turned up each month as they'd always done, without anybody in the administration organising anything); his role in the great river of supply was to be held responsible for the fall in output when the charcoal ran out.

(I could write a memorandum, he thought. But who would I send it to?)

He heard the sound of a boot-sole on the iron grating outside his door, and looked up. He saw a man he didn't know standing in the doorway; a round, soft, balding man in plain, clean clothes and thin boots, so obviously a Guildhall clerk. Nobody wore anything except steel toecaps in the factory.

"Yes?" he snapped.

"You're Falier."

The voice was mild but not weak. A senior clerk, then; although it was hard to believe that anybody of any importance in the clerical grades would come here himself, unannounced, soiling the soles of his fine shoes with oil and swarf from the factory floor. "That's right," Falier said. After a night in a chair followed by the depressing implications of the breakages list and the charcoal figures, he wasn't in the mood for Authority, and he guessed that anybody who climbed his stairs, even in fancy shoes, was somebody he could be rude to without getting into trouble. "What do you want? Only I'm very busy."

"My name is Lucao Psellus."

Wonderful, Falier thought. I've just insulted the head of state. He jumped up out of his chair and tried to make his mouth work, but it wouldn't.

"Sorry to disturb you." Psellus took a step across the threshold, then stopped. "I know you must be rushed off your feet right now. If it's a particularly bad time . . ."

"No, really." Falier practically spat the words out. "Anything I can do, obviously. Please, sit down."

There was, of course, only the one chair, and he was standing directly in front of it. Given the size of the office, he'd have to leave the room to give Psellus enough space to squeeze in behind the desk, and then come back in again. Psellus stayed where he was and pretended not to have heard him. It was a moment of great tact, but Falier couldn't really appreciate it. He felt as though he was sharing his office with a tiger.

"If you can spare me a few minutes," Psellus went on, "before the start of the first shift, there are a few questions I'd like to ask you."

Was he asking permission? Would it actually be possible for Falier to say, No, go away? Not really. "Yes please," he heard himself say.

"About a personal matter, really."

That didn't make much sense. "Yes?"

"About your wife."

Oh, he thought; and instead of mere panic, he felt fear. "What can I . . . ?"

"Perhaps we can talk outside, on the landing," Psellus said. "It's a little cramped in here for two people."

Falier wasn't quite sure he could walk. His legs felt weak, and the joints seemed frail under his weight. He had to lean on the desk with his hand to get as far as the door.

"Splendid work you're doing here, by the way," Psellus said, sounding like he meant it. "I realise it must be terribly difficult, with the demands we're making on you and the problems with supply."

"Oh, it's . . ." Falier suddenly couldn't think of anything to say.

"Materials must be specially frustrating," Psellus went on, looking straight ahead, along the gallery towards the frames of the five giant drop-hammers they used for drawing down armour plate. "All my fault, of course. I've given priority to food shipments, so there just aren't the ships or the carts to carry iron or fuel. It's a wretched business, but I don't really have any choice in the matter. Our food reserves are deplorably low, and there's no telling how long we've got before the enemy arrive and cut us off from Lonazep. In fact, I'm surprised they haven't done so already. If there's anything I can do about getting materials, of course, you only have to ask."

Oh well, Falier thought, and said, "Charcoal."

"Yes?"

"We're getting very low." He spoke as though he'd just been running; the words were too big for his throat. "I don't actually know where it comes from . . ."

"There's a syndicate," Psellus answered crisply. "They have a long-standing contract with the charcoal-burners of the Hobec – don't ask me where that is because I haven't a clue. Actually, I asked the Cure Doce ambassador only the other day, and I don't think he knew either. But it's quite some way away. The convoys take six weeks to get here, longer if there's heavy rain. The impression I get is that we buy everything they produce; there simply aren't enough of them to make any more, and if there were, they don't have any more carts. The syndicate asked them quite some time ago if they could increase production, but they didn't sound very keen on the idea. Why bother, was their attitude; why take on more men and build more carts when we're quite happy as we are?" He shook his head with mildly exaggerated sadness. "That's foreigners for you," he said, "they simply don't think like us. Imagine putting happiness before expansion. But anyway, even if we could induce them to change their whole way of life, it'd be months before we saw the benefit; and quite possibly, if we asked them, they'd take bitter offence and refuse to deal with us at all."

He stopped talking, and Falier groped for something to fill the silence. "I see" was the best he could do.

"Meanwhile," Psellus went on, "I've been making enquiries. You know, I do find it odd that nobody ever seems to have considered this before. Even if there wasn't a war, it strikes me as . . . well, curious, that we've been quite happy all this time to rely on a single limited source of supply for something as essential as charcoal. Anyway, it seems that they used to burn charcoal in northern Eremia, decent quantities, enough for their own use, and they could have produced more if they'd had any call for it. But that's no good to us, obviously. I'm told there are colliers in the old country, and they have whole-salers there with their own ships, for making bulk deliveries up and down the coast. If we can get in touch with them, we'll make them a better offer. But as to when all this might start happening . . ." He shrugged. "The tiresome thing is, we're having to do so many new things, we're making it all up as we go along, and there's really no *time* . . ." He stopped, and sighed; he'd been thinking aloud, Falier realised. "But that's not your problem," he said. "Nobody can expect you to work steel without fuel. All I can ask of you is that you do the best you can with what you've got, and it seems to me you're doing just that. For which," he added with a smile, "thank you."

Falier found that as disconcerting as a punch in the mouth. "That's all right," he said. "What I mean is—"

"Now then." No change in the pitch of his voice. "About your wife."

Later, when he'd recovered a little, Falier understood. The unannounced visit, the praise, the frankness and sympathetic reassurance about the charcoal situation, had all been to put him at his ease, let him know he was dealing with a man who was both intelligent and reasonable, before he closed in for the kill.

He told him everything, of course.

"We were in love," he said. "We just wanted to get married and be together. And Ziani . . ." It crossed his mind that he could lie at this point, but he realised it wouldn't be possible to make Commissioner Psellus believe something that wasn't true. "Ziani was in the way. So we had to get rid of him."

He waited for a reaction. Nothing.

"I don't mean murder him, or anything like that," Falier added quickly, appalled by what he'd just said and how it must sound. "We didn't want to hurt him, either of us. But the way things were was just – well, impossible."

A slight movement of Psellus' head told Falier he was about to speak. "She could simply have left Vaatzes and come to live with you," he said. "That sort of thing has happened before, I believe."

"Yes, but . . ." Falier began, then hesitated; because, now he thought about it, that would have been the obvious thing to do. But it hadn't occurred to him at the time. Or she hadn't let it occur to him. She'd insisted . . .

"But never mind that," Psellus went on. "Vaatzes had to be disposed of. What happened then?"

Falier hesitated again. He wasn't quite sure, now he considered it.

"Things happened quickly," he said. "It turned out Ziani was making that stupid doll . . ."

Psellus' eyes were on him now; they were pale and cold, like something dead. "How did you find out about that?"

"She told me."

"That he was making the doll, or that it was . . . ?" A pause. "That it wasn't quite right."

Falier struggled to get the right words. "She told me he was making it," he said. "And I suppose she said how he was spending hours over it, trying to solve problems about how to make it work. And I must have thought about that – at the back of my mind, you know, the way you do; and I suppose it struck me as odd, because if he was following Specification, there wouldn't be any problems to figure out. I mean, you look at the diagrams and the dimensions, it's all there. You don't need to think about it."

"And that led you to believe he was . . . ?"

"I suppose so, yes."

"You suppose so."

The fear, which Psellus had been to so much trouble to dissipate, came back so hard it made Falier catch his breath. "I don't know," he said weakly. "It's hard to get it straight in my mind, somehow; what I figured out for myself and what other people told me . . ."

"What other people?"

"Well, she told me about how long he was spending on it, and . . ." He dried up. No other people. Just her. And how many times had she mentioned it to him? More than once. Quite a few times; almost as if . . . "Just her," he said. "And I must have figured it out for myself."

"All of it?"

"Well . . ." Falier struggled to clear his mind, as though he'd woken up suddenly. "She and I talked about it. I said how I couldn't understand what could be so difficult about it, if he was following Specification. And she . . ."

"She reached the conclusion."

A statement. "Yes," Falier realised. "Yes, she did."

Psellus nodded slowly. It was as though he was being told something he already knew, but the hunger with which he'd been asking the questions contradicted that. "She's an intelligent woman," he said. "I know, I've spoken to her myself, as you know. But even so, I find it hard to accept that she formed that particular conclusion from that particular evidence, if you follow me. But if you say it was her and not you . . ."

Falier nodded eagerly. "I'm sure it was her," he said, "now you mention it."

"I see."

"Well, it seemed so *convenient*." Again, his choice of words disturbed him. "Here we were, trying to find a way of getting him out of the picture, and suddenly this came along. It was . . ."

"A stroke of luck."

"Yes." Falier realised he was feeling painfully cold. "Just what we needed, at just the right time."

"Indeed. So," Psellus went on, "did you go straight to the authorities, or did you investigate further, to make sure the accusation was well founded?"

He wasn't quite sure what to make of how Psellus had phrased that. "I didn't ask Ziani about it, if that's what you mean, or go poking about in his workshop to see if I could find anything wrong. I went to see the people at Compliance, and they told me I needed to talk to the Justice department."

Psellus nodded. "I know about criminal procedure, thank you. But I find it strange: you decided to go straight to the authorities, just on the basis of a conclusion – a guess, really – instead of looking for solid evidence."

Falier frowned. "I . . ."

"It wouldn't have been very hard," Psellus continued. "You were his friend, I assume you visited him at home often enough for your calling there not to seem unusual. His wife could have found some way of making sure he was out of the house for long enough for you to look in his workshop. You're an engineer; you could have taken measurements, interpreted the specifications well enough to detect violations. But you didn't do that."

"No. It didn't seem necessary."

"She told you it wouldn't be necessary."

"Yes."

Fear was thawing his mind now, instead of freezing it; and he couldn't help feeling a desperate kind of admiration for this man who understood him better than he understood himself. Because until Psellus started asking his questions, it simply hadn't occurred to him.

"She thought you had enough for an accusation," Psellus said. "No evidence, just your suspicions."

"That's right."

He nodded slowly. "And the clerks at Justice," he said. "How did they react?"

"They listened to what I told them, and said they'd look into it."

Psellus nodded firmly, as though Falier had given the right answer. "They didn't ask if you had any kind of proof."

"No." Falier felt as if he was sliding on ice. "I assumed that that's how they usually . . ." He shook his head. "I don't know what I thought, at the time. It all seemed to happen so fast, and it meant we could be together; I suppose I didn't want to think about it too deeply, because of what I'd done to Ziani." He twisted, as though trying to get away from something. "And it was the right thing to do, wasn't it? I mean, he was breaking the law."

Psellus looked at him, and he wished he hadn't said that. "Yes," Psellus said. "He was breaking the law, so it must have been the right thing to do. And you sent him to his death, but you didn't try and murder him." Suddenly he grinned. "We did that." Then the energy seemed to leak out of him, and he leaned against the gallery rail. "I met him, you know. I went all the way to Civitas Vadanis, and I met him. We plotted the death of an innocent man together. And he gave us Civitas Eremiae; we'd never have taken it without him, but we'd have wasted thousands of lives trying. He's really a quite extraordinary man; he's done almost as much to help this city as he has to harm it. I hope they'll be able to say the same about me one day, when I'm gone."

Chapter Three

Next morning, Psellus met the architects. He was already tired when the meeting began; he'd been up most of the night reading. The book was on his desk in front of him when they arrived.

It was a long meeting. At first they said it couldn't be done. Then they insisted it couldn't be done in time. After that, they argued that it couldn't be done with the manpower and resources available. For example, there simply weren't that many picks and shovels in the City—

"True," Psellus interrupted. "We're forty thousand shovels short, but I'm seeing to that. By the time they're needed, they'll be ready. Let's see, what else? Wicker baskets, for moving earth. I can lay my hands on ninety thousand, and I've got another twenty thousand on order; they won't be ready in time, so we're going to have to requisition. Watchmen going from house to house, ordering people to hand over their laundry baskets. Lumber; you're about to tell me we need huge quantities of lumber for propping and shoring, and of course it's in desperately short supply and we can't spare the transport to bring any in, even if we could get hold of any at such short notice. That means we'll have to scavenge what we can from shacks and sheds and fences; if needs be, we'll pull the roofs off houses and take the rafters. Gentlemen, since we haven't got everything we need, we're going to have to do what the farmers do, use what we've got instead of what we wish we had. I'm sure you'll cope. After all, you're experts."

After two hours they stopped arguing and started writing down what they'd been assigned to do. Somehow it was harder to cope with them once they'd stopped fighting him. A fight is a dialogue, once you're used to it practically a conversation; he'd met married couples who had no other form of communication except fighting, and they seemed to get on pretty well. Silence broken only by the sound of his own voice was considerably more intimidating.

And, he reflected nervously when they'd all gone, everything's based on the premise that what I've chosen to do is the right thing; and that's crazy. I've just commissioned the biggest building and engineering programme in the history of the Republic, on the authority of a two-hundred-year-old book I found in the library, written by someone I know nothing about, whose only qualifications for advising me are the fact that he wrote a book, and that it's survived two centuries without being cut up and used to mend shoes.

We can't win this war by force of arms, or even by digging. Only one man can save this city, and he's the enemy.

But Psellus didn't have time to sit thinking about one man; he had to figure out how to convince half a million men to drop everything and start digging trenches. And after that; well, he had the book.

Under the piles of papers on his desk a single sheet lay hidden. He found it, made a space and laid it down. It was blank, apart from six words:

Lucao Psellus to Ziani Vaatzes, greetings.

He'd written that a month ago. Since then, whenever his mind was quiet for a moment, he found himself hunting for the words that should follow. He had constructed sentences and paragraphs in his mind, complex as the best Guild clockwork, phrases that were springs, cams, sears, pawls, hooks, lifters, escapements, pushrods and connecting rods, axles, bearings, flanges, shoulders, tumblers, flies and ratchets. He could see the shape of the letter when he closed his eyes, but when he came to assemble the components, he could find no way of fitting them together; because there was no standard, no specification for a letter like this. It wasn't a diplomatic communication, a commercial negotiation, a legal pleading, a dispatch from a spy or a note to a friend, a love letter or a challenge to a duel. There could be no precedent, because the circumstances were unique.

Even so . . . He stood up and crossed the room to his small shelf of books – not the splendid and comprehensive personal library of the

Commissioner of War, but *his* books, which he'd bought with his own money. He thought of them as his toolchest: tables of weights, measures and equivalents, epitomes of regulations and manuals of procedures, almanacs, forms and precedents of all manner of legal and official documents, mathematical tables, indices, bibliographies and prosopographies, the complete Specification (in nine volumes), and a shabby, home-made book that had once belonged to Ziani Vaatzes, the famous abominator. His hand lingered over that one, but he passed on and picked out a thin, red-bound book, patched on the spine with salvaged parchment. It was the first book he'd ever bought.

The Scrivener's mirror, being the complete art and practice of all correspondence formal and private, by an officer of the Scriveners' Guild of the Republic of Mezentia; restricted.

He opened it and smiled. It was more than a book; it was a whole living. The book, a pen, ink and some decent paper, Pattern Seven or better, your Guild ticket, and you need never think again.

He turned to the back, for the list of contents:

*   *From the directors of a company to a creditor, seeking indulgence*
*   *From the directors of a company to a debtor, refusing indulgence*
** *From a bank to the holder of an equitable mortgage on copyholds*
    From a father to his son at the university, politely refusing money
    From a student to his father, passionately requesting money
** *From a resident alien to the residency commissioners, seeking leave to renew domiciliary status*
    From a woman to a man of equal status, declining marriage
    From a woman to a man of superior status, declining marriage
*   *From a manufacturer to a prospective customer, listing and commending products*
*   *From a manufacturer to an existing customer, excusing late delivery*
    From a host to a recently departed guest, tactfully requesting return of household objects
    From a bailiff to his master, conveying respectful congratulations on the birth of (a) a son (b) a daughter
    From a friend, concerning a miscarriage
*   *From a trader to a carrier, disputing the rebuttal of a claim for breakages*
    From a lover; general

> *From a prisoner to his judges, beseeching clemency*
> *From a condemned man, an open letter of (a) repentance (b)*
> *defiance*
> * *From a vendor of dried fruits to the market commissioners, con-*
> *cerning allegations of short measure*

Only the forms marked with a double star had the status of specifications; a single star meant strongly recommended. A triple star meant the form could only be used by a senior member of the Guild in good standing, but there weren't very many of those. He turned the pages slowly, looking for a phrase or a happy collision of words that would at least get him started.

(What were you supposed to do, when you were called upon to make something for which no specification existed? It was a question that was regularly set in the ethics papers of Guild professional exams, and it was an open secret that all the possible answers to it were equally wrong; the purpose of the question was to gauge the candidate's tolerances of error when error was inevitable.)

Lucao Psellus to Ziani Vaatzes, greetings.

First, I expect you'd like to know that Ariessa and Moritsa are both well. I have this from your friend Falier, whom I spoke to this morning.

(That was from Form 207, a parent to his son abroad on behalf of the family business. Not inappropriate, as far as it went.)

With regard to the present crisis

The nearest anybody ever came to a correct answer was that no citizen of the Republic would ever place an order for an artefact for which there was no specification (excluding, of course, military equipment reserved for the defence of the City). The order would, therefore, inevitably have come from a foreigner, and the appropriate response would be to persuade him that what he'd asked for didn't and couldn't exist, and to encourage him to order the nearest equivalent from the authorised catalogue; failing that, show him the door.

With regard to the present crisis, I find it impossible to believe that it is your intention to destroy the City and murder your fellow citizens. I appreciate that you may believe you have a grievance against us

He sighed, and drew a line through the paragraph. Another sheet of paper wasted. Fortunately, paper was made from old rags, boiled, crushed and rolled. The siege could last a hundred years and there'd still be enough rags in the City to make all the paper they needed.

We do not have to agree on the causes or the right and wrong of the present crisis. I refuse to believe that you want to see the City destroyed and your fellow citizens slaughtered. I prefer to think that there must be something else that you want. Tell me what it is; if I can get or arrange it for you, I will. In return

He frowned, bit his lip and leafed through the red-bound book until he found what he was looking for.

In return, we would – scratch that – I would only ask that you use your best endeavours to rectify the present situation, bearing in mind the mutual benefit that must accrue from the cessation of the current

It was a one-star precedent, which meant he could change it if it was demonstrably necessary. He drew another line.

In return, stop helping the Vadani and the savages. Better still, do what you did at Civitas Eremiae. I am now in a position to give you assurances you can rely on. You know me. We've already worked together. I can guarantee your safety, arrange a full pardon. If you want money, I can arrange that too.

Again he paused, lifted the pen to draw another line, hesitated and left it alone. He could always come back to it later.

You may wish to consider other possibilities; for example, the reaction of your present allies should they ever find out who betrayed Civitas Eremiae to us, or who contrived the false evidence against Duke Orsea, which led Duke Valens to have him killed. I understand that Valens is now married to Orsea's widow; an uncomfortable alliance, I can't help thinking, and one which might not survive the revelations I'm in a position to make. From what I know of him, I believe Duke Valens is the sort of man who would spare no ingenuity in finding a suitable way to express his feelings towards someone who'd placed him in such an impossible position. There are many ways to die, some of them considerably more distressing than others. (I would also suggest that as soon as you have read this letter, you should burn it. Were it to fall into the hands of your new friends, the consequences are all too easy to imagine.)

He wasn't at all happy with that. Too crude; an open threat, practically a challenge to Vaatzes' proven resourcefulness. Also, there was the very real possibility that the letter might be intercepted. He drew a thin line through the paragraph, to remind him to tinker with it later.

You may ask yourself why, if it's in my power to destroy you, I have not already done so. You may believe the answer I'm about to give, or not, as you see fit.

There are two reasons. First:

(He liked that way of structuring a proposition. Businesslike, unambiguous, easily grasped. The book recommended highlighting each subsection with an illuminated capital letter, but he knew his own limitations when it came to freehand drawing.)

First: if I betray you, you will die and my enemies will lose a most useful adviser, but I do not believe they will abandon the siege, or the war. If you can be induced to betray them,

Back to the book. He liked this phrase so much he'd turned down the corner of the page.

(You will, I trust, pardon my bluntness; this matter is too important to both of us for me to afford myself the luxury of polite circumlocution.)

Yes, but would Ziani know what circumlocution meant? He sighed, and crossed it out again.

If you can be induced to betray them, we stand some kind of chance of beating them, winning the war and saving the City. I say "we"; at some level, I regard you as a potential ally as much as an enemy, which brings me on to my next point.

He shook his head, and put a line through everything after "City".

Second: whether or not you choose to believe it, I would prefer so to arrange matters that you survive this crisis and find some sort of resolution satisfactory to yourself. Being realistic, you must understand that you can never come back to the City; anything else, however, that you may reasonably aspire to is eminently possible, provided you have the goodwill of a powerful friend. I would invite you to consider me in that light. What you have already done in the service of our enemies reveals you to be a man of exceptional abilities. To waste those abilities

He read what he'd just written; then, slowly, he tore the page across and dropped it on the floor. Then he stooped, picked it up again and screwed it into a ball.

Time for his fencing lesson. He hadn't had time to practise the exercises. Most likely the instructor hadn't expected him to.

"Today," the instructor said, "I'd like to explain the theory of time and distance."

Psellus felt quietly relieved. He liked theory. He had no trouble understanding it, and it meant he could sit down, rather than floundering about along the chalk line.

"In fencing" – he was looking past Psellus, over his shoulder, as though addressing an invisible class – "time and distance are so closely related that we can barely tell where one ends and the other begins. Time is distance, and distance is time. Distance matters, because you can't stab a man if he isn't there. So, if I have time to take a step back, so your sword can't reach me, I can always be safe."

Psellus nodded eagerly.

"Distance," the instructor went on, "in fencing parlance, is the space between two enemies. Full distance is where neither man can touch the other without moving his feet. If you're at full distance, he has to take a step forward before he can reach you; and of course, that gives you time to take a step back, which maintains the distance." He paused. "Are you still with me, or . . . ?"

"That's fine," Psellus said happily. "Go on."

The instructor nodded gravely. "Close distance," he went on, "is where both men are close enough to strike each other. When you close the distance, he can hit you, but you can hit him too. In fencing, danger is mutual; you need to bear that in mind at all times."

"Of course," Psellus said. He liked the sound of full distance much better, of course.

"Now then." The instructor's voice became brisker. "Suppose you're at full distance, and you believe your enemy's about to move towards you. There are three options. You can move back – safe, but it means he's safe too – or you can stay where you are and try blocking his attack with a defence – what we call a ward – or you can move forward at the same time he does, hoping to block his attack and make an attack of your own simultaneously. That is, of course, a dangerous choice; it can end up with both of you killing the other, for instance, and you'd be surprised how often that happens. But if you can make it work, it's the best choice of all, because as you close the distance you also close the time. He's got no time to defend himself or get out of the way, and so you win. We call that an action in single time, as opposed to where he attacks and you retreat, then you attack and he retreats; that's double time. All right so far?"

Psellus nodded, but he wasn't quite sure; the implications were too broad to be assimilated so quickly. He'd have to think about it later, if he could remember it all.

"For an action in single time," the instructor went on, and his voice suggested that he was reciting a scripture long since learnt by heart, "we can either simultaneously block and strike, or simultaneously avoid and strike. This is where the two main schools of fencing diverge. In the Eremian school—"

"I'm sorry," Psellus interrupted. "What did you call it?"

"The Eremian school. They have – well, had, I suppose – a long and rich tradition of fencing. The Eremian school" – he's lost his place, Psellus thought guiltily – "is up and down a straight line, because after all, a line's the shortest distance between two points, and the shorter the distance, the less time you need. The Vadani school is based on a circle. Basically, you avoid the attack by moving sideways and make your own attack by going forward; so, if you imagine a circle drawn on the ground—"

"I'm sorry," Psellus said. "A circle."

The instructor looked sad. "Well, strictly speaking, more of a hexagon, or an octagon, even, but a circle's easier to picture. Imagine the centre of the circle is a point exactly between the tips of the swords of two men at full distance." He frowned, then added, "It's much easier if I draw a diagram. If you've got some paper . . ."

The end of the lesson. Half a dozen sheets of paper, covered in lines, circles, hexagons (Psellus had insisted), some plain, some with arrows to show the direction of the defender's feet. An insincere promise to review it all before the next lesson and ask about anything he hadn't understood.

It had all been perfectly fine until the circle. If you don't want to get hit, be somewhere else; he'd grasped that just fine (except how can you move an entire city out of the way? You can't, especially if there's no time, less than nine days before close distance). He could understand staying put and blocking, which was, after all, what walls were for – walls and bastions and ravelins, and all those bizarre shapes in the two-hundred-year-old book, that could be the wild sketches of a lunatic for all he knew. Staying put, blocking and hitting back all at the same time; he understood that, and they ought to have superiority in artillery, although with Vaatzes out there they couldn't be sure. But the circle (or, properly speaking, the octagon), the move sideways and forwards in single time . . . If only, he felt, he could understand that, all his troubles would be over. And the volte – well, he'd been told to forget about the volte, since it was intermediate going on advanced, and they wouldn't be getting on to it for some time, so it'd only confuse him, but it did illustrate the principles perfectly, so they might as well just touch on it briefly; the volte, where you swing sideways out of the line of attack and watch the enemy walk blithely on to your sword-point, so that his own movement impales him . . .

Psellus picked up the diagrams, stacked them neatly, put them on his desk and covered them with a twenty-page report, so he wouldn't have to see them. The volte, he thought. The volte is the essence of single time. The volte is where you and your enemy *co-operate* . . .

Ziani Vaatzes. He wants to walk into my sword, provided he can get to where he wants to be. Not wants; needs. (It was a moment of revelation, purely intuitive, though he didn't realise that until later.) Ziani Vaatzes is a man with no choices; a man in single time, at all times. His line is straight, and that means that somehow I have to get my poor muddled head around this business of the circle. Or, properly speaking, octagon.

The quickest way to a man's death is through his heart, but if you want to get into his brain . . .

The work, they'd confidently told him, would take a year. That had depressed him, before he learned the truth about time and distance.

He'd sent for the master instructor of the Potters', and ordered him to build a model of the City out of clay. The master had replied that there was no specification for anything like that, but he'd convinced him that it came under the heading of military engineering, so that was all right.

And here it was; built to Guild standards, which meant it was beautifully detailed and immaculately glazed (they'd wanted to paint it, too; he'd had to be quite firm. Foliate scroll and acanthus motifs picked out in gold leaf weren't going to help him beat the savages), it stood on a Pattern Sixteen square beech table in Necessary Evil's cloister in the Guildhall grounds. Two worried-looking men stood by with buckets of earth dug out of the flowerbeds as the rest of the committee assembled for the briefing.

Psellus cleared his throat. They'd come to recognise the significance of that mild, sheeplike noise. Bizarrely, they'd come to trust it, too.

"Well," he said (how tired he sounded, they said afterwards; too tired to be nervous or scared), "here's the City." He paused, briefly reflecting on the absurdity of that statement. "While I think of it, formal vote of thanks to the Potters' for this fine model." A quick, low mumble of agreement, and the secretary scribbled something in his book.

"Now then." Psellus sighed. The temptation was to gabble, get it all over and done with. He wasn't used to speaking slowly. All his working life, he'd had to talk fast, to get his information across before someone more important interrupted. "As we all know, our ancestors of blessed memory fortified the City to the highest possible specification. We have the four concentric circles of main walls; the outer wall, which is thirty feet high and five feet thick; the outer curtain, twenty feet and four feet, the inner curtain, likewise, and the citadel, forty feet high and eight feet thick. At the time . . ." He paused, to let the words soak in. "At the time, the specification was more than adequate to cope with any possible threat the City could ever face from its potential enemies: the Eremians, the Vadani, the Cure Doce, even the savages beyond the desert. Our engineers designed our defences to withstand the methods of direct assault available to such unsophisticated attackers; attempts to batter down the gates, to scale the walls using ladders or primitive towers, and to undermine the walls by tunnelling under them. For obvious reasons" – he paused again – "they didn't bother to consider an assault by artillery, since only the Republic had the knowledge and capacity to build siege engines, and it was unthinkable that either of those could ever be acquired by an enemy."

He looked round. He had their attention.

"All that," he said, "has changed. The abominator Ziani Vaatzes has proved, at Civitas Eremiae, that he can train primitives to build functional artillery; that he can do so, furthermore, in an appallingly short time. I have reason to believe," he went on, looking over their heads, "that at this moment, the bulk of the savages' army is at a place called Vassa – you won't have heard of it; there's a map in my office if you want to look it up, but it's about half a day from Civitas Vadanis, it's the site of the second largest Vadani silver mine, and it's beside a big river, with a very large forest on the other side. You may find this news comforting, because it means the enemy are far away and in no hurry to come here. I'm afraid I don't agree."

A few of the older committee members were starting to fidget. The traditions of Necessary Evil didn't include long speeches.

"Here's why," Psellus went on. "Vassa is a silver mine, as I just said. That means it has the best the Vadani have to offer in the way of industrial facilities: furnaces, some established workshops, above all men who have a degree of experience in rudimentary engineering. There are already a number of quite large mills on the river, built to crush ore for smelting, but easily converted by a man of Vaatzes' abilities to run saws, trip-hammers, anything he wants and can make. The forest is an unlimited source of lumber. Also, according to what we know about the region – very little, of course, a few references in some very old books – silver isn't the only metal in the ground in those parts. There's also a very old abandoned iron mine, the Weal Calla. Two hundred years ago, it provided us with a quarter of our second-quality raw iron, until we found a cheaper supply in the old country and stopped buying. The mine was closed down, but it's still there."

They'd stopped fidgeting now.

"So," he went on, "at Vassa, Vaatzes has almost everything he needs. He has water power, some plant and machinery, iron, lumber and charcoal, a core of semi-skilled workers and unlimited unskilled labour. With these, he can start building siege engines. In fact," he said, raising his voice just a little, "we have every reason to believe he's already doing so. Our scouts – we have scouts now, by the way, thanks to our new best friends, the Cure Doce – tell me that smoke is visible from long distances – our scouts aren't keen on getting too close – and that road-building parties have been out in all directions, working with rather alarming speed and efficiency, presumably to make it possible for Vaatzes to cart in the food and supplies he needs for the very large number of people he's gathered there."

He stopped, drank a sip of water, took a moment to rest his voice. He'd never imagined talking could be so tiring.

"What this means," he continued, "is that our enemy isn't coming here quite yet. I believe that the cavalry squadrons posted nine days away are there simply to scare us; to make us think we have barely any time to prepare ourselves. I'm proposing to test this theory, now that we have the Cure Doce field army at our disposal, but that's a subject for another day. I believe that Vaatzes is taking his time, because he knows that without artillery, the savages can't take the City, even though there's close on a million of them and we have no trained soldiers, because the existing fortifications are such that they can't mount an effective assault in the time available to them; time which is very closely restricted by their own problems of supply. Put simply: they can't get enough food here to feed an army big enough to storm the City without artillery. By the same token, they can't lay a siege, because they'd starve long before we do.

"With artillery, however, our enemy's success isn't just possible, it's practically certain. We designed the weapons Vaatzes can bring to bear on us. We designed them to trash the sort of walls we're relying on, in weeks, maybe even days. Not to make too much of a song and dance about it: our walls are two skins of stone holding in an infill of earth and rubble. Smash up the bottom of the outer skin sufficiently, and the weight of the wall, particularly the loose infill, does the rest. Once the walls are breached, of course, we're done for. We have no trained soldiers to defend a breach. It'd be like punching a hole in a bucket of water."

He stopped talking and looked at them all, and for the first time, he didn't feel in the least intimidated. That in itself was faintly disheartening. All these wise men, but none of them with any more brains than he had.

"But we have time," he went on, "time and distance. If I'm right, it's a race. We have to learn how to fortify against artillery and get the work done before Vaatzes can teach the savages how to build siege engines. It's a race I think we can win. I believe so, because we already have all the information we need" – he picked up the book and held it so they could see; of course, it could have been any old book, for all they knew – "and the tools, and the manpower. Basically, it's just digging, carting earth from one place to another and dumping it. It's not difficult to learn. In fact, I believe that, given time, training and the right incentives, even the members of this committee could manage it."

Silence. He made a mental note: no more jokes.

"Vaatzes, on the other hand, faces a rather greater challenge. We can all dig, and we can all read the book. In what he's got to do, a huge part of it can only be done by Vaatzes himself. He's got to teach miners and village-level blacksmiths and carpenters how to be engineers; he's got to design the machines he needs, probably build the prototypes mostly by himself; he's got to organise and supervise a workforce of a million men, see to every detail, hold it all in his mind all the time. Also, he's got supplies to worry about, more so than we do. He has to get food from somewhere, food for his men and hay and fodder for the savages' herds of livestock. I believe he'll need to get the silver mine at Vassa working again, on top of everything else he's doing there, just to pay for what he needs to buy. But even then, he can't feed his people on silver. He must be planning on trading with the coast, through Lonazep, like us; essentially, shopping in the same market as us, which of course makes him vulnerable. Whatever he's paying, we'll have to pay more. That, at least, is one kind of war we understand.

"So, like I said, we probably have a little time. Now, if you'd care to look closely at the model here, I'll show you what I have in mind."

The men with the buckets, who'd nearly gone to sleep, sprang forward. They dumped their earth in piles, and the two representatives of the Architects', who'd been sitting quietly at the back, set to with little rakes and trowels, moving the earth around like children playing sandcastles. For a while it was just a silly mess; but then shapes began to form.

(What we need, Psellus thought as he watched, isn't engineers so much as gardeners.)

"This," he said as he pointed, "is really just a great big bank of earth, all round the City. You'll have to imagine the equally big hole out here somewhere, which is where we'll take the earth from. In point of fact, that'll be our first line of defence, since we'll divert the Brownwater and the Vane into it and flood it to make a nice wide moat, which ought to make Vaatzes' life rather more interesting. Now, these wedge-shaped bits sticking out of the bank are called bastions; the idea is to put our own artillery on them, and you'll see that, because of how they stick out, the engines will be able to shoot in all directions; there won't be any blind spots or safe areas where sappers can hide while they're digging under the walls. The great thing about making the bastions out of plain old ordinary earth is that they'll be soft. Vaatzes' engines can pound them with rocks and they'll just sink in, rather than smashing them up, which is what would happen if they were made of stone, like the walls. Obviously, sooner or later a continuous bombardment will shatter the brick and timber frameworks that keep the earth in, or else shake the earth loose; but that'll take time, which is the rarest and most precious commodity in this whole business. Time is the key, you see. We don't have to keep them out for ever; only for long *enough*. We all know the saying, time is money. It's a lot more than that. Time is distance; time is flour and animal feed and firewood, it's the patience of Vaatzes' barbarian allies – they're nomads, they aren't used to staying in one place. Time is overflowing latrines and a sudden flood of rain, leading to dysentery and plague; it's the grain surplus of the faraway places we don't even know about, where they grow the wheat that's shipped to Lonazep, and which isn't infinite." He paused, smiled a little. "It's a paradox," he went on. "Here in the City we make weapons out of steel, the best anywhere, which we don't know how to use; but what we've never realised before is that everything in our lives is really a weapon – the food we eat, the earth we stand on, lumber, bricks, shovels, buckets, carts, horses; and of course time." And one other thing, he thought but didn't say; the one thing that'll win this war for us, if anything can, the deadliest weapon of all. "Now we know we're not soldiers," he went on, "because we don't know a lot about spears and bows and arrows, or drill, or cavalry tactics. So, we can't expect to fight a war with soldiers and their kind of weapons. So instead we'll fight with the weapons we do know how to use, or those we can learn about quickly and easily: food, earth, water, money and time. The whole point of the Republic is knowing what to do and doing it well, doing what we know best. That's why we have the Guilds, and Specification. That's all we've got; we don't have armies or generals, just as we don't have dukes and princes and kings. Well; we don't have them, we don't need them, we don't even want them. We can win this war, beat the savages and save the City, just so long as we do what we're best at: ingenuity, resourcefulness, and plenty of hard, gruelling work. Or," he added, with a little nod of his head, "we can all give up, wait for the savages to come at us with Vaatzes' engines, and die. I think it's a fairly straightforward choice, but what do I know, I'm just a clerk who never wanted this job. I suppose it's up to you to decide, but you'd better do it quickly, and once you've made your decision, you'd better stick to it. Otherwise . . . well." He shook his head. "Unless someone else has any ideas. I'd be delighted to hear them."

Nobody said anything, of course, and Psellus thought: well, so much for politics. We've always had so much of it, we've been so busy about it all these years, and it turns out we were wasting our time. Now it's suddenly turned serious, and they'll follow any bloody fool, so long as someone else'll do all the dangerous thinking for them. At any rate, if we do lose, it takes the sting out of it, a bit. After all, if we're this pathetic when it really matters, maybe we wouldn't be such a great loss, after all.

They were waiting for him to say something.

"I think that's all, really," he said. "I take it nobody's got anything else to contribute; in which case, we might as well make a start. I've taken the liberty of writing up a schedule – we'll need to alter it as we go along, naturally, at this stage it's more guesswork than anything, so please don't feel afraid to say what you think about it. I've also given each of you your own specific assignments. I'll be talking to you about those over the next day or so, after we've all had a chance to reflect on what I've just told you. First priority, I think, is to organise the workforce, get everybody's names on a register and assign them to where they'll be needed. Aniaces, that'll be your job, you'll want to talk to the Guilds, they know everybody's names and where they live. It shouldn't be too hard really, all the infrastructure's in place already. Maybe you could see me around ten this evening, once you've had a chance to gather your thoughts, and we'll go through it together. Pazzas, I want you to take charge of the food supply, getting in as much as we can, storage, distribution systems. Oniazes, I'd like you to handle material procurement – speak to Alexicaccus at the Foundrymen's, Falier at the ordnance factory, Zeuxis at the Carpenters', you know who to talk to as well as I do. I suggest we meet again the day after tomorrow, when we should all have a clearer idea of what we're about, and we'll take it from there."

Later, when he was back in his office and alone again, he started to shake. It took a while for it to pass, and then he felt terribly cold, especially in his knees and hands. He thought for a while about Ziani Vaatzes, who'd escaped from the Guildhall by jumping out of a window.

It's tempting, he thought, but I'm too old to jump.

He wasn't quite sure what happened to the next fortnight. It didn't seem to have passed, because the enemy were still at Vassa, still only nine days away. Only nine days to go, then, before the end of the world, in single time. The trick, according to the fencing master, was to step a day back for every day forward taken by the enemy. So far, it seemed to be working, but it was making him feel dizzy.

At some point during those fourteen days, the members of Necessary Evil (his colleagues; dear God, his *subordinates*) had been busy. Each Guild had produced a register of all its members who were able-bodied and available for work, arranged and subdivided by factory, chapel, ward and lodge; each subdivision had its work assignment; all the assignments had been co-ordinated into a Grand Over-Arching Schedule (either a work of genius or the biggest joke ever perpetrated, but only time would tell); the necessary tools and materials for each job at each stage of the Schedule had been sourced, located and batched for delivery. From the gatehouse towers, you could see a forest of sticks standing up out of the plain in front of the City like some bizarre failed crop, each stick flying a little coloured pennant, each colour having its own secret significance to the surveyors' branch of the Architects', and between the taller, thicker sticks were strung taut lines of red and blue twine, marking sites of trenches, foundations, bastions, supporting walls, so that the observer from the tower might easily believe he was looking at a technical drawing, a lifesize blueprint. So far, of course, nobody had actually sunk a spade or filled a bucket. But there was still time.

His colleagues, subordinates, subjects had done all that; Psellus, by contrast, had spent those illusory fourteen days doing very little, at least by his own reckoning. He'd met people – the Cure Doce ambassador, scouts, the heads of departments – all of whom had told him in great detail what was being done, by other people. He'd listened and soaked in the information, until he felt quite bloated with details; but he hadn't actually *done* anything.

Instead, he'd sat and wrestled with the book. The text was bad enough; he'd finally figured out what palisades, cuvettes, cordons, scarp and counterscarp revetments, embrasures and escalades were, but he still couldn't get his poor head around counterforts or ecluses. It was the pictures, though, that haunted him. The shapes were just shapes; abstracts, symmetrical patterns of lines, essays in the geometry of violence, manmade and unnatural – except that they kept reminding him of things, and that was what was so disturbing. The bastion with complex ravelins assailed by saps and defended by countermines, for example, put him in mind of the head of an insect, with multiple eyes and projecting feelers, while other formations and patterns were stars or snowflakes, perfect but encumbered with strange and malevolent growths swelling out of them, grotesque and disgusting in a way that no picture of people or animals could ever be. At times, he caught himself feeling afraid of the book; savages and primitives believed in books that could suck your soul out through your eyes as you read them, books that could wrap their pages round your head and swallow you, words that crawled into your brain like tapeworms. Of course, he wasn't a primitive or a savage.

Saps; they, he was beginning to understand, were the real danger. If everything in the Grand Over-Arching Schedule actually happened, the City would be safe from Vaatzes' stone-throwers (not for ever, but for long enough; query, however, whether time fences in a straight line or a circle); and all the enemy had to do in order to be safe from the City's engines was to fall back a hundred yards or so. Artillery, then, was a negatable threat, and once both sides had figured that out (he had a depressing feeling they wouldn't take his word for it and save themselves the effort), the war would go underground and start burrowing, like maggots.

The book had plenty to say about sapping; about mines, countermines, camouflets, petards, galleries, stanchions and globes of compression. The basic idea was very simple: dig a tunnel under a wall. To keep it from caving in while you're building it, you need to hold up the roof with wooden props; when you've finished, you pack the end of the tunnel, directly under the foundations of the wall, with straw, brushwood and scrap lumber, all thoroughly soaked in lamp oil. Strike a spark and run; the fire burns through the props, down comes the roof, and the ensuing subsidence topples the wall.

Try that with a solid bank of earth, of course, and you achieved very little – a few dimples, maybe a crater, but nothing you could send an army into and hope ever to see it again. The book was ruthlessly straightforward when it came to proposing a countermeasure: *first, storm the bastion.* That was the point at which Psellus closed the book. He wasn't quite sure why, or at least he couldn't reduce it to words, but it was something to do with the thought of the unspeakable degree of effort involved – *first* storm the bastion, *then* start digging tunnels, where necessary chipping through any solid rock that might be encountered in the process. The thought of it – the work, the slaughter, the sheer weight of dirt to be shovelled into baskets in the dark and carried – made him feel sick. He looked at the pictures and saw the heads of insects; he read about sapping, and thought about ants. It was all too inhuman.

(Also, pointless; but it would have to be done, even though it wouldn't win the war. Only a letter could do that.)

Well, there was still time. He could force himself to read the rest of the book later, when it became unavoidable. In the meantime, he submerged himself with an enthusiasm little short of joy in banal, tedious administration, like a fish thrown back into the water by an angler. His clerks glared at him behind his back, of course. They felt that his insistence on doing routine paperwork that should have been their job was intended as a criticism. He felt bad about that; but he needed the columns of figures to soak up the diagrams that lingered in his head, like sawdust on spilled blood.

From time to time he wasted a sheet of paper trying to write the letter. The clerks learned to stay out of his way on such occasions.

Iosao Phryzatses, chief scout. As the door opened, he was expecting to see a spare, weatherbeaten man in worn buckskin and knee-length boots. Instead . . .

"Thank you for finding the time to see me," he heard himself say. "I'm sure you're very busy at the moment."

The little round man frowned, very slightly. "No, not particularly," he said, and stood perfectly still next to the empty chair, until Psellus remembered his manners and asked him to sit. He sat down – *expertly*, there was no other word for it. The slightest of movements, and he'd gone from a man standing to a man sitting. Psellus was tempted to make him stand up, just so he could watch him do it again.

"Now then," he said, trying to sound brisk. "Your latest report."

Phryzatses nodded, another tiny movement, then went back to being perfectly still. He was dressed in ordinary City clothes, plain but brand new and of the best quality of cloth allowed for that particular cut under Specification. His shoes glowed.

"The situation at Vassa," Psellus said. "I don't suppose you remembered to bring—"

Before he had a chance to finish the sentence, Phryzatses' rather chubby hand vanished inside his jacket and came out with a slim brass tube, which he tapped smartly on the edge of the desk. Out of one end popped the edge of a roll of paper. He teased it out with his precisely trimmed fingernails, unrolled it and smoothed it out with the side of his hand. "The map," he said.

"Thank you." Psellus reached for it, glanced at it. He had trouble with maps.

"That's north." Phryzatses touched one edge of the paper with his fingertip.

"Ah, yes."

The whole idea of maps was somehow disconcerting; because how could you possibly draw one? You'd have to breed giant eagles whose backs you could ride on, to get up high enough to see. Otherwise, he couldn't figure out how it was possible. It'd be like drawing with your eyes shut (though he believed that was possible, too).

But never mind. "So this is the river," he heard himself say, "and these must be the new roads they're building. Sorry, where's the iron mine?"

"Weal Calla," Phryzatses said. "There, look."

"Oh, I see, that sort of star shape is a mine." Psellus frowned, aware that he probably wasn't making a terribly good impression. But that didn't matter any more, did it? "So this must be the silver mine here. What's the scale, by the way?"

"An inch to a mile." From inside his coat, Phryzatses produced a small, elegant pair of callipers, Pattern Ninety, with an incised calibrated scale. Psellus took them and twirled them about for a bit, to show willing. "Thank you," he said. "So much easier if you've got a map," he lied. "Now, you said in the report, about these new buildings here . . ." He touched the little blobs which he took to represent the buildings with the leg of the callipers. "I take it . . ."

"The new buildings aren't actually shown on the map," Phryzatses said. "What you're pointing at is a string of dew-ponds, as you can see from the key at the bottom. There's a little number seven, look, and—"

"Ah, yes." He didn't bother looking. "So these new sheds would be . . ."

"Here."

A fingernail, pressed on a piece of paper. Psellus looked at it anyway.

"And you believe," he said, "that these sheds are where Vaatzes is building the siege engines."

"It seems likely." Phryzatses settled back into his chair. It was a perfect fit, tailored. "That's only an inference, of course, drawn from the proximity of the existing waterwheels at Nine, the furnace complex at Five" – oh, I see, Psellus realised, he's talking about the little numbers drawn on the map – "and the barracks at Three. As to whether production is actually under way, I have no information as yet. The sheds would appear to be complete, but it seems logical to suppose that it will take him a while to set up his production line. How long exactly, we can't really say. Here in the City, it could easily take six months. But we know that Vaatzes has the ability to do these things remarkably quickly. Note also," he went on, "how close the sheds are to the river; this will make it possible for him to ship in materials by barge."

Psellus frowned. "Oh," he said. "But surely not, the water-mills are in the way."

"I don't think so."

"But . . . Oh, I see, the river flows down the page, not up. No, that can't be right, or it'd be flowing uphill. Here, look – I take it these little lines mean a hill?"

"That's correct, yes." Phryzatses was scowling at the map. "Yes, you're right. The current must run east–west."

"You don't . . ." Psellus didn't say the rest of it: *you don't actually know, you haven't actually been there yourself.* Well, why should he? It didn't matter, after all. But for some reason he felt surprisingly disappointed. "I'm only guessing the mills are big enough to block the river," he heard himself say. "You might get that checked, if you wouldn't mind."

Curt nod (he doesn't like being found out, Psellus guessed).

"It's actually quite important," Psellus went on, "because the ambassador is talking about trying to get his men in there by water, rather than on foot. He doesn't think there'd be much hope of getting there from the south; coming down through the forest from the north would be better, but even so he's afraid his people would be seen by the logging teams on their way. But if they could float right up to the sheds on barges, he feels they're in with a chance, of sorts. Hence," he went on with a smile, "we do need to know which direction the river runs, and since we don't seem to have any other reliable maps . . ."

"Understood," Phryzatses said. "I'll see to it." He hesitated, then added: "I should point out that we don't actually know these sheds are where the engines are going to be built, it's just a supposition at this point. I wouldn't want—"

Psellus nodded. "Quite," he said. "But obviously he needs large buildings to make the engines in, and you tell me there aren't any others that'd be suitable. So it must be these."

"It would appear likely, yes."

It would appear likely; but of course, that's one of the tiresome things about war. So much guesswork and supposition, when it'd be so much more civilised to write the enemy a polite letter and ask him if the sheds really are his arms factory. Even more civilised, of course, and hugely more sensible not to have a war at all. "Let's hope you're right," he said wearily. "They may be Cure Doce, but they're the only soldiers we've got. The days when we could afford to be extravagant with our armies because there's always plenty more where they came from are over, I'm sorry to say. Still, I'm sure you've done everything possible, so we'll leave it at that. Just find out about the river, please, if you could. How long will that take, do you think?"

When Phryzatses had gone, Psellus sat and stared at the map for a long time, screwing up his eyes to read the little numbers, and looking them all up in turn in the key at the bottom. He tried to distil the lines and colours into a picture, but he couldn't. Hardly surprising, he told himself. Apart from his visit to Civitas Vadanis, he'd only been out of the City a few times in his life, and never so far that he couldn't see the top of the gatehouse towers in the distance. Great rivers, hidden valleys, forests – he believed in them, the same way men believed in gods they knew they'd never see, but his imagination skated off them, like a file off hard steel.

Later that evening, he sent for the Cure Doce ambassador, showed him the map, promised him a copy by morning, and gave the formal order to proceed with the raid. Afterwards, he walked slowly down the hundred and seven granite steps from the reception rooms to the courtyard. It was a clear night, and the stars were shining; their light shocked him, and for a moment he had an unaccountable feeling that they were falling down on him, like snow, or the shining heads of a volley of arrows.

Chapter Four

Linniu Matsinatsen was the eldest son of a fairly large farm in the Coinsolinnsa valley, the soft, misty heart of the rambling Cure Doce country. He was nineteen years old, which meant he knew how to plough and harrow, cut and stack hay, feed and herd cattle, carry water, castrate and dehorn the young bullocks, plane and mortice wood and forge nails; in a few years' time, he'd inherit the duties of pruning the fruit trees, looking after the bees, cutting the bracken for winter bedding, taking the pigs to the wood in acorn season and raising and killing the geese. After that, nothing would change until his father got old, at which point he'd take over the sowing and the harvest, slaughtering, malting, and the rest of the major work, subject to his father's instructions as to when, where and how. By then, of course, he'd have a son of his own, who'd start with feeding the poultry and slowly work his way up. Before the summons came, he'd never been more than seven miles from the farm, and he could remember the names and faces of everybody he'd ever met.

Now he was an archer in the People's Defence Force. He wasn't quite sure why; it was something to do with a vast army of savages who'd burst out of some place he'd never heard of and were planning to destroy the great city of Mezentia, where the axe-blades, hammerheads, saws, chisels, kitchen knives and needles came from, and this clearly couldn't be allowed to happen. Why this was clear he didn't know and didn't like to ask.

Being a soldier was something he'd dreamed about, needless to say. His uncle Loimen had been a soldier, for a month, thirty years ago. Loimen was older than Father, who'd been too young. He'd gone with fifty or so other sons of other considerable farms to fight the Vadani duke over something to do with water, and it had been the turning point in his life, for several reasons. He'd been away from the valley, for one. This automatically made him the district's leading and only authority on world affairs, strange and obscure customs in foreign lands, medicine, history and geography. He'd acquired (accounts varied as to how) a vast treasure in gold, silver and bronze, looted from the dead: buckles, buttons, a penknife with stagshorn scales, a fork and two pairs of scissors, together worth more than forty pence, and this wealth had made it possible for him to buy the pedigree Swayback bull on which was founded the celebrated Matsinatsen herd. He still owned a genuine Mezentine sword, which hung in stupendous honour over his fireplace. Finally, he'd lost an eye, and three fingers from his left hand, which meant he'd forfeited the main farm when his father died, since he wasn't up to running it, and was packed off to Lower End.

Such an ambiguous precedent left Linniu feeling uncertain when the summons came, and his parents' reaction hadn't helped much to clarify his mind. Mother had burst into tears and declared that he couldn't possibly go; he'd die, or come back horribly mutilated, and then there'd be nobody to run the farm and they'd all starve to death and Rinoj would never get a husband and it was the end of the world. Father hadn't said anything much, but Linnui got the distinct impression that he was pleased, because once Linniu came back he'd be the soldier, with a sword of his own for the fireplace, and Loimen wouldn't be able to throw his useless weight around quite so much in future; also, if there was any vast treasure in gold, silver and bronze to be had (and to hear Loimen talk, all you had to do was bother to fill your pockets), he had plenty of ideas on what it could be spent on, starting with a thoroughbred boar and a new share for the second-best plough. As for getting killed: well, the world was a dangerous place, but only idiots like his brother let it hurt them.

So far, it hadn't been so bad. Mostly it had been walking, and Linniu was good at that. He'd walked from the farm to the muster at Watersmeet, where he'd met the other soldiers. It had taken him a while to get used to so many strangers, but once he'd accepted the fact that he couldn't learn all their names or ask them all about their farms and herds, he'd realised that mostly they were just his own reflections in water; sons of other farms, his own age or thereabouts, most of them wearing older boots or shirts than him. He'd insisted on dressing in his best, of course. The pleasing thing was, so had they.

The camp at Loigna had been the same, only more so. The People's Defence Force had given them tents to sleep in, and stale bread and very poor bacon to eat (just as well, since his three days' rations from home had had to last him the best part of a week), and a genuine Mezentine helmet that was too small and hurt his head, but he didn't actually have to wear it all the time, so that was all right. He'd brought his own bow, naturally, and all seventeen arrows. He was a bit concerned on that score. They'd told him he was unlikely to have a chance to find them again after the battle (indeed, there might easily be more than one battle), and the arrows they'd brought along in big birchwood barrels were no good at all, warped in the shaft, the wrong spine for his bow and fletched with feathers from some bird he'd never heard of before. He had an uneasy feeling that when he got home, a fair slice of his vast treasure of gold, silver and bronze would have to be spent getting a decent set of arrows from the fletcher at Gollinagap. He'd tried to raise the issue (tactfully) with the officer, but the man had just looked at him.

Then came basic training, which left him more bemused than ever. Most of it seemed to be learning how to stand (something he'd been doing since he was a small child, but not the right way, apparently), walk up and down in an artificial manner, and hold the spear and shield he hadn't got in the approved manner. It was comforting that none of the other farm boys understood it or managed to get it right, but he couldn't help wondering. If a battle involved standing with your feet together until a sergeant told you to stand with your feet apart, it couldn't be anything like what he'd imagined. Eventually, however, they moved on to archery, which was reassuring, since he knew all about that. Indeed, to his great surprise and lasting joy, he came third, with eight golds out of ten at seventy-five yards. For that they made him a lance corporal, an honour he'd have appreciated even more if they'd explained what it meant.

After the archery competition, they were declared fully trained. After all, the sergeant told them, they were all country lads; they were fit, they knew how to move quietly, how to shoot; they'd all been beaters on driven days, or long-netted rabbits, so they knew how to work as a team, obey the line captain's orders, be where they were supposed to be and not make a noise. As far as the sergeant was concerned (he was Eremian, in his early fifties, with a scar on his face you tried not to look at), that made them better soldiers than arrow-fodder recruited in some town. Their officer wasn't so bad, he added, as officers went. They'd be all right.

From Loigna they moved on to Sicrypha; not walking, riding in carts, which made him think of haymaking when he was a boy. By now he was something of a hero, because of his eight out of ten, and because his boots were practically new and not hand-me-downs, and because when the cart got stuck in deep ruts in a stony lane, he'd taken charge and got it out again by rolling it back just far enough to pack the ruts with withy brash – didn't everybody know that was what you did? Apparently not.

At Sicrypha, they got paid. That made him very happy. Twelvepence in coined money, not lead tokens; vast treasure already, and they hadn't so much as seen a single marauding savage. He tied the coins up securely in a bit of cheesecloth.

From Sicrypha they went to Doulichar, where they got off the carts and walked for two days until they met up with the rest of the army. That was a remarkable thing. Later, someone told him that they'd mustered over two hundred, something he found hard to believe, even though he'd seen the huge sprawl of tents with his own eyes. Two hundred people, all in one place. It was impressive, even magnificent, but it made him feel uneasy.

Doulichar (he'd heard the name often enough, never expected to go there) was a river town, built around a wharf where the Lonazep barges stopped to load. The carter who collected their malt, oats and honey came here twice a year; he'd talked about the rows of squashed-up-together houses and sheds, the strangers that not even the locals knew, the brown faces of the Mezentine buyers who came down once in a blue moon. He'd always listened to that sort of talk with a blend of wonder and scepticism, half believing it as though it was fairy-tales or his uncle's more extreme reminiscences. Actually to be there, seeing it, made him feel very strange, as if he'd wandered into a story himself, like the boy who fell asleep on the haunted bank and was kidnapped by the elf-king's daughter. It was all very wonderful, but he wasn't sure he liked it. It seemed like a terrible lot of trouble and expense to go to, if the job they were supposed to be doing was as simple and straightforward as everybody seemed to think. The impression he'd got from the sergeant had been of a slightly more dangerous version of a boar-hunt, but as he watched the other companies shooting at the butts or practising the standing-with-feet-together thing over and over again, he wasn't at all sure. Boar-hunting, after all, wasn't exactly difficult, so long as you observed a few simple rules. There had to be more to it than they were letting on.

Three days at Doulichar, very busy doing nothing; and then the barges the carter had told him about turned up early one morning, except they weren't there to load oatmeal.

"We're getting on that?" he heard someone say.

"Yes." The sergeant; an Eremian, like the one at Loigna. "What about it?"

"But I've never been on a boat before."

"So?"

Being on the barge was very strange indeed. They all had to sit in the hold – fancy name for the bottom of the boat; rather like being in a pit, because the sides of the barge were so high you couldn't see anything except other people and sky – and there wasn't a lot of room. When you needed to pee, you had to call to a man up the other end, who made his way down to you, treading on people's legs and feet, and brought you a bucket. When it was full he emptied it over the side; not a good thing if the wind was blowing. The sky was getting steadily darker all the time, and he could smell rain. He thought of wet days in the field: netting snipe on the marsh, clambering over tussocks of coarse grass and sinking past his knees in stinking black mud. Wherever they were going, he hoped it wouldn't rain there. Things always went wrong in the wet.

Two days on the boat; cheese like hard plaster, bread you could've sharpened knives on, cold sausages you wouldn't have fed to the dog back home. Which was odd; because a while back, when they'd loaded oats and cheese and bacon for the carter, he'd said something about prices being high because of having to feed the Mezentine army in Eremia, and the stuff they'd sent off had been plain but perfectly good, not like this rubbish. Maybe the army did something to the food, on purpose – God only knew why they'd want to, but everything they did was so totally inexplicable, one more mystery shouldn't make any odds.

On the third day, he woke up to find the boat wasn't moving. He started to ask the man next to him what was going on, but the sergeant hissed at him to be quiet. Talking wasn't allowed, apparently, and so they spent the whole day huddled in silence, going nowhere, nothing to see but the lead-black clouds. Just after noon it started raining. There was no cover on the boat, so they got very wet. Nobody explained why this was helping the war.

About an hour before sunset, the officer started picking his way along the hold, looking at them all. It was impossible to guess what he was looking at, and he didn't say anything, but he seemed preoccupied and a little bit scared. After he'd peered at them all, he climbed up on a barrel and started talking to them in a loud voice, which seemed a bit strange after they'd had to keep quiet all day.

They were here, the officer said, to carry out a daring raid into the heart of enemy territory. That, in fact, was where they were right now (oh, Linniu thought, not liking the sound of it much). As soon as it was dark, they were going to float downstream in dead silence until they reached the headquarters of the enemy army, where they'd disembark quickly and quietly and, fully exploiting the element of surprise, set fire to some sheds, shoot off as many arrows as they had time for, then back on the boats and away off out of it before the enemy had time to react. Provided they didn't make a noise and give the game away, there shouldn't be any problems. He had every confidence, their cause was just, they were fighting for the very survival of freedom and their way of life, and a lot of other stuff like that. Then he repeated: no noise, get off the boat when I tell you to, set fire to the sheds – great big things, couldn't miss them – shoot arrows, leave quickly. All there was to it.

During the very long hour of total silence that followed, Linniu contemplated the things the officer hadn't said: what they were to do if anything went wrong; who'd tell them what to do, and how he'd tell them, in the pitch dark, with people running in all directions as like as not, arrows everywhere, and burning buildings too; or (even more puzzling) what good getting back on the boats was supposed to do them, when the current would carry them further downstream, instead of back upstream, the way they wanted to go. It was, of course, impossible that the clever men who ran the People's Defence Force hadn't thought of something as elementary as that; in which case there was a plan, and presumably the officer hadn't had time to tell them about it. He wondered what it could be, and whether it had something to do with standing-with-feet-together – they'd gone to the trouble of teaching them how to do it, after all, so it had to come in somewhere.

In any event, he reflected sadly, he could kiss his seventeen arrows goodbye. Ninepence for a new set still left him threepence out of his pay, but Father wasn't going to be happy when he got home. He'd set his heart on the thoroughbred boar.

Very gently, without warning, the boat started moving again. He glanced up at the sky, because it was his only source of information. Getting dark – he realised he'd lost track of time, and tried to work it out. The heavy black cloud made the light an unreliable gauge, but his best guess was that it was past afternoon milking, getting on for shutting up the poultry and feeding the horse. In which case, dark in an hour. He wondered how soldiers managed to calibrate the passage of time, since their days were so often different. At home, if you knew the season and the time of day, you knew exactly where you'd be and what you'd be doing, and surely that was the way people were supposed to live. All the uncertainty of the military life must unhinge your head, sooner or later.

Movement or progress, there was a danger in confusing the two. They were moving, slow and steady, down the river and into darkness, but without knowing where he was or what was happening, he had no idea if things were going right or wrong. Not knowing where he was – he thought he'd been getting used to that, after a lifetime of certainty, but apparently not. He could feel panic stirring inside, but did his best to ignore it. If he had any part to play in all this, panic wouldn't help. For the first time, he was quite sure he regretted coming on this adventure, valuable treasure or no valuable treasure.

It was quite dark now, and he couldn't make out the man sitting next to him. He knew his name, where he was from, how many acres and the size of his herd, the bare essentials, but that was all. That wasn't good. When the time came, if there really was going to be fighting, he'd need to know a lot more about all his companions if they were going to work together. He'd never had to co-operate before with someone he hadn't known all his life.

From time to time he heard scraping, which he identified as the branches of trees brushing against the side of the barge. It sounded murderously loud, and weren't they supposed to be keeping quiet? It was just as well, he told himself, that the officers knew what they were doing. But they were proper soldiers, and there wasn't anything to worry about. If there was one thing he could rely on in this whole baffling, disconcerting experience, it was that they wouldn't have been entrusted with men's lives unless they knew everything there was to know about soldiering. That was why he'd been trained to trust them implicitly.

The barge shook; it must've hit something, or run into the bank. Someone shouted, and Linniu thought, no, be quiet; but whoever it was shouted again, and he realised they were receiving orders: get up, move, let's go. But the voice sounded scared.

He jumped to his feet, collided with someone, staggered, fell against someone else. A boot crushed his instep. He suddenly realised he hadn't even strung his bow yet; of course he hadn't, nobody had told him to, so presumably he wasn't meant to do it. He thought about the sergeant's much-repeated phrase, *wait for the command*. Someone shoved him in the small of the back, pushing him forward. He couldn't see where he was supposed to be going.

Shouting; not on the boat, and he couldn't make out the words. Then someone yelled. He'd heard a yell like that before, just once, a barn-raising at his cousins' place, when the youngest son of the farm fell off a scaffolding and broke his leg. It meant someone was in trouble; and then he thought, well of course, this is a war. A thought like that was an odd thing to have in his mind.

More pushing, shoving, stumbling. He barked his shin on something, and realised it was the rung of a ladder. Was he supposed to climb up it? Nobody had said. Then someone grabbed his arm and dragged him forward, and there was nowhere else to go but up the ladder. It was awkward, with his bow in his right hand and not being able to see. He climbed, and then ran out of rungs. Someone pushed him; he felt himself fall, thought, this can't be right, and landed in mud.

He expected people to laugh, because that was what happened when you did a spectacular belly-flop in deep, sticky mud; he must've got it wrong, and now they'd be ribbing him about it for ever. But no laughter, and he heard a body land very close beside him, felt muddy spray on his face. Apparently that was how you got off a boat in the People's Defence Force. Strange way to go about things.

Getting to his feet wasn't easy. His hands were full of mud. He paused, trying to wipe them clean, because you couldn't hold or use anything if your hands were clogged and slippery. He scrabbled about for his bow and found it. He'd landed on it and snapped it in half. Disaster.

Disaster, because a good bow cost tenpence; because the only reason for him being there at all was to use the bow, and he couldn't now, could he? Obviously he had to tell someone; they were relying on him to play his part in this manoeuvre, and before it had even started he'd contrived to render himself completely useless. They were going to be so angry; but first things first, they had to be told. Then, presumably, he'd have to get back on the boat and wait until it was all over. His boots were full of mud, and he felt completely stupid.

Finding someone to tell . . . There were shapes, bodies, moving all around him, and it suddenly occurred to him that he was out of position and in danger of being left behind. It'd be like getting out of line in a woodland drive, one man could wreck everything. Bad enough that he'd broken his bow. The last thing he wanted was to make it even worse.

Someone barged against him; he grabbed, found himself holding an arm. "The sergeant," he shouted. "Where's the sergeant? I need to tell him—" But someone's boot rammed into the back of his knee and he went down again, belly in the mud. He felt a kick; someone tripped over him and landed on his back, scrambled up cursing. This was terrible. He was ruining the whole mission, all by himself. He had to get out of everybody's way, then find the sergeant and be told what he had to do. The worst day of his life, he thought.

Light. Up ahead, yellow and orange, like a building on fire. But that was what they were there for, of course, stupid. By the glow he could see definite shapes, men all around him, moving forward. As a shape lunged past him he called out, "Hey, I've broken my bow, what should I . . . ?" but whoever it was didn't seem to have heard him. In fact, nobody was taking any notice of him at all.

Well, he thought, fine; and it occurred to him (a guilty thought at the back of his mind, wicked but tempting) that in all this darkness and mess, it didn't matter that he'd screwed up really badly and done everything wrong, because how would anybody ever know? If he kept his nerve, went along with the crowd, went through the motions, how would they ever find out? Later he could pretend he'd done his bit, shot off all his arrows, and then lost his bow right at the last minute. Damn it (he grinned stupidly into the dark at the thought of it), he could probably even put a claim in, get the People's Defence Force to buy him a new one, or at least pay something towards it. Well, it'd be worth a try; and it was their fault as much as his that it'd got broken. At the very least they should have warned him about the ladder.

So he started to drag his way forward, his feet desperately heavy with the weight of caked mud. Furtively he started pulling arrows out of his quiver and dropping them on the ground. A wicked waste, but he couldn't very well claim he'd fought like a hero till his bow snapped if he reported back with a full quiver. Uncle Loimen always said you had to be crafty in the army.

Something fluttered past him in the dark. A bat, only bats didn't whistle. He felt the cool air on his wet face and wondered what it could be.

Somebody screamed.

For a moment he froze, and then his better instincts took over. A scream like that; someone was hurt. He tried to place where it had come from. It changed everything, of course; his whole clever plan, pretending he still had his bow, but he knew what he had to do if someone was hurt that badly, even if it meant getting found out. He stopped moving. Someone bashed into his shoulder, though he didn't see him. The firelight was getting brighter, but he couldn't spot the injured man, there were too many moving bodies in the way. Over there, he told himself, that's where it came from. He started forward, tripped over something and fell.

This time, though, he didn't land in mud. His chin hit something hard, jarring his teeth. A man's head. He opened his mouth to apologise, then realised, though he wasn't quite sure how he knew, that the man was dead.

His first thought was: shit, I've killed him; knocked him over, made him bang his head on a stone or something. It was actually a relief, for a split second, when he saw the arrow.

Then he thought, what do I do? Well, obviously he had to tell someone; the sergeant, the officer, there's a man dead over here, what should I do? He hauled himself up on to his knees and looked round: in front, to the sides, over his shoulder. At which point, he noticed it.

First he thought, how the hell did that get there? It took a moment for his mind to clear; an arrow, or rather the foreshaft of an arrow, the rest of it had broken off, sticking out of his shoulder: impossible. For a start, it should be hurting like hell. Then he remembered the man who'd blundered into him, but whom he hadn't seen. Not a man after all. It had felt just like a shove at the time (but then, he told himself gravely, I've never been shot before, so how should I know?).

Like someone who'd fallen asleep on the job and been found out, the pain suddenly started and made up for lost time. He heard a whimper and realised it was him, but somehow it didn't seem like it was actually happening, though the pain was real enough. I've been shot with an arrow, he had to tell himself. Men were bustling past him all the time, and there was a lot of shouting now. I've been shot, he repeated; and then he thought, well, look on the bright side, it definitely means I'm excused duty. I can go back to the boat, and . . .

He remembered he'd left his helmet on the boat. Bloody fool, he thought; and his entire head started to itch, as he thought, there's arrows flying about all over the place and I haven't got my helmet. Fuck that, I could get killed . . .

(Yes, he realised suddenly. Of course he'd thought about that before, but never actually believed it. Now full, paralysing belief dropped down on him, like a bag over his head. I could die here, he thought; and he felt piss run down his leg.)

Excused duty; back to the fucking boat. He tried to turn round, but while he'd been standing still he'd sunk deeper into the mud than he'd realised, and now he couldn't move. Panic; he wrenched his foot up, felt it slide out of the boot, the hell with the stupid boot. He felt the mud squelch up through his bare toes. Just get back to the boat and everything will be fine.

A man was yelling at him, "Where do you think you're—?" but he didn't finish the question because he died. An arrow hit him in the face, his cheek, just under his eye. His expression didn't change, he just fell over. Linniu tried to run, but the mud was hands grabbing his ankles. He lost his other boot, which made the next few steps easier, but then he slipped and went down on his face. As soon as he landed he was scrabbling to get up again; he felt the arrowhead move inside him, the strangest sensation. He managed a few more steps, then something broke or failed. All his strength drained out of him and he was suddenly too weary to move. His legs gave way and he was kneeling in the mud. Any sort of movement was too much effort. Even the fear was gone. Nothing mattered.

(He thought about long-netting; how when you've walked up the line with the lanterns to drive the rabbits into the net, sometimes you find one that hasn't bolted but just sits there, frozen, until you grab its legs and it starts kicking like crazy till you pull its neck. Just sits there.)

At some point, he heard and felt a great thump. It came through the air and up through the mud at the same time. He had no idea what it was, but it made the firelight flicker.

Then it was as though he'd woken up (he thought, I can't possibly have fallen asleep, but I definitely wasn't here for a while), and there was a man standing a few yards away. Of course, he thought; it's all right. I'm not alone, there's other people here, someone will help me. He'd forgotten about help, because all through his strange and terrible experiences it was as though he was completely alone, the only man in the world. But that was just panic. All he had to do was call out, and the man would pull him out of the mud and help him to the barge, and then all his troubles would be over.

The man turned his head, and Linniu breathed in to shout. But there was something wrong about the man. He wasn't an archer. He was wearing armour and holding a blade on a pole, something like a long-handled billhook but with a spike on the front. There hadn't been anybody like that at Sicrypha or Doulichar. He wondered who on earth it could be, and then the answer came. The enemy.

He mustn't see me. If he sees me, he'll kill me. He felt an urge to flop down into the mud, lie flat; but that'd mean moving, and maybe, just possibly, the enemy hadn't noticed him yet. Movement got you noticed. He kept perfectly still and held his breath.

(The enemy; not something he'd given any thought to. In his mind, they'd been targets, concentric rings of colour with a yellow centre, things that only existed to be shot at; definitely not people, because the one thing you're taught before you get your first bow is, *don't point it at anyone.* The enemy. The same word, of course, for one man or the whole lot of them, a million savages, they reckoned. Perhaps it was just the confusion inherent in the word, but as he looked at the man with the billhook, there didn't seem to be any difference. He was one man, but he was also all of them: the enemy. The slightest movement, and the enemy will see me.)

The man seemed terribly calm. He was turning his head slowly as though looking for something in particular – me, Linniu thought; he knows I'm here somewhere and he's looking for me – taking his time, unafraid, a man who knew what he was doing. Then, after a very long time, he started to walk, leaning forward to break the suction of the mud around his boots. After a few steps he raised his arm and called out, then carried on, moving steadily away.

Relief made Linniu's head swim. The enemy had been there, but hadn't seen him; and while that had been going on, he'd had a chance to rest. He felt a little stronger, and he'd realised that not getting killed did matter, after all. And all he had to do was get back to the boat.

He looked round, trying to make out its shape, and realised that there was light behind him now – that was how he'd been able to see the enemy – as well as in front. Helpful. Maybe he could see the boat from here. Then it occurred to him that the light was coming from where the boat should be.

The light *was* the boat. Burning.

And where was everybody, anyway? Suddenly he realised there weren't many people about, which didn't make any sense. He looked at the few he could see. They were the enemy, too.

Oh, he thought.

As soon as he realised what had happened, he accepted it. His side, everybody except him, must all be dead; the battle's over, we've lost, everybody's been killed except me. The explanation was so very easy to believe. It slipped down into his mind without the faintest hint of a struggle, and the only question was, what's going to happen next? He felt quite detached about it, though there was a certain degree of general apprehension. Will they kill me here, or has something else got to happen first? He was prepared to accept it, but it bothered him that he didn't know the procedure.

There had been more than one boat. He hadn't been aware of that before. Somehow, he'd assumed that his barge was the only one, but there were five sources of glowing orange light in the direction of the river. He tried to work out how many men had been on the barge with him: forty, fifty? As many as two hundred and fifty men, then; they couldn't all be dead, could they (apart from him, of course), in such a short space of time? Everything changed, of course; each day on the farm was a slight turn of the wheel, one degree in three hundred and sixty-five. But so much change, so quickly. Then he thought about early summer, when it was time to kill the surplus cock-birds out of the spring hatching. It was always a morning's solid work, forty, forty-five necks to pull, each one a sombre repetition of the last sad panic and desperate, pointless flapping of wings. When it was done, you noticed the change. Stillness in the runs where there'd been movement, silence where there'd been sound. He thought about it some more. It was a job he neither liked nor hated. The grab-jerk-twist was fluent, second nature to him after ten years. He thought of the birds in his hands. They'd crouch still as he held them, wings clamped against the body, their eyes very wide open, until he started the procedure. Then there'd be the panic, every last scrap of the bird's strength applied pointlessly against him, because he was so much bigger and stronger, and that was all there was to it. The struggle did no good. In fact, it was counterproductive; death would come even quicker and easier if they didn't try and thrash about, though it made very little difference, usually. He wondered if he'd struggle when the moment came, and assumed he would. Instinct, after all.

The enemy were moving about; walking slowly and wearily, like men gathering up their tools after they'd finished a job. Every few steps they paused and stooped, examining something on the ground. He realised they were checking the bodies, looking for any of their own, not finding any. He heard the occasional groan, but not often. It was all surprisingly quiet. He guessed the enemy weren't in the mood to talk. Let's get it over with and then maybe we can get some sleep; he'd felt that way often enough at the end of a long day.

The pain was a nuisance, like a dog wanting to play, but not too bad. Maybe pain was only unbearable when you knew it mattered. He felt no need or wish to move, though his knees were starting to ache, and he was profoundly cold. It started to rain, just softly enough to sting his eyes. He tried to think about the difference his absence would make, at the farm, to his family, but it all seemed a bit remote, as if home was something he'd believed in when he was a kid, when he was too young to know better.

The enemy came closer; stopped, looked in his direction, saw him. Coming his way, trudging, worn out by the effort of pulling boots out of deep, sticky mud. He lifted his head to look at him; it was rude to stare, but it couldn't make things worse now, could it? The enemy came a little closer, then paused. He's afraid of me,

Linniu thought, amused; he's afraid I'll bite. He wanted to reassure him, but that would be ridiculous. He heard the enemy call out, and saw another one coming towards him. Oh come on, he thought scornfully, it doesn't need two of you.

He heard the newcomer say something; and, maybe because his voice was higher or clearer, he could make out the words: "Live one here, sergeant." For a moment he wondered what that meant.

A third man came into view. He moved quickly, a man in a hurry, and he didn't seem to be hampered by the mud as much as the other two. As he got nearer, Linniu saw that he had the knack of stepping lightly so as not to sink in so deep; he dug his heels in and hopped. He'd have smiled at the sight, under other circumstances.

The sergeant didn't seem to be afraid of him, at any rate. He came up close, and Linniu was able to make out the general shape of his face: a young man, quite thin, with hollow cheeks and a chin that tapered to a cleft point. He was clean-shaven, and his forehead was splashed with mud. He stopped just out of reach and peered at Linniu like a buyer at market examining a calf.

"He'll do," he said. "Him and three more, take them to the duty officer. If there's any more after that, stick them in the rope store." Quite unexpectedly he grinned wide. "They're all just bloody kids," he said, "that's all they are. And you'll need to get the surgeon to this one, once they've finished with him. There's an arrow sticking out of his shoulder, the poor sod."

Surgeon? He knew what that meant, some kind of doctor. He'd never met a doctor in his life, of course, but he'd heard about them. *Once they've finished with him* didn't sound too good, but even so . . . Oddly enough, he felt relieved, if only because here at last was someone who seemed to know what to do, even if he was the enemy.

Then an unpleasant thought struck him. "Excuse me," he heard himself say; at least, he assumed it was him. The voice sounded very small and sad.

The sergeant raised both eyebrows, as if he'd just been spoken to by an animal; animals shouldn't talk, of course, it was unnatural, but he was too intrigued to be angry. "What?"

"The . . . surgeon." He stumbled over the unfamiliar word. "That's a doctor, isn't it?"

The sergeant was having trouble not laughing. "That's right, son. So what?"

"It's just . . . I can't see the doctor, I haven't got any money to pay."

The sergeant's face turned into one enormous grin. "That's all right, son," he said. "It's free in the army, you don't have to pay. It's one of the perks, you might say. Go on," he continued, turning his head toward the two soldiers, "get him over to the duty officer, and see if you can find a bit of rag for that arm. No charge," he added gravely. "You can bleed on it all you want, and it won't cost you a penny."

The two soldiers were on either side of him now. They caught hold of him firmly but carefully, avoiding his wounded shoulder, and lifted him out of the mud on to his feet. "No boots," he heard the sergeant say. "Fancy sending kids to war with no boots."

"I lost . . ." he started to say, but they were marching him along, and the sergeant had turned his back on them. Probably best not to say too much, in any case. Amazingly, it seemed they felt sorry for him, and although he couldn't really understand that, he didn't want to spoil it.

They had to step over quite a few bodies. He tried not to look at them. The two soldiers hardly seemed to notice they were there.

It couldn't have been more than two hundred yards, but it felt like a day's march. As they got further away from the river, the mud turned into firm ground. Fewer bodies to step over, and more enemy soldiers hurrying backwards and forwards, busy, not stopping to look. He saw a row of tents, elaborate things with awnings held up by poles. Outside one a man was sitting on a rickety-looking folding chair, with an equally flimsy-looking table in front of him, covered in papers. The man's head was bowed low and his shoulders were hunched; he looked at though he'd just come in from ploughing. Apparently, that was who he was being taken to see. He raised his head as they approached, and Linniu was surprised to see how young he was.

"Prisoner, sir," barked one of the soldiers.

"What? Oh, yes." The man frowned. "Fine, well done. We'll take him straight to the duke." He paused, narrowing his eyes as he looked Linniu in the face, like someone trying to read small hand-writing in bad light. "Does he understand . . . ?"

"Seems to, sir. He talked to the sergeant."

The man nodded, cleared his throat. "My name is Colonel Nennius," he said, slowly and clearly. "Who are you?"

"Linniu Matsinatsen."

The man frowned. "Mat . . . ?"

"Matsinatsen." He didn't know if he was supposed to say "sir". At any rate, the man didn't seem offended or upset that he hadn't. "All right," he said. "This way."

More walking. They passed through groups of men walking or standing about, who quickly made way for them. Some of them did the standing-with-feet-together thing as the man passed. He didn't seem to notice, or care.

Another tent, much like the man's but about twice the size. A flap hung over what he took to be the entrance, and two soldiers with spears and shields stood in front of it, either to keep people out or to keep whoever was behind the flap in. They seemed to recognise the man, Colonel Nennius, because they stood aside to let him go through the flap. Linniu assessed his own state of mind and realised he was nervous rather than afraid. Curious, he thought.

There were lamps inside the tent, five of them; brass, and they didn't look anything like the City-made lamps they had at home. Cruder, if anything. In front of them, so his face was backlit and hard to see, a man sat in another of those funny-looking folding chairs. He had his feet up on a little stool, and Linniu could see his boots: old, scuffed, loose stitching around the point of the left toe.

"You found me one, then?" he said. He spoke strangely; a strong accent, but easy enough to understand.

"It wasn't easy," replied Colonel Nennius. "Not many left to choose from."

He heard a sort of muffled snort, acknowledgement of a grim joke. "Get him a chair, somebody." A chair appeared as soon as he said it; Linniu couldn't see it, but he could feel the front edge of the seat pressing against the backs of his knees. He sat down. The man nodded.

"Right," he said. "There's really just one question . . ."

" . . . just one question I want to ask you," Valens said, lifting his hand to stifle a yawn. He paused, glanced back at Nennius, who was hovering on his left. "He can understand me all right, can he?"

"As far as we know."

"Fine." He turned back and looked at the prisoner. Farm boy, he recognised. Somewhere under all that mud, he was probably wearing his best shirt, so as to look neat and tidy for the war. "All I want to know," he went on, "is this. What the hell possessed you to come all this way and launch an amphibious night attack, just to burn down a flour store?"

The farm boy stared at him as though he'd got two heads. Valens frowned. "You sure he can understand me?" he asked.

"The sergeant who caught him seemed to think so."

"Fine. He must just be fussy who he talks to." He sighed. "Hello," he said. "Allow me to introduce myself. My name is Valens Valentinianus, duke of the Vadani. And you are?"

The boy hesitated, then mumbled something. It was too long and complicated to be worth trying to remember.

"That's introductions out of the way," Valens said. "Now, I want you to tell me the purpose of your mission." Pause. The boy was still staring. "Can you do that?"

"No." Pause. "Sir."

"I see. Under orders not to, or you just don't know?"

"I don't know, sir."

Valens frowned, and said nothing. He had an idea that embarrassment would get him more information than five torturers with hot pokers. Sure enough, the boy couldn't resist the temptation to fill the terrible silence.

"They told us at" (somewhere he'd never heard of) "we were going to burn down a place where they make things, a factory. Where they build the stone-throwing machines for attacking cities."

"Ah." Valens smiled. "That's what they told you."

"Yes, sir."

The smile warped into a grin. "Well," he said, "it's always nice to know the enemy are idiots. You may be interested to know that what you thought were engine sheds were just general stores. You managed to torch a week's worth of flour, but that's all."

The boy seemed to be having trouble with that. "Flour?"

"Flour." Valens nodded. "Which is tricky stuff when it catches fire, mind," he added. "The shed went up like a volcano, we were lucky nobody got hurt. Nobody on our side," he added. "Your people weren't so fortunate. Tell me, do you happen to know the name of the military genius who organised all this? No? Pity. I'd have liked to write and thank him."

The boy's eyes had grown very wide and round; it wasn't fair, teasing him. "Right," Valens said. "I want you to tell me, nice and slowly, where you come from, where your unit was raised, the names of as many officers as you can, how long it took you to get here and the way you came. If you do that, I'll tell them to see to your arm and give you a blanket and something to eat. All right?"

As the boy answered the questions, Valens looked for the place-names on his map. It wasn't a very good map. Nobody had taken any interest in the Cure Doce for a very long time; there had been a border skirmish thirty-odd years ago, so there was a campaign map of that particular region, but the most recent general survey was a hundred years old, and the Vadani of that generation had been lousy cartographers. There were large areas of plain white in the middle, and Valens suspected that most of the drawn-in section was just plain wrong. A picture grew in his mind of the map-makers sitting in an inn on the border interrogating the local carters; plenty of scope there for rustic humour. But who cared about the geography of a nation of nonentities anyway? Nobody ever went there, and if you wanted anything from Cure Doce territory, they brought it to you.

Fine. He pushed the map away, made some notes, wrote down the few names of officers that the boy managed to come up with. That was all. Hardly worth the effort. He ran out of questions.

"All right," he said wearily. "That's it." He closed his eyes, rubbed them. "Now listen," he said. "This is important. I want you to take a message . . ." He paused. The boy was still staring. He wished he'd stop. "I want you to take a message to your leaders, all right? I want you to tell them I've got no quarrel with your people. Tell them they owe me for a shedful of flour, but apart from that there's no harm done, and I haven't the energy to go killing people for the sake of it, so if they mind their own business and stop helping the Mezentines, we'll forget this ever happened. But if I catch any more of your people playing soldiers, I'll make you all wish you'd never been born. Now, do you think you can remember that?"

The boy frowned, his head a little on one side, just like a spaniel. "You're letting me go," he said.

Valens nodded. He'd had enough of idiots for one day. "It would appear so, yes. They'll patch up that shoulder for you, dig the arrow out, and you can be on your way in a day or so. I don't suppose you know how to get home, so a couple of my scouts'll have to take you to the border. You can ride a horse?"

"Yes."

"Splendid." He looked up and caught Nennius' eye. "Don't bother bringing me any more," he said. "I've got a feeling they're all like this." He paused and thought for a moment, then looked at the boy again. "One other thing," he said. "Tell your lot to send half a dozen carts to the border. When we've got a spare minute, we'll send back the other survivors. I can't be bothered to feed them, and they're no good to anybody dead. But please try and make your people understand, I'm doing this because I'm too busy right now to wipe you off the face of the earth, not because I'm a nice, kind man. Quite the opposite. All right?"

He considered the look on the boy's face. Might as well talk to sheep. He nodded, and the two guards who'd brought the prisoner in took him away again. Valens lifted a finger to tell Nennius to stay behind.

"Well," he said. "What do you make of all that?"

Nennius sat down. "I think it's good," he said. "The Mezentines must be totally desperate, if that's the best they can do."

Valens smiled. "I'd like to think so," he said. "It's the old joke about lulling us into a true sense of security." He sighed and stretched his legs. "I don't suppose we'll be getting any more trouble from them, but keep the scouts out just in case. Commendations to them for tonight, by the way. I don't think that lot would have done us much harm even if we hadn't known they were coming, but it's always nice to be in control." The back of the chair was digging into him; he wriggled, and heard it creak. "What we need to do," he said, "is capture some actual Mezentine staff officers. I don't want the men, but I hear they've got really comfortable travelling furniture. Why can't any of our lot make a decent folding chair?"

Nennius smiled. "Get Vaatzes on it," he said.

"I might just do that. Or at any rate his sidekick, the creepy bastard. He'll do anything for anybody, that one." Valens closed his eyes. It'd be wonderful to get some rest, at some point. "Thinking about it," he said, "I guess we ought to make something out of this. Tell you what: I want you to pass the word around – usual channels, you know what I mean; let them think we're putting a brave face on it, but actually this raid was successful. Mission accomplished. It

wasn't just a flour store they torched, it was the main engine shed. All
the really important production machinery wrecked beyond hope of
repair. Six months' work gone up in smoke, right back to square one.
I think I'd like the Mezentines to believe that."

"But you told the boy the truth."

"Which means the Mezentines will automatically believe the
opposite, especially if we help them out a little. You might want to
get a couple of carts loaded up with scrap iron, take them out somewhere they can see you and dump them in a bog or something. Give
them a cavalry escort, to make sure they take notice. They'll think
we're chucking out the ruined machines." He frowned. "That's
assuming their scouts are bright enough to take the hint. But it can't
do any harm. I'm sure Psellus would love to believe it's true. I'm serious about the chair, by the way. This useless article's ruining my
back."

Nennius left. Valens stood up, whimpered at the stab of cramp,
and lay down on his bed. He still had a great deal of work to do, but
he absolved himself with the excuse that he was too tired to do it
properly. Instead, he reached out and tugged the latest scouts' report
from the bottom of the pile of documents heaped up on a stool
beside the bedstead. He opened it and began to read, though he
practically knew it by heart already.

The scouts were puzzled. He knew the men who'd made this
report; conscientious but unimaginative. They reported that the
Mezentines were apparently getting ready to dig holes in the plain in
front of the City. They'd gone to enormous lengths to organise work
details, mobilising every able-bodied citizen who wasn't actively
engaged in essential war work. The ordnance factory had assigned
one of its four volume production lines, and a large amount of hard-
to-come-by blade-quality hardening steel, to making shovels. Lines
had been surveyed and marked out (see sketch). Presumably all this
effort was to do with additional fortifications, but the stonemasons
were being issued shovels along with everybody else, and there hadn't
been any recent orders sent out to the quarries.

Valens took another look at the sketch. When he was a boy, there
had been these puzzles; sheets of thin copper foil pierced with tiny
holes. You laid them on a sheet of paper and stuck a pin through each
hole in turn. Then you took a charcoal stick, and you had to find a
way of joining the pricked dots on the paper to make a picture: a

castle, or a horseman, or a waterwheel. He'd never thought much of the puzzles. They were too easy.

The lines so meticulously sketched by the scouts could mean only one thing. He'd seen them before; in a book in his father's library, one of a job lot he'd bought – histories and ordinances of the famous wars, lives of the great commanders, soldiers' mirrors, didactic dialogues between A Master and Some Students concerning the various branches of the military sciences. Junk, most of them. He particularly treasured the explanation offered in one gloriously illustrated volume of why feathers on arrows and wooden fins on crossbow bolts make them fly straighter. The projections catch the air, making the missile spin. The spinning motion unseats the malignant spirits of inaccuracy who love to perch on arrows and make them fly wide of the mark. The tiny demons fall to the ground, allowing the arrow to fly unhindered towards the mark. There was even a picture, of weensy blue pointy-eared fiends scrabbling air as they fell, their lips curled in baffled fury. Obvious, really, when you thought about it.

Almost as ludicrous (he'd always thought) was the catapult book. It had been a particular favourite when he was ten years old, because it had lots of drawings of funny-looking machines. Some of them looked like carts with enormous spoons sprouting out of them, others reminded him of giant wheeled violins, complete with bows; there were things like cheese-presses with crossbows wedged between the weights, and a sort of bent-back sapling arrangement that flicked a giant arrow off a pole. Also, there were the weird shapes. Stars, crinkly wheels, zigzags, knobbly things like overgrown cogs. When curiosity drove him to read the accompanying text, he found that these were supposed to be ground plans of fortified cities. That was what made him classify the book along with the treatise on arrow-riding pixies, because nobody would go to the bother and ruinous expense of building a city like that. All those spikes and wedges and sticking-out bits, and hardly any room left in the middle where people could live. Some old fool with too much time on his hands, he'd decided. And now, here those shapes were again, unmistakable as footprints.

(The book was, of course, still on the shelf in the library of the ducal palace at Civitas Vadanis. He'd sent riders to find it and bring it back. In the meantime, he'd have to make do with what little he could remember.)

He considered his enemy, Lucao Psellus. Impossible that anybody, let alone the newly promoted clerk, could have reinvented those exact shapes from first principles. It followed, therefore, that Psellus had his own copy of the book, and enough sense (unlike the young Duke Valens) to appreciate the value of what he was looking at.

There was a bright side, though. As far as he could remember, the writer had devoted a whole chapter to demonstrating (with really impressive mathematical formulae that Valens hadn't even bothered to try and understand) that, in the absence of grossly disproportionate forces and various other material factors, an attacker who followed the book's precepts was likely to beat a defender following the same precepts six times out of ten. The list of possible vitiating factors was long and complicated, and Valens could only remember three of them (outbreak of plague among besiegers/defenders; failure of ammunition supply for one side's artillery; treachery). It'd be interesting to read the full list again, and see how many of them applied in this case.

Sandcastles, he thought; another game I used to play, in the big pit where the foundry workers dug out the fine white sand they used for filling mould-boxes.

Sending for the book was all very well, but he was realistic enough to know that it wouldn't be much use to him unless he also had someone who could understand it. For that reason, he'd also sent for Ziani Vaatzes. Both of them should arrive within the next two or three days, and then . . .

Valens growled, rolled off the bed and sat on the uncomfortable chair. And then, he'd have no excuse not to get started. The siege of Mezentia; it sounded like the title of a play. A tragedy in three acts, complete with hero, villain, love interest, hero's tragic flaw, betrayal, confusion and finally lots of death. He picked up a report, glanced at it; his father had enjoyed a good play, though he tended to talk to people during what he considered were the boring bits. He liked the fencing, he said, and the speeches before the battles, and the deaths, which were inventive, gripping and so much better than the real thing. Also, he'd been told once that a great duke should be a patron of the arts. It gave an impression of class, and the writers always found a way of getting your name in somewhere. When he'd died, Valens had paid off the Duke's Men, cancelled all outstanding commissions and made it known there weren't going to be any more.

He'd given no explanation for his decision, and apart from the actors themselves, nobody seemed to have minded or even noticed. There had been a very good reason at the time, which had since slipped his mind. Of course, nothing spoiled a good play as much as a bad performance of it.

The siege. It went without saying that the City had to be destroyed. If he let them off the hook, his Cure Hardy allies would probably push him out of the way and do the job themselves. Even if they simply gave up and went back home (which they couldn't do, of course), that'd only make things worse. If the savages withdrew, the Mezentines would have no trouble recruiting mercenaries, and then he'd be back where he started, postponing the inevitable annihilation of the Vadani. No, the City had to fall, just to secure some sort of future for his people, as tolerated satellites of the Cure Hardy in self-imposed exile. A pity, but there it was. It was unfortunate that his one act of impulsive folly should have led to all this, but at the time he'd had no choice. And besides, as a result of it, hadn't he gained the one thing he'd always wanted, and never thought he'd ever have? She was waiting for him back at Civitas Vadanis. As soon as the war was over and the City was rubble and ashes, they could at last be together, as they should have been from the very beginning.

Well, then; that settled it. If a city with a population of over a million had to be razed to the ground just so he could go home to his wife . . . sledgehammers and nuts, to be sure, but it wasn't his fault. There didn't seem to be any other way of achieving the objective, and it was something he had to do, just as a dropped stone has to fall.

Chapter Five

The messenger sent to fetch Ziani Vaatzes had left before the farcical night attack, but he heard the news from a dispatch rider on a rather more urgent errand than his own, at the Faith and Trust just outside Paterclo. The rider hadn't actually witnessed the raid himself, but he'd heard all about it from his friend in the Sixth Lancers. He passed on the word that the assault party had been wiped out without the loss of a single Vadani. The enemy were a joke.

When he reached Civitas Vadanis, the messenger repeated what the rider had told him four times; once to the city prefect when he reported in; once to Vaatzes when he delivered his message; once to the duke's new wife, at her personal request; and once in the taproom of the Unity and Victory (formerly the Quiet Forbearance) in Well Street. By noon the next day, half the city knew that Duke Valens had wiped out the enemy's new ally, and set out at once to tell the other half before they heard it from anyone else.

After the messenger left on his return journey, with a two-squadron cavalry escort to guard some old book the duke had sent for, the head of the Aram Chantat's informal but ferociously efficient intelligence service set out to report the news to his master, at the great camp on what had once been the Vadani–Eremian border. The old man (you could think of him as that as long as you were at least twenty miles away; definitely not when you were face to face with him) thanked him politely and told his secretary to make a note of it in the official record of the war. He also asked who the Cure Doce were, though he didn't seem particularly interested in the reply.

Although he'd been ordered to report to the forward camp as quickly as possible, Ziani Vaatzes hung on at Civitas Vadanis for one more day. There was a problem with the assembly line that called for his personal attention, he told the messenger; he knew the duke would understand, and of course he'd be on his way as soon as it was put straight.

"Do you want me to come with you?" Daurenja asked him later.

Ziani shook his head. "I need you to stay and look after things here. It's bad enough I've got to go. We can't both be away from here, or the whole job'll grind to a halt."

"Of course." Daurenja nodded briskly. "You leave everything to me. I'll manage."

Of course he would. Ziani knew exactly what the workforce thought of Gace Daurenja, but he understood how to keep them working. So far they'd got four hundred of the heavy engines finished, dismantled and crated up for carriage. Six hundred more to go. A miracle; Daurenja's miracle. Without him, Ziani knew, he'd probably still be fiddling about trying to fine-tune the prototype.

Daurenja licked his lips and said, "When you get back, maybe we could make a start on that other business. You know, the thing we talked about."

Ziani made a point of looking past him. "All right," he said. "You'll have to fiddle the work rosters if you don't want Valens knowing. And you may want to keep an eye on the rope shop foreman. I have an idea he talks to the savages."

"I know about him, thanks," Daurenja replied with a grin. "He meets them in the Charity once a week, but they don't pay him enough. I'll think of something else he can tell them, and then everybody'll stay happy." He scratched his chin; he was growing a beard. "I've got almost enough clean grey iron for the slats," he continued. "But I need time on the Mezentine lathe to finish up the mandrel. It's all right, we're ahead of target in the machine shop so we can miss a shift without holding anything up. But I thought I'd better just mention it."

Ziani nodded gravely. "Get it done while I'm away," he said. "And I don't know about it, all right?"

"Understood." Daurenja nodded again. "All being well, I should have the mandrel ready by the time you get back, and then it's just a case of getting the slats drawn down. I've already spoken to the men I want striking for us."

Ziani frowned. "That's a bit quick off the mark," he said. "The fewer people who know about this, the happier I'll be."

"They'll be all right," Daurenja reassured him. "Five Eremians and two Vadani. They know which side their bread's buttered."

"Just make sure their shifts are covered," Ziani said irritably. "We can't afford to lose production at this stage. I can handle Valens if I have to, but I really don't want to try explaining to the savages. They're not easy people to talk to."

"Leave it to me," Daurenja said. "After all, when have I ever let you down?"

I should poison him, Ziani thought, after Daurenja had gone. It'd work. I've watched him eat, he just shovels the food in his mouth and swallows, he doesn't give it time to taste of anything. Five drops of archers' root on a slice of salt bacon, and all my troubles would be over.

But of course he wouldn't do that. Too risky, for one thing. What if the monster's digestion was as prodigious as every other part of him? Even with ten drops it wasn't worth the risk, for fear of the look in his eyes if he survived and figured out what had happened. What if he couldn't be killed at all? People must have tried. Also, without Daurenja the horrendous balance of chaos and energy that kept the factory going would immediately collapse. He needed the freak, at least until the thousandth engine was packed and shipped; and by that time, Daurenja would be so deeply embedded, there'd be no chance at all of getting rid of him without wrecking everything. He knows that, Ziani reflected bitterly, that's why he dares to eat.

To chase the thought of Daurenja out of his mind, he grabbed the spanner and stripped the whole saddle assembly off the lathe he was working on. As he'd thought, the problem lay with the lead screw bushes; useless soft salvaged bronze scrap, doomed to failure the moment he'd fitted them. At home, he'd just take a replacement pair from the spares box under the bench. Here, he'd have to make them himself, out of salvaged bronze scrap, in the sure and certain knowledge they wouldn't last out the month.

Try explaining that to the Aram Chantat.

He fished about in the scrap pile for the nearest shape he could find, then took it over to the Eremian who worked the number seventeen trip-hammer. "I need it swaged down to two-inch round bar," he said, choosing to ignore the look on the man's face. "I know it won't be perfect but get it as close to round as you can. It'll be hard enough turning it on one of those bloody useless home-made treadle machines. Of course, I can't use the good lathe until I've made the bearings to fix it."

The man looked at him as though he was blight on winter barley. Behind him loomed the eight-foot-high frame of the hammer; green oak instead of cast iron, already starting to warp in the heat. Two months, and the tenons would spring out of the mortices. If it happened while the hammer was under load, it'd tear itself apart and be completely wrecked. In two months' time, of course, they'd have finished and wouldn't need it any more. He hated the sight of it. "Do I stop what I'm doing now?" the man said. "Only I've got the top on this anvil casting to do, and it's taken an hour to get it up to welding heat. If I leave it and let it cool down, I'll be standing around idle the rest of the morning while it heats up again."

Ziani tried to think, but couldn't. "This is more important," he said, uncertain whether it was true or not. "Get it done and fetch it over to me as soon as it's ready. I'm late enough for the duke as it is."

There was a fairy-tale, every kid in the City knew it. The gods made angels, moulding them out of sunlight. The dark elves saw the angels and were filled with jealousy, wanting shining servants of their own. They tried to make some themselves, but of course they didn't know how to mould sunlight, so had to make do with clay, That was how the first men came to be created; an ignorant fake, so wide of the mark it was almost a parody, but it worked, for a little while. Ziani looked down the long, high shed. It still stank of pine sap and tar. The engines, designed by him from memory, built by hastily trained Eremians and Vadani – even a few savages, they were so short of manpower – certainly worked, for the time being. The cupolas melted the bog-iron and scrap into brittle, impure blooms for the trip-hammers to beat out into sheet or form into round or square bar, or wire for the nail makers' draw-plates. The water-driven circular saws slabbed the newly felled pine trunks into beams and planks, cut them to size ready for the chisels and twybills of the joiners. The end product was an engine capable of hurling a two-hundredweight stone four hundred yards. You'd get fifty shots out of them, maybe half a dozen more if you were lucky, before the cross-beams split under the pounding of the arms and the stubs cracked in their sockets and the dovetails sprang and the dowels sheared and the nails pulled through and the hand-cut screws stripped out of the spongy green wood. That was as it should be. The main difference, according to the story, wasn't that men were ugly and stupid and bad and angels were beautiful and wise and good. The real difference, which defined them both, was that men were mortal. The Republic built machines that lived for ever.

He thought about that, and decided it was a viable hypothesis, though of course impossible to prove conclusively; the gods had made engineers, but Ziani Vaatzes had made Gace Daurenja.

(He examined one of the clapped-out bushings. From memory, he'd made them out of melted-down Eremian coins, in theory pure silver but in practice eighty-five parts bronze. It was the purest, most consistent bronze he could lay his hands on. Not good enough, though.)

No, that didn't work. He hadn't made Daurenja, he'd found him and used him, because he needed an engineer, and Daurenja was competent, more than competent. He was also resourceful, tireless, efficient, highly accomplished, extremely brave; in his own abominable way, even principled. And, like Ziani, he had a simple purpose to fulful that left him no choice of action. Was it just a coincidence that he was practically impossible to kill, like the angels in the story?

The hammerman brought him his swaged bronze bar; he turned it down and faced it off on one of the wooden-framed treadle lathes, drilled the hole, parted off four bearings, fettled and fitted them. That got the Mezentine lathe up and running again, and he used it to make another eight bearings, naturally much rounder and tighter; four of them to replace the treadle-made stopgaps, and four spares. He tested the result by fixing a half-inch round bar in the chuck and measuring the runout as it spun. Five thousandths of an inch at nine inches from the chuck; a criminal offence in the City, but good enough for Duke Valens and the Aram Chantat.

In the stories, of course, when the dark elves rebelled against the children of the Sun, it was inevitable that they'd lose and be thrown into the Pit, while their trashy, built-in-obsolescent handiwork was turned out to graze the Earth's rocky surface, since Heaven couldn't quite bring itself to put the wretched creatures out of their misery. But supposing the stories had got it the wrong way round? Supposing the dark elves rebelled, and won?

Well; he had the lathe back up and running, which meant he had no excuse for not going to see Duke Valens, as ordered. Get it out of the way and then it's done.

He left the factory, heading for the southern gatehouse, where the messenger had told him there'd be a carriage waiting. Since he was already hopelessly late, he took a short cut through the outer gardens of the palace. Pleasant enough if you liked that sort of thing; a gravel path ran through a series of star-shaped knot gardens, some raised, some sunken, edged with box and lavender. At least the shapes were neat and tidy, though the gravel looked as though it hadn't been raked for a week. Gardeners away at the war, presumably.

A woman's voice called out his name.

It took him a moment to find her. She was sitting in a small bower scooped out of a large privet bush. He hadn't seen her for weeks, not since he'd come back to the city to start up the factory. He'd been invited to the wedding, of course, but he'd been too busy to go.

(He tried to remember the proper way to address a duchess, but couldn't, so he improvised a small, respectful gesture, somewhere between a nod and a bow.)

"Sorry, did I startle you?" She was smiling awkwardly. He didn't reply; she went on: "I gather you're going south to join my husband. Do you think you could give him a letter from me?"

He repeated the gesture. "Of course," he said.

She handed him a small square of folded parchment. She knew, of course, that it had been him who had intercepted the letter that disgraced Miel Ducas. "I'll make sure he gets it," he said.

"Thank you. Usually I use the courier service, but I always feel guilty about it. It's supposed to be for important official business only, and I'm sure I don't come under that heading."

Fishing for compliments? Unlikely. He had no reason to linger, but he sensed she didn't want him to go just yet. Of course, he'd saved her life at the fall of Civitas Eremiae. Had she ever wondered about that, in the long hours of futile leisure that made up most of her life: how he'd come to be in the right place to lead her to safety out of the dying city, through the tunnels and cisterns that people who'd lived there all their lives didn't know about, but which he'd navigated with ease?

"If you've got a moment," she said.

"Of course." There was a stone bench. He perched on the edge of it, just close enough to be able to hear her without having to lean forward. For a man who'd spent his life among trip-hammers and mills, he had excellent hearing.

"About the war." She stopped, as though compiling an agenda. "What's going to happen? They don't tell me, you see."

"I don't know." Which was true. "Quite soon now, your husband will advance on the City and start the siege. He'll go through the motions of a direct assault, but I don't suppose he'll keep it up for very long. He won't want to waste lives pointlessly. An assault will tell him how many defenders there are, where the artillery batteries are positioned, their range, weight of shot and rate of fire. He'll need to know all that, and it doesn't come free, he'll have to buy it with dead bodies. Once he's got the information, he'll start the siege operations. That's a very specialised branch of military science and I don't know anything about it. The engines I'm building will be important. Given time, they could knock down the walls. But he hasn't got that long; he'll be limited by food supplies, mostly, and other stuff like that. My guess is, he'll use artillery to distract them while he uses sappers to dig under the walls. That's even more scientific than artillery, but he's got the advantage of having skilled men who know the work, the silver-miners. My people don't dig holes if they can help it. If he can undermine a gatehouse or bring down a large enough section of wall, he's won. Once his soldiers get inside the City, it'll all be over. If he fails, and the food runs out, he'll have no choice but to fall back, and I don't suppose the Aram Chantat will be pleased if he does that. I suppose everything really hinges on how badly they want to take the City." He paused. "Does that answer your question?"

She nodded, unconvincingly. "Will you be able to help?" she asked. "With the digging under the walls, I mean."

Ziani shrugged. "He's got men who're better qualified than I am," he said. "Obviously I'll help if I can."

"And your friend." She wasn't looking at him. "What's his name? The tall man . . ."

"Daurenja."

"Daurenja," she repeated. "Everybody speaks very highly of him. He told my husband he was working on some kind of new weapon; like a catapult, he said, but much stronger. Is that right?"

Ziani kept perfectly still for a moment or so before answering. "In theory," he said. "It might work. But he hasn't built one yet. There are technical problems."

"Oh, well." She smiled faintly. "I wouldn't be able to understand, even if you explained. Really, I was only asking about the war because I want to know how long Valens is going to be away. I simply have no idea: a month? A year? I'd go out and join him, but they say it's too dangerous. It's silly, isn't it? Here I am, hoping that a city will fall and goodness knows how many poor people will die, just so my husband can come home and everything can be normal. That seems very wicked, really, but I can't help it." She turned her head slightly and looked at him. "You understand how I feel, don't you?"

He nodded. "Daurenja wasn't really supposed to tell the duke about his pet project," he said, "not until we'd managed to build a working prototype. And that's still a very long way away, and we didn't want your husband getting his hopes up."

"Maybe I shouldn't have mentioned it," she said. "I'm sorry if I've caused trouble for anybody. And I suppose," she added, turning her head away again, "you might want it kept quiet so the Aram Chantat don't find out. After all, a weapon isn't made to be used just once, and we may not be friends with them for ever."

Ziani tried not to show any reaction to that. "Politics," he said. "None of my business. I just make things."

"You had Miel Ducas arrested." Her head hadn't moved. "Because of that letter. I've wondered why you did that."

He was short of breath, just when he needed plenty. "I'll be honest with you," he said. "I was sucking up to the boss. I wanted to be promoted, in sole charge of the defence of the city. I thought, thanks to my engines, we were going to win; and after the war was over . . ." He made a show of shrugging, overdid it a little. "A man like me, a factory worker, comes to Eremia and sees how the gentry live: fine houses, estates, lives of elegant leisure. It's traditional for dukes to reward their low-born but faithful servants with titles and endowments." Out of the corner of his eye he saw her shift a little. "It's not as though I laid a trap or anything. The letter came into my hands and I had a choice. Get rid of it, hurt nobody, gain nothing. Or else I could do what I did. I'll apologise if you want me to."

She shook her head. "I think it was Miel who betrayed the city," she said. "After Orsea turned against him, I mean. And if he hadn't done that, if the city hadn't fallen, Valens wouldn't have come for me. I'd still be married to Orsea, instead of the man I love. So no, please don't apologise. The city falling gave me my only chance of being happy." She laughed, from her throat only. "Listen to me," she said. "Two cities, mine and yours, just so I can have the man I want. I despise myself for it." She was speaking very clearly, shaping each word like a craftsman. "I know it's wrong, and really I must be a horrible person, *evil*, to think like that, but it doesn't make any difference. I tell myself none of it was my doing; it couldn't have been, because look at me, I've never *done* anything in my whole life. So where's the harm in passively receiving the benefits of other people's misery? But of course it's not true. Orsea wouldn't have become duke if he hadn't married me, and Orsea was to blame for the war, though he didn't exactly start it. And Valens wouldn't have joined the war except for me; and his joining in brought in the Aram Chantat, and now it looks like Mezentia will be destroyed as well." She paused, as though doing sums in her head. "Do you think someone can be blamed just for being born, or not dying? And then I ask myself, with all these terrible things on my conscience, if everything really did go right, and the City fell and Valens came home, could we ever really be happy together, after all that? And the dreadful thing is, I believe we could. I think he could walk up the stairs and shut the door and say, 'I'm home,' and none of it would matter any more. That's an extraordinary thought, isn't it?"

Ziani paused to rub his eyes. "Not really," he said. "I think you're only evil and wicked if you have a choice. If you do what you have to, it can't be your fault. I heard someone say once that there's no such thing as a weapon; there's just tools, and men who decide how they're going to use them. And even then sometimes the user doesn't have a choice. He picks up a chisel and stabs a man in self-defence. He had no choice, and the chisel's just a tool. The evil came from the man who attacked him in the first place. Now suppose the attacker was a general, the only man who could have saved the city, and without him the city falls. In that case, it's still the general's fault, for attacking the man who defended himself. If the Mezentines all die, they brought it on themselves. It's very simple, when you think about it."

She stood up. "Thank you for taking the letter," she said. "Have a safe journey."

Valens took the letter from him without looking at it and tucked it under the stack of reports on the rickety folding table. "You took your time getting here," he said.

"The roads," Ziani replied. "You said something about a book."

"Yes." Valens reached down and picked something up off the floor. "I read it while I was waiting for you. I was surprised how much of it I remembered. I can't have looked at it for years. They say the things you read when you're a kid stay with you."

Ziani opened it. Diagrams. A mechanism? "What's it got to do with me?"

Valens smiled. "Let's say I wanted a Mezentine perspective." He picked up a cup, realised it was empty. "Suppose the Republic had put you in charge of the City's defences. You know that your artillery monopoly's a thing of the past. You send to the library for anything they've got on defending against artillery." He leaned over, turned the pages back to the flyleaf. "This book was copied by the Guild, so there has to be a copy in the Guildhall library. Or there's other books on the same subject, presumably saying much the same sort of thing. I want you to read it, then tell me how much of it the Republic's capable of doing in the time available with the resources it has to hand. Also," he added, as Ziani took the weight of the book from him, "I remember you telling my great-grandfather-in-law that you knew a way of breaking the City's defences. I think it's time you told me what it is."

Ziani leaned back, thinking of what the duchess had told him. "Oh," he said. "That."

"That."

Deep breath. "You know my assistant, Gace Daurenja?"

"Oh, I know him."

Ziani couldn't help smiling at that. "Quite," he said. "He's a nasty piece of work. But that didn't stop you listening to him when he offered you his new weapon."

Valens nodded. "Does it work?"

"He hasn't even built it yet. There's . . . ."

"Technical problems?"

"Yes." Ziani ran his finger down the spine of the book; rough, starting to crumble in places. "Imagine a man-made volcano. Very useful, but only if you've got a container to put it in. Daurenja thinks a metal pot will do the trick, but he doesn't know how to make one strong enough. He's tried, but the volcano tears them apart and throws the bits hard enough to take your head off. He thinks I can figure out how to make a stronger pot."

Valens' eyebrow rose. "Can you?"

"Stronger, yes. Strong enough . . . That's not the point, though." He scowled for a moment. "Daurenja's a very clever man. Brilliant, really, a genius. But he's set his heart on getting his idea to work, and that limits him. Now me . . ." He shrugged. "It's not my idea, I'm not in love with it like he is. I'm quite happy to explore the possibilities of what his idea can do if it *doesn't* work."

Valens sighed. "You're not making sense," he said.

"Oh, I think it's perfectly simple," Ziani replied. "To make the volcano, you mix stuff together to make a powder, and when you set light to it, you get an eruption. According to Daurenja, it's like what happens when water falls on a crucible full of molten metal, only much, much stronger."

"I see." Valens sighed again. "What *does* happen?"

"Lots." Ziani smiled. "The crucible cracks, burning hot liquid metal flies everywhere. It can crack walls, punch holes in roofs. The water turns to steam, you see, in a tearing hurry. The steam sort of pushes everything else out of the way. I imagine Daurenja's powder works the same way, except it makes smoke instead of steam. But the principle's the same. It's strong enough to smash a brass pot with sides an inch thick. Daurenja wants the pot to trap the smoke so it's only pushing one way, pushing against a stone lying on top of the powder, so the stone goes flying through the air. He reckons it'd have many times the force of the biggest siege engine ever built."

Valens' eyes had opened wide. "Would it?"

"I don't see why not." Ziani shook his head. "But even if it does, that's not much use to you. Suppose I could make a strong enough pot. To set up a forge to make a hundred of the things would take six months to a year. We haven't got that much time."

"That's true enough." Valens drummed his fingers on the table. "But you . . ."

"I can't help thinking," Ziani said. "Dig a hole under the City wall and stuff it full of barrels of Daurenja's powder. Stop up the hole with rocks, but leave a little gap, just enough to poke a burning rope into." He drew a little closer, knowing he had Valens' undivided attention. "The problem with sapping under the City walls is that they're built on foundations of solid rock. You remember how we sabotaged the silver mines, to stop the Republic getting them. We packed the mine shafts with brushwood and set it alight, to burn through the pit props and cave in the roof. But even if you had the time to cut a tunnel through solid rock, how are you going to collapse it? Oh, there's ways, according to your miners. There have been accidents in the past, where sloppy practice left gallery ceilings weak and they've caved in. But it'd need a lot of time and effort to do it on purpose. When they built the City, they thought about sappers, you can count on it. They built the walls where they are because they reckoned it wouldn't be practical for an enemy to undermine them. And without some new ingredient, like Daurenja's volcano dust, they'd have been right. That's what I had in mind when we were talking to that old man."

Valens thought for a long time; then he said, "Nice of you to tell me about it, finally. I'd have been really quite upset if you'd kept it to yourself all this time."

Ziani looked at him. "You've met Daurenja," he said, and left it at that.

Valens nodded very slightly, as though he didn't want anybody watching to see. "He's your man, though," he said. "You can handle him. I don't see a problem."

"No." Valens looked up as he said it. "I can't handle him. He scares me. I'd have had him killed, except I don't know the recipe for the volcano powder."

Valens turned away, as though suffering from cramp. When he turned back, he said, "Make him tell you. If you need help; soldiers . . ."

"He'd die first," Ziani said with conviction. "He knows he's dead anyway without the secret. No, the deal is that I help him make his stronger pot. When I'm doing that, he'll have to share the secret with me, I'll tell him I can't help him unless I know it too. Once I know, of course, the situation changes. We may even succeed. The stupid thing is, all Daurenja wants is the stronger pot; not money or power or anything like that. He just wants to make a pot that can throw big heavy stones. I guess you could call him a visionary." Saying the word forced him to smile. "So, let him have his pot. It'd come in very useful, I'm sure, in future wars, assuming there's anybody left alive to fight once we're finished here. But there's always someone to fight, isn't there? Anyway, that's nothing to do with me. I just want fifty standard-size apple barrels full of his magic powder, and then I can get my job done and go home."

Valens picked up a goose quill and sharpened it, slowly and precisely. I could have trained him to be a useful engineer, Ziani thought; he doesn't hurry, and his hands don't shake, even when he's shocked or disgusted. "Fine," he said. "If what you say is true, it makes sense, and I'm very pleased to hear we've got a secret weapon that can crack the City wall, because without one we'd be completely screwed." He looked down at the point he'd shaved on the quill. "Why didn't you tell me before?"

Oh well, Ziani thought, and said: "Because Daurenja knows something about me that'd get me killed."

"I see." The pad of his index finger, pressed gently on the point; just enough pressure to prove its sharpness without causing damage. "Who by?"

"You," Ziani said. "Among others."

"It must be a very bad thing, then."

"It is."

"Not something you'd care to tell me about."

"No."

Valens looked up. His eyes were bright, as though he'd just been crying, but his face was completely blank. "But I can't have you killed," he said. "I need you to take the City for me."

"You'd just have to find another way," Ziani said. "You'd have no choice."

A shrug; graceful, as if he was dismissing trivia. "And Daurenja knows this dark secret of yours, but he won't tell me because he needs you to make him a stronger pot. I need you to crack the City wall. You need him to tell you how to make the magic dust. I know Daurenja's a rapist and a murderer; in fact, I had the devil of a job getting out of doing something about it, but fortunately I have resourceful people on my side who can do wonderful things with legal technicalities. So here we are," he went on calmly, "all of us turning a blind eye to every form of evil under the sun, because we don't have any choice in the matter. Take me," he added, looking down at his hands. "I killed my cousin Orsea so I could marry his widow. I knew Orsea wasn't guilty of treason. The evidence against him was far too glib, if you see what I mean. I knew you were lying. But I had him killed, all the same. And now Veatriz and I are married, and we love each other, and as soon as this bloody stupid war's over . . ." He looked up. "I suppose everybody asks himself at some time or other, what wouldn't I do to get what I want? And the answer is, when I find out, I'll let you know. The depressing part is, I really don't care any more."

But Ziani shook his head. "If you found out the truth about me, you'd have me killed," he said. "After you've taken the City."

Valens smiled. "Do you really think so?" he said. "Of course, I'm in no position to offer an opinion, since I don't know what you've done. But you're a clever man, you haven't made this extraordinary confession just to cleanse your soul. You want to make a deal, presumably. Well?"

Ziani nodded. His mouth was dry, but he felt calm. The art of designing a mechanism lies in enclosing the components so that they can only move one way. "Very simple," he said. "If you find out . . . my dark secret . . . you won't have me killed until the siege is over and we've either taken Mezentia or given up in despair. In return, I'll build your siege engines and do everything else I possibly can. That's all. A stay of execution, not a pardon."

Valens stared at him for the time it takes to peel an apple. "That's it?" he said. "It's practically reasonable."

"I don't ask for something unless I know it's possible," Ziani said. "You can't promise me a pardon, because you couldn't keep the promise. But you can give me the time, because you need me alive and working, until the City falls. And," he added casually, "because you're a man of your word. Well? Is it a deal?"

Valens' eyes were very wide; he hadn't blinked for a long time. "I suppose it is," he said. "Because it's feasible, like you said. And because I don't have a choice."

Ziani dipped his head in formal acknowledgement. "Life's so much simpler without choices," he said. "Thinking about it, I'm glad I never had to make one. I'm not sure I'd have been able to." He nodded sharply. "Can I go now? There's nothing else I wanted to talk about, if you've finished."

"No, that's fine." Valens was still looking at him as though he was somehow impossible, the result of a conjuring trick. "I'd like a detailed report on the book in the next three days, if you think that's going to be enough time."

"Plenty." Ziani stood up. His knees were quite firm, but his feet felt as though he had lead blocks in his shoes. "I'm glad we've sorted that out, it was bothering me. Now I can help Daurenja make his pot. I've been putting him off, and he's getting impatient. It's strange, him and me: the more I grow to hate him, the more I admire his good qualities. He's like you, you know, a man of principle. It's just that he has different priorities."

"I'd rather not talk about him any more," Valens replied. "I don't like the fact that I don't care about what he's done as much as I should. Anyway, you'd better go. I've got a mountain of work to get through."

"Of course." Ziani was at the tent door when he turned back. "You weren't telling the truth," he said.

"Wasn't I?"

"No. You didn't know Duke Orsea was innocent when you ordered his execution."

Valens sat very still. "I knew later," he said, "when I asked Veatriz to marry me."

"That's different," Ziani said.

"Yes." Valens frowned. "It's the difference between shooting a doe in the close season and eating it once you've gone home and checked the calendar. The latter is better in some ways and worse in others, but it all balances out, more or less."

When Vaatzes had gone, Valens opened the letter. He read it three times, as he'd always done when she wrote to him. After the third reading, he held it for a moment over the lamp, so close that a smudge of soot formed on the bottom edge. He could think of no more appropriate way of punishing himself than to burn her letter and not reply to it. No, not strictly true (he pulled the letter away sharply and put it on the table). He could ignore the guilt of Ziani Vaatzes, the man who'd enabled him to kill Orsea and achieve his heart's desire. The thought made him grin. In his father's day, the punishment for forgery was disfigurement; the forger's nose was slit lengthways, his ears and lips were cut away, his cheeks sliced, his hair shaved and his forehead branded. He'd put a stop to that, of course, because he was a humane man, and the self-righteousness inherent in the punishment disturbed him. It wasn't good for people to be able to see justice gloating in another man's wrecked face. In which case, there was a fine poetic justice at work. Being a humane man, a good duke, he silently condemned himself to punishment by a disfiguration that only he could see.

He had a ridiculously large amount of work to do, all of it urgent and important. Instead, he answered her letter, indulging himself in every word he wrote, crossed out, rephrased. He knew how much it would mean to her; and if pleasing her meant allowing himself equal pleasure, he couldn't be blamed for it. After all, he had no choice.

As he wrote, he couldn't keep a small part of his mind from trying to guess what Vaatzes had done that could be so very terrible. That, he decided, was a bit like looking for one particular coin in a treasury.

The next day should have been a hunting day, according to his mental calendar. Instead, he started the war.

In theory, of course, the Mezentines had done that, by sending their half-witted Cure Doce to burn the nonexistent engine sheds. But that affair had been so pathetically ill-conceived that it didn't really count; the joke alone had been more than enough compensation for a shed full of flour. A war like this one had to be started properly, and since the enemy didn't seem capable of doing it, he'd have to deal with it himself.

The objective was to be the Mezentia–Lonazep road. Twelve miles from the City, according to his more reliable maps and the reports of his scouts, the Republic had built a customs house. Presumably they'd been trying to impress someone or other. By all accounts, it was the size of a small town, conveniently sited next to a river and all done in the pseudo-military style of architecture that the Republic seemed to favour – thin but grandiose walls, *trompe l'oeil* arrow slits, crenellated pepperpot towers, and a portcullis that didn't actually work. Tempting providence, really, since if you pulled all that rubbish down and replaced it with real defences, you'd have a castle that'd cut the road completely. Playing at soldiers, Valens decided, wasn't something he approved of.

The assault party was one hundred Vadani heavy cavalry supported by three hundred Aram Chantat. Assuming all went well, the

Vadani would stay behind afterwards as a garrison until the masons and carpenters arrived to do the makeover. The Aram Chantat had to be involved because they were restless and starting to be a nuisance. They didn't like the fact that the Mezentines were still able to bring in food and supplies, and they wanted something done about it. Valens had tried to explain – only once – that it didn't matter because starving the enemy out had never been an option, and he wanted the City to have good stocks of food in hand, since he'd need them himself, once the City had fallen, to feed the army and his own people while they were being resettled. They hadn't listened, and he wasn't in the habit of repeating himself. By his calculations, there was now enough food in the City for his purposes. Time to start the war.

The raid was an open secret around the camp; nevertheless, Valens was more than a little disconcerted when he was told, the night before the raiding party was due to set off, that Daurenja the engineer wanted to talk to him about it.

"I thought you were back at the city, looking after things while Vaatzes is away," he said.

Daurenja stood over him like a spider up on its back legs; intimidating, but he was damned if he was going to let him sit down. "That's where I should be," Daurenja replied. "But actually it's quite quiet there at the moment. There's been a hold-up with the lumber supply – I've seen to it, and we'll make up the lost time, and to be honest with you, we can do with a rest. The men aren't used to working flat out like they've been doing, work's getting sloppy and there's been a lot of waste in materials. A few days off will put that right."

Valens shrugged. "Sounds fair enough," he said. "That doesn't explain why you're here. By your own argument, you should be resting too."

Daurenja grinned. "I don't need rest," he said. "Not good for me. Too much energy, my father used to say. Which is why I'd like to ask a big favour."

"Something to do with the cavalry raid – how the hell did you find out about it, by the way?"

"I hear things." Big smile. Charm, Valens thought. But he does charm the way an illiterate craftsman copies letters; everything perfectly replicated, but he doesn't know the meaning. "I gather you're sending an expeditionary force to cut the Lonazep road. I'd like to go along, if that's all right."

Valens' eyebrows shot up. "You?"

Eager nod. "I'm a good horseman," he said. "My father bred horses, we used to send five destriers and two palfreys a year to the fair at Goyon and I helped break them in. And I'm not a complete novice at soldiering, either. I spent six months with the Tascon scouts, though I don't suppose I ought to tell you that."

He's not lying, Valens thought. He doesn't lie much, that's the extraordinary thing. And the Tascon heavy cavalry were at least as good as the Vadani, as he knew to his cost. "Really? When?"

"About eleven years ago," Daurenja replied. "In your father's time, and I'm sorry to say we did have one or two unfortunate episodes with your people. Nothing serious, but . . ." The smile broadened. "Good experience, anyway. Mostly we were annoying the Eremians, if that's any consolation."

Valens leaned back in his chair. "You do like to keep busy, I can see that. But no, you can't go. I need you here."

"But it's only for a few days. I'll come back with the Aram Chantat after the—"

"What I mean is," Valens said slowly, "I can't afford to risk you getting yourself carved up or killed. I've been thinking about the weapon you told me about. The brass pot that throws stones."

If he'd been a cat, his ears would've gone back. "You've spoken to Ziani about it, then."

Valens nodded. All this openness was making him dizzy. "He said the idea's worth developing. In fact, he's quite impressed."

"Really." For a moment, Daurenja's eyes shone. He's pleased, Valens thought; like when a mutual friend tells you the girl you're after really likes you. "So we can make a start, as soon as the siege engines are finished?"

"That's between the two of you," Valens said quickly. "But you can see why I don't want you galloping around the countryside playing at knights in armour. Vaatzes said he can't build this weapon without you."

"That's true." Faint smile. "But you don't want to worry about me, I'll be fine. My mother used to say I slip in and out of trouble like an eel in a net. And I really do want to go. I need to . . . well, stretch my legs a bit, before we start building the weapon."

"Fine," Valens said. "Walk back to Civitas Vadanis. But you're not going on the raid."

He went anyway. He stole a helmet, coat of plates, arm and leg harness from different tents during the night, and at dawn presented himself to the Vadani captain as the duke's special observer.

"First I've heard of it," the captain said.

"Maybe you weren't paying attention," Daurenja replied pleasantly. "If you like, we can go and wake the duke up and ask him to confirm."

The captain didn't think he wanted to do that. "Why's he sending you, though?" he asked. "You're that engineer."

"He wants a report on what's going to be involved in refortifying the station once you've taken it. I know about that sort of thing."

The captain shrugged. "Just do as you're told and don't get in the way," he said. "And if I want advice, I'll ask for it. All right?"

They followed the river as far as the Cure Doce border, then headed south, making good time over the top of the moorland ridge that ran parallel with the mountains. Strictly speaking they were trespassing, but if the Cure Doce wanted to make anything of it, that'd be fine too. Not surprisingly, they had no trouble. Valens had decided on the route himself, and though he hadn't shared his reasoning with the captain, the likeliest explanation was that he wanted the Mezentines to know they were coming. Why that should be desirable, the captain didn't want to speculate.

They arrived on the plateau above the station with half a day in hand, and the captain decided to use the time to rest the horses, since they'd been at grass for months and weren't yet back to full campaigning fitness. The Aram Chantat captains didn't agree; they were uneasy about the fact that the Cure Doce must have seen them coming and would undoubtedly have reported back to the Mezentines. Sitting about doing nothing for several hours would only give the enemy more time to react. The Vadani captain said that that was quite likely, but he had his orders. He was lying, but something about the Aram Chantat brought out the worst in him. "In fact," he added, "I think we'll spend the night here and attack first thing in the morning. I want the horses completely fresh."

"Unnecessary. Our horses don't need rest. We don't let them get fat like you do."

The captain smiled. "We'll wait till morning," he said.

He spent the afternoon watching the mountains behind and the road below. Four parties of riders, none of them more than a dozen strong, came and looked at them and went away again. He assumed they were Cure Doce – could the Mezentines even ride horses? – but he reckoned they couldn't see anything they wouldn't already have known. When it got dark he had something to eat, checked his armour by feel one last time for loose rivets and snagging joints, then went to sleep.

It was still dark when he was woken up, but he knew intuitively who was shaking his shoulder.

"What do you want?" he growled.

"Thought you might like to know." Daurenja sounded horribly cheerful. He smelt of blood. "There's a large force of infantry camped on the road from the City. Two thousand, maybe three; I've been counting campfires."

"Mezentines?" He reached up to disengage Daurenja's hand from his shoulder. It was sticky.

"Yes. Full infantry armour, and a field artillery train. Scorpions. My guess is, they'll try and lure you into a killing zone and shoot you up."

The captain propped himself up on one elbow. Very bad. An artillery ambush wasn't something he'd anticipated. "How long . . . ?"

"I've just come from there," Daurenja replied. "Still three hours before daylight. I imagine they were planning to set up the pieces – well, round about now, actually, so as to be ready for a dawn attack. They'll be running a little late, though. I made a bit of a nuisance of myself while I was there, let the horses out, did what I promised my mother I wouldn't and played with fire. Oh, and I took the liberty of sending some men down to keep an eye on them. It'd be a good idea to know where they're planning to lure us, don't you think?"

An unpleasant thought occurred to the captain at that point. "The savages," he said. "Did you tell . . . ?"

Daurenja laughed softly. "Sleeping like babies," he replied. "I thought it'd be a shame to wake them. So as far as they'll know, you figured all this out for yourself."

"I see." The captain didn't want to say it but he had no choice. "Thank you."

"No problem. I have trouble sleeping."

He started to straighten up, but the captain grabbed his arm. "What are you doing here?" he asked. "Really."

"Observing. You'd better get up now. You don't want to have to rush."

*

"You're not supposed to be here," Valens said, looking up from a map on his knees.

The captain gave him a worried look. "I know, sir, but if I could . . ."

Valens nodded him into a chair. "That's all right," he said. "Nobody seems to do what I tell them any more, so don't worry about it. Congratulations, by the way."

"Thank you." The captain seemed more worried rather than less. "I know I was meant to stay behind with the garrison," he said nervously, "but in the circumstances, I thought I'd better report to you direct. I didn't want . . ."

"Quite." Valens smiled. "I was just about to write to you ordering you to get back here on the double, so you've saved me a job." The smile vanished like spit on hot iron. "What the hell happened?" he said. "That lunatic . . ."

"Did you send him with us?"

"Me? God, no. In fact, I expressly told him not to go."

The captain took a deep breath. "Just as well he disobeyed orders, then. If it hadn't been for him, we'd all be dead by now."

A look the captain couldn't read passed over Valens' face. "Is that right?" he said. "The report said—"

"With respect." The captain realised how loudly he'd said that, and cringed. "With respect, the report was for the Aram Chantat – well, in case they got hold of it. I don't know if it's procedure for them to see direct-level dispatches, but I didn't want to take the chance. So I came myself."

"Ah." Carefully, Valens rolled up the map and slid it into its brass tube. "So, what really happened?"

The captain shifted slightly. "We got there early," he said. "I thought it'd be a good idea to rest the horses overnight and attack at dawn." He looked down at the desk, then back up again. "May I ask a question?"

"If you like."

"You wanted them to know we were coming."

(He'd said it, then. And he was still alive, and not on his way to the guardhouse.)

"That's a statement, not a question."

"Yes, sir. You wanted them to have time to get ready, do something. Capturing the customs post was a minor objective."

"That's not a question either. But yes, that's right." Valens sighed faintly, as though knuckling down to a chore he'd hoped to avoid. "I wanted to get a taste of how the Mezentines are coping on their own, without mercenaries," he said. "For one thing, I wanted to test their reconnaissance and intelligence system. I wanted to see if they'd notice you and if they'd be able to send a message back to the City before you got there. Next, I wanted to see how they'd react. I guessed it was fifty-fifty whether they'd panic and assume you were the advance party for an attack on the City, or guess we were planning to cut the Lonazep road. Finally, I wanted some idea of how they fight. Cutting the road was important too, of course, but it wasn't uppermost in my mind, if you follow me."

A brief nod, as if to agree that the subject was now closed. "Well, sir," the captain said, "now you know. Either word got through fast enough for them to put together a pretty sophisticated response force, or else they're in constant readiness. They were there fairly quickly, and they had a good idea of what they were about." He paused, then went on: "If I'd done as the Aram Chantat wanted and gone straight in instead of resting the horses, we'd still have beaten them to it, though I'm not sure that'd have been a good thing, seeing as they had all that field artillery with them. It wouldn't have been much fun if we'd already been inside the station and they'd opened up on us with that lot. As it was, they came up during the night. Very professional job, getting a force that size so close to us in the dark, plus they had the artillery train."

Valens nodded gravely. "Stupidest thing a soldier can do, underestimating the enemy. Hence my experiment."

The captain acknowledged that with a slight dip of his head. "We were that close to riding straight into it," he said. "There's a bend in the road half a mile or so short of the station from where we were. They were going to plant their scorpions about a hundred yards back – plenty of cover, but all loose stuff and rubbish, not the sort of thing that'd put you on notice. I assume they'd have sent a few sad-looking infantry up the road to meet us. They'd have run for it, we'd have followed up, straight into the scorpions' cone of fire. If they'd timed it right, they could've wiped us out."

Valens didn't say anything for a while. Then he reached for a jug and two cups, and poured them both a drink.

"Daurenja," he said.

The captain nodded. "Him," he said. "I still don't have a clue what he thought he was playing at. As far as I can make out, he either saw or heard them coming in the dark, watched them pitch camp; instead of coming back and telling me about it straight away, he snuck in there, stalked and killed at least half a dozen sentries, drove off the limber horses, set fire to a dozen or so tents, pulled the linchpins from eight or ten limbers, then just calmly strolled back and woke me up. And now you tell me he wasn't even supposed to be there."

"He's a character," Valens said quietly, after a pause. "So," he went on, "after that it was all fairly straightforward, I take it."

"Very much so." The captain lifted his cup, put it down without drinking. "We were able to come up behind the scorpions while they were still setting up – the Aram Chantat did a very good job there, makes me really glad they're on our side – while we had fun with the poor bloody Mezentines." He paused again. "I imagine some of them must've got away, but it can't have been many. Beautiful armour and kit they've got, mind, but it's like fighting a bunch of kids."

Valens put his cup down. "That's what I was expecting you'd say," he said. "The interesting thing is, they seem to be well aware of that, but they aren't letting it panic them. Hence the field artillery. Why send an untrained scared-to-death man where you can send a three-foot-long steel arrow?" He frowned. "Someone up there in the City's got a good head on his shoulders, and for once it looks like the politicians are prepared to listen instead of trying to score points. If it hadn't been for that freak . . ." He paused, as his frown deepened into a scowl. ". . . I'd have had to pay full market price for my lesson, instead of getting it cheap." He wriggled his back against the chair, which creaked dangerously. "I think we may yet have a war on our hands," he said. "I hope not, but from now on I'm assuming we're fighting grown-ups. For all I know, they've got the stuff out of books, but that doesn't really matter if the books are any good."

Daurenja was saddling his horse when they came for him. They took the reins out of his hand and led him across the camp to one of the grain sheds, where a blacksmith was waiting with a small portable forge and anvil.

"What's going on?" Daurenja asked.

"Sit down on the floor," they told him.

As the blacksmith was riveting fetters round his ankles, he asked them again. "Your execution's scheduled for noon tomorrow," they replied. Then they left him in the dark.

Fifteen hours later, the shed door opened and Valens came in. Daurenja was sitting on the floor, exactly where he'd been. The chain they'd attached to his ankles had come from the silver mines, where it had been used to raise a seventy-ton ore skip from the bottom of a deep shaft. It was too heavy to move. Valens didn't need to look down to know that Daurenja's bowels and bladder had been active while he'd been sitting there.

"Had enough?" he said.

Daurenja's eyes were closed against the sudden bright light. "Yes," he said.

"Good. Don't do it again." He sighed, and perched on the rim of a flour barrel. "I've been trying to figure you out," he said. "Vaatzes came to see me, when he heard I'd ordered your execution. Basically, he talked me out of it. You should be grateful."

"I am," Daurenja said.

"I doubt that, but never mind. At any rate, I pride myself on only making bloody stupid mistakes once. I suggest you follow my example."

"I'll do my best."

Valens laughed. "You know," he said, "that could easily be construed as a threat. I'll say this for you, Daurenja, your best is very good indeed. You're very good at all sorts of things, so I understand. Vaatzes tells me you're a very fine engineer – he reckons you're better than him, only you don't know as much, not having had the Mezentine training. My cavalry captain tells me you're a first-class scout and definitely officer material, apart from this tiresome habit of not obeying orders. My wife told me how you fought off those Mezentines, on my wedding-day hunt. Saved her life, she says, and I believe her. You're a good falconer, too, by all accounts. Do you fence?"

"Yes."

"Play a musical instrument?"

"Six."

Valens nodded. "I envy you," he said. "I learnt the rebec and the violin, but I haven't played for years, never was any good at it; forced myself to be competent, when I was a kid, but I couldn't do it now to save my life. You're clearly what my father used to call an accomplished man."

"I had an expensive education," Daurenja said.

"I can believe it," Valens replied. "I believe every accomplishment you've gained has cost someone a great deal. It'd be a shame to waste all that trouble and expense, but I will if I have to. Do you believe me?"

Daurenja smiled, his eyes still closed. "Yes," he said. "Do you think you could get someone to take this chain off?"

"I expect I'll get round to it at some point," Valens replied. "If I had any choice in the matter, I'd leave you there for a week to think about what we've just been talking about, but I don't. Vaatzes wants you back at the engine factory. Oh, and there's a little job I want you to do for me before you go."

"Certainly. What can I . . . ?"

Valens stood up. "Make me a chair," he said. "Something that folds up small for transport but doesn't wobble about when I sit on it. Can you do that?"

"Of course."

"Fine. I'll tell them to get that chain off you." He grinned. "You'll have to be quick about it, because Vaatzes wants you back on the road to Civitas Vadanis by nightfall. He reckons that if you ride through the night, you can be back at the factory in time to start the first shift after the lay-off. Won't leave you any time to get cleaned up or have anything to eat, I'm afraid. Still, you won't mind that, a rugged character like you."

He walked to the door, then stopped.

"I know why you did it," he said. "You wanted to show me how much I need you; not just at the factory, but everywhere. You wanted me to see what a brilliant soldier you can be. I imagine you're after a command of your own, once the fighting really starts. Yes?"

Daurenja nodded. "Yes," he said. "I want to lead the sappers when we attack the City."

"I thought you might say that." Valens nodded slowly. "Vaatzes told me how useful you were when he was sabotaging the silver mines. All right, then," he said crisply. "If that's what you want."

"Thank you."

Valens smiled. "Any time," he said.

He spent the rest of the day with the Aram Chantat. They weren't happy. They acknowledged that he had finally done as they'd asked and cut the City off from Lonazep, although he'd wasted far too much time; also, according to their captains, he'd sent the raiding party out under the command of an incompetent fool who nearly led them into a massacre, and it was fortunate that the excellent engineer whose name they couldn't quite pronounce had been there to save the day.

"Quite," Valens said. "I think very highly of Major Daurenja. In fact, I'm putting him in charge of the sappers, once the siege is under way."

They were delighted to hear that. They thought very highly of him too. Nevertheless, they were unhappy about the general conduct of the war, which they felt was proceeding without any sense of urgency or any real direction. Yes, thank you, they'd heard his explanations before, and certainly they couldn't proceed until the siege engines were ready – it was a blessing that Major Daurenja was personally supervising the work, since they weren't at all happy with the Mezentine engineer Vaatzes – but surely more could have been done in the interim, by way of moving troops into position, preparing the ground, drawing out the enemy forces and so forth. They were disappointed, not just with Valens' actions but with his attitude. Sometimes they wondered if his heart was really in this war. Also, they felt compelled to mention, they disapproved of the haste with which he'd married the Eremian duke's widow. It was disrespectful to the memory of his dead wife, for whose sake they were fighting the war. He was, of course, at perfect liberty to remarry, as obviously the succession had to be provided for, but he should have waited until the City had fallen and the war was over. Indeed, under those circumstances, he might have had an incentive to progress matters at a rather more acceptable rate.

When he got back to his tent, the chair was waiting for him. It was beautiful. Daurenja had used a dense, honey-coloured wood that seemed to glow like amber in the lamplight (later he realised it was barrel-stave oak, salvaged from junked nail-barrels). The curved uprights reached up like two hands cupped to catch an apple falling from a tree, and in the middle of the back Daurenja had somehow found time to carve a fallow doe, frozen in the moment of surprise as she senses the approaching hounds, her head lifted and turned, her whole body tense and perfectly still.

Chapter Six

Two horsemen. For a long time they were black dots on a green and brown background. Then they grew vestigial arms, legs and heads. The sun helped, flashing obligingly off steel, to show they were probably soldiers, though that was more or less inevitable, in context. The colour of their horses came next (one chestnut, one grey), and after that the pointed profile of their helmets, which meant that they were almost certainly Aram Chantat. At four hundred yards, the hypothesis was confirmed by the length of their coats, reaching almost to their ankles.

Today the hunt would be bow and stable. He didn't mind that. It suited the nature of the quarry. Parforce against dangerous game was all very well if you had twelve couple of hounds, a small army of beaters and a dozen huntsmen to ward the angles, but for one man on his own it simply wasn't practical. Jarnac would've agreed with him, if he'd been there.

Quickly, now that they were closing, he chose the ground. Assuming they were following the road, as they'd been doing for the past hour, they would cross the little river at the ford and start to climb the winding path that led up to his vantage point among the granite outcrops. His choices, therefore, were up here among the rocks, or down at the ford itself, where the stream had scooped out an embankment just large enough for a man to crouch under, if he didn't mind getting soaked. He consulted his knowledge of the quarry species: wary, intelligent, quick to bolt and dangerous once engaged. They'd see the outcrops and be on their guard, reasoning that the great stones provided excellent cover. They'd assume that an attacker would choose that advantage over the very meagre conceal-ment offered by the river bank. Therefore, as they entered the ford, their eyes and minds would be on the high ground, rather than their immediate environment. So, he'd engage them at the ford. No choice, really.

To get from the hilltop to the ford without breaking the skyline meant scrambling down the shale on the south-east side of the mountain, cutting across the dead ground under the lee of the reverse slope, then splashing up the river bed to the ford. The horsemen weren't in any hurry, but he was on foot. He'd have to run.

These days he was fast and nimble, in spite of the lingering bother with his right ankle (which would heal itself with a month's rest, but he had to hunt at least once a week or starve). He made good time down the shale, put on a spurt on the flat and forced himself through the water, which was chest-high in places, nearly sweeping him off his feet. Even so, he only just made it in time. As he stood on tiptoe to peer ever so cautiously over the lip of the embankment, the horse-men were less than thirty yards away. Cutting it very fine indeed.

He thought hard and quickly. Could he still abort and get away? Probably; if they saw him, they wouldn't be inclined to follow him up the river. Should he abort, or could he still make it? Yes, he could, provided the first shot was dead on target at twenty yards and he managed to renock smoothly without fumbling. Being in the river bed gave him the slight but deciding edge. A sensible rider wouldn't try and take his horse down into the water. Accordingly, if he missed one of them, he'd still have a better than half chance of making time and distance for a third shot, before the horseman could dismount to come after him.

The mental staff meeting had lasted five yards (a hunter learns to measure time in units of distance), so it had to be now. He drew the prongs of the nock over the string until he felt them engage, and pic-tured the target in his mind as he stood up. A nice touch, and one he'd figured out for himself; it wasn't in *King Fashion* or the *Art and Practice*.

His head cleared the top edge of the bank, and his mental image of an armoured horseman's chin and neck merged with the real thing. A quarter of a second saved at the point of target acquisition makes all the difference in the world. He'd begun the draw as he started to rise, combining the two movements so as to share effort; the straightening of his knees and back fed power into the draw as well as standing him upright. As soon as his spine straightened, he felt his right thumb brush the corner of his mouth, which told his three fingers to relax and allow the string to pull away. He must have taken aim, but he couldn't remember doing it.

This time, he actually saw the arrow bend. They said it wasn't possible, the movement was too quick for the human eye to catch. But he was sure he saw it (his hand was already drawing the next arrow out of his belt), the fishtailing of the arrow as it straightened out of the flex imparted to it by the violent impact of the string. When the arrow hit (inch perfect, just below the chin, the blade cutting the helmet strap before disappearing into the flesh), he'd got the nock of the second one between his fingertips and was feeling it on to the string.

The second horseman (the first no longer mattered) must have heard his danger before he saw it. His reactions were superb. He'd lifted his shield to cover his neck and upper body before he even started to turn his head, and by the time his comrade-in-arms hit the ground, he'd already pulled his horse round to face the attack, thus presenting a much smaller target.

As he pushed his left hand against the bow, he knew he wasn't going to make it. The shot would go home, but either the shield would blank it off or it'd hit armour and only wound instead of killing. Dangerous game with reflexes that quick wouldn't allow him enough margin for a reliable third shot. So, in the last fraction of a second before his thumb stroked his lip, he pulled the arrowhead down on to the forehead of the horse. As the arrow flew (he didn't see the flex this time), he assessed the consequences of the change. He'd lose the value of the horse, a third of his catch, but he'd survive. No option.

The arrow hit the horse in its right eye; not where he'd aimed, but the effect was better, since it had time to rear before it died. Instead of throwing its rider, therefore, it fell on top of him. There was a clearly audible crack as the rider's thigh broke. Suddenly, there was all the time in the world.

He walked three yards down the river bed to the ford, saving himself the effort of scrambling over the embankment, and stopped to look. No movement. The first rider lay on his face, the arrow shaft flat on the ground, at right angles; probably broken, which was a pity. His horse had run on a few paces and then stopped. It lifted its head to look at him, then stooped gracefully to feed. All he could see of the second rider was an arm sticking out from under the fallen horse, which was shuddering the way dead bodies do and living ones don't. The arm was completely still, suggesting it too was broken.

Even so. Instead of walking straight up to it, he circled, to get a clearer view. He didn't have to go far. The rider was still alive, but he wasn't even trying to move. His eyes blinked and squinted, implying that his vision was blurred. Safe enough, then, to close the distance to five yards before taking the third shot.

Plenty of time for a careful, deliberate aim; so, of course, he missed, by a handspan, pulling left and burying the arrow deep in the crupper of the saddle. That made him swear out loud. Half the value of the saddle wasted. He nocked his fourth and last arrow. If he missed again, he'd have to make the dispatch with a stone or a weapon taken from one of the bodies, and there was always a chance that arm wasn't really broken after all.

But the fourth shot, though not perfect, was close enough; it hit the forehead just under the rim of the helmet, slightly gashing the steel (but two minutes with a file and a bit of brick would see to that) before the taper of the arrow blade fed it into the skull. Job done.

Now, of course, the panic started. First, catch and secure the horse. Mercifully it held still and let him grab the reins; he found a heavy stone, wrapped the reins round it three times and put it on the ground. Next, strip the first body, because the second was going to be miserably complicated by the dead horse, and he might have to abandon it and run if he caught sight of anyone coming on the road. Boots first; he had the knack of the twist and jerk that frees a boot easily from a dead man's foot. Next the helmet (damaged strap; easy to replace), then the mailshirt. A bit like skinning a deer; you start at the knees and work it up over the neck (a foot on the chest helps with leverage) before the final tug to free the sleeves from the elbows, taking care not to fall over backwards when it finally comes away. Similar procedure for the padded arming doublet: trousers just a straight pull, after you've lifted the body and put a big stone under the small of the back. One ring, bronze, on the left hand. Then the trousers go inside the helmet, which rolls up inside the arming doublet, which in turn rolls up in the mailshirt, secure into a bundle with the belt, which forms a handy carrying strap. Load it on to the horse, along with the sword, bow, quiver, spear and shield. Everything else is waste; leave it for the crows and foxes to clear up for you.

Number two was going to be a real pain. At first he thought he was going to have to saw the arrow out of the skull, but miraculously it came away on the third tug, without even breaking the shaft. It was a good arrow, numbered seven out of the original sheaf of twelve. He wiped it on the grass, and turned his attention to the problem of shifting the dead horse off the body. Just grabbing a leg and hauling didn't get him anywhere, and he gave up when his back started to give notice. Then he realised he was being stupid. He stripped off the dead horse's bridle, unbuckled the reins, tied them together. Not long enough. After a minute of painful indecision, he decided to risk it and took the living horse's reins off as well. Just as well the horse was docile and good-natured; it stayed where it was, happily munching the coarse, fat river bank grass as he tied one end of the improvised rope to its girth. Then he led it by its throatstrap over to where the dead horse lay, and tied the other end to the outstretched back nearside hoof.

Problem solved, but it all took time; as did putting the reins back on the good horse and securing them with a stone, as before. When you're in a hurry, of course, inanimate objects start picking on you. The mailshirt simply didn't want to come, and he ended up having to cut the laces at the neck. By the time he'd wrestled off the arming doublet he was starting to get uncomfortably nervous, so he decided to abandon the dead horse's saddle (damaged, anyway) Then, just to be awkward, the piled-up stuff wouldn't sit right on the horse. He'd only gone five yards when half of it slithered off on to the ground, which meant unloading the whole lot and stowing it all again, this time using the spare reins and the uncut mailshirt laces to tie it down.

With all the delays, no wonder it was pitch dark by the time he got home. He led the horse into the stable, took off the bundled gear, dumped it in the feed bin and covered it over with hay, not that that was going to fool anybody if they came looking; then unsaddled, hid the harness, gave the horse its hay net and bucket of water, stuck his bow and quiver up in the rafters and stomped back through the muddy yard to the house.

As he opened the door, she called out, "Miel, is that you?"

"For crying out loud," he sighed. "Who else would it be?"

"Any luck?"

Her choice of words made him smile. Fifteen years ago, his mother always asked him the same question when he came back from the hunt, exhausted, his clothes ruined, usually dripping blood from some alarming-looking cut or other. What she meant was, "Did anybody die, have you been disfigured or maimed for life, am I going to have to think up endless ways for the kitchens to deal with mountains of perishable dead animals and birds, and *do* try not to track blood across the carpets." The same words; but now they meant, *you'd better have got something this time, or I don't know what we're going to do.*

"Yes," he said, stepping out of his boots and checking them for splashes of blood. "Is there anything to eat? I'm starving."

"Not unless you brought it with you."

Good point. He hadn't checked the saddlebags. "Just a moment," he called out, and squirmed his feet back into his boots. Easier to get a dead foot out of a boot than a living foot into it.

It was noticeably darker now, and he had to grope around in the feed bin till he found a saddle. A quick fumble with the saddlebag straps. Yes!

Back in the house, in the light, he examined his trophy. Oh well, he thought, better than nothing. By all accounts the savages thrived on it.

"Well?" she said.

She had a blanket, Vadani military issue, over her shoulders, her hair tucked in under it. Her eyes were red from the smoke of the peat-fed fire and its thoroughly inadequate chimney. She couldn't understand why he kept making excuses instead of fixing it. He was ashamed to admit he was scared to death of fooling about up ladders.

"Cheese and smoked meat," he said cheerfully. A sort of truth.

Her eyes narrowed. "Oh," she said. "The savages again."

Of course she had every right to complain. Mares'-milk cheese and wind-cured smoked horsemeat; you wouldn't feed it to a dog, and if you did, the dog would just look at you. But it was the way she said it, and the look on her face. "I can't help it," he snapped (the Ducas is always courteous and polite, especially to ladies). "I was lucky to find anything at all, and even luckier to get away with it. I can't just send a runner down to the market and tell them to send me up a colonel's wife and a couple of merchants."

"It's all right," she said, meaning the exact opposite. "Get any horses?"

"One."

She didn't sniff, but the effort cost her dear. "It's not branded, is it? You did check."

Of course he hadn't, and he should have. The savages branded their horses, quite a complex vocabulary of dots, dashes and squiggles. Nobody would dare buy a branded horse, not even for the bones and hide. "I didn't have time," he replied lamely. "It wasn't exactly straightforward."

Her expression told him she was in no mood for hunting stories. Needless to say, Cousin Jarnac wouldn't have taken any notice. If he really wanted to tell you, nothing short of feigning a stroke would get you off the hook. "Oh well," she said. "We'll get something for the boots, at any rate."

They ate the mares' cheese and horsemeat in solemn silence, apart from the grimly resigned sound of chewing. One good thing about horse jerky: it left the jaws too weary for talking afterwards. When he went out to fetch more fuel for the fire, he noticed the peat stack was getting low again. Another of his favourite jobs to look forward to.

That night, in bed, she said: "We can't go on like this much longer."

He'd be hard put to it to disagree with that, on several levels. "Got any better ideas?"

She appeared not to have heard him. "It's five days before the buyer's due back again, assuming he's still coming. He said last time it wasn't really worth his while coming out this far."

"That's just bargaining talk."

"And quite apart from that, there's the risk. He said he can talk his way round Eremians, and Vadani take bribes, but if he gets stopped by the savages, he doesn't want to think what'd happen. And fairly soon, of course, the war's going to start up again and then the market'll be flooded. And if it's true the Cure Doce have sided with the Mezentines, will their buyers still be able to cross the border? And if they close off the Lonazep road—"

"All right," Miel grunted, "you've made your point. There's no future in it, I entirely agree. But what the hell else am I supposed to do?"

"I'm not blaming you, I'm just saying." That flat tone of voice, more corrosive than any reproaches. "We aren't making ends meet now, and it's only going to get worse. That's all."

"I'm not doing this because I enjoy it, you know. It's bloody hard work, and most of the time I'm scared out of my wits. I'd love to do something else, it's just that there isn't anything. Well, is there?"

Silence. If such a thing were possible, her silences were worse than anything she could find to say. Well, fine, he thought. If that's the end of the discussion, I'll go to sleep now.

"By the way," she said, "I think I'm pregnant."

The Ducas is always positive, upbeat and optimistic. Even when he has personal misgivings, he's under an obligation to uphold the morale of those around him and put the best possible interpretation on any given turn of events.

"Well? Aren't you going to say anything?"

"Are you sure?"

"Not yet." A slight sharpening of the voice, as she added: "But I thought I'd better let you know there's a distinct possibility. Just in case you give a damn."

The Ducas is always positive; the Ducas is always courteous; the Ducas is always considerate of the feelings of his household and inferiors. "Of course I give a damn," he snapped. "It's just . . . well, I don't know what to say. I wasn't expecting anything like this."

"Really?" Now it was a voice he could've shaved with. "You surprise me. I'd have thought at some point someone would've briefed you on where little aristocrats come from. I thought it was such a big deal, ensuring the succession."

Mere vulgar chiding; he was under no obligation to reply to that. He lay still in the dark, trying to think. Correction: trying to care.

"We could go to the Vadani," she said.

He was too tired to be angry. "No we can't."

"We can. It's the only—"

"For crying out loud, they were going to kill us."

Patient sigh. He found her patience almost unendurable. "First, they won't remember me. Second, things are different now. The duke's married *her*." Pause. "Your girlfriend."

"She was never—"

"You were going to marry her. You were best friends when you were kids. You got arrested because you hid that letter, for her sake. She's not going to let him have you killed." Another pause. Perfect timing, like a great actor. "We'd be safe," she said. "You wouldn't have to stay with me if you don't want to."

"It's not like that, of course I want to stay with you, that's not the *point* . . ."

She ignored him. "If we stay out here, we're going to starve to death. Or one day a soldier's going to kill you, instead of the other way round. Or the savages will catch us with a branded horse. There's loads of ways it could all go wrong. But if we go to Duke Valens, at the very least he'll feed us, he'll give us a place to sleep, even if it's in a prison. It's got to be better."

He felt like he was choking on feathers. "I can't go to the Vadani," he said. "For God's sake, I've been murdering their soldiers for the last four months."

"They don't know that."

"Maybe not, but what if one of the buyers shows up and recognises me? I don't suppose Duke Valens is going to be very impressed, do you?"

"That's hardly likely, is it?" He felt her move beside him. "And even if it did happen, she could protect you. She could, I'm sure of it. Think about it, will you? He had her husband killed, that's got to be a really serious issue between them. You were her husband's best friend, you and she were going to get married, it was because of that bloody letter he wrote that you nearly got killed then. If you deny it, say you never killed any soldiers and it's all a mistake, he'll have to pretend to believe you, for her sake." Even in the dark, he could feel her tears coming. When she started crying, all he wanted to do was hit her. "If you're going to let your stupid pride stand between us and our only chance of staying alive. . ."

"All right," he said. "All right, I'll think about it."

"I know what that means. It means no."

"No it *doesn't*. I'll think about it. There may be another way, something else we could—"

"No there isn't. You said there isn't. You said so yourself."

"For pity's sake," he groaned, "have we got to do this now, when I'm completely exhausted? You always do this, start on me when I've had enough, when I'm too tired to think."

She laughed. "The only time I ever see you is when you're worn out," she said. "The rest of the time you're out, hunting soldiers. God almighty," she added, "will you just listen to that? Out hunting soldiers, what a bloody ridiculous way to make a living. All right, my husband used to go round battlefields robbing bodies, but at least they were already dead. And look what happened. They caught him and cut his head off for it. You're killing live soldiers just to get their boots, and you're saying we can't go to the Vadani because it's too *dangerous*."

Tears any second now; anything rather than that. "You don't understand," he said. "It's . . ."

"It's what? Well? Are you going to try and tell me you're scared? Like, more scared than picking off soldiers, two, three, four against one? No, it's that bloody pride of yours, the whole idiotic Ducas thing. You'd rather be lynched as a highwayman than dishonoured as an aristocrat. That's it, isn't it?"

Well, of course, he thought. Of course it is, and if you weren't a stupid, ignorant low-class woman you'd understand that; because if a soldier kills me or I'm caught and hanged, all they kill is a body. But if I go to Veatriz like you want me to, it's the real me that'll die; the real me that you could never possibly hope to understand.

And, of course; in the last resort, where necessary, it's the duty of the Ducas to die for his people; his household, his inferiors. People like you.

"Fine," he said. "If that's what you want, we'll go to Duke Valens. Just don't . . ."

Pause. "Don't what?"

He sighed. "It doesn't matter. We'll do it because . . ." He couldn't think of a reason, not one he could say out loud. "Because of the baby. Because I love you."

Silence; then she said, "I love you too."

Yet another attack on a routine patrol, the third in as many weeks; it couldn't be allowed to continue, the Aram Chantat liaison insisted, something had to be done about it, particularly since the insurgents had once again singled out Aram Chantat rather than Vadani as their targets. Examination of the bodies suggested the work of a band or bands of light, mobile snipers. It was well known that the Cure Doce trained as archers and hunted extensively with the bow. Most likely this was their way of striking back after the destruction of their sneak attack on the allied camp. At the moment it was only a nuisance, but it had to be stopped before it escalated into a significant annoyance. The liaison also felt constrained to point out that by sparing and releasing on parole the prisoners taken during the night attack, the duke would appear to have given the Cure Doce an unfortunate impression of leniency bordering on weakness.

Duke Valens replied that he accepted the points so ably raised by the liaison, and in the circumstances he felt it appropriate that the Aram Chantat should take such action as they saw fit. There was no need to keep him informed. He had every confidence in their capabilities.

The very next day, therefore, a squadron of Aram Chantat (ten lancers and thirty mounted archers) crossed the river at dawn and rode over the crest of the moor into Cure Doce territory. Reports said that the villages nearest the border had been abandoned after the night raid as a precaution, but a substantial farm only twelve miles from the river was still occupied.

Following the scouts' directions, the squadron's two outriders picked up the farm track where it left the road, until the ground levelled out and they were in danger of being seen. Taking their bearings from the helpful column of chimney smoke that rose calmly into the still morning air, they drew a wide circle under the lip of the surrounding hills, in doing so encountering a substantial brook which they assumed to be the farm's water supply. This brook ran down through a deep, narrow combe, lightly wooded with rowan, ash and willow coppice, showing signs of carefully managed cutting. Venturing a little way down the combe, the outriders decided that it would afford the necessary cover for the approach, and reported back to their captain, who agreed.

The outriders' assessment proved to be correct. With the smoke column to guide them, the squadron followed the brook down, satisfied that they were adequately concealed and would therefore have the element of surprise. When they eventually cleared the coppice, they found themselves barely two hundred yards from the fences of the home pastures, with the farm buildings directly ahead of them.

The captain made his dispositions quickly, sending five archers out on each flank to encircle the building and act as stops. He deployed the remaining twenty archers to ring the pastures and work inwards, and himself led the lancers in a dash for the main yard around which the buildings were grouped.

The plan worked efficiently. Four hours after dawn, the farm inhabitants had finished the early chores and gone indoors for breakfast. The alarm was, therefore, only raised when the lancers rode into the yard. Four men dismounted and broke into the smallest of the three houses whose chimneys were smoking. They killed the people they found there, two men, five women and a boy, lit torches from the hearth and came back outside. The screams drew out the remaining inhabitants, of whom approximately half were immediately cut down, the rest running out into the pastures or heading for barns and outbuildings. As soon as the firing party had remounted, the lancers set about kindling the thatches, by which time the twenty archers of the inner encirclement had drawn the pastures and arrived in time to shoot down the fugitives trying to escape in the open. The rest either were shot as they tried to flee the burning buildings, or perished in the flames. Fifty-seven bodies were recovered, twenty-five males and thirty-two females, with an estimated twelve additional males burnt in the buildings. Aram Chantat casualties were limited to one arrow wound, superficial, friendly fire, and a small number of inconsequential burns and bruises.

A search of the buildings and bodies revealed a pair of Vadani military boots and, even more significant, an Aram Chantat saddlecloth, apparently used as a bedspread in the main house. An elderly male, interrogated prior to execution, claimed to have no knowledge of hit-and-run raids against allied forces. Confronted with the boots and the saddlecloth, he was unable to account for their presence, asserting that he had never seen them before.

Returning by the main farm track, the squadron rejoined the road and proceeded to cross the river at an established ford, with an abandoned border station. There they encountered a man and a woman who demanded to be taken to Duke Valens, claiming to have vital information about the war. In their possession was found a branded Aram Chantat horse, which they asserted they had found wandering loose near the river. The man claimed to be Miel Ducas, the former leader of the Eremian resistance. They were taken into custody and escorted back to the camp.

Valens stared at him for a moment, then said, "Hello."

It was all Miel could do not to laugh. Fortunately, he was the Ducas, trained from birth not to register embarrassment. Really the only thing he'd ever learned worth knowing. "Thank you for seeing me," he said.

Valens nodded at the empty chair. Miel thought it didn't look as though it'd bear his weight, but he took a leap of faith and sat in it. "That's all right," Valens said. "I was wondering only the other day what the hell had become of you."

He had to smile at that. "After you ordered my execution, you mean?"

Valens nodded. "I seem to remember a guard got killed. I'm assuming that was nothing to do with you."

"Of course not."

"As I thought. Fine, we needn't mention it again." Valens frowned. "You look dreadful," he said. "What've you been doing to yourself?"

Miel grinned. "Living the simple life. I read about it in Pannones' *Pastoral Eclogues* when I was a kid, and I thought I'd try it: the open air, the stars my ceiling, the meadow my pillow. You know the sort of thing."

"Actually, I quite like Pannones," Valens said gently. "I've always taken his romanticised version of the rural idyll as an extended metaphor for the inner tranquillity that comes from the renunciation of worldly ambition in reformed Substantialist philosophy." He frowned and sniffed. "I'm glad you didn't bother getting all dressed up," he said. "We're informal here these days, it saves so much time and energy. Drink?"

"Yes please," Miel replied.

Valens nodded at the jug on the flimsy-looking table. Miel stood up – something had happened to his knees, but he made it, just about – filled a cup and sat down again.

"They told me you had some information for me."

Miel shook his head. "I'm afraid not," he said. "That was just a little white lie, to keep your Aram Chantat from slitting my throat. The fact is, I've invited myself to stay. Mostly," he added with a sheepish grin, "because I've got nowhere else to go. I hope that's all right."

"Sure," Valens replied casually, his eyes fixed on Miel's face. "After all, you're a hero of the Eremian resistance, you're entitled. And we've agreed to forget all about that other business, so that's fine. Who's your girlfriend, by the way?"

Miel smiled by way of parrying. "My girlfriend, actually," he said. "Where is she, by the way? I asked the guard, but . . ."

"I'll tell them to let her go," Valens said quickly. "Sorry. But you know how it is in a war, everybody gets so jumpy and serious about everything. They'd lock up their own grandmothers if they found them out without a pass." He leaned back a little, carefully, almost as if he didn't trust his chair. "I suppose I ought to try and explain to you about Orsea," he said.

"No, please don't."

"Fine."

Miel looked back at him, a riposte in double time. "How's Veatriz?"

"She's well. I had a letter from her two days ago, actually."

"She's not here, then?"

"No." Slight crease of the forehead. Probably he didn't realise he was doing it. "We decided it'd be better if she stayed in Civitas Vadanis for the time being. A bit too much war in these parts, and besides, the Aram Chantat don't really approve of her."

Miel nodded. "Do please send her my best wishes."

"Of course. She'll be glad to hear you're all right."

Miel remembered he had a drink in his hand. It had been a long time since he'd tasted wine. He drank it, trying not to let Valens see how much he enjoyed it. "Well," he said, "thank you very much for your time, and your hospitality. Is there anybody we should report to, or . . . ?"

Valens grinned. "Tell the guard who brought you to take you to one of the guest tents. When you've decided what you want to do next, tell the duty officer and he'll tell me. Anything within reason."

"I think I'd like to help with the war, if that's all right," Miel heard himself say. "I don't know how many Eremians you've got with you still, but—"

"Two full infantry regiments and a cavalry division," Valens replied promptly, "and I'm sure they'll be delighted to have you. And there's a lot of your people with the engineers, too."

"Ah." Miel tried to keep his face perfectly still. "I think I'd be happier serving with a field unit," he said. "I haven't had the happiest of experiences around engineers in the past."

"Of course." Valens looked away. For some reason, that gave Miel tremendous satisfaction. "Well, it's good to have you back with us. And if there's anything you need, just tell the duty officer and he'll see to it."

"Thank you." Miel stood up. For some reason he felt an urgent need to confess, to tell Valens about the Vadani and Aram Chantat soldiers he'd hunted and killed for their skins, just to spoil the look on his face. But that would be an appalling breach of good manners, and therefore unthinkable. "You've been very kind, I appreciate it. I'm sorry to be a pest."

Valens' expression said, that's enough, I've got no quarrel with you but I'd like you to go away now. "That's perfectly all right," he said. "Now I expect you'd like to get settled in."

Which was a pleasant, affable way of putting it, Miel supposed. He nodded, turned and left the tent. It was only when he emerged into the light and air that he realised he was still holding the cup. He hesitated, but going back in and returning it would be faintly ridiculous. He'd give it to the duty officer later, explain. He looked for the guard.

"The duke said to take me to the visitors' tents," he said.

The guard had noticed the cup; he glanced at it once, then looked straight past it, the way guards, chamberlains, footmen and door-keepers learn to do. "Very good," he said. "This way, please."

Please, Miel noted, and for some reason he tried to call to mind the face of at least one of the Vadani soldiers he'd killed: the sentries when he'd escaped, the men he'd murdered for their shirts and boots. But he couldn't. He was disappointed with himself for that. The Ducas should pay attention to his subordinates, make a habit of remembering their faces and their names.

The visitors' tents, a whole row like a street, were Aram Chantat by the look of them, spongy black felt an inch thick overlaying a sturdy square frame of poles. Inside, a small but efficient-looking brass stove, with a flue sticking up through a hole in the tent roof; Miel looked twice and saw that the flue pipes were designed to slide inside each other for compact storage and transportation. A heap of cushions; the floor completely covered by a plain dark green rug. A spindly-legged table, on which he found a tall brass jug and a brass plate of some kind of crisp white cakes. The jug turned out to contain water. Otherwise, not bad at all.

The guard was leaving. Miel remembered something. "Just a moment," he said. "My . . ." His what? Friend? Wife? Neither. "The woman who was with me when I arrived," he said awkwardly. "The duke said to bring her here."

The guard nodded and withdrew. Fine. All words are conventions, more or less arbitrary compromises. No two people ever said *I love*

you to each other and meant exactly the same thing by it. The Ducas
especially; in the nobleman's lexicon there were at least two dozen
different subcategories of love, ranging from the over-riding love of
duty and country down to the affection one naturally felt for one's
former nurse. All genuine, all perfectly valid, all quite different. It
was not only possible but obligatory for the Ducas to love people he
wouldn't dream of having dinner with.

Now then, he told himself, he had to report to the duty officer,
who'd get him assigned to an Eremian unit.

In any military community, finding the duty officer's quarters is
easy. Just spot someone walking briskly and follow him. "My name's
Miel Ducas," he told the short, thin-on-top middle-aged Vadani sitting behind another of those rickety tables. "Duke Valens said I
should see you."

The duty officer pursed his lips. "I see," he said. "What about?"

"Assignment," he replied. "With one of the Free Eremian units."

Something clicked into place in the duty officer's memory.
"Ducas," he said. "You were the leader of the resistance."

"That's right." He frowned slightly. "I've been on sabbatical, as
you might say, but now I'm back. I don't want to be anybody important, I just want a job of some kind. Can you arrange that?"

Dubious nod. "It may be a bit sensitive," the duty officer said.
"What I mean is, the senior staff might feel uncomfortable giving
orders to their former leader. And weren't you high up in the government, before the . . . ?"

That called for a smile. "Before I was attainted for treason, yes.
But that doesn't matter, does it? I mean, the city's gone, tens of thousands of us have been slaughtered, I think those of us who're left can
afford to take a few liberties with strict-form protocol."

The duty officer didn't look convinced. "You wouldn't prefer a
Vadani unit?"

"No."

"Leave it with me," the duty officer said sadly. "I'll talk to the
Eremian colonel-in-chief. You'll be . . . ?"

"Guest tents," Miel said. "I'll stay there till I hear from you, shall I?"

"Probably best if you did."

Well, quite, he thought, as he left the tent, aware but not particularly concerned that he'd just ruined someone's day. Thoughtless of
me to still be alive, but there. Some people have no consideration.

Finding the duty officer had been easy. Finding his way back to the guest tents, on the other hand . . .

The Ducas, unlike lesser men, isn't embarrassed to ask for directions. He stopped two Vadani, who didn't know, and an Aram Chantat, who looked straight past him and walked on. A third Vadani gave him directions, but talked so quickly he couldn't follow them; he smiled, thanked him politely, waited till he'd gone and tried again. An extremely polite and courteous Aram Chantat gave him clear and concise instructions, which he followed exactly, and found himself on the far edge of the camp, standing outside a latrine.

The hell with it, he thought; I'm a trained military officer, formerly commander-in-chief of the Eremian cavalry and a distinguished guerrilla fighter. I ought to be able to find a tent in a field.

He took a step back for a better overview of the camp's street-plan, and accidentally barged into someone coming out of the latrine. He was already apologising before he realised who he was talking to.

"My fault," the familiar face said. "I wasn't looking where I was going." Hesitation; recognition.

Miel nodded. "Yes," he said, "it's me. Hello, Vaatzes."

For a disturbingly long time he had no idea what to do or say. Luckily, Ducas didn't seem to be about to attack him; if he had, there wouldn't have been anything he could have done about it. Since he could neither move nor speak, he waited to see what happened next.

"I don't suppose you know the way back to the guest tents, do you?" Ducas said. "I know it's silly, but I'm lost."

"Follow me," he heard himself reply. "I'm going that way myself."

A grin. "You're a guest too, are you? That's lucky. Right, lead on. I'll be right behind you."

Of course he would. Ziani led the way, quickly dismissing any thought of trying to lose him in the maze of tented streets Even if he managed it, he couldn't simply steal a horse and gallop away. He had to stay here. No choice.

"Ah," the Ducas said, just behind his shoulder, "I recognise this bit."

"That's the guest tents, just behind the sergeants' mess," he replied, pointing. It was a pathetic attempt. Ducas was right behind him, only moving when he moved, like a shadow.

"Are you terribly busy right now? Only if you aren't, I'd like to talk to you."

No choice there, either. "Come to my tent and have a drink," Ziani said.

"Thanks. I'd like that."

Absurd; a parody of friendship. He waved Ducas into the chair, and sat on a cushion on the floor. "Help yourself to wine," he said. "The jug's on the table."

Ducas smiled and poured. "You having one?"

"Not right now."

He watched Ducas drink. He seemed to be enjoying it. Judging by his appearance, he'd been living rough for a while. "It sounds dreadful, but wine's one of the things I've missed most," Ducas said. "I don't mean getting blasted; just the taste. Sure you won't join me?"

"Quite sure."

"Suit yourself." Ducas poured a refill, slowly. Wine-drinkers did that, Ziani remembered. Something to do with not disturbing the sediment at the bottom. "Right," Ducas said. "I imagine you're surprised to see me."

"Yes."

"I'll bet." Ducas drank, and put the cup down carefully on the ground at his feet. "Last time we met, you were good enough to explain exactly how you betrayed me. Made Orsea think I was a traitor."

"So I did," Ziani said.

"And then," Ducas went on, "the city conveniently fell. You escaped, went off with Duke Valens. I stayed behind, you may have heard. Had a sort of half-hearted go at carrying on the war. Didn't make much of a job of it. Wandered around for a bit," he went on, when Ziani didn't react. "Lost interest, I suppose, for a while. Joined up with Valens – our paths didn't cross, but I'm sure you heard about it. Got in trouble, needless to say. But it seems like that's all forgiven and forgotten, and now here I am. Here we are." His eyes were suddenly fixed and still. "All friends together, I dare say."

He was waiting for a reply, but Ziani couldn't think of one. Ducas drank a little more, then went on: "I guess you could make out a case for saying that none of it matters a damn any more. I mean, Orsea's dead. Veatriz is married to Valens. Civitas Eremia's gone, of course, in fact so's the whole country. I mean, it's still there, but for all the good it'll do, it might as well have fallen through a bloody great crack in the ground and disappeared. They're saying the price for the Aram Chantat helping Valens wipe out your lot is Eremia, for them to settle in afterwards. Is that right? I'm a bit out of touch."

"Yes," Ziani said.

Ducas nodded. "Don't suppose they'll be satisfied with just Eremia," he said. "Not nearly enough pasture for a whole nation of nomads. They'll want the Mezentine plain as well, and probably a fair old slice of the Vadani country. Which won't be any bother to anybody, given how many Vadani have died in this war so far. Plenty of empty land, so that's all right." He put his cup back on the floor and refilled it. "Really," he said, "everything's changed so much, it'd be pointless harping on about the past. It's become – what's the word? – obsolete. No longer relevant. Wouldn't you say?"

"No."

That made him smile. "I don't think so, either. But, changing the subject, there's something I'd like your opinion about, if you wouldn't mind. Not in any tearing hurry, are you?"

"No."

Ducas nodded. "A bit silly," he said, "but it's one of those things that's been nagging away at my mind all this time, like the words of a song, where you know the verse and the chorus but not the middle bit. Nobody to ask, though, because they weren't there. Apart from you. So," he added, straightening up a bit and resting his hands on the arms of the chair, "what I've been trying to figure out is, who opened the gates of Civitas Eremiae that night and let the Mezentines in? You see, until we know the answer to that one, I really can't see how we can dismiss it all from our minds and move on to the next item on the agenda."

"I take your point," Ziani said.

"Thought you might." He reached down towards the cup, stopped, left it where it was. "There's theories, of course. I mean, at some point Valens seemed to believe Orsea had something to do with it. Don't know if he still thinks that, but I reckon we can forget about it as a hypothesis, because it's clearly not true. Same as the school of thought that says I did it." Faint smile. "Slightly more of a possible motive, but of course I was in prison at the time, so I propose we dismiss the charges against me. Agreed?"

"Yes."

"Very good. So then I thought, how about simple bribery and corruption? Always a possibility. One of my ancestors used to say, no city is impregnable, no matter how well fortified, if a man can get inside it carrying a shitload of money. So that's one we need to consider, even though I can't see how our traitor or traitors planned on getting out alive. No point being rich for ten minutes and then getting your head stoved in along with everybody else."

"There's that," Ziani said.

"Of course." Suddenly Ducas laughed; something between a bark and a growl. "Look at me," he said, "a couple of drinks and I'm starting to go all to pieces. Comes of drinking nothing but water for God knows how long. You'll have to forgive me if I don't make much sense. Anyway, where were we? Ah yes, the big question, who opened the gates? I've thought about it a lot, you know, and I keep coming back to the same wretched difficult problem. Whoever it was, how could he do it and get away with it? I mean, the moment the gates opened, in came the Mezentines, killing everybody they could find, I mean, they weren't stopping to ask names. So whoever the traitor was, he was running a really terrible risk, because how the hell were the Mezentines supposed to tell him apart from the others? You know, soldiers, civilians, people who just happened to be passing." Ducas paused and looked at him. "You got any ideas? I'm sure you must've thought about it too."

Ziani shrugged. "There must have been some kind of signal arranged in advance," he said. "Or else whoever it was simply didn't care."

Ducas nodded gravely. "Someone who hated his own people so much he was prepared to be killed along with them just so long as they died too. I thought about that, and it's a possibility. I mean, there's always someone, isn't there? Could well be. But another possibility did occur to me. Like to hear it?"

"Why not?"

Ducas smiled. "This is just a theory, mind," he said. "No proof, no evidence. But it strikes me that there was one man in Civitas Eremiae that night who looked completely different from everybody else; so much so that a Mezentine soldier who'd never seen him before in his life, never even been given a description, would know who he was straight away, the moment he set eyes on him. And why, you ask? Well, because his skin was a different colour. You know, brown, like theirs. A Mezentine, in fact. The only one in the city." He paused, perfectly still. "That's right, isn't it? You *were* the only Mezentine in the city?"

Ziani nodded. "I was. But your theory's a bit far-fetched, if you ask me."

"Of course it is. Just a wild notion, you might say. Because, after all, why the hell would you do such a thing, you of all people? I mean, the whole war was about you. You'd been condemned to death by your own government, I expect the soldiers'd have had orders to kill you on sight just for that, let alone the fact that you built the engines that shot down thousands of the poor devils. I expect they'd all been given orders to find you, top priority, a hundred thousand gold pieces to the man who brings me the head of Ziani Vaatzes. Don't you think?"

"I wouldn't be surprised," Ziani said.

"Quite. So it was really pretty remarkable, you managing to escape. Extraordinary. How did you manage it, by the way?"

"Luck," Ziani said.

"Well, indeed. But what kind of luck? I mean, did you just head for the gate and keep walking, or did you give luck a bit of a helping hand? I don't know. I mean, in your shoes, I'd probably have tried to pass myself off as a Mezentine soldier, except of course they'd all have been in armour and uniform. Maybe you found a dead one and took his kit off him. Was that it?"

Ziani shook his head. "If you must know, I found a way out through the underground cisterns."

Ducas nodded approvingly. "Not a bad idea. Still, you were pretty lucky, finding a way out that way. I never went down there much, no call to, but I seem to remember it was a fair old maze. And you a stranger to the city. Very lucky indeed."

"I had the duchess with me."

"Ah, right. Only I wouldn't have thought she'd have known her way around the cisterns. Hardly a suitable place for the duchess to take her daily exercise."

"It must have been luck, then," Ziani said. "And once we were outside, of course, we ran into Duke Valens' men. I don't suppose we'd have lasted very long otherwise."

"Ah well." Ducas yawned. "The strangest things happen in battles and sieges. And like you said, you had absolutely no reason at all to want to open the gates, so it can't possibly have been you, could it? I did wonder, you see, if maybe you'd done a deal with your people, given them the city in return for a free pardon or something like that. But here you still are, no pardon, helping the Vadani and the savages to build more engines to smash down the City walls, so that rules that out. Unless, of course, they double-crossed you, I wouldn't put that past them for a second. But then," he went on, his eyelids starting to droop, "you'd have gone straight to them after the city fell and said, here I am, I want my free pardon, and they'd have laughed in your face and chopped your head off. So no, it can't possibly have been you, could it?"

"That's right," Ziani said. "It couldn't have been me."

"So there we are." Ducas groped for his cup on the floor, knocked it over, tutted, picked it up and emptied the jug into it. "Of course, I still owe you for getting me arrested and disgraced. I know there's no point bearing a grudge now everything's changed so completely, but I'm afraid that's not the way my mind works. It's an honour thing, you see. Generations of ancestors looking over my shoulder and all that. All accounts to be settled in full, like it's a point of honour always to pay tradesmen, if you've got the money."

"I see," Ziani said. "So what do you propose doing about it?"

"Right now?" Ducas smiled wearily. "Nothing at all. If I killed you, Valens'd have me strung up like a flag; and besides, you're needed, for wiping the Mezentines off the face of the earth. Bloody fool I'd look if I killed you and then we couldn't take the City. No, it'll just have to wait, that's all. One of those things I'll get round to one of these days, when conditions permit. Assuming I live that long, of course. Dangerous times, these, what with the war and everything. But I don't need to tell you that, do I?"

Ziani shrugged. "You didn't have to tell me anything," he said.

"True. Anyway, I won't keep you any longer, I'm sure you must be very busy. Thanks for listening. You know, it's quite strange talking about the old days. I can barely remember what it was like, everything's changed so much. Me too, I suppose. And if you do happen to have any ideas about, well, what we've been talking about, I'd love to hear them. Any theory from an intelligent chap like you's bound to be worth hearing. And I'd love to know what really happened. Wouldn't you?"

"Naturally," Ziani said. "But here's a thought for you. If Civitas

Eremiae hadn't been betrayed and hadn't fallen when it did, I wonder what would've happened to you. Would Duke Orsea have had you killed for treason, do you think? Or would he just have left you in prison until the Mezentines eventually broke in and killed everybody? Strange as it may sound, perhaps whoever it was did you a favour, after all." He stood up. "Like you said, I really am very busy. And maybe you shouldn't think too much about all that stuff. It'll only upset you."

Ducas looked up at him. "Perhaps not," he said. "But it's not like I've got anything else to do. I have this depressing feeling of being left over, like a cold chicken after a banquet; like I've been killed, and plucked and stuffed and cooked and served up on a plate, and then nobody's got around to eating me, and I'm sent back to the kitchen for the dogs."

Ziani took a couple of steps towards the door, extending the distance like a fencer. "I take your point," he said. "But revenge; it always struck me as pointless, somehow. Back home we have all these legends and stories about the great heroes of the old country. Princes, mostly, and when they're kids their fathers are killed by wicked uncles and they only just manage to escape into exile, so they spend years plotting vengeance and contriving a way to bring it about; and when they finally manage it, things still always end really badly, and everybody dies tragically so there's nobody left alive at the end. I always thought it'd have made much more sense all round if the dispossessed princes had stayed in exile, learned a useful trade and settled down. When you come right down to it, after all, what actual use is a dead body to anyone? Can't eat it or skin it or boil the bones down for glue. All you can do is bury it, or leave it lying around for someone else to clear up. Maybe I'm just a bit stupid, but I really don't see the point."

Ducas smiled at him. "Settle down and get a job?" he said.

Ziani nodded. "Like I did. Like I'm trying to do now."

"Really?" Ducas frowned. "I wonder what your fellow citizens in the Republic would say about that."

This time, Ziani smiled. "I can't help it if my trade's making weapons," he said. "I'm good at it, and it pays well. I mean, look at me. From humble factory foreman to chief engineer to the Vadani coalition. If the folks back home hadn't tried to kill me, I'd still be slogging my guts out for twenty quarters a week."

Chapter Seven

After an uneventful ride, Ziani arrived back at Civitas Vadanis shortly before sunset and went straight to the factory. Daurenja was there, of course, in his office, sitting in his chair, checking through materials requisitions. It was a job Ziani particularly hated, and he usually made stupid, time-wasting mistakes. Daurenja always did them flawlessly in half the time.

"You're back," Daurenja said, jumping up out of the chair. "Excellent. Good trip?"

Ziani closed the distance but Daurenja didn't move. "What the hell were you playing at?" Ziani shouted, squeezing his voice to make it louder. "You must be out of your mind. I had to beg the duke not to have you strung up."

Daurenja looked back at him solemnly. "I know, he told me," he said. "I owe you my life. I promise you I won't ever forget—"

"Shut up, you bloody lunatic." Shouting at Daurenja was like trying to swat flies in the dark. "I've heard some stupid things in my time, but someone going absent without leave to *join* a battle is just perverse. What were you trying to achieve, for God's sake?"

He wanted to build up and maintain a good head of anger, to gain the advantage. But all the time Daurenja was watching him; bright, sharp eyes, missing nothing. "I've learned my lesson," was all he said, "and no harm done. But I'm sorry if I disappointed you. You know I have the deepest admiration—"

Ziani winced, as though he'd lashed out at Daurenja, missed and barked his knuckles on the wall. "Be quiet," he said. "And tell me what's been happening here while I've been away."

Immediately Daurenja changed, from humble penitent to invaluable assistant. "Steady progress," he said. "Shop seven have finished the torsion capstan bearings, I've got the night shift fettling and assembling the completed mechanisms. The lumber for the crossbars came in early, so shop five are shaping, planing and cutting tenons. Shop three, we found out what the glitch was with the rope-winding loom, so it ought to be up and running in time for the swing shift." He gulped down more air, like a frog swallowing a fly, then continued, "Shop two's standing by waiting for material for the stone-turning mill, so I took the liberty of putting them on preparing for a test of that theory of mine I mentioned a while back, coating the balls. You remember?"

Ziani frowned. "No."

"Ah." Daurenja's eyebrows flickered. "Well, the idea is, a smooth, uniformly round ball will fly faster and straighter than an irregular one, because it slips through the air easier. Turning the balls perfectly spherical takes too long with the men and machines we've got, so I thought, if we rough-cut the balls and then coat them with clay or, better still, lead, we can get much closer to a perfect sphere and save time in the process. I've arranged a test-firing from the prototype five-inch engine, noon tomorrow, if you can spare the time. I hope that's all right."

Good idea, Ziani thought; a very good idea, which I should've thought of myself. "Fine," he grunted. "If it works, we'll need to add another process line. Use the spare corner of shop eight, you can borrow time on the forge for melting the lead. There should be enough—"

"Eight hundredweight, in number nine shed," Daurenja interrupted promptly. "We got it in for making slingbolts for the staff-slings, but they got cancelled and we're stuck with it. Actually, I was wondering about casting round shot out of solid lead for the modified Type Three scorpions. It'd mean sparing a couple of the best masons to carve soapstone moulds, but it'd be one less calibre to turn, which'd save time in shop two. With your permission . . ."

"Yes, fine. Let me know how you get on." Ziani sat down in the chair. "Now, listen. I promised the duke we'd have sixty Type Two scorpions for him in six days. He wants to set up fixed artillery positions on the Lonazep road, in case they try and get it open again. Can we do that?"

Daurenja thought for a moment, a perfect study in concentration. "I believe we can," he said. "If you can let me have an extra two dozen unskilled for packing and loading. I'd rather not take skilled men off the lines."

"Use soldiers," Ziani said with a faint grin. "There's enough of them hanging about, and they must be good for something. Right. Anything else?"

Suddenly Daurenja smiled. "One other thing," he said. "You're not going to like it."

"Then what are you grinning for?"

The smile widened into a grin. "The prototype of the Class Six heavy bombard," he said. "They got it finished."

"About time."

Daurenja nodded. "The thing is," he said, "the project captain was so pleased at getting it done at last, he couldn't wait till you or I got back to test it, so he did it himself. Only," he went on, "he doesn't seem to have understood how the recoil dampers are supposed to work, because he didn't bother to tighten them right up before setting the thing off. As a result, when he pulled the lever . . ."

"Oh for crying out loud."

Daurenja nodded. "Exactly," he said. "The damper threads stripped, the cradle went right back against the stop, and so, of course, instead of shooting out at an optimum forty-five degrees, the ball flew straight up in the air." He paused. "According to the captain, it went up a good four hundred yards, which is very encouraging. But then, of course, it came straight down again. Nobody hurt, I'm delighted to say, but the machine's firewood."

Ziani was silent for a moment. "You know," he said, "I'm sorry I missed seeing that."

"Me too," Daurenja said. "I imagine it was quite a sight. Anyway, we'll have another prototype assembled by the morning. And at least we know the torsion spring's up to scratch. Four hundred yards straight up; that's better than I was expecting."

"Quite," Ziani said. "You'd better put the captain on report, though. Teach him not to play with things."

"Actually, I've already dealt with it," Daurenja said. "He was no good anyway."

Ziani froze. Daurenja was tidying up the papers on the desk, putting the stopper back in the ink bottle. "You dealt with it?"

Daurenja nodded. "I had him flogged and branded and discharged," he said. "There's a report in the personnel file. As a replacement, I was thinking, there's that Eremian in shop eight, he's showing a lot of promise. I'll send him up to see you when his shift ends, or I can see to it if you're busy."

Ziani let him go. It was easier; and, after all, the captain had been responsible for the destruction of a valuable piece of equipment . . .

(I'm afraid of him, Ziani thought. Every time I'm in the same room with him, I can't help watching him, following everything he does. I could've been rid of him so easily; Valens was furious, he didn't care about the volcano dust, but I said no, we need him. And we do. I do.)

It was dark, and the lamp was burning down; the flame struggled as it starved and died, flicking yellow light around the walls. Ziani let it go out. There was more oil in a bottle somewhere, but he couldn't be bothered. Besides, in the dark he could see more clearly.

He traced out the lines, as though drawing a sketch. For each function, a mechanism. For each process, an assembly of components working together within the constraints of a frame. He labelled them in his mind: Eremians, Vadani, Cure Hardy; Valens, Orsea, Ducas, Veatriz; an unwieldy, unsatisfactory but functional sub-array designated Psellus; a system of belts, gears and shafts to drive them all from the power source. A group of functions economically combined in the ingenious component Daurenja, which he hadn't designed himself but rather cannibalised from an existing, damaged machine. He considered issues of tolerance and stress, with particular reference to bearings and strength of materials. He thought briefly about the disgraced project captain, tied to a door, flogged bloody and burned with a white-hot iron; about the shot fired straight up in the air, because a part of the mechanism hadn't been properly understood.

I have no right to do this, he thought.

He got up, groped around in the dark, found the bottle of oil and refilled the lamp. He had a genuine Mezentine flint-and-wheel tinderbox, a Type Sixteen. The light burned away the shape of the machine, like a sheet of paper turning to ash.

They had no right. They were going to kill me; and all I want is what was mine anyway. The stories about heroes who came back;

Ducas understood. You can't run away, go somewhere else, settle down and get a job like nothing has happened. It's like tensing a spring and just leaving it cocked. The steel has a memory. It has no choice.

But he didn't really believe it; because of course they had the right. Abomination can't go unpunished, or the stone flies straight up and smashes the machine. Daurenja understood that (but in that case, why did he run off and play at being a hero, when he knew that offences must be punished? Simple; because he's the crime and the punishment all rolled into one, a complex assembly performing many functions simultaneously. Leave him out of it).

The stone flies straight up, and when it lands it smashes the machine that launched it. Well of course, Ziani thought, as he trimmed the wick. That's what it's supposed to do. No choice.

Shop thirteen was making the drills.

Ziani had seen a picture in a book, fifteen years ago. It showed a machine like a battering ram on a wheeled chassis, but it wasn't for bashing. Brick, the book explained, crumbles when hammered but doesn't shatter like stone. To wreck a brick wall, the approved procedure is to drill in it a series of three-inch holes no more than eight inches apart. Before drilling the next hole, insert a log, three-inch diameter, steeped in tar or pitch. Light the log-ends; by the time you've withdrawn to a safe distance, the logs will have burned through, leaving the now-unsupported wall to collapse. The book had been written for builders and stonemasons needing to demolish old buildings, so of course the ordnance department had never heard of it. A friend of his who worked the same shift at the ordnance factory had won a copy of it in a game of knucklebones and sold it to him for two quarters.

To make drills, he'd sent for the Vadani foresters. They knew exactly where to find what he needed: a stand of oaks planted on a steep hillside and neglected, never thinned out, with the result that they'd grown tall, straight and spindly, fighting to get above the forest canopy into the light. Ziani specified trunks seventy feet long, twelve inches in diameter at the base, eight at the top where the branches started to spread out. He had them cut off six inches short of that point, so that the end-grain would be tangled with knots and pins, and therefore resistant to splitting. The trunks were rolled down the hill to the river and floated to Civitas Vadanis in rafts of ten. The derricks and cranes built into the outside wall of shop thirteen lifted them easily and laid them down on the shop's long central floor, where they were planed and dressed. The carriages were ash; simple rectangular frames, inside which the oak trunk lay on an extending trolley with a bed of rollers. A cat's cradle of ropes running in pulleys turned it, and into its end was fitted a flat steel drill-bit three inches wide. The carriage had its own roof, tiled and sloping so that anything the defenders chose to drop or pour on it from above would slide or dribble harmlessly off. There wasn't time to build a geared transmission to drive the wheels, so it'd need forty men to push it along and twelve more to work the windlass that turned the drill. Jobs for the Aram Chantat.

With Duke Valens' book under his arm and a small bundle of sketches in his hand, Ziani went to see the foreman of shop thirteen. Yes, they'd just finished making the drill bits the previous evening; as it happened, they were just about to start fitting them. Ziani told the foreman what he wanted done instead, pinned him down to a firm time estimate and promised him a dozen blacksmiths to do the additional work.

Blacksmiths were, of course, in desperately short supply, but Daurenja's personnel roster showed him a dozen men he could reassign with the bare minimum of disruption and chaos. The men reported to him in the empty lumber store at the back of shop nine. Its principal merit was a long, plain plastered wall, which he'd had whitewashed. By the time the men arrived, he'd already drawn out the diagrams on the wall with a stump of charcoal.

He explained what he wanted, with reference to the diagrams. The men stared at him as though he was mad. But he was getting used to that sort of thing.

"Fine," he said. "All right, how many of you know how to forge a ploughshare?"

Eleven hands went up; there is, of course, always one who never admits to knowing anything.

"That's all right, then," he said. "Basically, it's just a toy windmill with four ploughshares instead of sails, rotating round a hub with a spindle stuck in it. Now, anybody got any problems with that?"

If they did, they kept quiet about it, so Ziani dismissed them and sent a note round to the stores, requisitioning fifteen of the large sheets of quarter-inch steel armour-plate. The quartermaster would, of course, scream and yell like mad and swear blind there weren't that many sheets left, and if there were, they were already earmarked for shop sixteen and the armourers. Daurenja could sort all that out. No point keeping a dog and snarling yourself.

Other calls to make. By the time he'd finished, the day shift had gone and the night shift had started up. He felt tired, so that his eyes itched and his knees ached, but he had six hours completely free; and, more to the point, nobody was using the toolroom at the back of shop seven.

Forty-eight lamps, set up in four racks of twelve, lit the toolroom, which had no windows or skylight. Another borrowing from standard practice at the ordnance factory. Changes, even slight, in the angle of sunlight coming in through a window can distort the way the fine calibrations on a dial or handscrew stand out, which can in turn lead to error. A constant, controllable level of artificial light makes for consistent work.

In the middle of the room stood the Vadani alliance's one and only Type Twenty-Three engine lathe; seventy-two inches between centres, swinging twelve inches over the bed, back-geared, as specified, perfect. Sometimes he came here just to see it; other times, he couldn't bear to look at it. How it had found its way to Civitas Vadanis he had no idea. It was at least ninety years since the Mezentines had stopped exporting them, on the grounds that nobody outside the Republic could be trusted with the potential of such a perfect artefact. Judging by the serial number, this one was at least a hundred and fifty years old. At some point, a blasphemer had oiled the bed, a crime to which the grooves scored in it by particles of grit and swarf embedded in oily paste bore silent, grim witness. Ziani himself had turned new headstock bearings for it and replaced the saddle shims. Apart from that, it had suffered no violations beyond the usual gentle, even wear of long, respectful use. Ziani had heard stories about the temples of the ancient heathens, in which the god was believed to be present, sublimated in the eucharist. Until he'd come here, he hadn't really been able to understand what that was supposed to mean.

There was a simple block-and-tackle hoist on the far wall, and he used it to lift the length of steel bar into position. He'd chalked his initials and his personal requisition code on it just before he left, to make sure nobody interfered with it; the chances of getting another one were practically nonexistent. It was round stock, six-inch diameter, eight feet long, best hardening steel; he'd tested it himself on the edge of a grinding wheel, and the shower of fat orange sparks had confirmed it: nothing less than a section of overhead shaft from one of the Republic's own factories, and how it could possibly have found its way here, he couldn't begin to guess.

Very slowly and carefully, he guided it into place over the bed of the lathe. You and me, he thought; we shouldn't be here, but here we are, and we've got work to do.

He clamped it to the faceplate with cramps and dogs, set the tailstock live centre in the dimple he'd already drilled in the other end, slacked off the winch and unbuckled the sling. Then, hardly daring to breathe in case the whole thing shook loose and wrecked the lathe, he let in the drive and watched it start to turn. A minute studying it by eye, then the necessary checks with gauges; it was set up straight and running true. He wound in the compound table and set the screw for a five-thousandth-of-an-inch cut.

Two cuts, two hours each; another two hours grinding, lapping and polishing. He'd been tired out before he started work. By the time he'd finished, winched the bar out of the machine and up on to its place in the long rack, he was in that rare but unmistakable state where exhaustion no longer matters. He was drawing his strength directly from the work, concentrating so intensely that he simply didn't have attention to spare for anything else. Dimly he heard the sound of voices; the swing shift taking off their coats and changing their boots on the other side of the toolroom door. He tried to chalk on the bar, but the surface was too smooth, so he wrote on the rack instead.

The last thing he did before he dragged himself back to his office and fell asleep in his chair was to scribble a note for Daurenja and give it to one of the messengers. As he handed it over, as his fingertips lost contact with it, he felt a dreadful surge of fear, and knew he was making a terrible mistake; as if he'd written out a death warrant, and carelessly put in his own name instead of the condemned man's.

The mandrel's ready, he'd written. *We can start whenever you like.*

He woke up. The messenger was standing over him, looking worried.

"He said to give it to you right away," the messenger said defensively. "Said it was very important."

The messenger's tone of voice made it unnecessary to ask who he was talking about. "All right," Ziani grumbled. "Give it here, thank you."

Daurenja's handwriting – neat, pointed, sloping at an exaggerated angle – across the bottom of the scrap of drawing paper Ziani had used for his note.

As soon as possible. Now. G.D.

Ziani groaned, reached for the top of the ink bottle, stabbed about in the ink like a woodpecker in a rotten tree, and scribbled:

Don't be bloody stupid. I've had a long day and I'm going to get some sleep. We'll start the forging an hour after sunset tomorrow. Get everything ready for then.

"No rush," he said, as the messenger took the paper from his hand. "Make the bastard wait."

Then he dragged himself to his feet, went outside on to the gallery, climbed the spiral stone staircase to the tower room where he slept, and went to bed.

Much to his surprise, he slept well, and woke up in daylight. His room in the tower was circular, with one small, strangely shaped window about a foot off the floor. After a month or so of wild speculation, he'd got around to asking someone about it, and was told that the factory building had once been the keep of the citadel, before Valens' great-grandfather built the ducal palace on the other side of town. The upper gallery, where his office was, used to be the intermediate defensive ring, where archers shot down at besieging enemies and pushed scaling ladders away from the walls with long poles. The room he slept in, his informant added, was the watch platoon garderobe.

"I see," he'd said. "What the hell's a garderobe?"

Basically, military terminology for a toilet; which explained, among other things, the position and shape of what he'd taken for a window. Boiling oil and molten lead weren't the only things you dropped on besiegers' heads, apparently.

He changed his shirt and trousers and put on a heavy-duty leather apron, and boots with steel toecaps, then went down to the gallery and along to the corner tower, where there was usually something to eat. Today, it was salt bacon, more salt than bacon, a basin of grey slop under a thick knobbly skin, and grey bread you could've sharpened axes on. He was hungry, but he couldn't bring himself to burst the skin on the grey slop. An earlier diner had left a hacksaw beside the bacon. It got the job done, eventually.

A little later, his mouth tasting uncomfortably of salt, he went to his office and attacked the paperwork for an hour, at the end of which his early-morning freshness had all gone. He felt blunt, like a knife misused for cutting lead, and he still had far too much to do.

The foreman of shop eleven rescued him in the nick of time; something about the bearings on the reciprocating saw, which nobody else was allowed to touch if it went wrong. Ziani smiled, abandoned the paperwork and spent a pleasant couple of hours in the small toolroom, turning up new bearings on the little toymakers' lathe he'd built himself. He stretched the job out a little, pretending to himself that a mirror finish was essential for the smooth running of the saw. Once upon a time, he thought, there was a man who worked in a factory rather like this one, only better; he checked tolerances and fought his way through paperwork, and when something broke he fixed it himself, because that was quicker and easier than explaining to someone else how to do it; he didn't like the administration much, and when he found an excuse to get away from it for an hour or so and spend time actually cutting and shaping metal, he used to wonder why the hell he'd ever wanted to be the foreman instead of an ordinary engineer; once upon a time, in a distant land, and also here, now, where the avenging hero had finally settled down, made new friends and got a job. The difference, the tolerance, the margin of error, was something you checked with a simple piece of metal, a yes/no gauge. If you put the gauge over the finished component and it fit, the piece was good. If not, scrap. Yes or no; no tolerance.

The bearing fitted perfectly, which was how it should be. After all, he thought, I do good work, and everything I make fits and does its job; which is why I can't be satisfied with sleeping in a toilet in a watchtower, while my wife and daughter think I'm dead or never coming home again. No fit; scrap.

The rest of the day passed rather too quickly. He knew the sun was setting when the light through the arrow slits in the wall of shop nine blazed a garish orange in the freshly cut steel of the catapult ratchets. An hour to go. He went back to the corner tower and ate some more of the grit-hard bread.

Then Daurenja came for him, like an executioner.

There was a big covered space at the back of the factory. In the old days, they'd told him, it had been the castle mews, where the hawks and falcons were kept, a dark, quiet place, suitable for savage, neurotic creatures in captivity. Now it was just a shell with a high roof and no windows. On Daurenja's orders, they'd cut a hole in the roof for a flue, rising up out of a broad funnel-shaped canopy, hung by wires from the rafters. Directly under it they'd dug a wide, shallow pit, lined it with firebrick and run in two-inch-bore clay pipes to conduct the blast from four enormous double-action bellows. Surrounding the pit like a moat was a channel, six inches deep and three wide, filled with water. Against one wall lay a mountain of charcoal.

Two heavy A-shaped iron frames stood a little to the right of the pit, supporting the two ends of the tool-steel mandrel Ziani had turned on the lathe. Next to that, two five-hundredweight double-horned anvils, and lying on the floor around them buckets of water, mops, bundles of cloth, wide-mouthed pails of water, with whole fleeces stuffed in them to soak, iron cans and dippers fixed on the ends of long poles. Two dozen men in aprons stood by the far wall, looking nervous.

"I've already hardened and tempered the mandrel," he heard Daurenja say, and for a moment he couldn't think what he was talking about. "It's going to be tricky keeping the frames from burning through. We'll just have to make sure they're damped down all the time."

A table, liberated from somebody's kitchen. On it lay eight pairs of tongs, sixteen sledgehammers, a big stone pestle and mortar, clay jars, rolls of three-sixteenth iron wire, a clutter of small, commonplace tools, a tinderbox, two fire-rakes, four wire brushes. "I think we've got everything," Daurenja was saying, and Ziani realised he sounded worried, the first time ever. It reminds me of something, Ziani thought, and realised it was two things, not one: preparations for an execution, and the midwife getting the kitchen ready, the day Moritsa was born.

"Swage blocks," Ziani said. "You've forgotten the swage blocks."

Daurenja shook his head. "Over there," he said, pointing into the shadows. "It's so dark in here you can't see them. Look, will somebody get some lamps lit, for crying out loud?"

It'd have to be dark once they started, of course; they needed to be able to see the fine differences in the blinding white of iron at welding heat, and the soft glow of a single candle might be enough to deceive them. "Get the blocks over here by the hearth," Daurenja was telling someone. "And have the staves laid out in order, we don't want to be fooling about dry-fitting once we're up and running. And then you might as well get the fire lit. The sooner we start, the sooner we'll see."

Someone picked up the tinderbox, but Daurenja took it from him. They were laying kindling in the middle of the pit; first small dry twigs and hay, then thin splinters of scrap planed wood stacked in a cone. Daurenja turned the tinderbox handle, blew on it, swore, called for more dried moss and shavings (Ziani smiled; he always had trouble getting a fire going himself). Someone leaned over his shoulder, offering to help, and was pushed out of the way. A little curl of smoke from the box. Daurenja took a long stride towards the pit and dumped the smouldering rubbish out of the box into the hole in the top of the stack of kindling. One of the bellows wheezed gently. An orange glow swelled and burst, like over-ripe fruit, into flames.

Two men started shovelling charcoal, sprinkling it slowly on to the fire as the second bellows started up. Apparently satisfied, Daurenja turned his back on the fire-pit and shouted something Ziani couldn't catch over the huff and roar of the bellows. Four men dragged a long wooden box out of the shadows, and two of them stooped and lifted out an iron plate, bending their knees and straightening up under the weight. The plate was five feet long, about a handspan wide, two inches thick. They laid it down on the table and stepped back, as Daurenja darted forward to examine the edges.

"Bloody rust," he shouted. "I thought I told you to keep the staves dry." He was scrubbing the edges with a small chunk of brick. "Got to keep the edges clean or the welds won't take." Someone handed him a clay pot, flux mixed with water to the consistency of thick porridge. He scooped out a thick blob with his finger, examined it and started smearing it on the freshly scrubbed edge.

"In the fire," he snapped; two men clamped heavy tongs on the plate, locking the handles shut with rings, and heaved it into the fire-pit, while other men raked orange-hot charcoal over it until it was buried. The bellows sighed, provoking the fire into a wild outburst of flame. Five men were dragging up the massive square iron swage block. A wide groove, like a gutter but shallower, was cut into the upper face. Daurenja nodded to two of the men, and they each took a sledgehammer from the table. Daurenja himself lifted the top swage, a half-round bar on a long handle; it must have weighed forty pounds, but he moved it easily. He rested it in the groove on the top of the block, and peered into the fire as the third and fourth bellows started to blow, stirring up six-foot plumes of flame.

"Keep the charcoal coming," Daurenja yelled. "Got to keep the heat even." Sweat was pouring out of his face, as though he was melting or leaking. "Right, that'll do, get it out."

The iron plate rose out of the fire-pit like the sun rising, a blazing yellow shape that defeated the eye as it swooped down on top of the groove in the block. Daurenja set the curved face of the top swage down lengthways, exactly in the middle, and nodded to the hammermen, who started striking the swage's flat back, squeezing the hot, soft plate down into the groove, as the men with the tongs drew it down the block, an inch between the fall of each hammer blow. By the time they were halfway down, the bright yellow had faded to orange; Daurenja lifted the top swage clear, and the plate went back into the fire to heat up again. Men came forward to scrub clinker out of the groove with wire brushes.

"You could have done this bit earlier," Ziani said. "You don't need me here for this."

Daurenja swung round and looked at him as though he didn't recognise who was talking to him. "I'm sorry," he said, "but I wanted to keep the heat in the fire. Once this lot cools down . . ."

It was a fair point, but Ziani made no sign of acknowledging it. "How many staves?" he asked.

"Eight," Daurenja replied.

"Fine. I might go outside for some air."

But he stayed, as they swaged down all eight staves, quenched them, cleaned up and squared off the edges and laid them one at a time on the mandrel to make sure they fitted snugly on the curved face. He wasn't sure why; it was painfully noisy and unbearably hot, and there was nothing for him to do except stand still and quiet and admire the frightening intensity of Daurenja's concentration. For once, he felt no desire whatever to take part, not even to set a square or a pair of callipers on the quenched, fettled staves to test them for straightness or uniformity of thickness. He found his own reluctance disturbing, but couldn't decide why.

"As near as makes no odds," Daurenja panted in his ear; which was his way of saying that the staves fitted together perfectly around the mandrel, their long edges lying so tight that the blade of a rule wouldn't slip in between them. Ziani nodded grudgingly (was it simple jealousy, he wondered; because this was the greatest, most ambitious piece of work he'd ever seen, and all he could do was watch? A part of it, yes, but only a small one), as Daurenja ordered the staves laid flat on the ground, dropped to his knees and began smothering the edges with flux. He worked quickly but with extraordinary care, verging on tenderness, like a mother feeding her baby some pulped-up mess with her fingers. Behind him, everybody was moving; carrying water, shovelling charcoal, damping down the mandrel, the tongs, the air-pipes, brushing off and sweeping up scale, grinding flux, laying out tools in order for the next stage, while Daurenja knelt beside the components of his dream like a man at prayer. Ziani glanced at him as he looked up, and saw that he was wide-eyed and pale with fear.

He's vulnerable now, Ziani thought, for the first time ever. I could get to him now and hurt him. He thought about that, as unconsciously he counted the slow, even gasps of the bellows. A few sharp, insidious words to wreck his confidence, get him worrying; pretend to find fault or foresee a problem. He was so tense that the slightest thing would break him, like a single drop of water on the red-hot air-pipes. It was like watching a lover waiting for an answer (yes or no, like the gauges; either everything fits together or it doesn't), one man kneeling still and quiet while everything behind him was fire and movement. Two possibilities. A genuine choice.

He tried to think straight. If Daurenja failed, what would he do? It was impossible to say. Valens would want to know, would want an informed and reasoned opinion, whether it'd be worth letting him try again, or whether the project was impractical, a waste of precious time and resources. But it wasn't about rational decisions; it was whether to kill the monster now, while he was weak, his guard down, stripped of his impenetrable armour by love and desire. It's the only thing he wants, Ziani thought, so is it better to stop him having it, or let him win his beloved and hope he'll be satisfied and go away?

"Right," he heard him say, in a voice as hard and brittle as glass. "We've only got one chance. If anything goes wrong, we're screwed." He wasn't talking to anybody; he mouthed the words like the responses in a religious service, a prayer, a general confession.

Two of the staves were in the fire, buried under a glazed roof of glowing charcoal. Ziani forced himself to clear his mind. When the staves were white hot, at the precise moment when the surface but not the core of the iron was just starting to melt, they'd be hauled out of the fire and held on the mandrel side by side. In the two seconds during which the surfaces were still molten, they could be joined by firm but gentle hammering, little more than a brisk smack; and that was what Daurenja didn't know how to do.

Success or failure; yes or no.

Rather than choose, Ziani watched the fire, looking for the stray white sparks drifting lazily upwards out of the charcoal oven that would tell him the iron was approaching welding heat. Apart from the snoring of the bellows there was dead silence. They'd put the lamps out, so he could judge precisely the colour of the glowing iron. As he waited, he could feel the tension in his mind, yes or no, the gauge set on the work, and he desperately wished he knew the grounds on which he was supposed to decide.

The sound of welding-hot iron is unmistakable; almost a crackle, almost a smacking of lips, against a background of hissing. Ziani took the rake from someone's hand and gently opened a window in the roof of shining coals. Almost immediately a spark shot up, bright as a star, burst and went out. He could hear the hiss but not the crackle. The problem was the thickness of the staves. Welding thin pieces was easy enough, so long as you didn't let them get too hot and burn; but thick pieces like these had to be welding-hot all the way through, or else the seam would be weak and false. The biggest risk lay in waiting too long once the sparks began to fly, burning the outside while waiting for the inside to run. Then there was dirt, rust or scale in the seam, which would stop the edges merging into one piece – the flux was meant to guard against that, but if you waited too long the flux would burn away, scale would start to form. Pull the staves out too soon, before the melt started, and you could hammer as hard as you liked and nothing would happen. He felt the skin on his forehead burn, and his eyes were bleached from staring into the painful brightness of the fire, but he found he couldn't move away, not until the moment came . . .

(It was yes, then. He took it calmly, with resignation, putting the implications away at the back of his mind for later.)

Seven plump white sparks soared up out of the fire, and the crackle was like snapping twigs. "Now," he heard himself yell. He felt a hammer-shaft in the palm of his hand – someone must've put it there – as the two staves rose up from the glowing heap, white as the moon. As they moved through the air towards the mandrel, he noted dispassionately the slimy, wet look of the surfaces where the iron was softening into liquid. Everything was perfect as the staves slid gently on to the mandrel and the edges to be welded nudged together and touched, needing only his gentle strokes, his caress, to join them inseparably for ever.

I know how to do this, he thought as he lifted the hammer; not a prayer or an exhortation, a simple fact. He struck, and a shower of burning white stars, droplets of molten iron, shot up in front of his eyes like a fountain. He felt some of them on his cheeks, his wrists, the backs of his hands, melting his skin as he struck again, patting and squidging the wet staves together like a potter moulding clay. There were good smiths, excellent smiths, who never managed to learn the knack of the forge-weld, lacking the touch, the passion, the love. One blow slightly too hard would spring the joint before it had a chance to form; slightly too soft and the skin on the wet surfaces wouldn't burst and open up to each other. The sparks scattered and buzzed round him like furious bees, sweat flowed down his forehead and the bridge of his nose – one drop on the seam could ruin it, but he didn't dare wipe his face or move his head at all – while his arm rose and fell, his wrist delivering the delicate pecks, like kisses. People who believed in gods reckoned that a creator made the world. For a short while Ziani was prepared to believe in something like that; a god who gripped the Earth in mighty tongs, lifted it white hot out of the sun and joined its seams with careful, passionate taps, filling the night sky with sparks, somehow made sense; and whether he made it as a paradise for the righteous or a trap or a weapon had no bearing on the holiness of the moment when the edges fused into a seam, and the mountains sank hissing into the sea.

"Well?" Daurenja's chin was on his shoulder. "Has it taken?"

He didn't know; unbelievably, he wasn't even looking. "Too late now if it hasn't," he shouted back. "You'd better look for yourself, I can hardly see."

Which was true enough. He closed his eyes, but the all-consuming white glare was still there. "It looks fine," Daurenja yelled in his ear. "It's taken, we're all right."

Ziani opened his eyes, but he couldn't see anything. "Good," he said. "Now for the tricky bit. Get the mandrel in the fire, quick, before it takes cold."

The tricky bit; because to weld on the remaining five staves and close up the final seam, they had to keep the piece he'd just welded at or just under welding heat for the rest of the procedure; and that, as far as Ziani knew, was impossible. Someone was pouring water over his head and shoulders; someone else was binding strips of soaking wet cloth round his forearms. They'd lifted the two staves he'd already joined off the mandrel and nestled them back into the fire, a little further out towards the edge, while the next stave was buried deep in the heart of the coals, close to the mouths of the four air-tubes. His forehead was already dry again. Someone took the hammer from his hand and quenched it in the water-filled trench. It hissed, and a round ball of steam drifted upwards.

As he listened for the iron, he allowed his mind to wander. He tried to picture the City – the factory, his home, the Guild school, the house where he'd been born – but the light was too bright. So he searched in it for the faces of his wife and daughter, and found he couldn't quite form their shapes. They were two white pools, two pieces at welding heat, but however hard he tried (though the edges were clean as arrow blades and he was using blood as a flux), nothing he could do was quite enough to form a seam. Right at the heart of the fire was a cold spot. No matter how forcefully the bellows blew (they were piling on the charcoal, they were throwing on cartloads of sawn timber, wrecked wagons, smashed arrows, dead horses, dead men, whole cities, and each breath of the bellows bathed the fuel in white light and burned it away), still the cold spot was there, in his house, in her eyes, the night they came to search for the illegal mechanical doll. He could see it clearly now that the light had bleached his mind. He could see the door opening, the faces of strangers, a cold draught blowing into the warm house, lamplight on a halberd blade. I don't understand, she says; Ziani, what are they talking about, I don't understand. He understands, of course; he's guilty, he shares a truth with the strangers but not with his wife. He looks at her, sees fear and confusion and a refusal to believe, but something else as well, a cold spot. But it's a totally new procedure, an innovation, an abomination, and so he has no frame of reference, not until now, when he sees the same flaw in the white iron, and the two moments touch and weld . . .

He was hammering. The sparks lashed his face like rain, and he couldn't tell for certain whether the salt he could taste as he licked his lips was sweat or tears or just the last of the salt bacon. But somehow the cold spot had collapsed; he pecked at the growing seam and watched the shadow inside the translucent iron wince, as liquid metal flowed from one piece into another. "It's taken," Daurenja howled, and quietly, in the back of his mind, Ziani agreed. Not a thunderbolt or a sudden stab of understanding; it was more that, when he probed the thought, like a man with toothache feeling with his tongue, he knew that he could no longer believe in what he used to believe. The cold spot was still there, as thought cooled and it became too late to make it good.

It was her, the cold spot said. She told . . .

The hissing again, like the voices of other people who knew something he didn't. Sparks; he could smell his own hair burning. "Now," he called out without even needing to look; and they dragged out the two pieces; seven eighths of a cylinder, and the missing eighth stave. There were a dozen men straining on the tongs now, staggering under the weight of the blurred white shape as they slid it over the mandrel like a sleeve and Daurenja laid the eighth stave gently on top. Two seams to make in one heat, there wouldn't be time. He worked them alternately, hardly thinking about what he was doing, going by the feel of the soft iron under the hammer, since he could no longer see. His face was raw from the heat, even the hammer's wooden handle was too hot to grip. His throat and lungs were burning, he was drowning in heat and light, but all he could think about was the cold spot, the flaw in everything. It was her, she told them; in which case . . .

Suppose (in his mind, by contrast, it was bitter cold) he was Duke Valens. Suppose he found out that Ziani Vaatzes opened the gates of Civitas Eremiae. Just suppose. Needless to say, it would change everything. It was a cold spot in the war, a flaw in everything. But the

war must be fought to the end, and without Ziani Vaatzes it couldn't
be won, and so the cold spot had to be overlooked, the seam had to be
closed up around it, he had to forget about it or pretend he didn't
know it was there. Now (let's suppose) he's Ziani Vaatzes, staring at
the cold spot in the heart of the white glow, knowing that everything
he's done is unsound, so brittle that one tap in the right place will
shatter it. If the cold spot had been in the first seam, or the second,
the third, the fourth, fifth, sixth or seventh; but the eighth seam, as
they shovel the last city on to the fire and lean on the bellows handles,
with Daurenja standing over him twitching and whimpering with
lust . . . The eighth and last seam, closing up the tube.

"That's it." Daurenja's voice, raw as though the lining of his throat
had been scraped with glass. "That's it, leave it, you've done it."

"It's no good." Daurenja was trying to pull him away, take the
hammer out of his hand. He struggled, put his hand on Daurenja's
face and shoved him. "There's a cold spot. There's a fucking cold
spot in the last seam."

Daurenja shouldered past him, thrust his face, his bright eyes and
his stupid little button nose, so close to the yellow iron that his eye-
lashes shrivelled. "Where?" he yelled. "Where is it? I can't see
anything."

Funny joke. Ziani could barely see at all, only round the edges of
the terrible white hole. He wondered how he could possibly explain.
"It's there," he said. "I felt it."

Daurenja was huddled over the glowing tube like a mother over a
cradle. He was bathed in the steam from his drenched clothes, the
wet sheepskin he'd draped round his head and shoulders. The light
from the bright iron shone in the cloud. "There's nothing there," he
said. "It's all right, you're imagining it. It worked, you did it. I knew
you could do it. It worked."

Two men were trying to pull him away now, before he scorched
his face and ruined his eyes, but his skin hadn't burnt and he wasn't
even blinking. Only a hero or a monster could get that close to yellow
iron and not burn. (Wasn't that what the savages believed, that you
could try a man with hot iron? If he burned, it meant he was guilty,
or was it the other way round?) "You bloody genius, Ziani," he was
yelling, his voice high and shrill, "I knew you'd be able to do it, I
knew all along, right from the first time I saw you, and I was right,
wasn't I? I knew there had to be a reason, I knew it was the right

thing to do." They were trying to make him move, hauling at his shoulders and arms, but they couldn't shift him, and as the iron gradually cooled, he seemed to grow even stronger, as if the heat was leaving the tube and draining away into him (but he didn't burn, only sweated).

"Right." Ziani heard his own voice, barely recognised it. "Get the hoops in the fire, I want this job finished. Wait till the tube's gone dull red and then quench it; oil, not water. I need to sit down for a bit and close my eyes."

"Yes, of course." Daurenja was still staring into the light, cooling it with his eyes. "Get the first hoop up to white, and for crying out loud keep them in order." At last he turned his head away, looking at Ziani. "There wasn't a cold spot, was there? I looked, but I couldn't see anything."

"I don't know," Ziani replied. "I could've been wrong. I thought I saw it, but . . ."

"There wasn't one," Daurenja said. "You imagined it. Hardly surprising, staring into the weld all that time, it's enough to screw up anybody. Look, we can finish now, shrinking the hoops on is no big deal. Why don't you go and lie down or something? You must be wrecked."

"I'll just go outside for a while," Ziani replied. "It's a bit too warm in here."

The night was dark and cold, and the stars were just sparks from the weld, he knew that now, just as the moon was hot iron and the clouds were steam. He stared into the darkness until the white rip began to heal, gradually shrinking until all that was left of it was a scar, a blemish, like a fault in a seam. It was still there when he closed his eyes. It was her, then. She told them.

Well, then. The City would still have to fall, he couldn't prevent that; no choice now. He'd condemned it to death a long time ago, in the bright white light of his lamp, when he changed the specification. By the illuminating glow of the cold spot – how much would he be able to see before its light faded? – he saw her standing in the door-way of his workshop, a silhouette with the firelight behind her, her head a little on one side as she watched him.

"What are you doing?" she said.

"Just drawing."

She came a step closer. "Work?"

"No. Actually, it's for Moritsa. Something I'm thinking of making for her."

A step closer still, and her body was between him and the yellow glow, so that he could only just see the paper in front of him on the table. "That's nice. What is it?"

Carefully he put the pen back in the ink bottle. "You remember when we went to the Guild fair, and they had those dancing mechanical dolls?"

A pause; then, "Oh yes. They were funny. She really liked them."

"I know." He looked for her face, but it was in shadow. "I thought I'd make her one."

"Really? Do you think you could?"

The surprise in her voice delighted him. He'd always known she admired him, was proud of having such a clever husband. It'd be a present for them both, in a way. "I don't see why not," he said. "Basically it's just clockwork, with some cams and levers. I got the specification from the library this afternoon, I was just drawing it out. Here, take a look if you like. Don't suppose it'll mean much to you, though."

He felt her hair on his shoulder as she leaned over him. "It's all just lines and squiggles," she said. He laughed. "Will it dance like the ones at the fair?"

"Well, no. They were Type Sevens, this is a Type Four. Type Seven is a restricted pattern."

"Oh." It wasn't much. A little inflection, probably not even intended. A cold spot. "Well, never mind. Will it be able to turn its head and move its arms?"

"Of course. Here, look, this is the linkage mechanism. This arm here bears on this cam, which raises this pawl here . . ."

She giggled. "If you say so," she said. "But it looks really difficult and fiddly, all those bits and pieces. It'll be a lot of work, won't it?"

"I'll just do a bit at a time, when I've got a spare moment. I'll enjoy it. It's been ages since I did any small work."

"I know she'd really like it," she said. "But you work so hard as it is, at the factory. You'll wear yourself out, you will."

He smiled. "You know me," he said. "I hate just sitting still. Anyway, I like making things. That's why I became an engineer, right?"

He wasn't looking at her face, but he could feel the warmth of her smile, like the heat of a fire making his cheek glow. "It'd mean a lot to her," she said. "Specially if *you* made it for her. She's very proud of her clever daddy."

"Well, then."

She neither moved nor spoke, but she didn't need to. The moment's hesitation, a cold spot, said it for her: *it's a shame it won't dance, though, like the ones at the fair.* And at that moment (the white rip was fading from his vision, he could barely see) it occurred to him that it would be better if it could dance, even though it was a Type Four. Why couldn't a Type Four dance? Well, because it wasn't a Type Seven. Sevens dance, Fours turn their heads and move their arms, that's why we have types. Dumb question. You might as well ask why the sun doesn't shine at night.

She left him, and when she'd gone the light came in through the doorway and he could see the machine again, lines on paper. Why couldn't a Type Four dance? But it *could*, if you duplicated the pivot-and-socket assembly, driving it off the main spindle with an auxiliary train . . .

He froze in his seat, suddenly cold all over. Just thinking about it was enough to make him shudder. Type Four was the kind that didn't dance; for dancing, there was the Type Seven, and that pattern was restricted. It wasn't hard to understand, for crying out loud. He could almost feel pain from the guilty thought, lodged in his head like an arrowhead in a wound; as if they could cut the top off his skull and find it there in his brain. He screwed his eyes tight shut, as if concentrating could crush the malignant thought like gallstones.

But it could be done. Worse than that; if it was done, the result would be *better*, an improvement, just like the modifications to scorpion mechanisms he'd submitted to the governors of the ordnance factory. Yes, he told himself, but that's permitted, one specific exception to the otherwise inviolable rule.

It would mean so much to her. He thought about that. To deviate from Specification was forbidden; but just because a thing's forbidden doesn't mean it's not possible. Quite the opposite. Murder, for example. Murder was forbidden, but it was possible and it happened. There was no need to prohibit walking in fire or flying through the air. Murder happened all the time. It was possible to do it, and possible to get away with it, provided that nobody ever found out.

"Dinner's ready": her voice from the other room. It would be as bad as murder; worse, in the eyes of the Guild, since it was a crime against the whole Republic rather than just one man. Very well, he thought; I've been tempted, just as I've been tempted to kill people, and of course I've resisted the temptation; because I know right from wrong; because I daren't run the risk of getting caught.

It would mean . . .

He blinked. The great white glare was closing up, and he couldn't see through it any more. Suddenly he realised it was raining. His hair was dripping wet, and water was running in streams down his forehead into his eyes. Only an idiot stands out in the rain when he doesn't have to. He opened the door, and heard the dull, heavy sound of hammers on hot metal.

They were shrinking on the strengthening bands. He watched as someone lifted a white-hot hoop out of the fire, carried it gripped in tongs to the mandrel and slid it tentatively on to the tube. Someone else teased it quickly down the tube with a length of brass rod, until it rested up against the previous band; straight away, someone else stepped forward and poured water on to it from a brass jug, quenching it so that it shrank, gripping the tube so hard it could only be removed by cutting. It would be a long job, since every inch of the tube had to be reinforced, but it was straightforward enough, just a slight variant on the technique used for fitting an iron tyre to a wheel. Another hoop went in the fire; further back, two men were welding hoops over the horns of the anvil, scattering white sparks as they patted the glowing iron. But he didn't want to watch. Simple welds, they didn't need him for that. He yawned.

Someone walked past him, stopped. "Are you all right?" He thought about that and realised that no, he wasn't. Every square inch of his exposed skin was scorched, and the muscles and tendons of his arms were aching horribly. He looked down at the palm of his right hand, then at his forearm, where the welding sparks had pitched and raised fat white blisters. "No," he said.

"You want to get those burns seen to," whoever it was said. He sounded concerned, which was strange. "And then you want to get some rest. You've earned it."

He recognised the voice. It was Daurenja. "You look terrible," he said.

Daurenja laughed. "Quite likely," he said. "But who gives a damn? It worked, that's all that matters. You did it."

Ziani shook his head. "There's a cold spot," he said.

The words melted against Daurenja's smile like drops of water falling on the hot iron. "No there isn't," he said. "And if there is, it'll be all right, the bands'll hold it. Tube and bands together, that's three inches of forged wrought iron. Nothing on earth's going to get through that."

"Maybe not," Ziani replied. "But there's a cold spot."

Daurenja turned away and walked past him without another word. That pleased him, and he thought about something Duke Valens had tried to teach him, about the way to a man's heart. Through the eye, into the brain, deep into the mind until you reached the place where the staves didn't join and the seam was weak. Valens hadn't seen fit to mention that the entry channel of the wound closed up once the sword was pulled out, like an underground shaft caving in, leaving the damage buried deep inside, stoppered like a bottle with a scar until something, a bright light perhaps, opened it up again, and for a moment or so you could look into the wounded man's eye and see the damage looking back at you from the mirror.

Chapter Eight

Sixty siege engines, dismantled, left Civitas Vadanis, heading for the war. They rode, like princesses sent off to be married, in great canopied wagons borrowed for the occasion from the Aram Chantat, escorted by a troop of Vadani cavalry with polished breastplates and banners. At the head of the convoy rode Gace Daurenja, seconded from the factory to supervise their reassembly and installation. Somehow he'd managed to get hold of a nobleman's blue cloak, extravagantly embroidered with gold thread and seed pearls. At his side he wore an ivory-handled sword in a scabbard covered in red velvet, while on his left wrist he carried a hooded goshawk, a present from the duchess to the duke. The inhabitants of the few remote villages the convoy passed through turned out to stare and cheer; and if some of them mistook the strange, magnificent creature leading the column for the duke himself, there was probably no harm done.

Because of the size of the wagons and the weight of their loads, it would have been foolhardy to try and force the pace on the soft, rutted roads. Progress was accordingly slow, and Daurenja (a captain was nominally in charge of the cavalry escort, but he had the common sense not to press the point) sent out scouts and outriders to watch for any signs of hostile activity. On the evening of the third day, one scouting party reported having seen horsemen in the distance, keeping pace with the convoy. They were too far away to identify, but there was no reason why Vadani or Aram Chantat riders should act in such a fashion, and the convoy was significantly close to the Cure Doce border.

Daurenja held a brief council of war, making a point of seeking the captain's approval before issuing his final orders. The next day the convoy moved on as usual, but conscientious spies should have noticed that the escort was riding in rather more open order than before, without taking up any more space on the road.

Shortly before mid-morning, the convoy approached a sharp bend in the road, where it followed the bottom of a steep-sided combe. Without warning, two parties of armed horsemen appeared on the crests of the combe and rode frantically down the slopes to take the column in front and rear. The escort halted immediately, dismounted, turned the front and rear wagons side on to form barricades, and opened up from cover with their bows. At least a dozen attackers were killed; the rest wheeled to withdraw along the road, only to be taken in flank and rear by a detached squadron of the escort, who'd left camp in the middle of the night and looped round, following the contours of the combe. Caught between arrows and lances, the attackers crumpled in a few minutes. The few survivors were interrogated by Daurenja in person and told him they were Cure Doce, in the service of the Perpetual Republic, and that they'd been sent to capture or destroy the siege engines before they could be brought to bear on the City. After a brief consultation with the captain and his staff, Daurenja gave the order to kill the prisoners, since it would be irresponsible to burden themselves with encumbrances on such a hazardous road. Only one survivor was sent back, his nose and ears slit, to advise the Cure Doce of the dangers involved in carrying out unprovoked acts of war against the Alliance.

"For God's sake," Valens said angrily. "You're not defending him, are you?"

On his wrist, the goshawk bated, startled by the tone of his voice. Thoughtless of him. He remembered King Fashion; never shout in the presence of the hawks, or display strong emotion. A calm and quiet demeanour soothes the hawks and befits the huntsman.

"Maybe it isn't what I'd have done," Colonel Nennius replied cautiously. Valens noticed that he was watching the hawk nervously. He suppressed a smile. Unless you'd been brought up with them, they could be rather alarming. "But in the circumstances it's under-standable. For all he knew, there were more raiding parties waiting for him on the road; he couldn't really spare the men for a prisoner escort. And we did try being nice to the Cure Doce, after that farce when they burned the flour shed, and it doesn't seem to have worked. A more robust approach . . ."

Valens sighed. All perfectly true; and if Nennius had done it, or one of the regular-army captains, he probably wouldn't be working himself up into such a state. He'd done worse things himself, of course. "What the hell was he doing giving orders in the first place?" he said irritably. "He's really only a jumped-up blacksmith in any case, not a commissioned officer."

Nennius dipped his head in acknowledgement. "Mind you," he said meekly, "it was a textbook response, neatly carried out. He didn't lose a single man, he made a real mess of the enemy, and the cargo was never in any danger. But you're right, he shouldn't have done it. Strictly speaking, though, it was Captain Brennus' fault for letting him. So, if there's going to be any charges . . ."

Valens shook his head. "We can't go punishing people for win-ning victories," he said. "All right, formal reprimand for Brennus but buy him a drink afterwards, and I expect some idle bugger in the clerks' office will forget to put it on his record." The goshawk shifted, tightening and relaxing its grip. "And we'd better have more patrols, just in case the Cure Doce are really bad at taking hints. I'm a bit concerned that they were able to get that many men across the border without us knowing about it." He yawned. It was a fine day, bright and fresh after the rain, and he had a new hawk he hadn't flown yet. He'd seen pigeons in the forest, feeding on the first of the acorns and beech mast, and the day before yesterday he'd fancied he'd heard a cock pheasant calling as it flew up to roost. Instead, he was going to have to talk to Daurenja about deploying the siege engines.

But not yet. With the goshawk had come a letter:

. . . *Saw the doctor again today. He said* . . .

Valens frowned, folded the scrap (she still wrote very small on tiny bits of parchment) and put it in the rosewood box on his desk, then turned the key and took it out. It was a long time before he managed to divert his attention back to the war.

*

Later, after he'd seen Daurenja, he sent out five scouts. They were Eremians, from the cavalry squadron he'd assigned to Miel Ducas. He tried not to let the word *expendable* into his head as he gave them their orders.

They rode along the Eremian–Vadani border as far as the Butter Pass, then branched off, following a succession of droves and sheep tracks until they reached the plain. No cover there, so they put on speed, crossing the battlefield where Duke Orsea's men had once been cut to pieces by the Mezentine artillery. The bodies had gone, but there were still thickets of steel scorpion bolts, brown with flaking rust, all leaning at their angle of impact, so that they looked like a cornfield in the wind. The scouts had to slow to a walk and thread their way through them.

After that, a fast gallop until they came to the Lonazep road. If the Mezentines were sending out cavalry patrols, they were in trouble. But the straight, flat road was empty in both directions for as far as they could see. They crossed it, heading over the downs for the long, slowly rising hog's back separating them from the broad plain and the City.

No soldiers; nobody at all. Near the top of the ridge, they stopped, dismounted, hobbled their horses and walked to the skyline, where they'd be able to look down on the City. They went slowly and carefully, like burglars in an unfamiliar house, as if any noise they made would wake the sentries on the walls a mile away.

The duke had shown them a map, with the shape of the City marked in red. Being skilled at their trade, they'd memorised it at first glance, along with the contour lines and the location of coverts, rines, drains and outcrops big enough to provide cover. What they saw now bore no resemblance to the red outline in their minds.

The first thing they noticed was a river, where no river should be. It was broad, curving gently in a wide loop, the sun's dazzle on the water blurring the line where it merged with the bottom of the sky. Beyond it, they saw hills where no hills should be; sharply sloping banks of newly dug earth, escarpments partially tiled with turf, topped by a perfectly flat plateau. The curious thing about the banks was their shape. Not circular; great wedges stuck out at regular intervals, like the legs of a starfish; at the point of each wedge, a five-sided finial, like excessively ornate decoration. On each finial, a palisade of thick stakes masked building work still in progress, the scaffolding frames of guardhouses or redoubts.. Further back, where the banks lay against the city walls, they saw a black swarm of men, some digging a ditch, others heaping the spoil up into a rampart. At that distance it was impossible to attempt any sort of accurate assessment of the number of workers. All they could make out was a dark, moving shape on the ground; at a guess, hundreds rather than tens of thousands. Behind them, the City itself squatted under a frayed black cloud, the smoke from thousands of chimneys. They stared at it for a long time before sitting down to make their detailed sketches.

Those sketches lay on the table in the vast Aram Chantat pavilion, as Duke Valens briefed his allies on the defences of the City.

"First," he said (he was aware of the catch in his voice, but didn't make the mistake of trying to override it with mere volume), "there's the ditch, here." He pointed at one of the sketches, realising as he did so that only two or three of the men in the front row could see anything at all. It was the Aram Chantat's custom in such gatherings for the important men to sit at the back, so as not to get sprayed with spit by impassioned speakers. The front row was filled up with retainers, aides, younger sons and other makeweights. "It's roughly seventy-five yards wide. We can only guess at how deep it is, but since the earth taken out of the ditch is what they used to build the banked-up platforms under the walls" – this time he didn't point at the sketch – "we can assume the ditch is something like twenty-five feet deep. They've flooded it by diverting the river Mesen, which rises in the chalk downs facing the city."

He paused, looking for a reaction. Waste of time.

"These banks," he went on. "Actually, the proper word for them is bastions. You'll notice" (no, not from back there they won't) "that the bastions are triangular, sticking out all round the walls like the points of a star. Our scouts counted forty of them, and they estimate that they're something in the order of eighteen feet high. The purpose of a bastion is to give their defensive artillery the widest possible field of fire. I think that's pretty self-evident. At any point where our forces approach the walls, they'll come under fire from both sides, more than doubling the firepower that can be brought to bear on them. The bastions also cut out the blind spot at the base of the walls. I'll just explain that: with an ordinary straight wall, once you get up close to it, you're reasonably safe, because the engines can't shoot vertically downwards. The base of the wall is a very sensitive area, because if you can get right up to it, you can dig under the wall and collapse it. The bastions make this impossible. Basically, anything within seventy yards of our side of the ditch is in range, and is likely to be shot to pieces in a matter of seconds."

Still no reaction.

"The bastions serve another purpose," Valens continued grimly. "As I'm sure you know, our best bet isn't storming the city walls with ladders and siege towers, or even getting sappers to the foot of the wall to dig it away. The most promising approach will be to dig tunnels twenty feet or so under the foundations of the wall and collapse them; the resulting subsidence should then make the wall fall in under its own weight. The bastions mean that if we want to do this, we're going to have to dig much longer tunnels than anticipated to reach the walls. If they detect our mining operations – which isn't difficult: you just fill bowls with water and put them on the ground; if someone's digging twenty feet directly under one of these basins, the vibrations ripple the surface of the water – all they've got to do is dig straight down and break through the wooden props of the tunnel. The tunnel roof collapses, earth from the bastion pours in, the tunnel's blocked, the miners working forwards of the breach are trapped. Simple and effective."

His throat was dry from all this lecturing. He looked round for a jug of water, but there wasn't one.

"Storming the bastions," he said, "wouldn't be easy. Apart from their sheer height, by the time we get there they'll be fringed all round with a palisade of sharpened stakes. If we get over that and go hand-to-hand with them on the flat top of the bastion, we'll find ourselves facing another ditch, with a palisaded bank on the far side of it, not forgetting constant artillery fire from the scorpions on the City wall. Trying to knock the bastions down with artillery would be a waste of time. Masonry shatters when you pound it with rocks, but a great big mound of dirt is soft and absorbs the shot. Tunnelling under the bastions won't be easy, as we've already seen.

"Behind the bastions, there's the wall itself. We know the wall's twenty feet thick at the top, thirty feet thick at the bottom. There are artillery towers at fifty-yard intervals, as well as a range of ingenious devices to guard against ladders, siege towers, rams and all the other usual stuff. The city has four main gates, which ought to be the weak spots in the defences. Not so. Each gateway is flanked with massive square towers and topped by a gatehouse. The gates themselves are eighteen inches thick, made of six layers of three-inch oak ply, each layer running crosswise to stop it splitting. Behind the gate is a hardened steel portcullis. Each gatehouse is fitted with an unpleasant device called a wolf; basically, a very large iron frame like a harrow, fitted with lots of long spikes, hinged, so all you've got to do is release a catch and it swings down, crushes or impales anybody standing in front of the gate, trashes battering rams, siege drills and so forth; then it's hauled back up again with chains and winches ready for the next wave of attackers. As well as the wolf, there's other machinery for dropping rocks or boiling water, there's cranes and hooks that pick up rams and pavises, haul them up in the air and then drop them, other things like that. Even if our artillery manages to smash the gatehouse into rubble and we succeed in bringing up rams, by the time we've bashed through the gate and portcullis, they'll have had plenty of time to build a stone block wall across the inside of the gateway, dig trenches, raise barricades, and anything else their ingenious minds can think of. All in all, I believe the gates are probably the hardest points to crack, and I propose leaving them well alone."

Some reaction, at last. A certain amount of muttering at the back, restlessness at the front. Valens leaned forward on the table and waited. As he'd anticipated, a man in the back row stood up.

"With all due respect" (a tall, thin man with a bald head, very plainly dressed; Valens was sure he ought to recognise him, but didn't), "your information is admirably detailed and thorough, and your scouts are to be commended. By ascertaining the scale and nature of the defences, they have undoubtedly saved many hundreds of lives. I feel, however, that I might be forgiven for forming the impression that you are trying to persuade us to abandon the attempt on Mezentia by stressing the difficulties and dangers. I would like to remind you that the logical approach, starving the City into submission, is not available to us, thanks to your delay in cutting the Lonazep road and allowing them to lay in supplies for a long siege. This, I feel sure, you would not have done without a reason, but I confess I am unable to guess what that reason might be. Perhaps you would be kind enough to explain it."

Valens hid most of his smile. "Starving them out was never an option," he replied. "Our supply lines are tenuous, and even if they held, there simply isn't enough food and fodder to be had to supply our forces for that length of time. Put simply, if we'd tried that game, we'd have been the ones who starved first, even if I had cut the road as quickly as I possibly could. Which brings me, in fact, to my next point. Whatever we do, we've got to do it quickly. At the moment, I can't tell you precisely how long we can keep the army in front of the City. It depends on too many factors. Even if everything goes as well as possible, though, I can tell you for certain it won't be any longer than three months."

"Three months," the thin man said. "That's not very long. Why three months?"

Valens shrugged. "It's an educated guess."

"Perhaps you'd care to share your reasoning."

Valens paused. He could hear the patter of rain on the pavilion canopy. Somewhere outside, someone was hammering steel on an anvil, a flat, harsh sound like the warning cry of a bird. He looked at his allies, with whom he had so little in common, apart from a number of deaths. "The country on our side of the desert is quite different to what you're used to," he said. "As I understand it, your country is big and empty. You drive your cattle in a wide circuit across broad plains, going where there's grass for them to graze. On this side, we've got little fields and meadows in among the mountains. Over the years we've reached a balance, a certain number of people living on land that can just about feed that number. True, a lot of people have died in the war and don't need feeding any more; by the same token, there's fewer people to sow and reap corn and cut hay. You brought close on a million more people across the desert, and over a million head of cattle. There's only so much grain and hay on our side, even in peacetime. We can't ship food in from overseas as the Mezentines do. A maximum of three months, after which we either crack open the city and feed our people from their stores, or we starve. I left the Lonazep road open because the Mezentines can accumulate food faster than we can, and they've got sources of supply we can't access. Gentlemen, we've reached the point where taking the City isn't a matter of avenging the death of your princess or my late wife. It's not even about stopping Mezentine aggression against the Vadani or liberating Eremia, or finding a new homeland for the Aram Chantat. We have to beat them and break into their city because either we steal their food or we die. You don't know about winter in the mountains. Possibly you could feed your people till the spring by slaughtering your cattle, but that'd just make the problem worse; we can't grow enough grain to feed all of you, and without cattle you have no livelihood. If we'd taken the city a month ago, we'd have signed our own death warrants. Three months, gentlemen; if we haven't captured the City granaries intact by then, we won't survive the winter. Really, it's as simple as that. To be honest with you, compared with seeing to it that your people and mine have enough to eat, breaking open the City is a trivial problem, the sort of thing I'd normally delegate to someone else who's not got as much on his mind as me. Which, in fact, is what I've done." He smiled, straightened up a little, took a deep breath. "Allow me to outline for you the plan of campaign drawn up for us by our expert engineer, Ziani Vaatzes."

The hammering Duke Valens had heard came from an anvil under a big, splay-limbed beech tree on the northern edge of the camp. There, a farrier was shaping shoes for a rather fine chestnut gelding, assigned to the new commanding officer of the fourth Eremian light cavalry division, Major Miel Ducas. Having nothing else to do, the major sat and watched, while an armourer finished the alterations to his issue mailshirt. The major was taller and more slightly built than the notional average soldier for whom the shirt had been tailored; the rings cut out of the waist would more or less provide the necessary extra length. Meanwhile the woman generally referred to as the major's wife, at least in his hearing, was weaving straw to pad out his helmet.

"They're always too big," she said, as she paused to flex her sore fingers. "When we were scavenging on battlefields, we saw it time and again. You'd find a man with his head smashed in, and his helmet lying next to him without a scratch on it. They make them a big standard size so you can pad it to fit, but I guess they don't explain that properly when they hand them out. Silly, really. You should talk to the duke about it, it'd save a lot of people from getting killed."

Miel snuggled his back against the trunk of the tree he was sitting under. "Not my place to bother the duke with operational details," he said drowsily. "The chain of command says I should report something like that to the quartermaster general's department, through my immediate superior."

"Oh," she said. "Who's that?"

"Ersani Phocas," Miel replied, yawning. "But he's too embarrassed to talk to me, because before the war he was a third cousin of a minor collateral branch of the Phocas, and I was the head of the Ducas, so strictly speaking I shouldn't even be able to see him on a sunny day, let alone take orders from him. Also, the Ducas and the Phocas hate each other, except when we intermarry. All that's gone now, of course, but Ersani Phocas is an old man, set in his ways. These orders he's given me read more like a dinner invitation I'm expected to be too high and mighty to accept. All very charming and nostalgic, but it means I'm still not sure exactly what it is I'm supposed to be doing."

"Well, then," she said, tucking one end of the plaited straw under the leather rim of the liner. "It's like my father used to say. The aristocracy's just a waste of space."

He frowned, watching a bird on a branch overhead. "We ran Eremia fairly well, all things considered. Not perfectly, but as well as anybody could. Most people had enough to eat, and we kept the roads safe from robbers."

"Very true," she said placidly. "You did a marvellous job, and you never got any thanks for it."

He nodded. "And we spent your rents on tableware and cushions and falcons and parade armour, mostly imported. We ate too much and made our wives and sisters waste their lives embroidering samplers, we fought our rival families like lunatics and we let Orsea lead us into a war that finished us. But I think the worst of it was, we never enjoyed what we had."

"Of course," she said. "Everything else pales into insignificance in comparison."

He smiled. "I think so, yes," he said. "We had so much; we had everything. I owned huge areas of land I'd never even seen. I could've snapped my fingers and said, Bring me a lifesize gold statue of a horse, and they'd have apologised for the week's delay. Instead—"

"What good would that have been?" she asked pleasantly. "It'd take up a lot of room, and what could you use it for?"

"Instead," he went on, "I spent my whole life worrying. I shouldn't have had a care in the world, but I worried every day of my adult life; because I might've done something inappropriate, or someone else was sneaking past me in the advancement stakes, or I wasn't giving the right advice in council. I worried because I hadn't got married like I was expected to, and then I felt guilty because I couldn't face the prospect of being lumbered with any of the small number of dreadful women who were suitable for me. We used to have the most amazing dinners, but I can't remember what we ate because I was worried about everything going right, not offending the guests. We used to hunt at least once a week in the season, but I was worried about making sure my guests got more of the action than I did. I worried like hell I wouldn't get to be chief adviser to the duke; then, after I got the job, I never got another good night's sleep. I worried myself to death about the war. Then we lost, and suddenly I didn't have to be the Ducas any more, I could actually choose for myself for the first time; and now look at me, getting ready to go off to fight, which is the one thing I hate above everything else."

"Fine," she said, looking away. "Don't go, then."

He sighed. "I've got to," he said. "I won't make any difference, nobody really cares if I don't, my superior officer hates the fact that he's got to order me around and would far rather I just went away somewhere. For the first time," he added, his voice suddenly flat, "I'm scared I'll get killed, because of what might happen to you and . . ."

"That," she said. "That's what you were going to say, isn't it? You and *that*."

He nodded. "I'm sorry," he said.

"Don't be. I understand."

He shut his eyes and scowled. "But I've got to go," he said. "I've got to go and be a small, unimportant part of a war that doesn't really concern me. I don't even know who I'll be fighting – could be the Mezentines or the Cure Doce or some other ally they may have kidded into joining them. You'd think that if you've got to kill someone, if they're that important to you, at least you'd know who they are. Killing strangers without even knowing why is really rather ridiculous, don't you think?"

She frowned at the inside of the helmet, then pulled the plaited straw out and twisted it a little tighter. "Not so long ago you were killing men for their boots," she said.

"Yes." He nodded, staring straight ahead. "In comparison, that was practically honourable. We needed to kill to stay alive. There's far worse things in the world than honest predators."

"So," she said. "Don't go. We can go back to hunting soldiers for a living. Better still, you could get the duke to make you an ambassador or something: Eremian diplomatic representative to some country they haven't discovered yet. Then we could stay home all day and not do anything."

"I could," he replied.

"But you won't."

"No."

"Well, there you are, then." She stood up and held the helmet out. "All done," she said. "Try it on, see if it fits better now."

He tried it. Still a little too big. "That's fine," he said.

"No it isn't. Give it here."

She sat down again and pulled the straw out. He looked at her but couldn't see her face.

"Fine," he said. "So what do you think I should do?"

"Not up to me." Her hair, usually stretched tightly back and stabbed with a comb, was coming loose, like stuffing from a frayed cushion. "I'm not even your wife. And *that* doesn't really change things so much, does it? I mean, the Ducas must have left little souvenirs right the way across Eremia."

He scowled. He could tell her it wasn't true, but she'd choose not to believe him. "I don't suppose the apple wants to fall from the tree," he said. "But it has no choice."

"Bullshit." She looked up at him and smiled; a bleak, angry smile that hit hard and deep. "You're going because you want to. You're an aristocrat, all your noble ancestors fought in every war there's ever been, so you're going. Simple as that."

He nodded. "That's right," he said. "Like I said. No choice."

She sighed. "Well," she said, "at least when you get bashed on the head, your helmet shouldn't fall off. Don't suppose any of those blue-blooded suitable cows you ought to have married would've known how to line a helmet."

"Quite true." He took it from her and settled it on his head. Perfect fit. "Don't worry about me," he said. "I'll be back soon enough. I've made arrangements. . ."

"Of course you have." A different smile this time. "You're the slave of duty, you told me so yourself. The farrier's finished, look. Give me twelve quarters and I'll go and pay him for you."

She left him then. He waited for the armourer to finish the work on his mailshirt. In the distance he could see Aram Chantat leaving their gaudy pavilion; the big meeting breaking up, presumably. He caught a glimpse of Valens, hanging back to talk privately with one of them. Someone walked past, blocking his view. By the time he was able to see again, Valens had disappeared.

He looked up. The man who'd walked past him was the murderer, Daurenja.

Without thinking he jumped to his feet. He knew that Daurenja was very much in favour with the duke, which meant nothing could be done about him, and he'd heard he was back from Civitas Vadanis, having ridden in with the first shipment of artillery from Vaatzes' factory. Actually seeing him, on the other hand, was something he hadn't expected, and he found it intensely disturbing.

But so what? He knew for a fact that some years ago Daurenja had killed a man and raped his sister; that Valens knew about it and had hidden behind some abstruse technicalities of legal jurisdiction to avoid having to take action. He was also well aware that, since the crimes had been committed on Ducas land, before the war, he was the legal authority and instrument of justice. Properly speaking, he was duty bound to chase after the man, grab him by his ridiculous ponytail and cut his throat, like a butcher killing a calf. Instead, he trotted after him and caught up with him just as he was about to disappear into one of the storage sheds.

"Oh," Daurenja said. "It's you."

"Yes."

He paused, licked his lips like a cat. "I gather you've been given a command."

"That's right."

Daurenja frowned. "Congratulations," he said. "Was there anything you wanted?"

Miel looked at him, but it was like trying to see through mist. "I just thought I'd let you know I haven't forgotten about you."

"I should think not. People tell me I'm a memorable character. Rather a mixed blessing, but on balance I'd rather be notorious than a nonentity. If that's all, you'll have to excuse me. I'm rather busy."

He moved, but Miel put a hand on his arm. "I guess you should know," he said, "I'm filing a formal request with Duke Valens to be recognised as the official representative of the Eremian government in exile, now that Duke Orsea's dead. There's nobody left except me, you see, and somebody's got to do it."

Daurenja frowned. "What about the duchess?"

"Remarried," he replied. "Under the Act of Settlement, if she marries a foreign head of state, she forfeits her rights as trustee of the succession. That means we have to fall back on the heirs in the third degree, which in this case means the head of the Ducas family. Me."

Daurenja looked genuinely interested. "Does that make you the duke?" he asked.

"The proper term is Lord Protector," he replied, "meaning I'm responsible for safeguarding Eremian interests while the dukedom is in abeyance. There can't be another duke until all of the former duchess's sisters have officially passed the age of childbearing; after that, there's a complicated formula for working out which of their children is the rightful heir. Since we don't know what's become of any of them, it's all a bit academic anyway. Meanwhile, there's just me."

"Fascinating," Daurenja said. "I've always had a soft spot for that sort of thing: genealogy and heraldry and rights of succession to thrones that don't actually exist any more. I once met a man who told me he was the rightful king of Palaeochora, which is the old name for what's now Mezentia. He had letters and charters and all manner of old documents to prove it. Not much practical value, of course, unless there's money involved."

"No money," Miel said. "Just obligations."

Daurenja grinned. "Isn't that exactly like life," he said. "Well, nice to see you again. I really must get on now, though. Ever such a lot to be done."

Miel didn't move. "Once Valens has given me official status," he said, "I intend to prosecute you for the murder of Framain's son. I thought I ought to warn you, so you'll have time to prepare your defence."

"No defence." Daurenja shook his head. "I confess, I did it, I'm guilty. It's a pity you're not actually the duke, otherwise you could issue a full pardon. Though if you're effectively the government of Eremia, I suppose it'd be valid. Especially if Valens confirms it. I'll have to talk to him about it. I think it'd be nice to get that business cleared up and out of the way." He smiled. "Is Framain still hanging round the camp, or is he back at Civitas Vadanis? I'd really like to do something for him, and his daughter. God only knows what they're doing for a living these days, now they haven't even got the pottery factory any more." He lifted Miel's hand gently off his arm. "Justice is all very well, but I believe in making amends. Practical help, instead of empty vengeance. I mean, revenge is fine, but it doesn't put food on the table, and isn't that all that really matters, in the long run?" He paused, and maybe he glanced down at Miel's boots; it was hard to tell. "After all, we've all done bad things at some time or other, because we've had to. Getting sanctimonious about it just makes things worse, if you ask me. Show a little remorse, make things better for anybody you've harmed in the past, do the decent thing and what more can anybody ask of you?" He reached out and pushed open the shed door. "Take care of yourself," he said. "There's a nasty rumour going round that the Eremian contingent's generally regarded as expendable, because the duke's promised your land to the Aram Chantat after the war; the more of you get killed, the fewer people he'll have to evict. It's not how I'd want to do things, but I don't suppose he's got any choice in the matter."

Captain Aureolus of the duke's general staff left the Aram Chantat pavilion after the briefing was over and went back to his tent. He sat down on the rickety chair and pulled the rickety table towards him. Farmhouses, he thought; here we are in the recently deserted Eremian countryside, scores of farms within a day's ride. It wouldn't be all that big a deal to send out a half-squadron with a couple of carts to round up some decent chairs and tables that didn't wobble like exotic dancers every time you breathed.

His job was to assign the various tasks on the agreed schedule of actions to the units best suited to undertake them. Not the hardest job in the world. He dipped a pen in the black oak-gall ink and drew a line down a sheet of paper to form two columns; at the top of one he drew a little sun, on the other side a little skull and crossbones. On the Sun side he jotted down the nice, easy tasks. On the Death's Head side went the rotten jobs. Then he took a new pen, dipped it in the green ink, to represent Vadani forces, and wrote the name and number of a unit and a commanding officer next to each Sun-side entry. A third pen went in the red ink, to represent the Free Eremians assigned to operations on the Death's Head side.

(Nobody had told him to do it that way. Nobody had needed to. You didn't have to teach a baby how to breathe, either.)

He assigned the Death's Head missions in reverse order of hopelessness and danger. When he came to the third from last, he paused, consulted his roster, gazette and army lists, then carefully wrote in: *Fourth Eremian light cavalry, Major Miel Ducas commanding.*

He paused. The name was vaguely familiar, but he couldn't remember why. Not that it mattered; the fourth Eremian light was an experienced unit, made up of pre-war regulars and men who'd seen action during the brief resistance. If they encountered enemy forces in the course of their reconnaissance, they'd put up a good fight. If they lost . . . they were Eremians, no doubt pleased to have the opportunity to give their lives for their horribly abused country.

There was also a bottle of blue ink, to signify Aram Chantat. He had specific orders not to use it unless explicitly told to do so.

A shadow fell on the page, and he couldn't read the words. He looked up, and saw him, whatever his name was: the duke's Mezentine engineer's assistant, the murderer, the freak. He was standing perfectly still, and Aureolus knew at once that he was one of those people who have the knack of reading upside down.

He didn't like it. Nobody knew for sure what the freak's rank, status or authority were. He was a civilian, but he reported directly to Vaatzes and the duke, nobody else. The general consensus was: if he gives you an order, better obey it just in case.

"Can I help you?" he said.

The freak nodded. "Let me see that."

Aureolus could feel trouble coming on, the way some people can sense an approaching thunderstorm when the sky's still blue. "I'm not sure I can do that," he said. "I'll need to see some kind of—"

"No." The freak reached for the paper, his thin, bony wrist emerging from the sleeve of his coat like a tortoise's neck from under its shell. The fingers tightened on the page, and Aureolus knew that if he tried to snatch it away, the paper would tear. It was an example of intuitive tactical thinking on a level Aureolus knew he'd never aspire to. In passing, he noticed that the freak chewed his fingernails.

"Fine," he said. "If anyone asks, I'll say you assured me you had clearance."

The freak wasn't listening. In fact, Aureolus realised, as far as the freak was concerned, he no longer existed. Galling, but on balance he preferred it that way.

"Just a moment," the freak said, and the skin on his fishbelly forehead tightened. "This entry here." He put the paper on the table; left hand pinning it down, right forefinger pointing to a name. "Pen."

Aureolus said: "What's the problem?"

The freak reached across him, so that the elbow of his sleeve brushed Aureolus' mouth. The coat, he observed, was best-quality Mezentine cloth, last year's fashionable cut, indescribably filthy with mud, oil and dried blood. He took the red-ink pen, crossed out an entry, paused for a moment, and wrote something in over the top in tiny, neat, spiky letters.

"What do you think you're . . . ?" Aureolus started to say; then the freak looked at him, and the words evaporated, like water on a stovetop. Carefully the freak replaced the pen.

"You made a careless mistake," the freak said pleasantly. "Lucky for you I was here to correct it. You could've been in so much trouble."

For some reason, Aureolus felt he shouldn't look down and see what had been changed. "You've got the authority to do that, have you?" he said.

The freak grinned. "Do what?"

Rumour had it that this man was guilty of murder and rape; that when his victim's father was captured by the Mezentines, he'd broken into their camp, killed half a dozen guards with his bare hands and rescued him. Since then, he'd disobeyed the duke's direct orders to assume command of a mission, turned a potentially disastrous ambush into a victory; and before that, when the duke's hunting party was attacked on his wedding day, something about saving the duchess's life; which duchess he wasn't quite sure, but that wasn't the point.

The freak was grinning contemptuously at him. "Thank you for your time," he said.

Aureolus felt his fist tighten, realised that the freak had seen it and now there was an almost hopeful look in his eyes: go on, they were saying, take a swing at me, I want to fight, I enjoy it. Aureolus froze. He'd fought in nine pitched battles and two dozen skirmishes in his time, been wounded twice, honestly believed he was a brave man. Now, though, he was scared. The feeling reminded him of watching dogs, the way the underdog backs down when the pack leader growls. He realised he wasn't brave at all.

The freak broke eye contact, turned away and left the tent. When Aureolus was sure he'd gone, he looked to see what had been changed. A line through the fourth Eremian light cavalry and Major Ducas; in their place, the seventh Eremians and Colonel Pardas.

He thought about that. Really, it didn't matter. The seventh were practically indistinguishable from the fourth, and he'd never heard of Pardas, but presumably he had to be reasonably competent or he wouldn't have been given the seventh to command. Then a wave of relief swept over him, making his knees tremble and his bladder ache.

God only knows what all that was about, he thought, but it's nothing to do with me.

He filled in the last two remaining assignments. To be on the safe side, he didn't use the fourth Eremians at all. Big army, plenty of other suitable units.

He made a fair copy, without the excessively frivolous sun and skull column headings. Then, just in case there was a problem, he burned the sheet of paper the freak had written on.

Later that day, he came back from the latrine to find the hated regulation-issue chair and table gone, and a solid Eremian rustic stool and small farmhouse table in their place. He made a point of not asking anyone if they knew where they'd come from.

At the next weekly briefing in the Aram Chantat pavilion, Valens reported the findings of the intelligence-gathering exercises agreed on at the previous meeting. As anticipated, the enemy had made various attempts to secure concealed defensive positions on the hog's-back ridge in front of the City. Predictably, these positions had consisted of hastily excavated and fortified artillery emplacements, mounting between twelve and twenty scorpions, supported by a platoon of heavy infantry and a company of archers. All the emplacements had been successfully taken, and it was encouraging to note that all of them were manned by Mezentine citizens rather than mercenaries or Cure Doce. The artillery had inflicted casualties, units of the Eremian second and seventh light cavalry coming under particularly heavy fire and losing a considerable number of men (their gallantry and sacrifice was duly noted in the minutes, using the usual form of words); the enemy archers too had proved unexpectedly effective. In hand-to-hand combat, however, the Mezentines had proved to be completely ineffectual, in spite of their best-quality arms and equipment. Accordingly, Valens felt able to describe the operations as a success. Not only was the hog's back now firmly under allied control; the principal objective, testing the enemy's ability to fight at close quarters, had been achieved, and the result was extremely encouraging. Naturally, it was safe to assume that the enemy would learn from the encounter and step up the combat training of their citizen levies. With only books to learn from, however, it was unlikely they'd be able to make any significant difference in the time available to them. Meanwhile, he felt confident that it was now safe to occupy the hog's back, prepare siege lines and deploy the first consignment of artillery. The siege of Mezentia (he allowed himself to indulge in a little melodrama at this point) was about to begin.

Chapter Nine

A woman was howling. She'd been doing it for over an hour (no consideration for people trying to sleep). He couldn't help listening, with a sort of revolted fascination. From time to time she'd subside, just long enough to catch her breath and rest her lungs and throat, and then she'd be off again, building up to a hysterical peak that was both embarrassing and disturbing to hear. Apparently she'd been told that her husband had been killed by the savages, out on the downs, so presumably he'd belonged to one of the levy units. He'd heard the neighbours talking, raising their voices to make themselves heard over the godawful racket: how she'd never seemed particularly fond of him while he was alive, how they'd quarrelled all the time, said all kinds of things behind each other's backs. The shock, someone said. Being left alone in the world with two small kids, someone else suggested; and that made more sense, in his opinion. He could see how she could work herself up to that pitch of frenzy if she was mourning for herself, rather than him.

When she finally arrived, the woman was still bellowing away, but he had no trouble hearing the grating sound of her fingernails on the doorpost. He stayed where he was, and waited. Her head appeared round the door, squinting in the dark he'd long since grown used to. "Where are you?" she said.

"You're late."

She nodded. "There's a crowd in the street, I had to be careful. What's going on up there?"

"A war widow, I believe," he said. "Did you bring the food?"

She handed over a basket, covered with a cloth. He grabbed at it, snatched the cloth away, tried not to pull a face. She must have seen something, though, because she said, "It was all I could get."

"It's fine," he said.

"Everything's so expensive now, with the war."

"I said it's fine, thank you." The ends of two loaves, some scraps of cold chicken, white with congealed grease. He knew she could do better than that, but it wasn't worth making an issue out of it and provoking a sulking war. "I know how hard it must be," he said carefully. "It's wrong of me to impose on you like this."

Something in his voice had snagged her suspicions. Her eyes were tighter, and her mouth was hardening. "It's all right," she said. "Tomorrow I'll try and bring some cold beef. That's what we're having tonight. A friend of Falier's brought some in to the factory, he's got a friend who works on the carts. He thinks he might be able to get other stuff, too, but what with the savages blocking the roads . . ."

He withdrew, letting her babble; it gave him time to think. When she paused for breath, he said: "Did you go and see the man I told you about?"

Briefly, guilt; then the shield came up. "I'm sorry," she said, "I haven't had time. It's difficult."

That told him she hadn't tried. "Do you think you could go and see him tomorrow?"

"I'll try."

Meaning no. "Please do," he said. "It's quite important. They're saying the savages have reached the downs; that's what that woman's making that noise for, her husband was killed in the fighting." He let the fact of a death hang in the air for a moment. Death by association. "It won't be long before they shut the gates," he said. "I've got to get out before then. You do see that, don't you?"

She didn't reply. She had that advantage. Silence was her way of falling back behind an unapproachable guard, forcing her opponent into an inadvisable attack.

"If I'm trapped in the City," he explained patiently, though of course she knew it all already, "sooner or later they'll find me. And when they find me, I'll be killed. Psellus will have me locked up in a cell, and then one morning, early, they'll come and take me out into the small courtyard behind the chapterhouse, and they'll put a rope round my neck, and that'll be that." He paused, but she was still in a posture of defence. "You don't want that to happen, do you?"

Or he could have hit her; the effect would have been the same. "They won't find you. They must think you've already gone. I haven't heard anybody say they've been looking."

He didn't bother to reply to that. "The man I told you about can get me out, quietly and safely," he said. "Once I'm outside, I can go where I'll be protected. It won't be for long," he added quickly, following up. "In fact, the sooner I leave, the sooner this whole stupid mess can be sorted out, the sooner I can come back, and then we can be together at last. Really together." He was able to say it as though he meant it, because he could remember the tone of voice he'd used when it did mean something, the precise level of controlled feeling. It worked; he'd got through. He followed up again. "That is what you want, isn't it?"

"Of course it is." Her voice betrayed her, finally. "Are you sure it's what *you* want? Really?"

Really? He was hungry. He was dirty, wearing filthy clothes, raw where he'd scratched at flea-bites; he was cold, wet, scared, furiously angry; he was ready to explode with rage and frustration, too frightened to poke his nose out of this unspeakable hovel in case someone recognised him under the dirt and filth. Was screwing her one more time what he really wanted? The question was, could he make her believe it was? Luckily, under all that cunning, she wasn't terribly bright.

"Of course," he said, and she believed him. Only because she wanted to.

"All right, then," she said. "I'll try and see him in the morning, after I've taken Moritsa to school. Will he want money? Only . . ."

He shook his head, careful not to let her see the relief. "That's all taken care of," he said. "Just say exactly what I told you; he'll tell you what to do. Really, it's for the best. It's the only way we can ever be together."

Her eyes narrowed again. He wondered if Psellus had cottoned on to that particular signal yet. He'd interrogated her often enough, by all accounts. He'd have to be blind not to have noticed it. No, belay that. What possible experience could Lucao Psellus have had with women? He knew what it meant, though: she'd seen something she

wanted, and was wondering what would be the best way to get it. Her
rodent look, was how he tended to think of it.

"Can I come with you?" she said.

His own fault, he told himself; should've seen that one coming and
prepared for it. Instead, his answer came out half raw, unrehearsed,
awkward. "God, I wish you could," he said (overdone; had she
noticed? She noticed everything, those dark, twinkling rat eyes,
unless it was something she didn't want to see). "Don't think I
haven't thought about it," he went on. "Just you and me, getting as
far away from here as possible, starting a new life. It wouldn't matter
what we did or where we went, we could forget all this . . ." He broke
off, trying to keep his eyes and face soft while he scanned her for
signs of suspicion. No; all clear so far. "But we can't," he said. "You'd
be missed. You know Psellus has got his eye on you. If you disappeared one day, just like that, we'd have no chance. It's wretched,
but . . ."

"You think they'd come after us?"

No words; just a grim nod.

"But if they close the gates," she said slowly, "seal off the city like
you said . . ."

It was an uncomfortable moment. He was sensible enough, pragmatic enough, to admit straight away that this stupid, common
woman had beaten him, tripped up his heels and knocked him down.
Stubborn pride and underestimating an opponent wasn't going to
break him a second time. "It doesn't work like that," he said, finding
a patronising smile from somewhere. "That's what the little gates in
the wall are for, the sally-ports; so that scouts and spies and messengers can slip out at night without the enemy seeing."

"Oh," she said, "I see." She was thinking, you could practically see
the wheels going round. "But would they bother? I mean, with the
war and the siege and everything? Surely it simply doesn't matter that
much any more."

He made an effort to moderate his response. "That's not how
they'd see it," he said. "Think about it. Vaatzes' wife sneaks out of
the City just before the gates close. Obviously they're going to
assume you've gone to him, taking plans of the defences with you.
There's nowhere on earth you'd be safe. Trust me, I know how they
do things. They'd find you, find us, and then . . ."

She frowned, her head a little on one side, like a dog. "They haven't found you, though," she said. "They looked, for a bit, and then they gave up."

"Because they think I'm with the enemy," he replied, perhaps a shade too quickly. "If they thought I was still here in the City . . ."

"In that case" – maddening, like arguing with a child's limited, impeccable logic – "in that case, wouldn't you be safer here, inside, if they think you're out there, and they're so good at tracking people down? If you leave, surely that'd be much more dangerous."

He felt as though he was wading in mud: the more you tug to free one foot, the harder you press on the other, the deeper in you sink. So he laughed instead. "It's all right," he said. "It's all arranged. The man you're going to see will get me out safe, and once I'm out I'll go where they can't reach me. But I can't take you as well, because it'd put both of us at risk. And I can't tell you what the arrangements are, just in case Psellus or his people trick you or force you into telling them. If you don't know, you can't tell. I'm sorry if it sounds like I don't trust you, but you know that's not true, I've trusted you with my life all this time, haven't I?" Pause; regroup, redeploy, counter-attack. "I'm doing all this for us," he said. "Otherwise . . . well, I'd just let them catch me and have done with it, save myself the grief and the aggravation of staying alive. You're all I've got, but that's all right, you're all I want, so long as we can keep our nerve, do this right. And then we'll be together and it'll all be over; just as long as you do what I say." Pause; smile. "All right?"

"All right. I'm sorry. I know I shouldn't make difficulties. It's just, I'm so worried."

"Of course you are. Me too. We'd be crazy if we weren't." Easily into his flow now, catching his breath. "But we're more than a match for Psellus and his cronies, so long as we stick together. We'll be free and clear, and then to hell with the lot of them. As far as I'm concerned, they can burn the City down. All I care about is you."

The newly widowed woman had finally shut up, and he could hear himself think. She nodded quickly, took back the basket, and the cloth; the scrupulous attention to detail of a born deceiver. "I'll go and see the man tomorrow, I promise," she said. "I love you."

"I love you too."

As she scuttled away, he wondered: what did I ever see in her? No idea, unless, just possibly, it was his own reflection in a distorting mirror. No, too complex. He'd seen a pretty face and nice tits, a pair of legs he could open like a padlock. Love was just something nasty he'd caught in the process, and he was better now.

He heard the clatter of iron tyres on the cobbles, and instinctively drew back into the shadows, his eye to the crack in the wall through which he could watch the street. He saw a carriage, recognised it, scowled. It had been his carriage once. He inflated with anger as it rattled past, sounding like a quarry, four white horses drawing a gilded box that swayed like a dancer on four slender curved springs. Guild officials' official transport; they built just one Type Sixteen a year, in the sheds south of the main coachworks in Tyregate Yard. He could just make out the shape of a man inside it: hunched, head forward, round shoulders. He didn't need to see the face.

Psellus still wasn't used to travelling in carts (to him, all wheeled, horse-drawn vehicles were carts); he knew about them only because he'd spent so many years as a young man scheduling deliveries. He knew practically to the ounce what weight of freight each of the twenty-six types could carry. He hadn't actually ridden in one until he was thirty-eight. Even now, when his duties required him to be bounced about in carts from one end of the City to the other, he always felt sick going round corners or over bumps in the road.

Glancing out of the window, he caught sight of a familiar face: Ariessa, the former wife of Ziani Vaatzes, now married to Falier, the foreman of the ordnance factory. She'd pulled her shawl up over her head to keep the drizzle off her hair, and she was carrying a basket. He saw her in the act of stepping gingerly over a puddle – why, he wondered, do women have such a morbid fear of getting their feet wet? Women and, he believed, cats – and as the cart passed her, she looked up and their eyes met. It was pure, unprovoked, uncharacteristic malice that made him smile and waggle his fingers in a cheery wave.

Well, he thought. Coincidence. Everybody has to be somewhere. The basket implied shopping, though she didn't seem hampered by its weight, suggesting it was empty. Coming back from shopping at this hour he could understand, but setting out just when the shops were shutting? He smiled to himself. No doubt she'd gone out to buy something and changed her mind, or they were sold out (shortages; don't you know there's a war on?). Something like that.

Ariessa; he couldn't help thinking of her as Ariessa Vaatzes. The facile but apt comparison was with an onion: peel away one layer to reveal another, and any contact with her ended in tears. He just had time to note the fear and hate in her eyes as she saw his little wave, and then she was behind him and out of sight. A fortuitous encounter, which pleased him. Quite soon now he'd be ordering her arrest, but certain things had to be done first.

She was still on his mind as the cart passed through the City gates and stopped to join up with its cavalry escort. They were a dreary sight: a dozen civilians perched on the backs of horses, dressed in the best Type Six armour and looking very sad. At the first sign of an attack, of course, they'd turn tail and gallop for home, assuming they managed to keep from falling off.

Surprisingly, he didn't feel afraid as they left the City behind, even though he was well aware that enemy cavalry – *real* soldiers – were lurking somewhere on the slopes of the downs, a mere two miles away. If they saw the cart, guessed what its ornate splendour signified and came thundering out to get him, he knew he'd be in a tight spot, very tight indeed. So he should be frightened, it was simple common sense, but he wasn't. He had no idea why not.

Half a mile from the outer defensive earthworks, the cart and escort fell in with a party of horsemen (the term used loosely). One of them dismounted awkwardly and limped over to talk to him. He opened the coach door, and the man climbed in, bumped his head on the door frame and sat down heavily on a cushion. Udo Streuthes of the Painters and Engravers'; formerly chairman of the mercenary recruitment oversight committee, now the extremely reluctant commander-in-chief of the Mezentine army; a short, fat man in his late sixties, round cheeks, curly black and grey hair.

"You look worn out," Psellus said.

"Yes," Streuthes replied. "I've been up since six, bouncing my balls on that damned hard saddle. I think horseback riding isn't something you should take up late in life. The body's too old to adapt."

Psellus nodded. "They say the savages are proficient horsemen at four years of age," he said. "Apparently it leads to permanent disfigurement, bow legs and curved spines. Is there any truth in that, or is it just propaganda?"

"No idea." Streuthes shrugged. "Chances are you'll be in a position to see for yourself soon enough. We haven't noticed any Aram

Chantat up there on the downs, though; Eremians, mostly, with a few Vadani heavy dragoons arrived around mid-morning." He sighed, and dabbed at the rainwater running around the edges of his eye sockets and on to his cheeks. "They don't seem to be massing for an attack. My belief is that they're an advance party sent to secure the ridge before the main force arrives."

"I see," Psellus said. "Thank you. Can we get any closer?"

Streuthes shook his head. "The danger zone starts roughly a hundred and fifty yards ahead of here, but we can't be precise about it. Just as well, really; this rain's helped, of course, damped down the earth so it's not immediately obvious where the traps are planted. They'll know we've been digging, of course, but what we've buried and where is something they'll have to find out the hard way."

Psellus dipped his head in acknowledgement. "How effective . . . ?"

"A nuisance, at best." Streuthes smiled thinly. "What it'll do, though, is slow up their advance, make them nervous and wary just knowing there's traps in there. The more time we can make them waste, the better our chances. And if we break a few axles and lame a horse or two, that's an added bonus."

Optimistic desperation; an acceptance of the inevitability of defeat, while doing everything he could possibly think of to avoid it. Well, Psellus thought; I've chosen the right man for the job, if my aim is to kill and maim as many savages as possible before they wipe us off the face of the earth. The thought made him feel ill, and he changed the subject.

"I've been meaning to ask you," he said. "Boioannes. Have you got any new leads yet?"

That made Streuthes frown. "We're fairly certain he's left the City," he said. "No sightings or reliable reports, but the general consensus is, it's just not possible for him to have gone to ground in the City this long without being found unless someone's helping him. We've identified and traced everybody who knows him and might have even the faintest motive for helping him, they're all being watched round the clock . . ." He made a vague gesture with his arms, weary and resigned. "He's not in the City, you can count on that. So, all we can do is wait till he turns up. By then, I imagine, it'll be academic anyway."

"I suppose so," Psellus said. "He's a luxury we can't afford any more, and being realistic, there's not a great deal he could do to harm us. Even if he was minded to betray the City, all the major defences we're going to be relying on have been built since he escaped, he won't know any more about them than the enemy does." He smiled. "Listen to me," he said, "trying to convince myself. I guess it's because I lived in awe and dread of him for so long, I can't believe he's simply stopped mattering. That's a very strange concept, you know; a state of affairs where I'm more important than Maris Boioannes. The world turned upside down, in fact. Not sure it's a place I feel comfortable in."

Streuthes made a valiant but unsuccessful attempt to hide the fact that he had no idea what Psellus was talking about. "He was a bit of a joke in the recruitment office," he said. "Everybody knew, of course, but he thought it was a deadly secret. Odd, really, because whatever else he was, he wasn't stupid."

Now it was Psellus' turn. "Knew about what?"

For a moment, Streuthes looked blankly at him, trying to decide if he was being sardonic or funny, or whether it was some kind of cunning trap. "About Boioannes having it off with . . . I'm sorry, I assumed you knew about it. I mean, everybody—"

"Everybody knew, yes. Everybody except me; but that was par for the course, I never knew any of the things everyone knew." He shrugged. "Boioannes was having an affair, then."

"Yes. Since before the war. We never found out who the woman was. Which told us it had to be somebody fairly unimportant; I mean, not the wife or daughter of anybody at the Guildhall, or we'd have found out who she was straight away; you know what a rumour-mill that place is."

Psellus raised an eyebrow but didn't comment. Something was out of place. He shuffled the facts in his mind until he found it.

"Everyone knew," he said, "but not who the woman was. That's odd. What I mean is, knowing Boioannes, if he'd wanted to keep it secret that he was having an affair, he'd have seen to it, but you say it was common knowledge. So he didn't care that people knew, and why should he? A man in his position indulging himself, it's practically expected of him." He paused, thought about the implications of that statement, and felt himself blush: embarrassing. "But clearly he took pains to keep her identity secret. Therefore, her identity must be important." He shook his head. "I think I'm losing my judgement," he said sadly. "The more I'm obliged to think about cities and armies and sieges, the more I feel the urge to immerse myself in little mysteries about people's private lives. I can't help it, though. It's attention to detail taken to a counterproductive extreme. Comes of putting a junior clerk in charge of a war."

Streuthes was silent for a while. Then he said: "Is it true you're learning fencing? Fancy swordfighting, I mean."

"Perfectly true." Psellus pulled a face. "I'm very bad at it, though. Why do you ask?"

"Oh, just idle curiosity."

"You're quite right," Psellus replied gravely. "I am wasting my time on pointless frivolities when I should be giving my full attention to the war. But I'm finding it helpful, even so."

Streuthes frowned. "Good healthy exercise?" he hazarded.

"Strategy and tactics," Psellus said. "Applied in microcosm. I've learned two important things so far," he went on. "First, you can't be hit if you aren't there. Second, if someone's close enough to hurt you, he's close enough to be hurt back. Either of those lessons is enough to justify the tutor's fee, don't you think?" Slowly he looked round: first at the line of the downs ahead, then over his shoulder at the newly dug bastions. "If we stay inside the defences, we're safe from a pitched battle, which we'd inevitably lose. And if their artillery can reach us, ours can reach them. We have plenty of food for a siege, which is more than can be said of the savages. I think we're wasting our time out here. Let them have the downs if they want them. I've lived here all my life and never felt the need of them." Suddenly he smiled; not the sort of expression you'd have expected from a faint-hearted clerk. "Let's just hope it rains," he said.

The next morning, the artillery (now entitled to call themselves the Artillerymen's Guild; military, therefore the innovation was permissible) staged a full-scale drill. The exercise began with ten rounds from the heavy long-distance mangonels, followed by the onagers, springalds, catapults, perriers and scorpions. Both rate of fire and accuracy were assessed by the newly appointed Guild inspectors and judged to be adequate. For some reason, the section commanders were under orders not to shoot at maximum range. Instead, they were told to pitch short, but no shorter than three-quarter range. The emplacements on the bastions were then inspected, to see if repeated loading and firing of the engines had shaken the fixtures loose. Some slight damage was detected, and orders were given to strengthen them accordingly.

Not surprisingly, the display was carefully observed by the Eremian scouts on the hog's back. They drew their meticulously detailed sketches, took some measurements with strange-looking shiny brass boxes on four spindly legs, and withdrew to report back to Duke Valens, who thanked them and sent for his mapmakers. They drew him a new map, with a dotted red line clearly marked.

Veatriz to Valens, greetings.

Confirmed. No doubt about it, he said, several times. I can only assume he thought I wasn't paying attention.

I wish you were here. I need to know what you think. What you really think. Oh, I know you'll write back straight away, saying how pleased and happy you are, how wonderful, everything I need to be told. You've always written me such beautiful letters, taken so much care over them. When we were apart, I used to wonder if our love could possibly survive us being together. That sounds ridiculous, doesn't it? But I knew it'd be different. Letters were our way of making love; secret, the pleasure of giving and receiving each other's thoughts. I used to ask myself if you'd still find me interesting if I was there all the time.

Now, though; I want to see your face when you tell me it's good news. In your letters, you took such trouble to tell me things you knew I'd want to hear. Now, that's the last thing I want.

I sit here, staring out of the window. I tell myself, of course he's pleased. He's the duke, a very conscientious man. He knows it's the duke's primary responsibility to provide an heir and secure the succession. Then I think, he's the duke, leading the Alliance in a huge, terrible war. His allies are only there to avenge the murder of his wife, they can't be happy that he's married again; and now this. How inconvenient. Then I argue that his dead princess was the last of the royal line, so when the old man dies, Duke Valens will become king of the Aram Chantat as well; so isn't it even more important that there's an heir? So they'll be pleased, won't they?

The worst part of it is when I catch myself wondering what Orsea would have thought about it. Dear, stupid, disastrous Orsea; always so desperate to do the right thing. He was so painfully aware that the succession was his duty, and of course he failed, just like he failed at everything. But, since the succession passes through the Sirupati line, it doesn't actually matter who the father is. So I can almost hear him saying, That's all right, then. Eremia's got its heir after all, though it'd have been even better if there still was an Eremia. Really; I think he'd have been pleased.

I know you did what had to be done; about Orsea, I mean. When he found out about the letters, I think it killed him inside. He knew that he'd lost me; and the wretched thing was, he couldn't ever put it out of his mind that he was only the duke because he was married to me. So, he thought, if ever he lost me to somebody else, he lost the dukedom too; he felt he wasn't entitled to it any more. Then you came, when the city was in flames and we were all going to die. He'd tried to die fighting – his duty – and made a mess of that as well as everything else. He survived, rescued by you, the man who'd taken me from him, and the dukedom as well, after he'd ruined it. His entire life was a wreck, because he'd tried to do his duty and failed. Then, suddenly, he was in Civitas Vadanis, a duke with no duchy, a married man with no wife, the slave of duty with no duty asked of him, just a stupid nuisance in everybody's way.

I know he didn't try and betray us to the Mezentines. He'd never have done that. Impossible, like breathing underwater. I think the Mezentines arranged it all, to make him look guilty, so you'd have to kill him, and that should have turned the Eremians against the Vadani, put us right back to where we were before the peace my father made. I think you knew that too. I think you killed him so we could be together. And I let you do it, for the same reason: because I love you, and because I loved Orsea. I wanted him to die; because he was in the way, between us, and because his life was such a misery to him, and nothing could ever put it right. Orsea had one good quality. He always knew when he was beaten, when he wasn't wanted, when it was time to leave, when he was more of a hindrance than a help. I'm thinking so much about him now because this has happened. Eremia will get its heir, Mezentia will be destroyed, what's left of the duchy

*will get a good, wise duke who'll do all the right things, bring
peace, make it so the fields can be planted again. Everything he
couldn't do; everything important, that couldn't happen as long
as he was alive. Most of all, he wanted me to be happy. And –
this is such a terrible thing, but I can't hate myself for it – I am.*

*I know; you can't leave the war just to come and talk to me for
ten minutes. I know you'll write me the most beautiful letter
instead. It'll have to do.*

I love you.

Valens to Veatriz.

*I've never lied to you. I could never lie to you. Like breathing
underwater.*

The news is wonderful. It's what I wanted.

*When I killed Orsea, I believed he was guilty. Afterwards, I
changed my mind. I believe that what I did was wrong. If I had
the same choice to make now, I couldn't give the order. I don't
regret having given it.*

*There's a meeting tomorrow I can't get out of; I'll leave as
soon as it's over, and I'll be with you as soon as I can. It probably
will be only ten minutes, though.*

I love you too.

The courier who took Valens' letter was a lieutenant in the messenger corps. He was shaken out of sleep by a sergeant of the guard, handed a dispatch case and given his orders: quickly as possible, urgent, vitally important, be on the road in half an hour. After the sergeant had gone, he swore, massaged his eyelids with the tips of his index fingers, and dragged on his clothes and boots, still sodden from a long day's ride in the rain. No time to eat or drink anything. To save weight and thereby increase speed, he didn't bother with a mailshirt or a helmet. A horse was waiting for him when he blundered out of the bunkhouse into the damp, dark night. A groom raised a lantern.

"Is that for me?" the messenger asked.

The groom grinned at him. "Duke's orders," he said. "His very own second-best hunter. You're honoured."

And stunned, too. Nobody rode Valens' horses except Valens. It was a beautiful animal, with the small head and long, tapered neck of the old Vadani bloodline. "I'm to tell you she'll take you all the way, no need to stop and change, if you take the old drove road."

The courier frowned. "On that?" he said doubtfully, thinking of the horse's slim, delicate-looking legs on the steep, rutted surface of the drove. At this time of year, it'd be more watercourse than road, as the run-off from the hills that formed the Vadani–Cure Doce border poured down to meet the Redwater: mud, stones loosened by the water. "That can't be right."

"Only passing on the message," the groom replied cheerfully.

The duke's own saddle and tack, too. It was almost worth being hauled out of bed for. "She been ridden lately?" he asked.

Short nod. "Half an hour a day, and she's been fed on oats and barley. She'll be glad of a chance to stretch her legs properly."

He'd been riding all his life, but this was quite different. As soon as the sun came up, he pushed her into a steady working gallop. Her pace was smooth and incredibly consistent, and he'd never ridden such a sure-footed horse. Even when he'd crossed the river and started the long climb up to the hole-in-the-wall where the cart road joined the drove, he was able to maintain the sort of speed an army horse could only manage on the flat. He wondered what the hell was in the letter that made it so important.

He let her rest and drink at Iselloen Top, where the cattle trail to the Cure Doce border branched off. From there, mostly downhill. He would have liked to know what the record was for this run. Every chance he could beat it, whatever it was.

From Iselloen down Cylinder Hill to the Hunting Gate, where the road cut a notch between two outcropped hilltops before descending into the wooded combe where he'd pick up the forest road that'd take him the rest of the way to Civitas Vadanis. The Hunting Gate marked the start of familiar country, and he allowed himself to relax a little. Even at this time of year, with the going soft, he could accurately predict how long each of the remaining stages would take. He looked up at the sun and congratulated himself on making such good time.

The sun was the last thing he saw. A twelve-inch crossbow bolt hit the back of his head, hard enough that the tip of the point broke through his cheekbone just below his left eye. He dropped off the horse like a sack.

The shot had been loosed by a captain of the Cure Doce rangers, a forester by trade, and an expert at shooting moving targets. He'd been aiming for the junction at the base of the shoulderblades, but he wasn't about to tell anyone that. He straightened out of his crouch and waited till the horse slowed down and came to a stop, dimly aware that the weight had gone from its back and something wasn't right. The captain sent two of his men to catch it, while he and the rest of his platoon went to see what they'd got.

"Vadani," someone said. "Military shirt and boots."

The captain stooped and eased the strap of the dispatch case over the dead man's head. "Duke's messenger," he said, smiling broadly. "Not something you see every day." His fingers were on the buckle of the case, but he hesitated. The satchel could well be worth a great deal of money if he could get it to Mezentia, but the seal would have to be intact; the officers of the Republic got upset if they thought someone else had read captured enemy dispatches before they did. But the City was a long way away; dangerous, too, now that the Lonazep road had been cut and allied cavalry patrols were moving about on the downs. He cleared his mind and did some calculations. He was assured of the ten-florin bounty for a Vadani messenger's badge in any event; the horse was a good one, say forty florins for a quick sale, add another ten for the tack and the dead man's boots, another five for his sword. If he took the satchel unopened to the City, that would probably bring the total up to the round hundred, but was the extra forty-five florins enough to justify the risk, or should he settle for what he'd already got?

"Now what?" one of his men asked.

"Shut up, I'm thinking."

Forty-five florins; a nice bit of money, which took some earning, but he really didn't fancy the ride down to the City. In which case, it'd do no harm to read the dispatches. Orders, troop movements, requisitions, whatever; the Mezentine agents would be bound to pay something for the information, even if the seal was broken. Not forty-five florins, perhaps, but at least ten. That cut the profit in braving the dangers of the City road down to thirty-five. No, screw that. He broke the seal, took out the single small packet and read it.

At first he couldn't make sense of it. Then he burst out laughing.

"What's the joke?" someone asked.

He nodded at the dead man. "It's on him, poor bugger. He died delivering the duke's love letter." He frowned a little. "Hell of a way to go. Here, get a look at this. His Royal Highness' own handwriting, most likely."

They crowded round, peering over his shoulder. "I love you too," one of them crooned in a comic falsetto, while another speculated as to what the Duke planned to do in ten minutes flat when he got home. The captain grinned; then, abruptly, he realised the implications.

I'll leave as soon as it's over, and I'll be with you as soon as I can.

The captain swore under his breath. A duke's messenger on the drove; not one of the usual routes, because it was rough going – also, these days, dangerous, as the poor sod had found out the hard way. But quick; on a good horse (a very good horse; too good for a mere army courier), and if you were prepared to take the risk, you could halve your journey time. *I'll be with you as soon as I can.*

He felt cold all over. Some opportunities are so good they're terrifying. If he was right about this, Duke Valens himself was about to leave the army camp and hurry back to Civitas Vadanis, taking the shortest, quickest route, the same one his messenger had taken. Ten florins' bounty for a messenger; so how much would the Mezentine agent pay for the commander-in-chief of the Alliance? There was an expression, the sort people used every day: *worth a king's ransom.* It'd be interesting to ask the Mezentines if they cared to put a figure on that.

They'd taken the letter to show to the two men who'd caught the horse. He dashed after them and snatched it back.

There's a meeting tomorrow I can't get out of; I'll leave as soon as it's over. He forced himself to clear his head and think. From here to the camp; assume the messenger left at dawn or thereabouts, because only a lunatic would try and climb the hill in the dark. Valens, inconsiderate bastard, hadn't specified when his meeting was due to start or how long it'd take. It was possible he could be here in as little as four hours. And would he have an escort with him, or was he in such a mad, desperate hurry that he'd come alone? Maybe, but he had to assume otherwise. If he planned for four hours and a minimum of a twelve-man escort, with any luck he wouldn't be facing too many unpleasant surprises.

A lot of work to do in four hours, most of it on the far edges of his experience. He wished, for the first time in his life, that his brother-in-law was there with him – a useless, idle, stupid excuse for a man, but at one time he'd been a huntsman in Eremia, working for one of the noble families there. He knew about hunting dangerous game at bow and stable, which was more or less the job he now faced. He tried to recall details from the idiot's interminable hunting stories: the driving zone, the killing ground (why hadn't he listened more carefully?). The trick, as far as he could remember, was to funnel the game into a drive by the skilful placement of obstacles, coupled with measures to induce panic, so that the quarry would seek to escape by the only route left open, mistakenly believing it had no other option. He thought about it, trying to press out the essence from the detail, like someone treading grapes.

First, he had to choose his place. Ideally (his brother-in-law's voice was bleating away in his head) you wanted something like a road through a wooded valley, a high-sided combe. Beaters up on the steep sides, to prevent the quarry from leaving the combe bottom; stops in plain view, to guard any rides or deer-paths that branched off the main road. The stable itself should be a bottleneck on the road, so that the quarry had to pass within comfortable range of the waiting archers; or you chose a sharp blind corner, and hung out nets. For choice, you wanted a long, straight stretch of road before the bottleneck (the elrick; the technical term floated into his mind out of some miserable boring evening at his sister's house; he grabbed at it thankfully, since it gave him the illusion of knowing what he was doing); the idea being that if the quarry was running flat out, he wouldn't have time to study the ground ahead for hazards, incongruities that would spook him under normal circumstances. Well, that was clear enough, made good sense. The problem was that he wasn't just hunting deer or boar in general. He had to take one specific quarry on one specific road; the wide range of choices available to the self-indulgent aristocrat wasn't open to him.

Choices: it all came down to that. If he'd understood the letter right, the duke was in a hurry. His own urgency would do the job of the hounds, which was just as well, since there weren't any. As for the road, there was only one, and the duke would be on it. A wooded, high-sided combe; now there he was in luck. He smiled, and relaxed a little.

He looked round for his men. They were standing round the dead messenger, stripping the body, quarrelling over a belt and a brooch like hounds over a carcass. "Leave it," he shouted, and they looked up at him, very much like hounds, he couldn't help thinking. "Clear that off the road," he said, "I want it out of sight."

A net, he thought.

Valens opened his eyes.

He could see through one of them. The other was blurred, some kind of liquid; not water, too thick. He could see grey sky through the thin branches of tall, spindly trees.

Then the pain came rushing back, and he heard himself whimpering. That surprised him, disappointed him, because he never made noises like that, and he'd been hurt often enough before. Not, he decided, like this. Calmly and objectively, he considered the possibility that this time, he wasn't going to survive. His mental commission of enquiry found that it had insufficient evidence on which to base any valid findings, and adjourned, allowing the pain to fill up the space it had been occupying.

On the edges of the pain, where he still had room to think (it was like an army of occupation; a strong garrison in the centre, but elsewhere its control was patchy), he felt for a sense of danger, but his instincts told him there was no immediate threat beyond the wound. That was all right, then. He didn't have to move or do anything right now. He let his eyes slide shut.

The pain came, he remembered, from an arrowhead. It was lodged, as far as he could tell, in the bottom edge of his left cheekbone. He was still a bit vague as to how it had got there; all he could remember was the astonishing force of the blow. At first he thought he must have galloped into a low branch. He remembered leaving the saddle, a dizzying moment in the air, landing flat on his back in the leaf-mould; two seconds, something like that, of simple empty-headed confusion, and then the pain flooding into him, like water into a jug.

He went back further. He'd been galloping because some men had jumped up beside the road and started shooting at him, no, them, there'd been others with him: Colonel Nennius and six dragoon troopers, his escort. He'd seen Nennius hit in the chest and arm, four arrows almost simultaneously, his eyes were already dead as he flopped off his horse. One of the troopers hit in the neck and elbow; he hadn't seen what happened to the rest of them, behind him. So, naturally, he'd kicked on into a gallop. The road ahead was straight downhill, into the trees. He'd heard shouting, the enemy in pursuit. He remembered his intention to get into the forest and lose them there. It had worked, apparently, until the arrow hit him.

He opened his eyes again and tried to sit up. Pursuit: but he remembered, and calmed down a little. He remembered opening his eyes as he lay on the soft rotten leaves, peering through the pain like fog, and seeing (of all things) a net stretched across the road, a few yards away. His horse was tangled in it, rolling on the ground, a leg clearly broken. A net; a hunting net. He remembered thinking he must have ridden into somebody's hunt – bloody careless fools, hunting on the highway, no wonder there'd been an accident – except that didn't fit the ambush (he identified it as such for the first time) back at the top of the hill. Then he'd heard voices, someone angrily shouting; someone had done something wrong, spoiled the hunt (he sympathised; there's always some idiot), and now there was confusion, things scrambling out of control, gaps in the line, the quarry able to escape. He'd realised the quarry was him.

A man had come running up the road towards him, a crossbow (unspanned) in his left hand, a hanger on his belt. He'd been fumbling with the hanger as he stopped and bent down; it was still half in the sheath when he'd noticed Valens' eye twitch, but he'd been careless, come a yard too close. Valens could remember the sound, like a thick twig snapping, as he lifted his leg and stabbed his boot-heel in the man's mouth, and the stupid expression on the suddenly bloody face as he staggered and fell backwards.

He remembered how he'd found out about the arrow. He'd jumped up, snatched the man's hand away from the hilt of the hanger, drawn it; then the man kicked him on the kneecap and he'd fallen on top of him. He'd realised about the arrow when the impact of the fall snapped off its shaft.

An arrow, he'd told himself, and then the pain was everything. It drained off, eventually, and he'd remembered about the man he was lying on top of, the predator, his enemy. The hanger was stuck right through his ribs, the pommel wedged into his own midriff; pure luck, or accident. He'd had no choice about the direction of his fall.

But that was all right. The enemy was dead, but (he remembered) there was an arrow in his face, the blood obscuring his left eye. The pain came back and closed him down. Before it wiped him out completely, he remembered, he'd moved, putting a little space between himself and the dead man, as though an accidental stab wound might prove contagious. His legs failed; he contrived to fall in a neat, convenient way, and remembered turning his head to look up at the sky, so that if the rest of the hunters found him, they'd see the stub of the arrow shaft sticking out of his face and assume he was dead. That was a small animal's trick, not worthy of noble quarry, but he couldn't care less. After that, it was all too much trouble.

And now, here he was; alive, for now, though that might well change. Pain and danger form layers of immediacy, like the core of an onion; they may come back but they aren't here now; I may die of this, but not yet. He looked round, and saw the man he'd killed. The body hadn't been moved. In passing, he scolded the dead man for ignorance and stupidity, getting too close to dangerous game without first making quite sure it was dead. He wasn't a soldier. His clothes and weapons weren't military. Obviously not a Mezentine; beyond that, his nationality had died with him. Who he'd been did have some bearing on the nature and immediacy of the threat, but Valens didn't have the energy to make a proper assessment. Just some dead man.

His horse was now hopelessly tangled in the net, worn out with struggling and the pain from its broken leg. He remembered that the dead man had been carrying a crossbow. Wearily – how expensive a simple thing had suddenly become, like bread in a mining camp – he hauled and stumbled to his feet, swayed like a drunk, waited for the pain to clear a little, looked round for the bow; the first duty of the hunter is to put a wounded animal out of its misery. Just as well his hunters weren't as conscientious as he was.

He found the bow, and there were two bolts left in the dead man's belt; but he was too weak to span the bloody thing. That surprised him. It wasn't much of a bow, not the kind that needed a winch or a cranequin or a goat's-foot, but today it got the better of him. He felt bad about leaving the horse, but he had no choice.

That reminded him. Danger; he didn't know what had happened, why he was still alive, why the rest of the hunters hadn't come to finish him off, or what the net had been for, but that sort of thing would keep. The next thing to do (he resented it; chores, before he could rest) was get away from here. Where to? Deal with that later. Walking, not really an option. He could think of two horses that might still be free and in the area; could he face walking back up the hill to where Nennius and the trooper had died, and would he be putting himself in worse danger? Question too difficult. He sat down on a fallen tree, and the pain took over for a while. It quietened down eventually, but it took rather too much of his remaining strength with it. Finding, catching, getting up on a horse now too expensive; in which case, he was stuck here, and the only issue to be settled was whether the wound or the remaining hunters would get him first.

He accepted the verdict calmly; it takes strength to panic, and he was too poor, couldn't afford it. He felt his body slip out of his control, muscles too weak to hold him still. He slithered sideways off the log. He knew what that meant, of course. He'd seen this sort of thing before: a pigeon struck by a falcon manages to get away, makes it as far as a tall tree, roosts motionless for ten, twenty minutes, then just topples off the branch. He thought about that. When he was a boy, he'd been terrified of the pictures in the margin of his father's copy of *King Fashion*; an old copy, heavily decorated, for show as much as for reading, made at a time when there was a brief revival of the Lonazep school. Accordingly, the capitals, margins and colophons were crammed with small, exaggerated, colourful scenes and sketches; the world turned upside down, the feast of all fools, the dance of death, all the standard themes of the Oblique movement. To a small boy they were rather disturbing; far and away the worst were the marginals and vignettes in which animals dressed as humans hunted small, naked men and women, illustrating the text in a kind of lunatic counterpoint. Even now he could close his eyes and see the tall, grinning hare, dressed in forester's green, ears lying back on its shoulders as it poked a hindpaw through the stirrup of a crossbow to span it; under a tree another hare crouched like a pointer, its head turned to stare up into the branches where a tiny man cowered in fear. On the opposite page, the same hare carried away its prey, trussed, head down, ankles hocked over a pole on the hare's shoulder. Elsewhere in the book deer and boar and wolves chased men and women parforce, or drove them into the elrick where the hares and foxes lurked with bows drawn, or dragged them struggling out of nets spanned between the trunks of trees. Of course it wasn't like that in the real world, it was just make-believe, intended to be amusing . . . But what if it came true, he used to wonder, lying awake at night staring at the darkness; what if something went wrong, and suddenly the animals changed somehow, got strong and clever and came to get us?

The pain was back again. It was like being in the presence of a king or a duke; everything stopped and went quiet while it was there. This time, however, it faded slowly and gradually, King Pain sharing his throne with Queen Weakness (and in the margins of their book, the hares and foxes hunted, and the doves swooped, and they solemnly portioned out the carcass between the rabbits and the partridges under the stern eye of the heron and the bear), until he slipped away into a kind of sleep, halfway between life and death, where he paused for a moment to consider his options. No choice, said the hare, with its flat ears, grin, and easily spanned crossbow. Even if the arrowhead didn't make it to the brain (and if you want to get into a man's brain, you should really aim for the eye socket), that's only the beginning. Just a little rust or dirt on the blade would be enough to poison the blood; and the longer it stays in there, the better the chances of the wound going bad, even if the hunters don't come back. A wounded man alone in a hostile place doesn't stand a chance. He has no choice; all he can do is suffer and hurt until at last he dies. A responsible hare should follow up the wounded game and dispatch it, clean and quick. Besides, added the dove (in the allegory of the hunt, the dove is the beautiful beloved, pursued by the amorous hawk; love is the predator swooping down on outstretched wings, love is the bent bow in the elrick, and all pursuit is the headlong chase after joy), this quarry is dangerous game, not food to be eaten but vermin to be controlled and wiped out; this killer of men and sacker of cities. A predator deserves predator's justice, a quick death if he ran well, the short, solemn nod to do him honour, the sprig of green foliage laid on his mouth before he's skinned, his teeth and claws pulled to mount as a trophy. He would have liked to argue the point with her, but the case she'd made was unanswerable. Respect for the dangerous animal, but no pity.

None of that need concern us, said King Pain, and the animals fell silent. All that matters now is that he should endure me in the same spirit in which he inflicted me, recognising the jurisdiction of the necessary evil. If he can manage that, we will forgive him for all those things for which he could never forgive himself, as he forgave those that roared and bared their teeth at him, killed his sheep and uprooted his fruit trees, trampled his standing corn and slaughtered his chickens in their pen. We will forgive him for the war, for killing her husband, for scrabbling with his claws on the gates of Mezentia, just so long as he admits the sovereignty of King Pain, by divine right the patron of the strong, fount of all justice, defender of the faith, chamberlain of life and death.

At which all the hares and doves and roe deer shouted; but Queen Weakness only smiled, and said: he endures you only because he has no choice, being too weak to struggle any more. You had better finish him now, because if he lives, I promise you he'll betray you, just as he betrayed your loyal servant his father. You must kill him or let me have him, one or the other. The choice, she added, smiling, is yours.

The animals groaned and stopped their ears, but the King grinned. No, he said. Let him choose.

He opened his eyes and saw them looking down at him. He recognised their faces straight away.

"He's waking up," the King said. "Can you hear me?" The Queen said nothing. Her eyes were red and wet.

Her, he tried to say, *not you*. His lips moved, but he couldn't hear words. Then he thought: what's he doing here? He's supposed to be back at the camp, assembling the siege engines.

"It's all right," he heard Daurenja say. "You're in the palace at Civitas Vadanis. You've been badly hurt, but you're out of danger." Her face told him he was lying. "They've given you something for the pain; it's probably making you feel a bit light-headed. You should go back to sleep now."

It was an order, from a superior officer, and he had no choice but to obey. He tried to smile, because they'd made the choice for him. Something for the pain, to drive the King away. In which case, why was he still there, staring down with that infuriatingly compassionate look on his face? He felt sleep coming in, filling the space where the pain had been, but before he gave in to it he made himself say, "I got your letter. It's all right. I wanted you to know."

He'd have liked to stay and see her reaction, but apparently it wasn't allowed.

Chapter Ten

The man in the common room of the Sincerity and Trust at Darrhaep was telling a strange story. He claimed to be the last survivor of a company of free rangers patrolling (the men listening to him knew what he meant by that word) the Vadani border. They'd intercepted a Vadani messenger, he said, carrying a letter in the duke's own handwriting, in which he wrote that he was on his way back to the capital and that he'd be taking the border road. The company sergeant, being a great patriot, had realised that here was a chance to capture a prize of incalculable value and win the war for the Mezentines at a stroke. The man paused just long enough for his fascinated listeners to buy him more beer, and went on to tell how they'd set a carefully planned ambush for the duke, and how he'd obligingly ridden straight into it. But . . .

(He paused again. More beer arrived.)

But the duke, he told them, wasn't alone. He was accompanied by a twenty-man escort, crack troops from the household cavalry. Instead of a simple ambush, the rangers faced a desperate battle against the finest mounted soldiers in the world. Did that deter them? Of course not. They knew their duty, and so forth.

As the rangers locked in desperate hand-to-hand combat with the dragoons (a moment ago they were household, a voice at the back interrupted, now they're dragoons; make your mind up, will you?), the duke spurred on like a madman, riding headlong into the rangers' cunning snare. That should have been the end of it. Unfortunately, things didn't go quite as planned. The sergeant, watching the duke hurrying towards the concealed net over the sights of his crossbow, accidentally squeezed too hard on the sear, tripping the tumbler and loosing a shot. The arrow hit the duke in the head. Running in to see if the duke was still alive, the sergeant came a trifle too close, and the duke, barely alive, cut him down before himself dropping dead. At that moment, the surviving members of the escort broke through the rangers' cordon, killing all but one of them, recovered the duke's body and carried it off, heading for Civitas Vadanis.

It was a fine tale and the survivor told it well. When he'd finished, a carter who'd been sitting at the back got up quietly and left the room. He went upstairs to the best bedroom and knocked on the door. A short, thin woman in a red dress scowled at him and asked him what the matter was.

The thin woman left the inn at first light the next morning, although she was supposed to meet a consortium of grain merchants there at noon to close a substantial deal. Instead, she drove her chaise rather too fast along the narrow back lanes of the Ashbrook valley, taking the dogleg route through the border country that was now the only safe way to Mezentia. When it grew dark she lit her lanterns and carried on, much to the distress of her driver and two porters. By mid-morning of the next day, she reached the customs house on the Mezentine border; abandoned, of course, but thankfully there were no allied patrols. She cleared the remaining miles over the flat at a pace that wrecked her cart's suspension and cracked two spokes, but the cart was a Mezentine Type Six and held together until she was a mile from the Westgate . . .

Which didn't seem to be there any more. In its place was a huge trench, with an enormous mound of earth behind it, its top fringed with a palisade of tall, sharpened tree-trunks. Baffled, she stood beside her trashed cart and stared, until a foreman from the earth-works hurried up to see who she was and what she wanted.

The news that Valens was dead took everybody by surprise. It was, Secretary Psellus said later, rather like being told by all your friends and relations that it was your birthday, when you knew perfectly well it wasn't. He managed to keep his fellow councillors reasonably calm and under control by urging them to consider the means by which the news had reached them. A man cadging drinks in an inn might well be telling the truth, or at least some things that were true, but on the other hand he might not. It wasn't, he reminded them, the first time Valens had died. In fact, if memory served him, it was the fifth, or was it the sixth, and on each previous occasion the duke had made a full, practically instantaneous recovery. This time, he went on, it was entirely possible that the report was true. Men die, particularly in time of war, and if the duke had been so rash as to go galloping through disputed country with an inadequate escort, he could easily have come to harm. Nevertheless, he argued, it would be foolish to do anything significant on the strength of one informal, unsubstantiated report. If Valens was dead, he pointed out, he'd still be dead tomorrow, and the next day, and the day after that. Meanwhile, it would probably be as well not to let the rumour spread through the City. For one thing, it wasn't immediately apparent what difference, if any, the death of this one man would make.

While Psellus was arguing these points in the chapterhouse, the woman in the red dress and her men were leaving the Guildhall. They weren't in the best of moods. Having repeated their news in full six times to six different officials, including the chief secretary himself (a pleasant enough man, the woman reckoned, though he struck her as a bit vague and woolly-minded for the ruler of the Perpetual Republic), they'd then been kept hanging about in various offices and waiting rooms until late afternoon. Eventually they'd been allowed in to see a senior clerk in the paymaster's office, but instead of hard cash for their reward and considerable expenses, they'd been given a paper draft, redeemable as credit against goods; the idea being that they'd take their payment in kettles, scissors, buckets, curtain rings, brooches, Type Seven travelling clocks and embroidery boxes rather than silver money. When they queried this arrangement, they were assured that Mezentine trade goods were in widespread demand all over the world (except in those countries currently at war), and they'd have no trouble disposing of the items at a considerable profit, assuming they could arrange transport to ship them out of the City; failing which, warehouse space could no doubt be arranged for them on reasonable terms. Silver money, on the other hand, was out of the question. There simply wasn't any. The government had spent it all, on food and iron for the war. So sorry.

The woman in red and her companions went to the nearest bar, where they pooled their actual cash money and found that they had rather less than they'd imagined: twelve Mezentine dollars, ninety Vadani quarters, sixteen Eremian doubles and twenty of the crumpled-looking brass discs-with-holes-in-the-middle that passed for money among the Cure Doce. Not good. Vadani silver was guaranteed ninety-six points pure and therefore ran at six quarters to the dollar, war or no war. The Eremian double was three points of silver to seven of copper, and the Cure Doce stuff was handy if you needed washers but otherwise useless. They asked the price of a room, and opted to sleep in the stable with the horses.

The next morning brought rather more cheerful news. Their cart had been repaired, the innkeeper told them, by special order of Secretary Psellus himself, and was waiting for them at the Westgate. However, if they intended to leave the City they should do so at once, since at noon precisely the dams would be broken and the outer ditch would be flooded, effectively cutting the City off from the world. The woman in red protested that that left them no time to buy any kettles, scissors, buckets, curtain rings, brooches and other junk with their precious credit notes, and if the City was about to be cut off for the duration of the war, she'd be left with a handful of worthless bits of paper. The innkeeper pointed out that it wasn't anything to do with him; then, after a significant pause, he offered to take the worthless paper off her hands for ten dollars cash. After a brief, bitter debate they settled on twelve dollars, one of which the innkeeper kept back to cover board, stabling and lodgings. They didn't part on the best of terms.

As they led the horses to the Westgate, they passed a shed in an alley. A tall Mezentine in very dirty clothes came out and called to them. He seemed nervous and walked as though there was something wrong with his legs, but the woman couldn't help noticing the quality of what was left of his coat, and the fashionably pointed toes of his boots.

"You're a merchant," he said. "Are you leaving town?"

It was the way he spoke; she was reminded of the lofty clerks who'd been messing her about all day. There were very few beggars in Mezentia, and they didn't talk like that or wear the remains of silk brocade morning coats. Nevertheless, she told him to go away.

"I want a ride out of the City," he said. "I've got money."

Normally . . . But these weren't normal circumstances. True, the cart had been fixed, the horses had been fed, just about, and they'd earned eleven miserable dollars. On the other hand, they'd had a long, gruelling dash for nothing, and she'd almost certainly missed out on the grain deal. "How much?" she asked.

The man grinned at her and opened his clenched fist. The brooch resting on his grubby palm was gold filigree set with a cluster of star-cut first-water diamonds supporting a large solitaire ruby; a hundred City dollars for a quick sale anywhere.

"Fine," she said. "Sevio, give him your coat and hat. If anyone asks, we've hired you to load the cart. Please don't tell me who you are, I really don't want to know." She held out her hand for the brooch, but the man closed his fist again. Well, fair enough.

"I want to go to Erbafresc," the man said, shrugging off his coat. "It's a small town on the Vadani frontier. I imagine you know it."

"I know lots of places," the woman replied. "We're going back to the Cure Doce, where it's safe. Once we reach the border, you can go where the hell you like."

He didn't seem happy about that, but he put on the carter's coat and hat. She made him walk in the middle, flanked by her men, so his appearance wouldn't attract attention. She made him carry her bag, which was rather heavy. He didn't like that, either.

When they got there, they found the Westgate jammed with carts and men heading for the dam workings. They struggled their way through to the gatehouse, where they found their cart. She stopped to inspect the repairs, and was impressed: new springs and carriers, new bearings, the damaged spokes neatly mended with spliced-in patches, and they'd even replaced the worn front offside tyre; say what you like about the Mezentines, they did good work. Getting the horses hitched up in the cramped gatehouse with men jostling past all the time wasn't easy, but nobody seemed the slightest bit interested in their new companion. The traffic jam escorted them slowly as far as the palisade, where they crossed the ditch on a plank bridge.

"You're getting out just in time," someone said to them. "After we've cracked the dam, this whole ditch'll be flooded. That'll give those bastards something to think about."

As she crossed the bridge, the woman looked down. The ditch was deep enough, but shouldn't they have faced the inside wall with something to stop the water washing it away? None of her business. There was a column of carts backed up on the far side, waiting to cross into the city; they were cutting it fine if they were planning on getting out again. Presumably they believed it was safer inside the walls than outside. Somehow, she was inclined to doubt that, but then again, she'd never been too keen on confined spaces.

There were guards on the other side, making a half-hearted attempt to marshal the traffic. Guards; they had armour and helmets but that didn't make them soldiers. She could tell by the fact that they were clearly not used to standing still for hours at a time. All their equipment looked far too clean and new: breastplates still mirror-bright from the buffing wheel, without the scratches that came from being cleaned off in a sand-barrel, spear blades with the packing grease still on them. And their eyes were wrong: they kept looking towards the downs, to see if the enemy were coming. It made her grateful she was leaving.

"Any sign of them?" she asked one of the guards.

He shook his head. "Not since yesterday afternoon," he said. "And that was just a handful."

Fine; a dash across the flat, and they'd be at the border. It occurred to her, not for the first time, that if they did run into an allied patrol, having a Mezentine on the cart with them wouldn't look too good. "Best of luck," she said to the guard as the cart moved off. He said something in reply, but she didn't hear it.

As instructed, the passenger kept his head down and his mouth shut all the way to the frontier post. Once they were five hundred yards or so past the Cure Doce side, she told the driver to stop the cart.

"Get off," she told the Mezentine.

He scowled at her. "No," he said. "I want you to take me to Erbafresc. Otherwise you don't get paid."

She sighed and nodded. The nod wasn't for him. Behind him, Sevio the carter recognised the signal. He picked up a small hammer from the floor of the cart, and bashed the Mezentine hard on the side of the head. He slumped forward, and Sevio and one of the porters pitched him out of the cart on to the ground. She got down, knelt beside him and prised the brooch out of his clamped fingers, while Sevio took back his coat and hat, and the other two searched his pockets and tugged a couple of rings off his fingers.

"Give me those," she said. They were good pieces, though not as valuable as the brooch. "Leave him his boots," she added. "We aren't thieves."

One of the porters was looking at the brooch. "How much do you reckon that's worth, then?"

"Forty dollars."

The porter whistled. "We did all right, then."

She nodded. "How much did he have on him in cash?"

"Ten dollars and change." The porter frowned. "That's odd," he said. "He looks like a tramp. What's a tramp doing with that kind of money?"

"Who cares?" She climbed back on to the cart. "We never saw him, all right? Come on, let's get going. If we're lucky, we might just catch up with the grain people at the Sincerity."

Which, as it happened, she did. Furthermore, they gave her a hundred and eighty dollars for the brooch, and seventy more for the rings, which paid for the grain with twelve dollars over. She sold the grain to the Vadani at the camp for two thousand Vadani quarters cash; she could have had three thousand in letters of credit but, as she pointed out to the supply officer, what could she buy for three thousand quarters in Vadani territory that anybody could possibly want?

The supply officer conceded the point gracefully. "Any more where that came from?" he asked.

"There might be," she replied. "What sort of quantity are you looking for?"

"Unlimited." He didn't smile as he said it. There, she thought, stands a worried man.

"Cash," she said firmly, "no paper. I've had enough of paper recently. It may take a while. Are you staying here or moving on?"

He did grin at that. "You'll have no bother finding us," he replied. "Just look for the smoke."

She nodded. "I'll see what I can do," she said. "It's getting harder all the time."

"I know," the supply officer said. "That's what I hate about this job. You wear yourself down to the bone getting food for this lot, and then the ungrateful buggers eat it all. Still, what can you do?"

Jokes, she thought. When they start making jokes to strangers, it means things aren't going well. "You won't be here much longer, though, surely," she said. "Not after what's happened to the duke."

His face changed. "What's that supposed to mean?" he asked.

They didn't know. Oh well. "I'd like to talk to the duty officer, please," she said.

When he woke up, his head hurt. That made him panic, in case he'd suffered some kind of permanent injury. He reassured himself with a quick inventory of his faculties. Even so.

They'd taken the brooch, naturally; also his rings and the money in his pockets. He sat down and pulled off his boots, shaking them until the pieces of jewellery he'd stuffed in the conveniently pointed toes came loose and fell out on the ground. Not so bad, then. He thought of the disapproving looks his former colleagues in Necessary Evil had given him when he'd started dressing up in flashy brooches, rings, bracelets, fobs and buckles; vulgar ostentation, they'd said behind his back, all that finery, like some duke of the savages; looks like the great Maris Boioannes has finally lost his grip. On the contrary, he thought, and smiled. A man who may need to leave home in a hurry can never have too much jewellery.

Of course he only had the vaguest idea of where he was. Somewhere in the Cure Doce country; all very well in diplomatic theory, but he fancied that national boundaries wouldn't be much of a deterrent to a Vadani patrol who spotted someone with a brown face just over the line. Besides, he'd overheard the merchant's people chattering, something about Cure Doce rangers having attacked the Vadani duke. In which case, the border probably didn't mean anything any more, which was extremely inconvenient. People could be so thoughtless sometimes.

He put his boots back on and stood up. The middle of nowhere. For a two-hundred-dollar brooch, they might at least have left him a horse. Walking, in his opinion, was strictly for poor people (to which category, in all fairness, he now belonged). Working on the hopeful assumption that the road must eventually go somewhere, he started trudging. Something (a diamond, or an emerald, maybe) was chafing his big toe.

Well now, he thought, more to occupy his mind than anything, suppose the Vadani duke really is dead. Does that mean the end of the alliance with the savages, or merely a change in leadership? Pointless, of course, to speculate without hard facts. The real question was what the savages wanted out of the war. Revenge for their murdered princess; well, he could believe that savages thought like that, took honour and blood-vengeance and the like quite seriously, but enough to bring their entire army, not to mention their herds and families, all the way across the desert? It was infuriating that he only had snippets of overheard gossip to go on. Nevertheless, he was inclined to favour the other theory he'd heard about: pressure on the Aram Chantat from other, stronger tribes; a need to find new land and new grazing, or be wiped out. It only mattered because it had a bearing on how serious they were about taking the City; and that, of course, mattered a great deal. More immediately relevant was whether it was true that Duke Valens had been killed by the Cure Doce. If so, some form of punitive action, swift and massive, was inevitable. A full-scale invasion? He thought about that. If they had the manpower to blockade the City while they were about it, then most certainly, yes; it was the best possible pretext for looting and foraging, thereby getting hold of the vast quantities of food and supplies they'd need for a sustained siege of Mezentia. If he was right about their motivation, the savages wouldn't object; more territory, more land they could depopulate and use to graze their wasteful, inefficient flocks and herds. Duke Valens was, of course, far too shrewd to embark on war on two fronts unless he absolutely had to; but if he really was dead . . .

These and other reflections turned over and over in his mind, like a woman making butter, and the more he thought about them, the harder and more elusive they became. His course of action, needless to say, was obvious, dictated by circumstances. Really, he had no choice in the matter, if he wanted to stay alive and salvage something from the ruin of his fortunes. Valens' death (if he really was dead) made little difference, unless it marked the end of the Alliance and the war. Once again he found himself frustrated beyond measure by the lack of reliable information. Without it, he was a bird with a broken wing, flapping wildly, knowing perfectly well how to fly but unable to get off the ground.

He walked on, curling his feet inside his boots to take the weight off the blisters. There were people, so he'd heard, who walked for pleasure; bizarre thought. He tried to recompile the map in his mind. An inch along this road (he struggled to remember the map's scale; was it two or five miles to the inch?) there ought to be a well-used, clearly defined cart track that went directly to Erbafresc. Or would it be more sensible to carry on to the next turning, which would bring him to the river that led, eventually, to the allied camp? Tactically, Erbafresc would be better, and in theory a Mezentine face would be safer in Cure Doce territory than across the border. On the other hand, if they were still actively looking for him and had notified their Cure Doce allies to watch out for a stray Mezentine wandering about on his own, he'd be far safer on the Vadani side, and to hell with the finer points of strategy. It'd be better to announce his presence to the allies from neutral territory than simply to allow himself to be picked up by a patrol, but if, after the Valens incident (if it had happened at all), the Cure Doce were now regarded by the allies as outright enemies, a patrol finding him in Cure Doce country would be more likely to kill him on the spot rather than accept his surrender. The train of thought made him grin: you wanted choices, you've got them.

He found the Erbafresc road, exactly where the mapmaker had shown it. Decision time. In the end, he chose to go on and take the shorter route to the Vadani border simply because it meant less walking.

There was a customs post on the frontier; abandoned, needless to say. More than that, someone had been to the trouble of setting fire to it, though it looked as though they'd been in a hurry and hadn't bothered to wait and see if the fire caught properly. The inside was gutted and blackened, but the flames had barely touched the rafters, so the roof was intact. He looked up at the sky and guessed it would be dark in a couple of hours; might as well spend the night here, under a roof. He went inside and sat down on the floor, his back to a wall. He was worn out, his feet ached even after he'd taken his weight off them, and he was miserably hungry. He sat still and quiet, trying very hard not to think about food, dozing rather than sleeping, until dawn.

Vaatzes, he thought as he woke up; through a gap in the roof he saw a grey sky, the colour of weathered lead. He'd been fretting over nothing, because Vaatzes, not Valens, was the key. Foolish of him to have lost sight of that, though such a lapse was forgivable in the circumstances. But of course, it could only be Vaatzes (poor Ziani, as he tended to think of him, even now), because after all, he'd studied him, analysed him, trained him to a certain extent, moulded and shaped him, designed the whole huge, intricate mechanism around him. In comparison, the Vadani duke was a nobody – he didn't even know his name when the groundwork for the plan was laid, he only knew that the Vadani had a duke, well thought of in some quarters, just sufficiently intelligent and capable to be useful in some capacity. Vaatzes, on the other hand . . .

He sat up, suddenly awake. Voices, not far from the customs shed; too indistinct for him to be able to make out what they were saying, or what language they were saying it in. He had no idea what the Cure Hardy language sounded like. Frustrated, he crept to the window and looked out.

A dozen or so soldiers were riding past; weary men in rusty Mezentine armour (but everybody wore it) on big, strong-looking horses, too military to be Cure Doce, therefore either Eremians or Vadani. He had his doubts about Eremians, because of the destruction of their city and the massacres during the occupation. They might just kill anybody with a brown face on principle, whereas he'd heard the Vadani were relatively disciplined, for savages. No way of telling. But the alternative was struggling on alone, and he couldn't face that. His feet hurt, and he was so very hungry.

He limped to the doorway. By the time he got there, of course, the idiots had ridden past, not looking round. He shouted, "Over here!" – stupid thing to say, but for once his usual knack for the right turn of phrase eluded him.

Two of the riders turned their heads. They hadn't seen him. Frantically, he jumped up and down and waved.

As it turned out, they were Eremians. His fears, however, proved groundless. The leader, a tall, skinny man with a badly scarred face, clearly understood the significance of a Mezentine prisoner, especially one who gave himself up voluntarily and promised valuable information, though the way he grinned was disconcerting, as though he was smiling at some private joke.

"Don't let it bother you," the leader replied, when he asked what was so funny. "It's just that you're not the first tatty-looking Mezentine I've picked up on my travels. My name's Ducas, by the way. You may have heard . . ."

"No," he replied honestly; then a faint echo in his memory prompted him. "Just a moment," he said. "You were a leader in the Eremian resistance. And before that, you were arrested for treason, during the siege."

"Quite right." Ducas smiled, twisting the scar tissue on his cheek. "And if you've heard of me, it bears out what you said, about you being somebody important. As I understand it, only the high-ups in your government know anything about what goes on outside the city walls. Or is it all different in wartime?"

"You know a lot about the Republic, for an Eremian."

Huge grin, rather disconcerting. "A friend told me all about you people," he said. "But he left before the war started, so maybe what he told me's out of date by now." The grin faded into a mere smile. "What did you say your name was?"

"I didn't. But my name is Maris Boioannes."

Ducas' face froze; he nodded slowly. "You can't prove that, I suppose? No, of course you can't. Let's see, who could vouch for you? I don't imagine Ziani Vaatzes knows you by sight."

He shrugged. "He may do. But I doubt it. The leaders of the Republic don't stroll about scattering coins to the mob or anything like that."

"I don't suppose they do." Ducas thought for a moment, then said: "We haven't got a spare horse for you to ride, so either we commandeer the first one we find, or else I'll have to send a rider ahead to the nearest inn to hire one."

"That'd be better. I don't like walking."

This time, Ducas laughed out loud. "I'm convinced," he said. "You must be Boioannes, or one of that lot. As far as I'm concerned, your arrogance vouches for you better than any witness ever could."

Ducas sent a rider ahead to the Patience Rewarded at Chora Vadanis for a horse, and settled down in the customs shed with the rest of his troop to await his return. Quite by merciful chance, he found a travelling castles board and pieces among the rubbish in one corner of the room. It was damaged but complete apart from the red angel; he carved a makeshift replacement out of a carrot. The downside was that none of his troopers knew how to play castles. Worse still, the prisoner did.

"Maybe we should have something on the next game," Boioannes said with a smirk, as he tipped over Miel's sun for the sixth time. "Make it a bit more interesting."

Miel scowled. "I haven't got any money."

Boioannes laughed. "I have," he said. "Well, not cash. Better than that." He pulled off his boot and produced a chunky gold ring. Miel had no idea whether it was worth anything or not. "Bet you this against . . ." He frowned. "I don't know. Your armour, perhaps, or your horse."

Miel shook his head. "Not mine," he said. "Government property."

"Fair enough. So what have you got?"

For some reason, he wasn't quite sure why himself, Miel laughed. "How about a manor house? I own dozens. Or the Tellwater estate: two thousand acres of prime upland grazing, or so they tell me; never actually been there myself, inherited it from an uncle. Or what about Middle Room? That's a forest, about twelve hundred acres of mixed beech and chestnut coppice. Take your pick. I really do own them all, freehold in sergeantry from the Duke of Eremia, who might just possibly be me, by the way. Tell you what," he added, with a rather disturbing smile, "I'll bet you Tellwater and Middle Room against that ring of yours. We can toss for who starts, if you've got a coin."

Boioannes shrugged. "It's a bet," he said. "And you can go first. I don't find it makes all that much difference."

They played and, after a long and hard-fought game, Miel won. He was surprised but (for some reason) absurdly pleased. Boioannes handed over the ring quite cheerfully and congratulated him on his closing gambit. "I don't feel like playing any more, though," Boioannes said. "Where did you learn to play like that, by the way?"

"My father taught me," Miel replied. He was setting the pieces up again. "He loved the game but not many people used to play it in Eremia, so he didn't get many opportunities. So he taught me."

Boioannes nodded. "Did you beat him?"

"Once or twice." He picked up a starburst and turned it round slowly with his fingertips." I tried not to, though. Discreetly, of course."

"You played to lose."

"I suppose so, yes."

"Why?"

Miel thought for quite a long time before answering. "I guess I was afraid of how much I enjoyed beating him," he replied.

Boioannes understood what he meant by that, apparently; he nodded and said, "We used to play it at school. We had proper tournaments and everything. I won for five years in a row."

"Really." Miel smiled. "What happened in the sixth year?"

"I left the school."

Miel thought for a moment, then held out the hand with the ring in it across the board. "Not allowed to accept gifts from prisoners," he said with a smile. "Besides, winning is its own reward, as they say."

"Do they?" Boioannes took the ring from him. "Not where I come from. Winning is about what you get when you win."

"I see. Hence the bet."

"Exactly."

Miel yawned. At the back of his mind, he was reviewing his calculations about how long it'd take for the rider to reach Chora Vadanis. "You realise all that stuff I promised you is useless. Nobody'd give me a copper double for the lot with the Aram Chantat in possession."

Boioannes was looking away. "And if they decided to leave here and go home?"

"I'm not actually sure," Miel told him. "In theory, I suppose it'd all revert to me, but even if it did . . ." He shook his head. "I'll say this for you Mezentines, you have a pretty uncluttered way of looking at the world. But I imagine it's founded on you always being the winners. We see things differently, I guess. We find it hard to forget that we have to live with the same people, go on seeing them every day, which means that victory is sometimes a bit of a mixed blessing. We'd rather come to an understanding than win, if that makes any sense."

"I see what you're saying, but I don't agree with it." Boioannes slid the ring on to his finger. It was tight. "Fairly academic, though, isn't it?" he said pleasantly. "After all, you must realise that as a nation you're finished."

Miel frowned, as if reproving a small, slight breach of good manners. "I grant you, rebuilding Eremia once the war's over . . ."

"Not just Eremia. The Vadani too. The savages, the Aram Chantat, will swamp you. Within fifty years or so, you won't exist any more. All this country from the desert to the sea will fill up with them." He laughed abruptly. "Which is why I lost the game just now, when we started betting. I couldn't get into it, because you haven't got anything worth winning."

The rider came back eventually, leading a sad-looking horse for Boioannes to ride. They didn't cover much ground the rest of that day, owing to Boioannes' lack of experience as a horseman. Although they kept the pace down to a brisk walk, he still contrived to fall off twice, though without suffering any injury. He was clearly terrified, and clung on to the pommel of the saddle with both hands.

It took them two full days to reach the Patience Rewarded. They arrived well after dark, and the night groom took their horses to the stable. He looked long and hard at Boioannes but didn't say anything.

The innkeeper was expecting them, and asked Miel if he was Major Ducas.

"There was a messenger here looking for you," he said. "Came in after your man there had gone back with the horse."

"Looking for me?"

The innkeeper nodded. "Duke's messenger," he said, "showed me his badge so I could tell you the message is genuine. I've seen enough of those badges over the years to know what they look like. He said you're to go back to Civitas Vadanis, soon as possible. Top priority, he told me, leave whatever you're doing and go straight there. Apparently there's riders out all over, looking for you."

Miel didn't know what to make of that. "Did he give any reasons?"

"Just said it was top secret and really important."

"I see." He shrugged. "Well, thank you. In that case, we'll be leaving early in the morning. Could you see to it that the horses get a good feed of oats and barley, and put up two days' rations for my men, so we don't have to stop on the way?"

The innkeeper nodded, then said: "About the prisoner. I've got some empty pigsties out back, but there's no bolt on the door or anything. You'll have to post a guard."

"Don't be stupid," Miel replied. "Give him a room. He's a very important man." He grinned. "If he hadn't been a bit careless moving a pawn he'd be one of the biggest landowners in Eremia right now."

In the morning, a stroke of luck: just as they were about to leave, two women in red dresses arrived at the inn in a chaise, accompanied by five outriders and an empty cart. Miel told his sergeant to make sure they didn't go anywhere, then rode over to the mounting block, where Boioannes was gazing wretchedly at the horse he was just about to get up on.

"Good news," Miel said. "You don't have to climb that thing."

"Really?" Boioannes looked as though he'd been reprieved with the noose already around his neck.

"Really. Just give me that ring I won off you the other day."

The women protested, of course; they said the chaise wasn't for sale because they needed it in their work, and even if they were prepared to sell it, the ring wasn't worth anything like enough. Miel replied that he wasn't buying it, he was requisitioning it in the name of Duke Valens, and the ring was just a polite way of saying thank you.

The women looked at him. "Duke Valens," one of them repeated. "Haven't you heard?"

Valens dead: as he rode, his knees and spine aching, his head dizzy from the relentless swaying, he tried to make a calm, rational assessment of the implications – for the war, for the Alliance, for his people, for himself – but all he could think was, *So she's a widow again*. It was a stupid thought and he was properly ashamed of it, but . . .

Instead, he made himself think: the Aram Chantat came into the war because Valens married their princess, the old chieftain's only surviving heir. When the Mezentines killed her, the succession passed, under their law, to Valens, her husband. He tried to remember what someone had told him about Aram Chantat inheritance law – he hadn't been listening properly, of course, at the time it seemed such a pointless, abstruse thing to be talking about. Under Aram Chantat law, when a man dies childless and without brothers or their issue, his widow inherits. In which case, *she* was now the heir to the kingdom of the savages; extraordinary thought, the girl he'd grown up with as ruler of a million barbarian nomads. As far as he could remember, she couldn't be Duchess of Eremia, but any man she married would be the duke. As for the Vadani succession, he didn't have a clue. Presumably Valens had cousins; everybody had cousins.

(His horse was getting tired, he could feel it in its pace and hear the tightness of its breathing. Give it another hour, then stop, and the hell with orders.)

Yes, now he came to think of it, Valens did have a cousin; just one, a child, six or seven years old. In which case – they'd made him learn all this stuff years ago, constitutional law of neighbouring countries, an hour a week wedged in between formal dancing and astronomy – in which case, there'd be a regency, and the duchess (dowager duchess, use the proper terms) would rule the duchy until the boy came of age. Which meant that she . . .

They'd make her marry, of course. It would be essential, a first priority. The savages would want her to marry one of them; but inevitably they'd have their own internal politics, especially since they'd been living with their own hideously fragile succession problem for a long time: there'd be factions, each one terrified in case the other snatched the prize. In such cases, they'd all prefer to see the heiress marry an outsider – that was why she'd married Orsea in the first place, because of the rivalry between the Phocas and the Ducas. As for what the Vadani or the Eremians thought, that hardly mattered. The Aram Chantat would want a compromise candidate, preferably someone from the least threatening, least significant element of the Alliance. He grinned; that could only mean an Eremian. In which case . . .

When they stopped, Boioannes climbed out of the chaise and came marching over to him, brisk as a woman complaining about faulty merchandise. "This isn't the road to the camp," he said.

"You're right," Miel replied. "We're going to Civitas Vadanis instead."

It wasn't so much a reaction as the exact opposite, a slamming of the gate through which any indications of feeling might escape. "I see," he said. "Sorry to have—"

"You knew, didn't you?"

Boioannes was motionless, completely still, for about five heartbeats. "Yes," he said. "At least, I'd heard a rumour, which I assume from your question is true. Duke Valens is dead."

The way he said it made Miel feel angry, though he couldn't really accuse Boioannes of any offence. He'd stated it as a fact of politics and diplomacy; fair enough. "So I'm told," he said. "It's what the merchant women back at the Patience were saying, and they're generally well informed."

"Indeed. I heard it from another merchant, in Mezentia."

You might have told me earlier; but why should he? It was just a rumour; and besides, with a mind like his, perhaps it might have given him an edge in some negotiation. He certainly wasn't the sort to go handing out information for free, and what did Miel have that he could possibly want to trade it for? "Well, I guess that's a sort of corroboration," he replied. "And it'd explain the sudden abrupt summons." He didn't say anything about her, naturally.

By the time they reached the hills above Civitas Vadanis, Boioannes was in a wretched state. He was convinced he'd caught some terrible disease, probably from drinking foul water. The Eremian cavalryman he explained his symptoms to just grinned.

"Dizzy," the cavalryman said, "headache, and you feel like you want to puke all the time. Is that about right?"

"Yes," Boioannes replied eagerly. "What is it? Mountain fever?"

The cavalryman shook his head. "Travel sickness," he said. "Let me guess. You haven't done much riding about in carriages before, right? Well, there you go, then. Don't worry, you'll be fine soon as we get there."

Boioannes scowled. Either the man hadn't been listening, or he was just plain stupid. "I'm sure it's the early stages of mountain fever," he repeated. "I need a doctor, right away. Where are we, exactly? We need to make for the nearest large town, where we can find a doctor. If I get sick and die just because you refused to help me, your government will hold you directly responsible."

"Travel sickness," the cavalryman said cheerfully. "Just stick your head out the window and have a good long puke. You'll be right as rain."

Civitas Vadanis. His first sight of it was a grey blur glimpsed through a dense veil of low cloud as they picked their way slowly down the long road from the top of the hills. When the midday sun finally burnt off the mist, the city proved to be disconcertingly small. Not a fortress perched in a superb defensive position on a mountaintop, like Civitas Eremiae. Instead it slumped in a valley, spread out on either side of a slow, fat river like jam around the mouth of a messy child. The surrounding landscape – wide, thick-hedged pastures spattered with dozens of small clumps of woodland; unimproved marshes, drainable but undrained fen – clearly demonstrated that the rulers of this country had always been more concerned about hunting than profitability per acre. Just as well for them that they had the silver mines. On the other hand, meagre and ramshackle as it undoubtedly was, it must house at least one competent doctor . . .

The strange thing was, as soon as they slowed down and the carriage stopped swaying about, he began to feel better. Not that he minded that, of course, but he couldn't understand how mountain fever could clear up so rapidly. The reports he'd read clearly stated that, unless properly treated, the patient grew steadily worse for three days and usually died on the fourth.

He'd expected people to stare at him, and the fact that he was riding in a carriage, with the cavalry troop apparently his escort, made it considerably worse. Presumably they thought he was an ambassador, come to sue for peace. Mostly they cheered, though a few shouted, and a few stones whistled past, too high or wide to cause concern. He felt an urge to wave, but resisted it. All in all, it was a strange way to arrive at the capital city of the enemy, escorted by misunderstanding and comedy. As he looked about him, taking note of the poverty of the architecture, the narrow streets, low buildings, miserably rutted and filthy roadways, he was appalled at the thought that something so wretched, so low-class, must now inevitably prevail over the Republic he'd served so proudly all his life. Still, he reminded himself, it was necessary, and he had no choice.

The confusion as to his status continued. Ducas was collected and whisked away by a party of grave-looking men (mostly Aram Chantat, he observed), and presumably didn't have time to explain properly who the man in the carriage was. A guard officer, quite junior, was hurriedly assigned to take charge of him, but presumably he either wasn't told the true position or hadn't taken it in; accordingly, he must have resolved to play safe and treat this unexpected black man as an honoured guest rather than a prisoner. It was "If you'd care to step this way" rather than "You, follow me", and the room he eventually ended up in, after an extended forced march through courtyards, up and down stairs, along passageways and cloisters, was really quite good for such an unsophisticated society. There was furniture – mostly crude local copies of Mezentine types, but a couple of genuine pieces – and an adequate-looking bed; a water jug and basin, towels; the piss-pot was a quite respectable copy of a Type Seventeen, though one handle had been broken off and wired back on.

"If you wouldn't mind waiting here," the officer said. "Someone'll be along to see you directly."

Directly: a vague term, in his experience, anything between fifteen minutes and five days. Still, it was better than the dungeon he'd been expecting, and a great improvement on the disused stable he'd been calling home for so long. He nodded and introduced the subject of food. The officer promised to take care of it, then fled. Boioannes counted up to fifty, then opened the door a crack. There was a soldier standing outside the door. Well.

He sat down on the bed, remembering that he was ill. It had slipped his mind. Still, when the food came, he'd send for a doctor. If it really was mountain fever . . .

There was a knock at the door. The food: wheat bread, cheese, salt pork, an apple, better than he'd been used to recently. A terrified-looking woman brought it.

"I need a doctor," he said, slowly and clearly. "Fetch one immediately."

Her eyes widened; she dropped an awkward curtsey and scampered away. He sighed, and started to eat, faintly ashamed at himself for being so hungry. The salt pork made him thirsty, and the water in the jug tasted strange. Nothing particularly sinister in that, however. People who'd been abroad on diplomatic missions had told him that foreign water always took some getting used to.

Being a realist, he had his doubts about whether the woman was capable of fetching a doctor. He was therefore pleasantly surprised when, a mere ten minutes or so later, there was another knock on the door. He stood up and opened it, to find a most unexpected sight: a face the same colour as his own.

"Are you the doctor?" he asked.

The Mezentine grinned at him. "No," he said. "Why, are you ill?"

Not the doctor; in which case . . . "You're Ziani Vaatzes."

"Yes."

He stepped back to allow him in. Ziani Vaatzes, the abominator, the cause of the war, her husband. But he was nothing special: a stocky man, medium height, middle-aged, hair thick at the sides but just starting to thin on top; a blunt, coarse face; big hands poking out of the sleeves of a shabby coat in the local style – a Mezentine in Vadani clothes couldn't help but look faintly ludicrous. All told, not really what he'd expected of such an important man, upon whom his hopes and fortunes had rested for so long.

"You're Maris Boioannes," Vaatzes said, sitting down on a chair like he owned the place. "Actually, I've been expecting you. They brought you something to eat, then."

Boioannes nodded. "I wasn't expecting to see you," he said.

"Ah, well." Vaatzes shrugged. "There wasn't anybody else, so they sent me. Seems to be a bit of confusion about what you're doing here. A worried-looking junior lieutenant told me you're a prisoner captured by a patrol, but someone else said you arrived in a carriage and four with cavalry escort, so he assumed you're some kind of envoy. That's not the case, though, is it?"

"No."

Vaatzes smiled. "No, of course not. You're probably the second most wanted Mezentine in the world," he said, with a slight dip of his head, "after me, of course. You were deposed in the coup that brought Psellus to power, and you've been on the run ever since."

"That's right," Boioannes replied.

That seemed to please Vaatzes a little. "There you are, then. You're neither a prisoner of war nor a diplomat. You're a – what's the word? – defector." His smile sharpened a little. "Also like me. We have a lot in common, it seems. Strange, really. Before all this started, the chairman of Necessary Evil wouldn't have had a word to say to someone who worked in a factory."

If only you knew, Boioannes thought. "Everything's changed," he said. "That's why I'm here."

"Ah yes." Vaaztes nodded. "We'd better talk about that. I must say, though, you aren't quite what I'd been expecting." He frowned. "First things first, though. You said something about needing a doctor."

Boioannes had completely forgotten about that. "I think I may have mountain fever," he said.

"I doubt it. How long?"

"A couple of days." Actually, he couldn't remember exactly. "Two days, perhaps three."

"That's all right, then. If you'd got the fever, you'd be at death's door by now. Besides, it's very rare, they tell me, four or five cases a year. Was that all, or is there something else?"

Boioannes shook his head. "I expect I'm just feeling run down," he said. "Things haven't been going well for me lately, not since . . ."

"Quite." Vaatzes was grinning at him again. "Being condemned to death and having to leave home in a hurry can have that effect on a person, I know. Also, the change in the water can turn you up: vomiting, the running shits. The stupid thing is, the water here is a damn sight cleaner than back home. But we're used to drinking our own sewage, so clean water makes us ill. There's a paradox for you."

"Is it true that the duke is dead?"

He hadn't wanted to ask it so abruptly. Vaatzes looked at him for a moment or so before answering.

"No," he said. "He was ambushed by the Cure Doce and badly injured, but he's alive. Whether he'll make it, they can't say. But fancy you knowing," he added, with a frown. "They've been trying to keep it quiet, obviously. Is it common knowledge back home?"

Boioannes shook his head. "I don't think so. At least, it wasn't when I left. Actually, I think the rumour may have started with the merchant who helped me get out of the City." The tone of his own voice surprised him; but how should he talk to Ziani Vaatzes, the abominator and traitor, currently the only other Mezentine in Civitas Vadanis and, presumably, the man who held his life in his hands? A fascinatingly complex question for a protocol subcommittee. "I asked because I need to know who to talk to," he said, and realised he'd gone too far in the other direction. Vaatzes acknowledged that with a slight widening of his grin.

"Me," he said. "Like I said, everybody else is busy. It's complicated by the fact that the chief of staff was with the duke when he was ambushed, and he didn't make it. The Aram Chantat are getting hopelessly worked up, because of the succession business – you know all about that, of course. Nobody's giving any orders, the career military are all for cancelling the siege and going after the Cure Doce, the palace is crawling with junior officers wandering around with bits of paper in their hands, looking for someone to sign them, and on top of that, suddenly we've got a high-level enemy defector, presumably wanting to sell us something." He shook his head, mock-woebegone. "I should be in the factory fixing a broken headstock spindle, but they figured I'm the only man in the city who might have a clue about what you're here to offer. Also," he added pleasantly, "I've got to admit, I'm just a tiny bit curious. I never imagined I'd ever get to meet the man who completely screwed up my life. Not living, anyhow. I'd sort of resigned myself to being content with mutilating your corpse. It's all right," he added, as Boioannes tried to suppress a flinch, "that's just the way people like me think. We know we'll never have a chance to get even in real life, so we daydream. These days, I don't do that any more. I gave up revenge a long time ago."

That seemed a very curious thing for Ziani Vaatzes to say, but Boioannes let it pass. He wasn't sufficiently interested in the man to care. He cleared his mind. "So, you're authorised to negotiate on behalf of the Alliance?"

"Yes." He said it without pride or guilt, as though he'd just been asked his name. "Now, then. Tell me what you've got, and we'll see what we can do."

Boioannes took a deep breath. "I want to go home," he said. "I don't just mean returning to the City. I want my life back. I want to be who I was, before that insufferable little clerk . . ."

"Yes." Vaatzes was looking straight at him. "I understand how you feel, as it happens. But maybe it's just not possible."

"No." He hadn't meant to shout. Shouting was loss of control, therefore weakness. "I don't accept that," he said. "I simply can't. I've got to get it all back, everything I used to have. So, whatever it takes . . ."

Vaatzes was nodding slowly. "Whatever it takes, meaning that we take the City and then give it to you."

"Yes." Not a shout. He said the word loudly, but without anger, fear, anything like that. "Once your savages have looted the place, killed as many people as they need to kill to satisfy their honour; you'll need a reliable man to put in charge of a provisional government, someone who'll do as he's told without question, keep the people under control, make sure there's no stupid dissent, nobody with dreams of driving out the invaders. After all, you'll need us, the City; we make everything, every tool, every cup and plate; I know you won't let the savages burn it all down. It makes sense. You can see that, can't you?"

No expression on Vaatzes' face. "So it's all right if the savages kill ten thousand citizens. Twenty thousand. Stop me when the number gets too big. Fifty thousand, just so you can have your old office back. Isn't that just a bit too much, even for—"

"Be realistic." His voice sounded cold, but he knew no other way to say it. "The alternative is a siege, an assault. Psellus can't defend the City. Nobody can. We aren't soldiers. The City will fall, and fifty, a hundred thousand people are going to die. Maybe all of them. Maybe, if we don't do something, the savages will burn it down and kill everybody. But if we can avoid that, you and me together, for the good of the City . . ."

Vaatzes was nodding, as though listening to the most reasonable proposition in the world. "I agree," he said. "Here we are, two outcasts, condemned to death, and we're the only ones who can save the Republic. Perfect irony, don't you think? So," he went on, sitting up a little straighter, putting his business face on, "what do you have in mind?"

"Quite simple." Just a little bit further, he thought. "I know how to get an assault force inside the City. They can go in, open the gates, it'll be easy. Just like Civitas Eremiae." He risked a smile. "Just like what you did for us at Civitas Eremiae. And in return, I get what I want, and you can have anything you want. You can be the military governor, the king, anything at all, just so long as I can be the chairman of Necessary Evil, like I used to be. Isn't that what you really want, after all? Well?"

Vaatzes sat perfectly still for a moment. Then he said: "You can do that, can you?"

"Yes."

"I believe you." Boioannes caught his breath. "And it'd make sense. Everybody would get what they want – part of it, anyway – and we'd avoid the worst of the killing, and the City would at least survive, and we could both go home. It does seem," he said mildly, "like the perfect solution."

"It is. Well?"

Vaatzes stood up and walked quickly to the door. "I'm sorry," he said, his hand on the latch. "I'm sorry, but the answer is no." He beckoned to the guard, and said to him: "Take this man to the cells and lock him up where he can't talk to anybody. Make sure there's nothing in the cell he can use to harm himself. No visitors except me."

"Vaatzes." He howled the name; Vaatzes paused on the threshold and looked back at him, as the guard came into the room. "That's insane. It's stupid. Do you really want to see the City destroyed, just so you can have your revenge?"

But Vaatzes shook his head. "Believe me," he said, in a voice that was pitifully weary, "revenge is the last thing on my mind. I've never believed in it, and I don't want it. Oh, I nearly forgot," he added, suddenly sounding almost gentle. "Thank you. You've done me proud, but I've got no further use for you now. They'll feed you, and you'll be safe, and there's not many people can say that these days." The grin returned, just for a moment. "The first thing they taught me when I joined the factory was, always look after your tools. Words to live by."

For a moment it seemed as though Boioannes might try some futile gesture of violence; but then he glanced at the guard and thought better of it. He walked out of the room like a bullock through the slaughterhouse gate; a little flourish of quiet melodrama, which Ziani quite forgave him, as he trusted Boioannes would forgive him the little lie he'd just perpetrated.

He sat down again. Some time later, a clerk came looking for him. He was needed in the duke's apartments, he said. Ziani nodded.

"I'll be there in a minute," he said. "But could you just quickly fetch me some paper and ink? I need to write a letter."

Chapter Eleven

His letter written, Ziani trotted down the stairs, across a courtyard, up more stairs, along a gallery, down more stairs, through a series of antechambers, until he met two guards. They stood back to let him through.

The duke's bedroom was dark, apart from one dim oil lamp, so he couldn't see the faces of the men crowded round the bed. There was only one woman, though. He threaded his way through and stood next to her.

"How is he?" he asked.

"The same," the duchess replied, her voice as dry as dead leaves. "They gave him something to make him sleep. They still don't know."

Too dark to see the look on her face. He wasn't sorry about that. "What can I do?"

"The doctors need you to make something for them," she replied, her voice quiet but perfectly clear and steady. "A special kind of tool. They'll tell you."

"Of course." He hesitated; one, two, three under his breath. "Can you arrange someone to do something for me?" he asked. "I'm sorry to bother you with it, but it's important. The prisoner they brought in just now, the Mezentine . . ."

"Oh yes, of course." She wasn't interested. "What is it?"

"Nothing very much. I need someone to carry a letter to Mezentia, a diplomatic envoy. Who should I see about that?"

He could almost feel the effort it took her to reply. "Major Penna, duty officer. I think," she added. "I don't know where he's likely to be."

"I'll find him," Ziani replied firmly. "Now, about this tool the doctors want made . . ."

On his way out, he passed Miel Ducas, coming the other way. Both of them pretended they hadn't seen each other. The second thing they'd told him when he joined the factory was to keep his bench tidy, don't leave your tools lying about in a jumble. But that was a counsel of perfection.

The doctors had been given a room of their own, apparently so they could shout at each other without disturbing the patient. He had to be quite abrupt with them before he could get any sense out of them.

"Basically," one of them told him eventually, "the position is this. There is an arrowhead lodged in the duke's face. It's gone in on the left side of his nose, and we believe it's buried six inches deep, embedded in the bone at the back of the skull. Remarkably, it appears to have missed the vital areas, the bleeding has stopped and at present there is no sign of infection. However, if it stays in place, the arrowhead will rust. Blood poisoning will inevitably follow, and the duke will die." He paused, as if he'd suddenly understood what he'd just been saying. "The shaft of the arrow was broken off during the fighting, which means, to put it crudely, we can't pull it out because we have nothing to hold on to."

Ziani nodded. The thought of it, steel wedged tight in bone, made him feel sick. The pain, he thought, must be unendurable, enough to make you choose death just to be rid of it. Then he realised the doctors were looking at him. Presumably it was his turn to say something, but he had no idea what.

"The arrow," he said. "Is it barbed?"

One of them replied: "We don't know, we can't see that far into the wound. But the duke believes he was shot with a crossbow bolt, and traditionally they have small, diamond-shaped heads, more suited to punching holes in armour than causing complex lacerations."

His throat itched and there was a sweet taste in his mouth. He swallowed. "How am I supposed to get a tool in there?"

One of them dipped his head, to acknowledge a valid question. "We propose to enlarge the entry channel by means of a series of probes. In these cases, we tend to use wood, elder for choice, usually the pith from well-seasoned branchwood. A simple disinfectant, such as honey—"

"How long have I got?"

The doctor looked at him, his eyes bright and steady. "No time at all," he said. "By rights the duke should be dead already. Unless we can remove the arrowhead and clean the wound out thoroughly, he will most certainly die. For all we know, infection has already set in. If that's the case, nothing any of us can do will save him. If you want my professional opinion, I believe we have hours rather than days in which to operate. Do you think you'll be able to make something that'll do the job?"

It was already there. He hadn't been aware of its arrival. He asked a few more questions, most of which they were able to answer. Then he made his excuses and left. It had started to rain, and he hugged the collar of his coat around his face in a desperate attempt to shield his skin.

(This is stupid, he thought. I've seen dead and injured men. I've killed two men with my own hands, and I'm responsible for more deaths and wounds than I can begin to imagine. The duke means nothing to me beyond his usefulness. I didn't even see it, I just heard a description. It makes no sense . . .)

He realised he was running, and made himself slow down to a brisk walk. It was dark, but he didn't need light to find his way to the factory. As usual, people in the streets stopped and stared at him whenever he passed through a beam of lamplight spilling out of a doorway or window; his face, the colour of his skin. He knew what they'd be thinking – a Mezentine, no, wait, it's *our* Mezentine, so that's all right. In the fraction of a second that the train of thought took to pass through their minds, he changed from monster to hero. That made him smile. Monster and hero. Neither and both.

Number three shift was in full swing in number seven workshop. They all looked up as he walked in, presumably fearing a snap inspection. He ignored them, marched over to an empty bench, found a crumbly stub of chalk and a scrap of steel sheet, and began sketching.

An arrowhead has a hollow socket, into which the shaft fits. Impossible to get tongs or pliers to grip it on the outside, since that would mean enlarging the wound, risking serious damage to nerves and blood vessels. Therefore he had to grip it on the inside (no choice in the matter). He fished about on the bench for a small offcut of two-inch tube, stuck his index and middle fingers inside and spread them, until they pressed against the tube walls. As simple as that.

The shift foreman came up, to ask him if there was anything he wanted. He nodded. "Get this shop cleared," he said. "Stop all the machines, move everybody out, but leave a fire in the main forge." It was only later that he realised how harshly he'd said it; at the time, he was slightly puzzled by the scared look on the foreman's face. Three minutes later he had the place to himself.

Two spring steel fingers slide up into the socket; fine. How to make them spread.

He scrabbled around in the trash bin under the bench until he found a little snippet of thin brass shim, scarcely thicker than paper. With a pair of tinsnips he cut a thin rectangular strip, punched a hole in the middle with a bradawl, and folded it lengthways. Let the strip be the two steel fingers. Further down in the trash he found two inches of eighth-inch wire; he straightened it, clamped it in the vice so that only an eighth-inch was showing, and peened it over with a hammer, giving him a disc on the end, like the head of a nail. He threaded the wire through the hole in the fingers, so that the disc pressed against them on the inside, gripped the folded shim at the base, and pulled gently on the wire. The disc slid down, pushing the fingers sideways; spreading them.

Then it was a matter of drawing, measuring, calculating, solving the inevitable small problems of application and fit; and for a while, the total concentration the process demanded acted as a kind of absolution. Let the hole be threaded and the shaft screw-cut; the disc, however, must float, therefore bore it five thousandths oversize. How thick is an arrow shaft? He could only guess; three eighths external diameter, so five sixteenths internal; five sixteenths decimal is three hundred and fifteen thousandths, therefore let the spread of the fingers at rest be two nine five to allow clearance; for strength, the fingers must be seventy thousandths thick; double seventy is a hundred forty, a hundred forty from two nine five is one five five, therefore let the shaft be one two five, an eighth, threaded standard Mezentine fine, forty-five turns to the inch; let the hole in the middle of the fingers be reinforced to one two five to keep it from stripping; spring steel throughout, tempered dark blue; a simple ratchet at the handle end, to maintain the tension; no time for that. Let the length of the fingers be eight seven five . . .

It was as though someone had crept up behind him and hit him over the head. For a moment, he couldn't think at all; then, instead of pain or fear, he was flooded with clarity. Numbers, he thought; numbers make up a specification, specifications define. That was the core of being Mezentine. A set of numbers encapsulates perfection in every circumstance where perfection is possible, and every such circumstance was reduced to numbers long ago, so that no progress or innovation is needed or possible. The only exception to the rule was war, and that anomaly had always puzzled him. It was clearly an important issue, this one exception; until now, he'd always assumed it was mere cynical expediency, but Boioannes, of all people, had shown him the true reason. *You can be the military governor,* he'd said, *the king, anything at all, just so long as I can be the chairman of Necessary Evil, like I used to be. Isn't that what you really want, after all?* It was highly unlikely that he'd meant anything profound by it, but that didn't matter. As soon as his mouth had shaped the words, Ziani realised, he'd understood, from that simple accidental juxtaposition: chairman of Necessary Evil, like I used to be; isn't that what you really want?

Presumably it had been intended as a small, sharp joke; an affectionate-derogatory nickname for the seat of true power, to which they all aspired. Necessary evil; in Mezentine terms, that could only mean the permitted degree of error allowed for in the specification, the tolerance. That was implicit in the paradox, necessary evil. Good and evil, perfect and imperfect, the simple gauge used in every process to check whether a component is the right size; either it fits or it doesn't. Between the component and the edge of the gauge lies the infinite space of necessary evil (because nothing is perfect, nothing ever measures exactly five thousandths; the limitations of the measuring tool are necessary evil), and the truth of the matter, the point he'd never grasped before but which shone in his face now like a glaring light, was what Boioannes had said. If anything is to be made, necessary evil must span the gap between specification and reality, one foot on the numbers, the other in tolerance, forming a bridge between the work and the edge of the gauge. For Boioannes and himself, for Valens and his duchess, even for Daurenja, in love with the weapon of his dreams, war was the necessary evil, the evil necessary in order to put right something that should never have been, something that violated the numbers, some abomination. To be what I used to be is all I really want; but abomination distorted the specification beyond tolerance, and so evil is necessary to put it right again. The arrow in the duke's head, the unimaginable pain, were clear breaches of specification; in order to pull out the arrow, here he was engaged in an act of pure abomination, designing and building an artefact for which no numbers existed, arrogating to himself the power of creation, which was vested in the Convention of Guilds. For every wrong crying out to be put right, there was a necessary evil. The mistake he'd been making had been to grieve for it, resent it, when he should have been accepting it as a fact.

Well; now he understood. Curious, that saving a life should help him to see the true justification for taking, wasting, wiping out lives in incomprehensible numbers. Let the dead Mezentines be thirty thousand; let the dead Eremians be a quarter million, Vadani twenty thousand, Aram Chantat forty thousand, Cure Doce . . . Not that it mattered. To make anything, take the solid material and cut away the waste. Let the waste be what it needs to be, so long as the finished work is perfect. Necessary evil.

He found that he had something in his hand, and looked down at it. Just a pair of brass callipers, Mezentine, Type Two. He stared at them for a long time, trying to remember what they were for, how they'd come to be there. Something made in the City had no place here.

Spring steel, seventy thousandths thick. He could draw down a piece of bar stock on the forge, but that would take too long. Instead, he opened the drawer under the bench, where the valuable tools were kept, and found a six-inch rule, also Mezentine; therefore made of the finest-quality hardening steel. He measured the thickness, though he didn't need to. A Type One rule would always be seventy thousandths thick. He frowned, but it was necessary and expedient.

A few cranks of the bellows handle and the forge woke up, blades of orange flame piercing the crust of the fire like arrowheads. Gripping the rule in fine tongs, he poked it under the crust and drew the bellows handle smoothly up and down half a dozen times, then waited. When the steel was yellow-hot, he laid it on the anvil and rough-cut a strip about the right size with the hot chisel. It was, of course, an act of murder; he'd drawn the perfect temper of the steel, hacked off the length he needed and discarded the rest as waste. He could feel the weight of the sin, but it didn't matter, because it was necessary. He left the steel to cool slowly, while he found an eighth-fine nut to weld in the middle of the strip.

Then it was just bench work: filing to shape, threading the rod, cleaning up, before the last step, hardening and tempering. He worked calmly, having perfect confidence in the specification he'd made and the adequacy of his own skill. When the blue-hot steel dipped into oil for the last time, whipping up a brief tantrum of flames that subsided immediately, he smiled. Every perfect work is born in fire, just as every human being is born in blood and pain, but the evil is necessary. As simple as that.

He wiped the oil off the finished fingers with a bit of rag, and tenderly compressed them, feeling their gentle, confident resistance. Then he screwed the rod into the nut; it spun freely, spreading the leaves as it went down, until, when it bottomed out, they were stretched wide under full tension, close to their breaking point but in no danger at all. He remembered the truth about spring steel: a spring bent is nine tenths broken, but if it's tempered right it'll stay that way for a hundred years. Sad, really. He'd been making springs all his life, and never understood them till now.

There, he thought, that's that done. He knocked the handle off a file and wedged it on to the end of the rod, to give the doctors something to hold on to. They'd have to burn the stub end of the arrow shaft out of the socket with a white-hot skewer, which would have to go up inside the wound channel; but that was all right, since the heat would help cauterise the wound. Then they'd be able to introduce the tool he'd just made, and everything would be fine. As for the pain, that couldn't be helped. You can only hurt, after all, if you're still alive.

Finished. Really, he ought to get the tool to the doctors as quickly as possible, but he felt curiously lazy, unwilling to stir himself. He realised it was a desire to prolong the moment, to savour it. Partly it was pride, satisfaction with his work, but those were trivial things, feelings he could easily over-ride. What kept him there was the sense of peace, as the last component of the design he'd begun so long ago slid gently into place, fitted and locked; the mechanism that delivered the power of the drive to the assemblies that would achieve the desired result; the escapement. Foolish (he smiled indulgently at his own stupidity): he'd been searching frantically for it, and here it had been all the time, wedged inside his head like Valens' arrow, only needing a simple mechanism to draw it out, with the attendant necessary fire and pain.

The duke, they said, had been wounded by an arrow in an unprovoked attack by the Cure Doce. Following a successful operation by his doctors, he remained in a serious but stable condition, and the prognosis was extremely hopeful. Throughout the long and painful operation, they lied, the duke remained calm and stoical, never once crying out. The success of the operation was due in no small part to special apparatus designed and personally manufactured by the duke's director of military engineering, Ziani Vaatzes.

"We got the arrowhead out, eventually," Ziani told them. "It took an hour, just waggling the bloody thing from side to side like a loose tooth until it finally came away. They doped him up with henbane tea and slapped on hemlock poultices, but I guess the pain was too much; he started yelling and thrashing about, and the doctors weren't having that, they said that if he moved while they were working they could nick a major vein and kill him. So they tied him to the bed and got the strongest man they could find in the palace guard to sit on his chest and hold his head absolutely still. When they finally got the arrow out, they washed the mess they'd made with white wine and stuffed up the hole with bog cotton soaked in salt water, which I gather is supposed to make him better. Anyhow, that's all I know. If you want details, you'd better ask the doctors."

There was a long silence. Then the oldest Aram Chantat cleared his throat.

"You should tell your doctor to mix bread sops, barley meal and honey into a smooth paste," he said. "We find it a most effective salve for deep internal wounds. The pain can be eased with a simple infusion of poppies." He gave Ziani a long, disapproving look, and added, "I confess to a certain degree of surprise that you are unaware of these basic remedies. Is this how you treat arrow wounds in Mezentia?"

Ziani smiled. "We don't have the problem," he said. "We pay other people to fight our wars, so Mezentines never get shot."

"That, of course, is no longer the case," the Aram Chantat said severely. "Still, if the duke is likely to survive, it is of no consequence. However, we must face the fact that he is in no condition to supervise the conduct of the siege." Beside him, the other Aram Chantat nodded gravely, while the Vadani representatives suddenly looked thoughtful. "We ourselves have no experience of this kind of warfare. Accordingly, we must have another commander, at least until the duke is well again."

A long, awkward silence. Then a Vadani cleared his throat and said: "Unfortunately, the duke's second in command, Nennius, was killed in the same ambush . . ."

A different Aram Chantat clicked his tongue. "So we gather," he said. "We would question the wisdom of permitting the commander-in-chief and his second to cross dangerous territory together without sufficient escort."

"What about the Eremian, Miel Ducas?" An elderly Vadani he'd seen before but couldn't put a name to. "He conducted the defence of Civitas Eremiae for a time, so presumably he knows about sieges. And a non-Vadani would mean there'd be no squabbling between factions."

The elder Aram Chantat sighed, as if the Vadani had said something embarrassing. "Major Ducas is not acceptable," he said. "His political record . . ."

"Excuse me." Ziani paused and looked round. He had their attention. "Sorry to interrupt, but it strikes me, for the siege itself you really need an engineer more than a soldier. I mean, once the army's in position and we start digging trenches . . ."

The looks they were giving him would have soured fresh milk. "You are proposing yourself, I take it."

Ziani laughed, then shook his head vigorously. "Absolutely not," he said. "I wouldn't have a clue."

"In that case—"

"But," he went on, speaking soft and low so they'd have to be quiet in order to hear him, "I have an assistant, Gace Daurenja. He's a first-rate engineer, and he's had military experience. With the right support . . ."

The Aram Chantat's eyes widened. "We have heard of Major Daurenja," he said thoughtfully. "We understand he took command of the raid against the Mezentines' communications, after the Vadani commander had allowed himself to be lured into a trap. He displayed great resourcefulness and personal courage." He frowned: a man who thought he knew everything, suddenly confronted with a new idea. "You believe the captain has a sufficient grasp of siege techniques?"

Ziani nodded briskly. "We're none of us experts on this level of siege engineering," he said. "It's a forgotten skill; basically, we're learning it out of books, and we think the Mezentines are doing the same thing. Daurenja's ingenious and imaginative, and a quick learner. Like you said yourself, he's proved he can lead soldiers." Slight pause; then, "He'd need guidance, of course. But that's where you come in. An advisory commission of your best officers, to help him with logistics, administration, basic stuff like that. That way, he'd be free to concentrate on the engineering side, but there'd still be one man in overall command."

Nobody spoke. The Vadani were staring at him as if he'd gone mad. The Aram Chantat were frowning, nodding. A good time, he reckoned, to say nothing.

"We will consider the proposal," the elder Aram Chantat said suddenly. "But we approve of Major Daurenja. From what we know of him, we believe he has the necessary qualities of courage, leadership, resourcefulness and determination; and, in the absence of any obvious alternative, and given that the duke's indisposition is temporary . . ." He fell silent, scowled, then shook his head. "You may inform the captain that we are giving serious thought to his nomination. We will need to speak to him ourselves, so ensure that he is available."

The meeting broke up. For a moment, Ziani was sure the Vadani were going to lynch him, once the savages were safely out of sight. But after a lot of intense staring, they walked away without saying anything, leaving him alone in the room. He sat down on the nearest chair, resting his face in his cupped hands. Well, he thought; the delivery mechanism, the escapement. It was there all along.

He sat there for a long time; then he got up and walked briskly across the courtyard and climbed the stairs to the duke's apartment. He met one of the doctors in the corridor.

"Well?" he asked.

"Better," the doctor replied. He looked like someone recently rescued from the desert: drawn, brittle and exhausted. "Sat up about an hour ago and drank some water. No sign of infection, thank God."

Ziani nodded. "For what it's worth," he said, and told him the Aram Chantat recipe for wound salve. The doctor shrugged.

"Actually," he said, "they're surprisingly good at treating wounds. Talked to one of their medics a while back; apparently they bank on saving one in three serious cases, which is a damn sight better than we can do. And I've heard stranger suggestions. There was some woman up here, don't know how the guards came to let her through, some Eremian; she said we should pack the wound with mouldy bread, of all things. Traditional remedy in her mother's family, apparently. It's a miracle the Eremians survived as long as they did, if you ask me."

Ziani smiled. "He also said something about poppy juice to soothe the pain," he said.

"Oh, we know about that," the doctor replied blandly. "Only you may have noticed, it's not poppy season, and I don't think the duke can wait that long. Henbane and hemlock, trust me, marvellous stuff. But you go poking a hot wire in an open wound, doesn't matter what kind of jollop you give him, it's still going to hurt."

She was there with him, of course. She smiled as he came in, which troubled him. "Is he awake?" he asked softly.

"Yes." Valens' voice; thin, as if watered down, six parts to one, but instantly recognisable. "No, it's all right. I want to talk to him. Two minutes won't kill me."

She stood up, and gave Ziani a ferocious glare. "Two minutes," she repeated. "I can't trust him, so I'm relying on you."

"Actually, I think you should stay," Ziani said. "You can make sure I don't wear him out, and I think you ought to hear this."

That worried her, but she sat down again. Ziani came a little closer, until he could make out Valens' face in the dim glow of the single candle.

He'd have preferred not to. Valens' face was a monstrous thing. There was a hole in it, plugged with coarse wispy cotton, the surrounding area hugely swollen, dark red. The swelling pushed his cheek up so far that it nearly closed his eye, and dragged down the corner of his mouth in an idiotic simper. He looked drunk or stupid, an idiot frozen in the moment of making a bad, crude joke. It was a nauseating sight, the sort that makes you feel guilty just for looking at it.

"I've come from the meeting," Ziani said. "With the Aram Chantat, and our chiefs of staff."

"Meeting," Valens repeated. "What meeting?"

"You didn't know." He said it without emphasis or inflection. "Well, the Aram Chantat called it. They're concerned about the conduct of the war, now that you're—"

"Not going to die," Valens said crisply. "Still, it's a fair point. What happened?"

When it came to it, he found it very difficult to say. "They've appointed Daurenja as interim commander-in-chief," was what eventually came out of his mouth. He wasn't happy with it, but there didn't seem any point in trying to wrap it up.

"Daurenja." She was staring at him. "That . . ."

"Yes."

"But that's *obscene*." She spat the word out at him. "It's crazy. He's not a soldier."

"He's an engineer," Valens said quietly. "Second-best engineer we've got." He shifted a little, trying to lift his back off the bed, but the weight of his own body was more than he could cope with. "Whose idea was that, anyway?"

Ziani looked down at him and said, "Mine."

She was about to yell at him, but caught sight of Valens' face and subsided at once, like a pan of boiling milk lifted off the hob. Then Valens smiled. That must hurt, Ziani thought.

"I don't understand," Valens said. "Why would you do something like that?"

A cue, obviously. "All sorts of reasons," Ziani said. "Clearly someone's got to be in charge while you're out of action. It can't be a Vadani. With the best will in the world, whoever they chose would belong to one of the main factions; you'd have civil war on your hands. The Eremians are all lightweights, even the Ducas, an Eremian'd have no authority. Obviously not an Aram Chantat. Daurenja's an outsider; for some reason, the Aram Chantat approve of him, and they can see you need an engineer to fight a siege. I can vouch for his intelligence, resourcefulness, determination – say what you like about him, he gets the job done." He paused, because Valens was looking straight at him out of that appalling face.

"Apart from all that," Valens said.

"Quite simple, really," Ziani replied. "If you've got to be replaced for a time, I reckoned it was a good idea to choose someone that nobody could want to have doing the job full time. Whether he succeeds or not, they'll all be counting the days till you're fit to take over again." He paused again, then added, "And he's up to the job, I'm sure of it. It's the best of both worlds, really. He can do it, I believe he'll do it well, but there's no chance at all of him replacing you permanently. Personally, I reckon it's a rather elegant solution to an awkward problem."

Valens laughed suddenly, and Ziani knew what his laughter meant: *I don't believe you, but what you say is true.* "That amazing weapon of his," Valens said. "What happened?"

"We made it," Ziani replied. "But he hasn't tested it yet. I'm not sure why. My guess is, he's convinced it'll work, and he wants it to come as a complete surprise to the Mezentines. If he tests it, no matter how hard we try and keep it quiet, they're bound to find out. As it is, only you, me and him know what it's for. Even the men who helped build it weren't told, and it's not something you can figure out from first principles."

Valens sighed. "I'm tired," he said. "You'd better go. Come back in the morning."

He was very glad to get out of there. To soothe his nerves, he went back to the factory and spent four hours realigning the tailstock of the genuine Mezentine lathe, after some Vadani had tried to adjust it.

Ziani Vaatzes to Lucao Psellus, greetings.

Boioannes is here. I'm letting you know partly so you won't tear the City apart looking for him, partly as a token of good faith.

He made us an interesting offer: to betray the City, in return for a key role in a provisional government. I turned him down. At the moment he's in the cells, no doubt feeling very much ill-used and sorry for himself. He gave me to understand that he has sympathisers in a position to open the gates to us as and when he says the word. I'm not inclined to take this at face value – in fact, I wouldn't believe him if we were standing under the big clock in the Guildhall and he told me the time – but I think it's safe to assume there's a grain or two of truth in it. You may want to investigate further.

Why should you believe me? Well, it wouldn't be the first time I've told you the truth. I gave you Civitas Eremiae. I gave you

*Valens' wedding party – it's not my fault that it all went wrong;
you should have sent a bigger task force. I tried to give you the
Vadani when they were crossing the desert. All before your time, I
know; but you can read the files. You already have, so you know
I'm telling the truth.*

In return, there's one little thing I want you to do for me . . .

Psellus read the letter again, and again, and again, until he could
recite it by heart with his eyes shut. Then he folded it lengthways and
held it in the flame of his lamp. It curled, went brown, caught fire.
When the flames touched his fingertips, he let go, and it fell to the
floor. He covered the ashes with his foot.

Half an hour later, he sent for his private secretary and ordered
him to cancel all his appointments for the rest of the day. Then he
opened his desk and took out a flat rosewood box. It had belonged to
Boioannes, and the wretched inconsiderate man had taken the key
with him when he escaped; they'd had to break it open, and now its
perfection was spoiled by cracked wood and twisted brass.
Nevertheless, he opened it, and took out an ink bottle, a pen, a sand-
shaker and a sheet of parchment. The ink bottle was solid gold,
profusely engraved with vine-leaf and acanthus patterns. The pen
was silver, with a gold nib. The sand-shaker, a tiny pot like a salt-
cellar, was gold, engraved to match the ink bottle. All three were
very old and exquisitely beautiful, conforming to no type, bearing no
Guild hallmark. As such, they were illegal to own; he soothed his
conscience by telling himself they were evidence, which he was pre-
serving for Boioannes' trial. He hadn't dared use them, of course; but
this letter seemed to call for them (and he remembered the home-
made book in which Vaatzes had written poems for his wife). He
unscrewed the ink bottle and peered inside, expecting to find that the
ink had dried up into sticky black mud. But the threads of the lid
must be airtight (more than could be said of any Mezentine-made
inkwell). With extreme care, he nudged the tip of the nib into the
ink, drew the sheet of finest-quality parchment across the desk until
it was squarely in front of him, and wrote:

Psellus to Vaatzes, greetings.

He froze. He'd had his opening paragraph all ready in his head,
but now that he was ready to start making irrevocable marks on the

parchment, he wasn't sure of it at all. He reached to the side, picked up the top sheet of the minutes of some meeting, turned it over and quickly scribbled:

So you've got Boioannes. Fine. You can have him. It'd have been a nightmare bringing him to trial, we'd have been facing civil war. If you cut his throat, you'll be doing us a favour.

Talking of favours . . .

Quite wrong, of course. He drew a line through it, and tried again.

Thank you for letting me know that you have Secretary Boioannes. We have, of course, been looking for him. I assume you have interrogated him and learned everything he knows about the defences of the City. I should warn you, however, that any such information is probably completely out of date by now. May I remind you of your duty to keep him safe and well. Please also regard this letter as formal application for extradition.

Wrong again. He crossed it out, turned the page sideways to make space, and wrote:

How pleasant to hear from you again. First: Ariessa and Moritsa are both well. Thank you for letting me know about Boioannes. I confess I have no idea what his motives were for coming to you, beyond his obvious need to get out of the City before we caught him. I suppose I ought to ask you to send him back to us, but I know you can't do that. Personally speaking, if I never set eyes on the wretched man ever again, I shall be only too pleased. We don't actually need him for anything; he can be tried in his absence, which is fine because it means I won't have to listen to his insufferably pompous voice.

Turning to your request . . .

He paused, and laid the pen down carefully on the edge of the desk, so any dribbles of ink would land on the floor rather than the desktop.

His request.

He remembered, a long time ago: he was sixteen and she (what was her name? Well, perhaps it would come back to him some day) was fifteen, and they weren't even supposed to know each other. Her family were factory people, his were clerks, and so he met her by accident every day on his way home from school. Sometimes she wanted actual money, other times it was just food or clothes. Her father drank, apparently; so did her brothers, and her mother. There was never anything to eat or put on the fire. Sometimes, she and her sister cried themselves to sleep because it hurt so much being hungry.

He wasn't inclined to believe her, because surely someone who was starving would be very thin, but that, like the bruises on her arms and neck, was none of his business. When it was money, that was all right; it was never more than a few coppers, which he could steal from his father's dressing table without him even noticing. Clothes were fairly straightforward, too, since anything a little bit old or faded went in the charity box and was promptly forgotten. Food was another matter, though. His mother was one of those women who planned out the month's meals in advance; she wrote it all down with a nail on a slate fixed to the kitchen wall – three columns: date, meals, ingredients required. If an egg or a dried apricot went missing, she knew about it, and once the crime had been discovered, the list of suspects was extremely short.

So that time he'd told her, "No. I can't. I'm sorry, but she'll know, and then I'll be in trouble again."

Silence. No words. She never *said* anything when she was displeased.

"Look," he said, "why don't I just give you the money, and you can buy it yourself? It's not dear. Fivepence a quarter. I can get you fivepence by the day after tomorrow."

Still no words. He didn't like her voice much anyhow. It always troubled him that someone so beautiful spoke in such a harsh, common voice, flat vowels and sloppy, elided consonants. In the daydreams, where he rescued her from her nightmare of poverty and they got married and lived happily ever after, the first thing he always did after he'd got her home was have her taught to speak properly.

"It's getting really hard," he pleaded. "She's starting to wonder what I want all this stuff for. I mean, if it was cakes or biscuits or fruit, she'd just think it was me stuffing my face, but flour and bacon and things like that . . ."

She said: "I see." That was all. Anything more he could have resented and resisted. His mother always said far too much when she was accusing him of something, so his anger was able to get the better of his guilt. His father, on the rare occasions when he was dragged into mere domestic bickering, never said anything at all. But "I see", in just that tone of voice, was unbearable, because the voice in his own head said all the rest for her: *you don't really love me, you're just using me, if you cared at all about me you'd do this one stupid little thing . . .*

"Fine," he replied, and he knew he sounded ridiculous, a sullen little boy. "Day after tomorrow. She's doing that lamb and pearl barley thing then. It's disgusting," he added, "looks like puke and tastes like goo. Anyhow, I'll be able to get it for you then. Maybe," he said without hope, "she won't notice this time."

She didn't say anything; and when she kissed him, it was like the scary stories his grandmother used to tell, about the foxes who could turn into women and who stole men's souls through their mouths. And he remembered thinking at that moment: this is what love is, it's the constant demands (give me money, give me food, give me happiness, keep me alive) and the incessant taking, taking and taking away until there's nothing left, but you keep on because there's no alternative; because you have no choice.

His request. Now, if he'd asked for money; nothing easier. If he'd asked for the City; well, that could be arranged, he felt sure. *Surrender the City to me, and I'll keep the savages from slaughtering everybody, I'll be their military governor, I'll double the taxes to pay their tribute, we'll double production to compensate and everything will be fine.* If he'd asked for revenge; what could be simpler than to sign a sheaf of death warrants, every official who'd been involved in his accusation, arrest, trial and punishment. Instead . . .

He could write, *Regarding your request, I'm sorry, but it's not possible.* No more than the truth; but in his mind's eye he saw her face and heard her say (in that unpleasant voice), "I see", and knew he couldn't do it.

(And why? He knew why. And it was absurd. All he'd done was investigate a mystery with his typical bureaucratic thoroughness. But in doing so he'd taken himself into every part of the man's life, to the point where he knew him better than anyone else he'd ever met, to the point where he was beginning to understand him, the way he'd never understood or been understood by anybody else. The City, he forced himself to admit, was neither here nor there. Ziani wanted this, the same way that girl whose name had slipped his mind had wanted money, clothes and food, and so he had no choice.)

As for your request, he wrote, *I'll see what I can do.* Then he took the piece of scrap paper, screwed it up and threw it on the fire. He watched it turn black and disintegrate. There were savages, he'd heard, who wrote prayers to their gods on bits of paper and burnt them, believing that fire took the words direct to the divine ear.

He thought about the other letter he'd burned. *In return, there's one little thing I want you to do for me. I need to talk to Falier. I promise you can have him back afterwards; or if necessary, I'll come to the City. I know I can trust you if you guarantee my safety.*

(Well, yes. He could do that. But . . .)

And I need to see her, as well.

Which was impossible; because one way or another, it would break his heart, and that was something Psellus couldn't allow. For entirely valid reasons of state: Vaatzes heartbroken and in despair would take no further part in the war, couldn't care less what happened to anybody, and Vaatzes was the City's only hope. And for the real reason.

He got up and went to the doorway. Just one clerk in the outer office at this time of day.

"Get me Falier," he said. "Straight away." The clerk stood up – they always looked so scared of him; they'd never been that scared of Boioannes. Why was that? – and headed for the door. He called him back.

"And when you've done that," he said, "arrest Falier's wife and have her put in the cells. Send a whole platoon of guards. I want her frightened out of her wits."

He sat down again, feeling sick. It was high time, he decided, that he got to the bottom of all this. Quite apart from everything else, it was the only way to save the City. What was preying on his mind, however, was nothing to do with the fate of the Perpetual Republic (a matter far too grand and romantic for a little clerk like Lucao Psellus). It was simply that lately, whenever he'd thought about the girl whose name had slipped his mind, the face he saw was that of Ariessa Falier, and the face reflected in her eyes was Ziani Vaatzes.

Chapter Twelve

The announcement that Major Gace Daurenja had been appointed supreme allied commander was greeted with stunned amazement, rapidly followed by the special blend of loathing and respect unique to the military. As one career officer on the Vadani staff remarked, the bugger was *everywhere*. He never slept; according to his staff, he sat up all night, sweeping through paperwork like a scythe through corn. When reveille sounded (an innovation of his own; hitherto, the military day had begun with a slouch and a crawl rather than the blare of trumpets), he held court in his tent, parcelling out the day's meticulously detailed assignments, all written in his own spiky, legible hand; in the morning he went through the camp like a ferret in a warren, suddenly appearing and asking the most difficult questions imaginable, ferociously well-informed, his disapproval oppressive but never voiced, his suggestions and recommendations admirably, infuriatingly sensible. At noon precisely he ate a basic infantry ration – bread, bacon, beans – while the heads of department reported to him. In the afternoon, five in-depth meetings of exactly one hour. The evening ration. Two hours kept free for matters arising. Three hours of briefings, policy debates, disciplinary and commissariat business. Then everyone else went to bed, leaving him alone to do the real work of the day, as he liked to call it. His final chore, meticulously observed, was the composition of a detailed report for Duke Valens, sent off at dawn each day by duke's messenger, with a dozen cavalry troopers as escort: and another, similar but even longer and more detailed, for the Aram Chantat liaison.

"We must admit," the liaison told him one evening, after an exhaustive discussion of the problems and practicalities of large-scale military laundry, "that had Engineer Vaatzes not recommended you for this post, we would not have considered you for it. True, we were greatly impressed with your skill and enterprise in the matter of the fortress on the Lonazep road. But we believed that you lacked military experience. Clearly that was not the case."

Daurenja smiled. "I'm fortunate," he said. "I've done a bit of nearly everything in my time. My rule is, always learn a new skill if you can, it'll come in useful sooner or later."

The liaison nodded gently. "You would appear to have had ample opportunity," he said. "We have been making enquiries about you." He paused, face expressionless. "An interesting life, so far."

"Yes," Daurenja said.

A slight movement of the head. "It's not for us to pass judgement," the liaison went on, "particularly as regards crimes – alleged crimes – committed by foreigners against foreigners outside our jurisdiction, long before this alliance was formed. They do not concern us, except insofar as they provide insights into the nature and character of the man accused of them. Any future misconduct, however . . ." (He paused: one, two seconds.) " . . . will be regarded as very much our business. In such matters, we are not tolerant people. There is almost no crime in our society. Murder, rape, theft are things we know about only by report; we find them impossible to understand, because we have no experience of them. You will ensure that from now on, your behaviour conforms to our standards and expectations."

Daurenja lowered his head; like a dog, the liaison thought, recognising the authority of the pack leader. "Of course," he said. "You have my word."

"Excellent. In that case, the subject is closed." He shivered a little, pleased to have got that out of the way. "Now," he went on, "we shall discuss your progress towards the next stage of the siege."

Twenty-five thousand men, with shovels.

The watchmen on the embankment saw them a long way off, and sent frantic messages to Secretary Psellus at the Guildhall. A vast army, they said, a cloud of dust that blotted out the sun. Anticipating the order, the colonel of the hastily formed first Mezentine cavalry commanded his terrified men to muster and saddle up. No order came.

Secretary Psellus came instead, puffing hoarsely as he climbed the steps up on to the top of the embankment (or *glacis*, as he called it; he used a lot of weird-sounding words, which people said he got out of old books). He didn't seem particularly concerned. "It's all right," he told them, after ten minutes of silent peering into the dust. "They aren't going to attack. There's not enough of them, and they haven't brought heavy equipment. Could somebody tell Colonel Sporades to let his men get off their horses, please? They'll only become restive if they're kept standing about like that."

Psellus was right. The column halted about fifty yards outside the extreme range of the heaviest trebuchets. They appeared to be doing something, but nobody could make out what. After an hour of agonising suspense, the watch officer sent out three observers, mounted on the fastest horses in the City. They walked out and galloped back.

"They look like they're digging a trench," was all they had to say for themselves. "Thousands of them, with picks and shovels, and there's a bunch of them unloading timbers off wagons."

The watchers on the embankment relaxed a little. The enemy had come, but they weren't going to attack; instead, they were digging a trench – a latrine, perhaps, or graves for their own dead, victims of a highly contagious outbreak of plague (wouldn't that be nice), or maybe they were planning on planting some climbing beans. Like it mattered. They weren't going to attack. Nothing to worry about.

But Psellus was worried, though he tried, hard and successfully, not to show it. He knew exactly what they were doing. The trench they were digging would run parallel with the embankment frontage for something like a hundred yards; it would be six feet deep by three feet wide. By the time they'd finished it, the watchers on the embankment would have lost interest, and so wouldn't notice when the line of the trench began to change, creeping gradually slantwise, approaching the embankment, one yard forward for every twenty leading away. Then it would stop and angle sharply back – thirty degrees would be best practice, though it depended on how stiff and rocky the ground was – and begin its slow zigzag approach to the

City: forty yards, an angled turn, another forty yards, and so on. Being mostly side-on, the trench would be sheltered from artillery fire (if it came on straight, at right angles, an expert artilleryman could shoot down into it), and the spoil would always be heaped on the side facing the City, to give additional cover. He'd seen it all, reduced to neatly ruled lines in diagrams, in the old book. Once the trench came within easy shot of the engines on the embankment, he'd start to see pavises (tall, broad wicker shields, mounted on wheeled carriages) put out to guard the sappers from arrows and catapult shot lobbed up high. Once the pavises appeared, of course, they'd begin their own artillery bombardment; its purpose not to kill men or damage machines or structures, but simply to keep heads down and rule out any risk of a sortie from the gates to force the trenches and kill the sappers. In all likelihood, if his enemy was proposing to do the job properly, when this trench was halfway another one would start off, aimed at a different point on the embankment; one of them would be a blind, to leave him no choice but to divide his forces. The other would be the real thing, and when it eventually sidled up to the base of the mound . . .

He didn't want to think about that. From the forward point of the leading bastion he could see nothing but small, teeming shapes, the very occasional flash of light on a shovel blade fresh from the forge. According to the old book, an acceptable rate of progress would be a hundred yards every twenty-four hours; so, with a scale map, an abacus and a protractor, it'd be an easy enough job to calculate exactly how long it would be before the trench reached the flooded ditch at the foot of the embankment, on which, he knew, his people were placing so much fragile hope. They hadn't read the book, of course. With cruel impartiality, the book told you how to build an uncrossable moat in chapter six, and how to cross it with minimal casualties in chapter nine. In chapter ten it gave instructions on how to disrupt the assault on the moat, to the utter discomfiture of the enemy – but not if they'd read chapter thirteen, countermeasures against disruption. So detailed, so clearly written, so authoritative; you could read the whole history of the siege there, from the first spade stuck in the ground to the collapse of the last undermined wall. You could figure out a precise schedule, with estimates of killed and wounded accurate to within five per cent plus or minus. Simply by reading to the end of the book, you'd know what was going to happen. Curious, that: a hundred years before Ziani Vaatzes was born, before Boioannes decided that the best way to advance his career was a war, before the minor clerk Psellus took the decision to invade Eremia and slaughter its people, the book had already foreseen and planned it all. The schematics, the working drawings, every detail of the design, the exact specifications of the death of the City of Mezentia had been there, pressed like dried flowers between the book's covers, all along.

Well, Psellus thought, I've been condemned to death by a man writing a book a century before I was born, and according to the specification there's nothing at all I can do about it. But (he smiled to himself) I've got something he never anticipated, which might yet render all this digging and building and piling up earth and burning completely irrelevant. I've got Ziani Vaatzes.

"Any idea what all this is in aid of?" Someone was talking to him. Oachem Phrazus, superintendent of mid-range artillery; an idiot, but too noisy not to be put in charge of something. The book-writer would've known all about him. Psellus pulled a grave face, and shrugged.

"Your guess is as good as mine," he said.

"Well, if it keeps them happy and out of mischief," Phrazus replied indulgently. "They can dig their little molehills all they like. Soon as they come in range of my Type Seventeens, they'll wish they'd never been born."

(No; because by then they'll be shovelling the earth from the trench into stout wicker baskets, called gabions, and stacking them five deep and three high on the lip of the trench. Your catapult stones will smash the baskets and spray dirt and gravel all over the place, but you'll be wasting your time. I know this, because to all intents and purposes it's already happened.)

"Let's hope so," Psellus said cheerfully. "Would you mind very much staying here for a while and keeping an eye on things? There's a job I've got to do back at the Guildhall. If anything important happens, send someone to let me know."

Phrazus nodded, looking over Psellus' shoulder at the swarming black dots in the distance. "Of course," he said. "But nothing's going to happen, I can promise you that. My guess is, they're building a bunker. Somewhere safe where their leaders can cower once we start bombarding the hell out of them."

Psellus smiled and left him. A covered chair was waiting to carry him back to the Guildhall, but he waved it on, preferring to walk. One good thing: he'd had more exercise in the time since he'd succeeded Boioannes than in the whole of the rest of his adult life. By the time the savages killed him, he ought to be splendidly fit and healthy.

"Falier's wife," he said to the Guildhall guard captain. "Which cell is she in?"

The captain gave him a number; a specified cell in a particular row in a block on the third floor of the west wing. "I'll have her brought up to your office, shall I?" he said.

Psellus shook his head. "I think I'd rather go to her," he said. "Thank you for the offer, though."

The captain looked surprised, but he couldn't be expected to understand. The reproachful look on his face said, *why would anybody want to go visiting in a dirty, smelly prison?* But, of course, he had no choice.

It was the first time he'd been in a place like this, and naturally he had no idea what it was like. He'd anticipated darkness, filth, damp, stench, rotting straw, the white leach of saltpetre streaking the walls, the olive-pit shapes of rat droppings. Instead it was well-lit, savagely clean, not a speck of dust or a cobweb anywhere. Of course. In real terms, the jailers were prisoners too. They swept and dusted and scrubbed because there was nothing else to do in their warehouse crammed with toxic human waste. That was the truly horrifying thing about it: the sense of time as an enemy, to be fought tooth and nail (but there was so much of it; you killed an hour, but what good did that do when there were thousands, hundreds of thousands, millions more hours just waiting to take its place? Like a siege).

The corridor his directions led him to had been whitewashed recently. It glared at him, and the sound of his heels on the brick floor was embarrassingly loud. The duty warder asked him if it was his first visit to the cells, as though he was here to cut a tape and open something. It took three keys to open the steel door.

She looked up as he came in. "Oh," she said. "It's you."

"Me," he confirmed. "Is it all right if I sit down?"

Whitewashed brick. Twelve feet by eight. A brick ledge stuck out of the wall, covered by a thin mattress. A water jug sat on the floor. That was it. All scrupulously clean, of course.

She sat down on the bed. "What on?" she said.

He conceded the first scratch. "The floor, I suppose," he said, and made the effort of folding his legs and back, settling himself as best he could into the corner by the door. "Are you warm enough in here?" he asked without thinking.

She nodded. "It's always the same," she said, and he thought: well, it would be. Just cold enough to be mildly uncomfortable, if you're wearing a plain white cotton bag with holes for your head and arms, and you have no blanket, but not cold enough to do you any harm. Everything always the same. Nothing, no defence, standing between you and infinite time.

"I expect you're wondering why you're here," he said.

"No," she replied.

He let that go. Just by being there, he knew, he was giving her the victory; every minute he spent with her was a massacre of her enemy. The almost impossible task he faced was turning that fact to his advantage.

"Moritsa's fine," he said. "I made sure. She's been well looked after, at the orphanage."

A tiny glow of anger in her eyes, quickly fading. "That's good," she said.

"I can get you out of here, you know," he said gently. "One word from me, and you can go home."

"I know."

He'd forgotten just how formidable she could be; and he'd made a mistake, he realised, by bringing her here. A place like this would only make her stronger. "I just need you to tell me a few things, that's all."

"You can ask."

He watched her closely. There was more to see in the whitewashed wall behind her head. "It's about your husband – your former husband, I mean, Ziani."

"I thought it might be."

He nodded. "I've thought about him a great deal," Psellus went on, "about the sort of man he was – good heavens, listen to me, I'm talking about him as though he's dead; the sort of man he *is*. I feel I've got to know him quite well. I met him; did I tell you that? Anyway, I've studied him quite carefully, ever since this whole wretched business began, and every time I try and make sense of it all, I keep coming up against a solid wall. You see, I can't for the life of me figure out why he did it."

Not a flicker. "Did what?"

"Why he built the doll. No," he corrected himself, "that's not it. He built the doll because Moritsa wanted one. What I can't under-stand is why he changed the design, improved it the way he did. That was so wildly out of character for such a sensible, law-abiding man. And there was no need for it, no need at all."

She shrugged, and he thought of a lizard on a wall, so frugal with its movements. Of course, he realised, it's no wonder she's adapted so well to this environment. She's been in one kind of prison or another all her life. "It's all right," he said pleasantly, "I quite understand. You don't have to say a word if you don't want to. I'll just tell you what I think, the conclusions I've reached, and maybe you'll feel like commenting. All right?"

Another shrug. "If you like."

"Thank you." He shifted a little; his left leg was going to sleep. When had he last sat on a floor? he asked himself. When he went to Civitas Vadanis to meet Ziani Vaatzes, of course. "Yes," he went on, "it's a mystery, isn't it? It's been haunting me, you might say, ever since I first looked into the case. Everything I've learned about Ziani – I mean Vaatzes – leads me to believe he'd be the last man on earth who'd ever do such a thing. He isn't a free thinker, a born rebel, the sort who breaks rules just because they're there. I think he genuinely believes in the Guild system, the inviolability – is that a word, I wonder? – of the specifications, all that rather high-flown theoretical stuff. I was so puzzled," he went on, deliberately allowing his voice to drone, "that in the end I turned to the charge sheet, just to have a look at these terrible illegal modifications he risked every-thing to make."

He paused. Of course she said nothing, gave no sign that he was there in the cell with her.

"At first glance," he said, "to a non-specialist like me, they simply didn't make any sense. An awful lot of work, the risk, needless to say, but they didn't actually achieve anything. What I mean is, they didn't improve the doll at all, make it work any better. I was starting to think I'd never understand when at last it came to me, the proverbial flash of lightning. When Compliance raided your house, the doll wasn't finished. The modifications didn't seem to do anything because they weren't complete. There," he added with a smile. "What do you make of that?"

She frowned. "Like I keep telling you," she said, "I don't know anything about it."

"Ah well." He nodded a couple of times. "In that case, I'll have to explain my theory. It's only a theory, of course; I can't prove any of it."

He took a deep breath, organised his mind; then he said: "Once I'd got that assumption, I started reading up in the Guildhall library, about design theory. Desperately complicated stuff, needless to say, and very difficult for an elderly clerk like me to understand. But I kept at it, whenever I had a spare half-hour or so, and eventually I knew enough about how mechanisms work to hazard a guess at what Ziani was up to. I think he was modifying the doll so it'd move its arms and head up and down, possibly its legs as well. Maybe it'd even dance, I don't know. Anyway, once I'd got that far – well, you don't need me to tell you what that suggested to me, do you?"

He got a cold stare for that. It was almost as good as a round of applause.

"All right," he said, "maybe you do. I think Ziani is a man deeply, deeply in love: with you, with his daughter. The two of you mean literally everything to him; a glib enough phrase, but when you look at it and try and think what it actually means . . ." He sighed. "Now, you aren't going to comment on that one way or the other, so it's just an assumption. So let's assume. Ziani's love for you is his entire world; but he's not a naturally romantic or outgoing man. In spite of the strength of his feelings, he doesn't know how to express them. That's why he spent hours and hours writing love poems about you, but never actually showed them to you. It's like an invisible barrier he can't cross. He can't tell you how much he loves you; so he goes away somewhere on his own and makes something instead, because making things is all he knows how to do. He made those poems. He even made a book to write them down in. And he wanted so very much to make something for his daughter. Really, it gives a whole new meaning to the expression 'making love'. Rather literal-minded, of course, but that's a sort of occupational hazard for an engineer."

She yawned; but not very well.

"He wanted to make something for Moritsa," he went on. "Probably he'd mentioned it a few times, asked you what you thought she'd like. And one day, you told him: she'd like a mechanical doll, like the one we saw at such-and-such a fair. He'd have thought, that's fine, I can do that, and the basic type's not a restricted design. And then you said it again, I expect; in passing, probably not looking him in the face: like the one we saw at the fair, just like that one. But the doll you were referring to wasn't the basic type. It was the advanced model – I ought to know the type number, but it's slipped my mind. But I do know that the advanced model moves its arms and legs and head, and it dances."

She was looking at him.

"Well," he continued, managing to drone although his heart was racing, "that must've been a blow to him, because the advanced model's a restricted design. He couldn't just go to the specification tables and copy it down. He probably said as much to you; and I expect you pulled a very small sad face and said, oh what a shame, she'll be so disappointed. You won't have made any big deal about it. You'll have touched his mind ever so gently, because you knew that'd be the best way to make him do what you wanted. Quite probably he doesn't even remember you saying it; he'll believe it came from him, not you."

"I'm sorry," she said, in a voice as brittle as glass. "You've lost me, I'm afraid."

He ignored her. "I imagine he let it prey on his mind for a week or so," he said, "like an arrow in a wound slowly going rusty, until it poisons the blood. Then he'll have made up his mind. He can't get access to the approved design, but he won't let that stop him. He's an engineer, isn't he? He's even submitted modifications to military designs – all done properly, of course, through channels – and a couple of them have actually been accepted. He knows he can adapt the basic model to make it do all the things he believes Moritsa wants. And why shouldn't he? Nobody will ever know, after all. He probably blotted the risk out of his mind; in fact, as I see it, he must have felt he had no choice, risk or no risk. His little girl wanted him to do it, and it was the only way he knew to show her how much he loved her. No choice at all, really."

Now she was looking away.

"Well," Psellus said, after making a show of clearing his throat, "that was my clever theory. Next I started wondering how on earth I could prove it. And then I thought of a way. I thought, I'll send someone, a nice friendly lady, to ask Moritsa herself. Not straight out, of course. She'd start talking about a mechanical doll she'd seen, and observe how the girl reacted. Splendid idea, I thought, so I made the arrangements. But when I got the results, it seemed like they contradicted my whole theory. You see, when the nice lady started talking about dolls, Moritsa got quite upset. She hated them, she said. Well, the nice lady said, was that because of what happened to Daddy? And do you know what she said? She said she didn't understand, because Daddy did a bad thing and ran away from home, but it didn't have anything to do with dolls. No, she hated dolls because they'd seen one at the fair, and it frightened her. The way it moved its arms and legs was creepy and scary, and she never wanted to have to see one ever again."

He looked at her face. Frozen. "I hope you're proud of yourself," she said, "bullying a little girl like that. I don't suppose she knew what she was saying, if you had your people persecuting her, asking her questions about her father."

It was all he could do to stop himself grinning and clapping his hands. It was a counterattack, but a frightened one, hurried, snatched, deficient in timing and direction. Instead, he said, "Of course you're angry, what mother wouldn't be? But I knew you wouldn't tell me the truth if I asked you; and I promise you, it was done very carefully so as not to upset her."

"So you say." Anger, yes, bitter anger, but nothing to do with the way her daughter had been treated.

"Be that as it may." Oh, but he enjoyed saying that. "That's what she said, and I believe her. In which case," he went on, taking his time, savouring it, "the whole idea of making a doll, let alone an illegal one, must have come from you. From you or through you, anyway. Clearly the girl didn't ask him for one, and I very much doubt he plucked the project out of the air, he's not that imaginative. So it must have been you," he said. "Mustn't it?"

He couldn't help admiring the sheer still force she was putting into her defence. But it's one thing to be impressed by a performance, quite another to be convinced by it. She was tiring rapidly, like someone who'd lost a lot of blood. "Really," she said – beautifully done – "you've got to have something more important to think about than that. They're saying the savages are about to attack the City, for God's sake. Shouldn't you be up there doing something about it?"

He smiled. "Mustn't it?" he said.

She shrugged. "Fine," she said. "All right, I admit it. I put the idea into his head. I just wanted to get rid of him, so Falier and I could get married. But I couldn't just walk out of the house. He'd have gone to law, they'd have taken Moritsa away and given her to him. I wasn't having that."

"So you decided to murder him, then."

A very wan, faded smile. "I suppose so," she said. "If you want to look at it like that. I never loved him, you know. But he just sort of took delivery of me, like I was a load of materials, to be signed for. That's really not very fair, is it?"

Psellus nodded slowly. "You trapped him into committing a crime which you knew carried the death penalty, just so you'd be rid of him." He looked carefully at her face. "So you could marry Falier."

"Yes."

He shifted again. The pins and needles were spreading up his leg, above the knee. "I suppose Falier thought up the idea of the mechanical doll. Being an engineer himself, of course. He'd have known about the two types, all the technical stuff."

She nodded. "He's a smart boy," she said.

"Quite." He smiled pleasantly. "And very brave. Like you. I mean, you must both have known what a terrible risk you were running."

She seemed perfectly relaxed, but the knuckles of her left hand, clamped around a handkerchief, were white. "Not so terrible," she said.

"Heavens," he replied, "you really are brave, aren't you? I mean to say, you must have known there was a very real chance that you, as the wife of an abominator, would've been executed yourself, or at least put in prison. And Moritsa too, of course. Well, I suppose I can credit you having that sort of nerve, but I wouldn't have thought Falier would've wanted to risk it. After all, he stood to lose the girl he loved. If you were both that desperate, why not just poison him? That way, you'd only have been punished if you'd been found out."

Winning is one thing. Daring to exploit the victory . . . "We didn't see it like that," she said.

"Obviously not." Psellus sighed, closed his eyes for a moment. "And you got away with it, so really, you were right all along. But, like I said, very brave. And by rights, nobody should ever have suspected anything. You've got no idea how much effort I've had to put in, just to get this far."

A grin. "Well, I hope it was all worth it."

"Absolutely. The truth is always valuable. My father used to say, you can't plan a journey unless you know where you're starting from." He tried to stand up, and found he couldn't. The pain of the pins and needles made him grunt, and just for a moment he panicked. He couldn't get up.

"Excuse me," he said. "I'm sorry to be a nuisance, but would you mind giving me a hand to stand up? My leg's gone to sleep."

She laughed. "You're pathetic," she said.

"Yes," he replied mildly. "Aren't I just? The ruler of the Perpetual Republic, and I can't even get myself up off the floor."

She got off the bed and held out her hand. He gripped it and hauled himself to his feet, wincing at the pain. "Thank you," he said. "You've been a tremendous help."

She hadn't let go of his hand. "What's going to happen to me?" she asked.

"Oh, you can go home now," he said. "I'll get them to bring Moritsa back in the morning."

He felt her fingers slacken and let go. "That's it, then. All this was just to make me own up."

"Yes." He took a step, and ended up leaning heavily against the wall. "And it doesn't really change anything. I mean, Ziani's still guilty. He committed the crime. He shouldn't have made the doll, no matter what pressures were brought to bear on him. I just needed to know *why*, that was all. And now I do know, so I know where my journey has to start from. Extremely valuable. Thank you." He reached out and banged his fist on the door. When he heard the handle turn, he added, "You know, you really have been most helpful. In fact, you'd have helped me far less if you'd told me the truth. You can learn so much more from lies, I always find."

They brought Falier to see him, before he left. He looked terrified, which was, of course, perfectly understandable. Not, he decided, a young man burdened by a dangerous excess of courage. Even so, it was probably just as well he didn't realise quite how much he had to be scared about.

"Thank you for agreeing to this," Psellus said gravely. "You realise I can't put you fully in the picture. But it is really very important."

Falier shuddered. Even now, though, Psellus could see in his mind the tiny grub of the thought, *how can I get something out of this, for me?* "I'll do my best, you can rely on me," Falier said, in a rather shaky voice. "And if, well, anything bad happens . . ."

"Oh, it won't, I'm quite certain of that."

"Yes, but if it does." Pretty to watch, the way he smothered the frown of annoyance. Like the old joke: there's far less to this young man than meets the eye. "You will see to it that Ariessa's looked after, won't you? And the kid."

"Of course."

"Thanks, you've set my mind at rest. I'm really not bothered about myself, but . . ."

Psellus smiled. The effort hurt his jaw. "Off you go, then. You'll be back again before you know it." And he thought, she must have loved him very much, to put up with having this buffoon in her bed. A remarkable young woman, that. But then, we've always made superb weapons here in the City.

They took Falier to the sally-port in the palisade of the front gate bastion. He couldn't have a horse, they explained, because there was no way of getting it down to ground level; and besides, how would it get past the ditch, ten feet deep, flooded, the bottom mined with sharpened stakes? Falier appreciated that, but how was he supposed to get across the ditch himself? Swim, they said.

"I can't swim," he pointed out.

You're an engineer, they replied. Resourceful. You'll think of something.

Their faith in him was entirely justified. He paddled across on an empty nail-barrel, which stayed afloat nearly the whole distance. As he squelched out of the torchlight into the darkness, he wondered why they'd all been so hostile. They think I'll desert, he realised. The thought hadn't actually crossed his mind before, but now they'd put it there, it'd be wasteful just to throw it out.

Not, he told himself as he walked, that he actually believed for one moment that the City could possibly fall. There were savages, primitive, superstitious, who believed that the sun was a cart driven across the sky by a god, and gods were forgetful creatures; if they didn't remind him with prayers every evening, maybe the sun wouldn't come up tomorrow. But Falier believed in the inevitability of the sun, and he believed in the inviolability of the City. Damn it, they'd never get past the ditch, let alone the bastions, let alone the walls. It simply wasn't possible that such a vast, extravagant expenditure of strength, effort and materials should go to waste (and besides, the enemy were savages, primitives, sun-worshippers or something equally ludicrous). He shivered as water ran down the inside of his trouser legs, and plodded on towards the dim glow ahead.

The light grew brighter. It reminded him a little of the glare on the skyline just before dawn. As he grew closer to it, he realised how big it was; a line of fires where the enemy camp was reported to be. With every step he took, it grew longer, and he thought: that's not a camp, it's a city; a city of fire, a city on fire, maybe he was walking across the present to the future, and what he was looking at was actually the City itself, Mezentia, captured and burning, a reflection in time as in water. Then he remembered that the inhabitants of the fiery city weren't the whole enemy army, just a relatively small force of sappers and diggers, twenty-five thousand. A quarter of a tenth of the full strength they were bringing against the walls of his home. In the dark, of course, you couldn't judge scale very easily. Behind him, the lights on the embankment were just a small glow, whereas the light ahead of him stretched out like a vast orange boulevard; and he thought, there's so many of them, such a huge army, the ditch and the bastions and the wall won't hold them up for more than five minutes. We haven't done nearly enough, and now they're here.

"Falier?" A voice from nowhere. In the dark, distances can't be measured, there's no scale, nothing to calibrate by, either in space or in time. The voice came from the infinite space between two lights in darkness, and from the past. "Falier, is that you?"

"Ziani?"

"Keep still. I'll come to you."

He froze. Gradually a scoop of darkness thickened into a human shape. When it was just close enough to make out its outlines, it stopped. "Thanks for coming," it said.

Ludicrous, talking to a shadow, in a place like this. "That's all right," he heard himself say. "Where are we going?"

"Here'll do." The shadow changed shape, got shorter and thicker. No magic, he realised. Ziani had sat down on the ground. He did the same, hating the feel of wet cloth.

"How's Ariessa?" Ziani asked.

"She's fine."

"Moritsa?"

"She's fine too. If she'd known I was going to see you, I'm sure she'd have sent her love."

It was a stupid thing to say, and a lie as well. Of course, he couldn't see Ziani's face, to judge the effect of his error of judgement. "What did you want to see me about?" he asked.

"I want you to cast your mind back," Ziani said. Unnecessarily; hearing Ziani's voice had done it for him. Just the voice, no face; voices don't change the way someone's appearance does. "When I was arrested," he went on. "You knew all about it, of course."

He dragged back the impulse to lie. No point. "Yes."

"You and she." He was finding it difficult. "You told Compliance."

"Yes."

"To get rid of me. So you and Ariessa could . . ."

"Yes."

Silence, and the block of clotted shadow didn't move. Then, "It's all right," Ziani said. "I'm not going to attack you. That's why we're meeting like this. If I could see you, I don't think I'd be able to keep from killing you. But knowing the truth's more important." Pause. "I need to know exactly how it happened," Ziani said. "The details. For instance, what made you choose a mechanical toy?"

That didn't make sense. "I don't understand," Falier said.

"Really?" No movement; and suddenly Falier panicked and thought: what if what I'm looking at isn't Ziani after all? What if I'm looking at a rock or a tree-stump, and Ziani's coming up behind me with a knife? But then the outline shifted a little and reassured him. "Let's get this straight. You and Ariessa wanted me out of the way. You, or you and she, decided to trick me into making something illegal, so you could inform on me. Why a doll, is all I'm asking. Why not a clock, or—?"

Falier couldn't help frowning. "It wasn't like that," he said.

"Really?"

"No." This was stupid, Falier thought. He'd been made to come here like this because Ziani knew, because he'd figured it out and needed confirmation; and presumably Psellus thought that once he'd had it confirmed that it was his best friend Falier who'd betrayed him and not the Republic arbitrarily condemning him to death for a mis-demeanour, he'd relent and give up seeking his terrible revenge. But that didn't work if Ziani didn't actually know the truth. "No," he said, "it wasn't like that at all. It was my idea, all me. Ariessa told me what you were doing. She said we'd be able to have more time together because you were so busy, making a doll for the kid. I must've said something like, what sort of doll – meaning, how long's it likely to take, how much time will it give us? And she told me you were making a special mechanical doll that could move its arms and legs and dance. And then it just sort of came to me: I knew you were doing something illegal, and if you were caught . . . I didn't think of it in terms of you *dying*, I promise you. I just thought, he'll be out of the way, like a piece in a board game. You know how you say, I'll take your castle, you've taken my knight. It's ambiguous, isn't it? So you don't feel guilty. You sort of assume they're captured, not killed, and when the game's over they all get to go home again, so no harm done really. Like fishing, when you catch them and throw them back. I just thought, here's a piece blocking me, but if it gets taken—"

"That's all right," Ziani said softly. "I told you, it's all right. But listen." His voice had changed: soft, but more urgent, the voice of a man who wanted something. "Tell me the truth. Was that really how it was? Your idea, to go to Compliance?"

"Yes. I promise."

"Quite. You wouldn't lie to me. After all, you promised me you'd take care of Ariessa and Moritsa, and you have."

There was no answer to that, so he didn't reply. After a moment, Ziani went on: "Just to get it straight in my mind. Ariessa happened to mention the doll. You realised it was illegal, and you told Compliance."

"Yes."

"Did you discuss it with her first? Did she know? Did she approve?"

He considered lying, but could see nothing to be gained by it. "Yes."

"Thank you. You've been most helpful. You can go now."

That was it? It didn't feel right. "Ziani . . ."

"One last thing, before you go. Tell Secretary Psellus there's only so much I can do, but I'll try my best. Tell him . . ." Hesitation; a tired man searching for a form of words. "Tell him, he and I have got to trust each other, no matter what. Will you do that? Those exact words?"

"Yes, of course. Ziani, I'm really sorry. What I did, it was very bad, it was evil . . ."

For some reason Ziani was laughing. "Don't be stupid," he said. "There's no such thing. No evil, no bad people, they're just a myth. Do you want to know something, Falier? Everything we do in this world, everything that matters, we do for love. It's always love, when you peel away the shell. There's that old song, it's love that makes the world go round. Well, it's true. Who'd have thought it? They didn't want us to know the truth so they hid it where nobody'd ever think of looking, in some stupid old song. It really is true, you know. Apart from mad people, and they're sick and can't be blamed, apart from them, everything bad – I don't mean just greedy or spiteful things; everything really bad that was ever done was done for love. You and me, we love Ariessa. The Eremian duke, Orsea, he loved his country. Even Maris Boioannes loved the City; he wanted what was best for it, and he really believed that he was the best. That's why there's no such thing as evil, Falier. Evil's just love in action, love on the move between wanting and getting. I mean, look at you. A man and a woman love each other, they've got no choice but to do whatever needs to be done. No, you mustn't blame yourself, really. Believe me. I've only just realised this, and it changes everything. You do see that, don't you?"

Falier didn't reply, and it occurred to Ziani that maybe he'd gone, leaving him to make his fine speech to empty air. Not that it mattered. If you tell the truth, does the fact that nobody's listening make it a lie?

He should be getting back, he thought. He had a long, miserable ride back to Civitas Vadanis ahead of him, and there'd be no time to rest once he got there. Too much to do. He was grateful for the darkness, which kept him from seeing Psellus' new defences. The more a dying thing wriggles, the less willing you are to finish it off. But he'd heard everything he needed to hear: solid data, measurements, specifications, numbers. Now he had that information, he knew he'd done enough. The ditch wouldn't be a problem, and neither would the bastions, and as for the wall, that was already taken care of. He looked towards the City, a vague blob of firelight, and thought, it'll be that much brighter when the whole City's burning. A man sitting where I am now should be able to read a book by that light. He smiled. No evil, except necessary evil; and what's more necessary than love?

He closed his eyes for a moment. A blind man could find his way back to the camp from here just by following the smell of woodsmoke. To pass the time as he walked, he compiled a mental nomenclature of parts. Daurenja. Secretary Psellus, Duke Valens, that Aram Chantat liaison whose name he couldn't pronounce. Maris Boioannes. In order to get this far, he'd had to rely to a certain extent on luck. He'd had to leave a few blank spaces in the design, vaguely labelled: transmission, gearing, escapement. It was a practice he despised. Instead of having the whole thing drawn out before you start cutting metal, leave the tricky bits till later and hope you'll think of something. Of course, he'd had no choice. Now that the design was complete, he reckoned he hadn't done so badly, considering the prototype had also to be the finished product.

He was close enough now to see men silhouetted against the firelight. He thought of her; at least, he tried to call her into his mind, but all he could see was someone standing in a doorway with the light behind her.

He stopped walking. I've failed, he thought. The design was good, I made the parts well and fitted them together all right, but the job turns out not to be possible after all.

No, there was no point thinking like that. Everything was possible. He considered the example of Duke Valens, who killed Duke Orsea so he could marry his wife. Now, she loved Orsea, but when he died, she loved Valens just as much, or more. Everything was possible, provided you arranged the course of events.

A sentry yelled at him. He called back his name, and walked slowly into the firelight with his hands on his head. Luckily, the sentry knew him by sight.

"I've been to look at the defences," he explained, when the sentry asked what he'd been doing. "Too risky in daylight."

The sentry nodded and let him pass. He walked slowly up the main roadway that ran through the middle of the camp, until he found Daurenja's tent. The flap was down; yellow light glared under it, seeping out like a spillage. There was a guard outside it, of course.

"I'm sorry," said the guard. "Orders. He's not to be disturbed."

"He'll see me," Ziani replied.

Daurenja was sitting behind a table; actually, a wide board resting on two sawhorses. On it was one large sheet of paper, covered with dozens of tiny drawings, columns of figures, notes, tables of parts.

"That's uncanny." Daurenja grinned at him. "The man I most

wanted to see in the whole world. Come in, sit down. Tell me what you think of this."

It was a design, but at first Ziani couldn't make out what it was supposed to be. A main drive unit, clockwork, powered by four coiled clocksprings in parallel. The takeoff connected to a complex gear train, supplying power to five spindles at three different ratios of conversion. A gearbox – why was it stuck right up there, requiring those long, fragile linkages? Cams and camshafts, with lifters and interrupters. By the spacing of the eccentrics and the complicated but ingenious travelling arm running down a series of zigzag keyways . . .

He realised what he was looking at. Not a machine after all. It was a plan of the defences, with the offensive trenches, saps and mines superimposed on it. A machine for defending and attacking a city. As he looked down at it, he realised why he'd made the mistake. Both functions, defence and attack, were part of the same mechanism. This machine was designed to do both.

Except that it wasn't a machine, of course. But it worked just like one.

"What do you reckon?" Daurenja asked anxiously. The fool, Ziani thought, he really does value my opinion. Of course, he was another example of the same principle: a device for being the hero and the villain simultaneously.

"You need to cap the approach trenches at the turns," he said. "Gabions'd do it, but you might want a few heavy steel pavises as well. Otherwise, a battery of scorpions here" – he pressed the paper with his fingernail, hard enough to leave a mark – "could shoot down into all your main trenches here, here and here, look."

"You're right," Daurenja said, scrabbling for his pen. "Thanks for pointing that out." He dipped the nib in ink and wrote PAVISES in big letters at the point of each angle of the zigzags. "Anything else?"

"Give me a moment," Ziani replied mildly. "There's a lot to take in."

Now there was a thought. Defence and attack working together to achieve the foreseen result; the machine wouldn't work without both of them, acting and reacting on each other. You could say the same about good and evil. He traced the sequence of events through the various stages and processes – the flooded trench, the bastions, the embankment, the walls. Then he stopped, and grinned. "It's not finished," he said. "No escapement."

"Sorry? I don't follow."

Ziani leaned back in his chair, which creaked. "You've got past the new defences, under the wall, but now you're stuck. You need to bring the wall down, and bring up foot soldiers right away to force the breach. But there's nothing about that here. Did you forget, or haven't you got around to figuring that step out yet?"

This time, Daurenja smiled. "Actually," he said, "you haven't read it quite right. All that bit there" (he pointed) "is really just a feint, to draw off their forces. But we're getting into the City through this gate here."

The Westgate; the strongest and the best defended of the five main gates. But it opened on to Guildhall Street, the widest, straightest thoroughfare in the City, leading directly to the Guildhall itself. Carry the Westgate with sufficiently overwhelming numbers, and a half-mile sprint up an unblockable, indefensible road would get you to the seat of government before anybody, even the best professional soldiers, could stop you.

"You're way ahead of me, I can see that," Daurenja said happily. "Once we've taken the Guildhall, we hold it until the sappers have brought down the walls here, here and here. While all the defenders are rushing towards the centre of town, three support parties are coming up behind them to take them in flank and rear. Then it'll just be a matter of clearing the walls themselves and mopping up. Well?" he added anxiously. "What do you think?"

It was a superb piece of engineering. A ram, a scoop and a pivot, then just tighten the collet and grip, equalising the inside and outside pressure. But he had to say something, so: "You're very laid back about breaking down the Westgate," he said. "I take it you're thinking of using a battering ram, presumably in a covered frame, but I suggest you may have overlooked the gradient of the embankment. You'd need, what, thirty couple of draught horses . . ."

"Nothing like that." He'd never seen Daurenja happier. "I mean, yes, you're right. You'd never get a ram up that incline under fire, and even if you could, it'd take too long. By the time you'd got through, they'd have had a chance to barricade the main drag, and then you're fighting every step of the way instead of making a quick, decisive dash to victory. And before you say it, I know the gatehouse is built on heavy clay, so undermining it'd be a nightmare. No, the hell with that. What I've got in mind . . ."

Ziani knew what he was going to say. The stone-throwing pot,

Daurenja's great invention. It was, of course, the answer, assuming it could be relied on. He watched Daurenja's face as he talked about it, like a young boy talking about his first girl, eyes bright, unable to keep the love from seeping past the seal of his mouth. He thought: this is a remarkable man, by any standards. Engineer, soldier, murderer, rapist, scholar, traitor, thief, hero, a man of ingenuity, resource, courage, determination, intellect; a passionate man, driven in everything he does by a ferocious pressure of love, like the poison under an abscessed tooth. He understood him now, clearly for the first time, his characteristics and properties. Daurenja was the two different kinds of love, the good and the evil. His life had been spent in search of a worthy object for his unlimited ocean of love, and he'd found it at last, in the weapon he'd conceived and brought to life. Well, Ziani thought, that's all right, I can handle lovers. Lovers are easy to use.

But, again, he had to say something; so he asked, "Have you tested it yet?"

Just a brief flicker; pain, fear. "Not yet, no. I want to keep it a secret, you see. The whole point is, it's got to come as a complete surprise. You and me, and the duke, of course, we're the only ones who know what it does or how it works. If I test it, the enemy'll find out about it, you can bet your life on it. Besides," he added, with a slight waver in his voice, "it doesn't need testing. It'll be just right, you'll see."

He'd heard that flicker in men's voices before, when they said things like, *Besides, I trust her, I don't need to know where she is all the time or what she's doing, there'll be a perfectly reasonable explanation, you'll see.* And that made him think of the cold spot. Love welds together, but a cold spot is where the seams and joins begin to tear apart. Poor Daurenja, he thought; he couldn't see it, just as I couldn't see the cold flaw in my own weld. Perhaps love blinds you to it, and only a stranger can see it.

"I hope so," he said gently. "Everything'll be depending on it. If it goes wrong . . ."

"It won't." Admirable, the way Daurenja dragged back the anger and replaced it almost instantly with gratitude for friendly concern. "Trust me," he added, smiling, "I've been really thorough. I did years of experiments, remember, I've thought about nothing else for – well, as long as I can remember, really. It's funny, when something like this comes into your life, it gradually takes over, and everything else gets pushed to the edges. It's all right," he added, "I won't let you down. I know you persuaded them to give me this chance because you believe in it too. I knew you'd come round, you see, once you realised what an amazing thing this is. You can feel it too, can't you? The sense that something incredible's about to happen."

Ziani nodded. He understood. The old contradiction: you want everybody, all your family and friends, to realise how wonderful she is, but nobody else is allowed to love her, only you. "So," he said briskly, "that'll take care of the gate, then. And everything else should go smoothly after that." He nodded, his seal of approval. "Yes, I think it'll work. You've done well."

A big smile spread over Daurenja's face. "I couldn't have done it without you," he said. "I mean that, I'd never have got this far on my own. And I'm sorry; I mean, I know I've not . . ." He pulled a face. "I've not exactly behaved well towards you, at times. I've pushed and nagged, and I've bullied you, done things I really regret."

"That's all right," Ziani said quietly. "You had no choice."

"Yes, exactly," Daurenja said excitedly, "I knew you'd understand. There were things that had to be done, so I did them. But all the same, I do feel bad about it. I mean, using people to get what you want, like they're tools or bits of a mechanism, it's deceitful. I can't help feeling bad about it, the way I've manipulated so many people, and you especially."

"No big deal," Ziani replied. "It's actions and outcomes that matter, not intentions. And when something's got to be done, it's no good killing yourself with guilt about it."

Daurenja laughed. He was happy. "I must say," he said, "I wish all my victims took such a pragmatic view of things."

Chapter Thirteen

On the twelfth day of the assault, the allies' approach trench came within range of the forward batteries on the point of the northernmost bastion. An engineer by the name of Tuno Belias of the Foundrymens's Guild, deputy night-shift foreman at the pipe and stove factory, loosed the first shot from a Type Nine scorpion. Later, he admitted that he'd neglected to allow for the moderate easterly side-wind; but that was all right, because he'd laid three degrees too far left in any case, and the wind drew the bolt straight and pitched it precisely in the heart of the sapper standing next to the man Belias had been aiming at. This early success was celebrated noisily all across the City, and Belias' colleagues at the stoveworks immediately launched a subscription to raise money to buy a suitable trophy or memento to mark the occasion. By the end of the shift, the fund stood at fifteen dollars, and a Type Seventeen commemorative silver salver was commissioned from the Silversmiths', to be engraved with Belias' name and a brief account of his notable deed. The rest of the shots loosed from the battery missed, and within the hour the sappers had raised a wall of gabions that protected the trench-head completely.

They waited until it was dark to take the dead sapper's body back to the camp. The stretcher party was met by General Daurenja in person; he took the front handles and helped carry the body to the fosse, where a grave had already been dug. He made a short but powerful speech to the crowd of soldiers and sappers who'd gathered there; the dead man, he told them, was only the first of many, and the priorities of siege and battle would mean that not every body would be retrieved or decently buried. Therefore, he said, it was important to mark their first loss calmly, solemnly, making no attempt to belittle the ugly realities of war and death. Every man lost was one too many, he told them, and every death would stay with him for the rest of his life, since he was their commander, responsible for everything that happened. Nevertheless, he went on, the war had to be fought, the power of the enemy had to be broken and made safe, if the horrors of Eremia were not to be repeated. As they buried their dead, so they must bury fear, misgivings, doubt and even compassion. They should mourn now, he concluded, for themselves and their enemies, and have done with it. From tomorrow, there would be no place in the army for sorrow or regret, only for courage, resolution and grim determination.

When the body had been buried and the crowd had broken up, Daurenja went back to his tent. He drank three glasses of wine and ate a little rye bread and cheese; then he got up and went quietly, without guards or staff, and climbed down into the assault trench. He moved so quietly that the sappers of the night shift weren't aware of him until he tapped the rearguard on the shoulder.

"It's all right," he said, as the man raised his lantern and recognised him. "I just came by to see for myself. How's it going?"

They stopped work and explained. There were five of them, they said (he could see that for himself, but he said nothing): four sappers, and a guard. The front sapper dug a trench eighteen inches wide and twenty inches deep. To protect himself from the enemy's shot, he pushed ahead of him a shield of half-inch steel plate, mounted on a wheeled carriage. As he dug, he threw the spoil to his left into a stout cylindrical wicker basket four feet high and two feet in diameter, known as a gabion; filled with earth, it was dense enough to stop a scorpion bolt. The line of filled gabions formed the core of the trench's defensive bank. The second sapper followed on behind, doubling the depth and width of the trench and helping to fill the gabion with his spoil. The third and fourth sappers deepened and widened the trench still further, until it was three feet deep and four feet wide, but they threw their spoil over the line of gabions to form an earth bank beyond it, to reinforce and stabilise it. The guard fetched empty gabions from the supply cart and topped off the bank with tightly

bound faggots of coppice-wood, called fascines. The resulting com-
bination of ditch and bank meant that a column of men two abreast
could march upright along the completed trench, almost entirely
safe from the enemy's tactical artillery. Each team of four worked for
an hour, and was then replaced. So far, they'd been averaging a hundred yards in twenty-four hours, but they felt sure that a hundred
and sixty yards was possible, maybe even more. At the angles, when
the zigzag line bent back on itself, they were exposed and in danger,
as had been demonstrated earlier that day. To deal with that threat,
they proposed to double-sap, building a gabion wall on both sides of
the trench; assuming, of course, that that met with the general's
approval. He then asked them where they were from, and they said
they were Vadani, formerly miners from the silver mines. Most of the
sappers were from the mines, though there were also some northern
Eremians, experienced in building terraced fields on the sides of
their thin-soiled hills, and a few peat-diggers from the marshlands of
the Vadani–Eremian border. They had all the equipment they
needed, though it was hard for just one man to keep them supplied
with gabions and fascines; sometimes they had to stop and wait, and
so it'd be a good idea to assign an extra guard. Daurenja nodded and
said he'd see to it; then he slipped off his coat, rolled up his sleeves
and took the front position for the rest of the hour, sending the lead
sapper back to help with the gabions, as they'd recommended. As he
left, he made them promise not to tell anybody that he'd been there.

Back at his tent, in front of a warm stove, he dragged and peeled
off his muddy clothes and changed into a blue velvet gown edged
with gold lace at the neck and wrists. It came from the Aram
Chantat. Properly speaking, that style, cloth and level of ornamen-
tation was restricted to counsellors, generals and members of the
royal family. It had been meant as a gift for Duke Valens, but he
hated that sort of thing and had packed it away at the bottom of a
chest, where Daurenja had found it and taken an instant liking to it.
He only wore it at night, so nobody would see him in it and tell the
savages, who'd be sure to be offended.

At dawn the next morning, Secretary Psellus made an unannounced
tour of inspection of the forward batteries. He was there when the
first shot of the day was loosed, and he followed its long, looping

trajectory, from the moment it left the slider to its rather anticlimactic impact in the bank of earth that hid the trench from view. He thanked the artillery crew and praised them for their diligence, then went back to the Guildhall.

"Useless," he said sadly to the assembled joint chiefs. "I saw it myself. It wobbled through the air and stuck in the big pile of dirt. We could bombard them all day long and they probably wouldn't even notice."

Orosin Zeuxis of the Linen Drapers', colonel-in-chief of the artillery, shook his head violently. "The plan is," he said, "to keep up a constant, hammering fire which will inevitably smash up those wicker basket things, loosen the earth and send it sliding down into the trench. We've run tests using donkey panniers, and—"

"Useless," Psellus repeated mildly. "We need to do a whole lot better than that. The scorpions are accurate, I grant you, but it's no good being able to pitch five shots in a foot square if they don't actually *do* anything. No, I think it's time we brought up the trebuchets and mangonels. I know," he added, raising his hand in a rather weak gesture; they stopped arguing at once, even so. "We were planning on keeping them in reserve, we don't want to let them know the true range we can achieve, so that when their main army gets close enough, we can take them by surprise. And no, ideally we wouldn't want to commit them to the embankment in case it's over-run, and there wouldn't be time to move them back again. All perfectly true. The fact remains that they're digging their wretched trench at an appallingly fast rate, and our only hope is to slow them down until their food runs out. Therefore," he said softly, so they had to shut up just to be able to hear him, "we will deploy the heavy artillery straight away. Orosin, that's your department. If you need help with transport and installation, feel free to use whatever resources you like. I know it's asking a lot, but I'd quite like to have at least one full battery in place and working by this time tomorrow."

Zeuxis glowered at him, then nodded stiffly. "I'll do my best," he said.

"I'm sure you will," Psellus replied. "And with any luck, that'll put a stop to their confounded tunnelling, for a while at least. Meanwhile, though, we need to do something else. I had a good look at the new trench they started the day before yesterday."

"Oh," someone said, "that. You know, I'm not too fussed about it. It's moving very slowly, compared to the others."

Psellus smiled. "That's because it's three times as wide," he said. "Which suggests to me that it's not for bringing up soldiers or sappers. I think that trench is going to be used for machinery of some sort. Artillery, perhaps, or some kind of digging or battering engine."

Someone else shrugged. "Maybe it is," he said. "But it's still a long way away. Out of range, even for the Type Twenties."

"Quite," Psellus said, dipping his head in graceful acknowledgement. "Which is why I think we ought to try a sortie."

This time they weren't so easily quelled. As their voices rose in protest and complaint, they merged, cancelling each other out, so that Psellus couldn't make out a word anybody was saying. He didn't need to, of course.

Manuo Phranazus, commander-in-chief of ground forces (not so long ago he'd been chairman of the Cabinetmakers' standards and quality control committee; war's strange alchemy, Psellus thought), eventually managed to make himself heard over the buzz, and the chorus gradually subsided. "We've been through this before," he said aggressively, "dozens of times. A sortie simply isn't practical. My men may be kitted out in the finest armour money can buy, but they're not soldiers. They've never seen action, their drill's still shaky, and the officers and NCOs have a long way to go before they're fit to be trusted to command a serious action. And on top of all that, trying to keep them in some semblance of order at night, in the dark—"

"I wasn't thinking of a night sortie," Psellus said mildly.

Now they were so stunned they couldn't even speak. "You can't be serious," Phranazus said at last. "You're actually thinking of attacking in *daylight*?"

"That's right, yes." Psellus' chin tended to wobble when he nodded. He'd noticed it in the mirror for the first time a few days ago, and was still painfully self-conscious about it. "Noon, to be precise."

"That's—"

"Recommended," Psellus interrupted. "In the book. It gives a whole host of excellent reasons: technical stuff, mostly, about shift timings. I've had someone keeping an eye on them, and there's always a shift change about a quarter of an hour before noon. The men coming off shift are worn out after working, and they tend to

stop a little early. Meanwhile, it takes the new shift at least ten minutes to come up the trench and relieve them. And of course the last
thing they'll be expecting is a sortie, in broad daylight, in the middle
of the day." From the bottom of his pile of papers, he drew out a
sketch. "If we come out of the sally-port and bridge the ditch here,"
he explained, "we'll be out of their line of sight until we actually
round the point of this bastion; then it's only, what, six hundred
yards, in a straight line, and then you're in the trench. At least, one
unit goes in and kills the poor sappers. A second unit follows the line
of their wall, bank, whatever you care to call it; the point is, they'll be
out of sight from the enemy camp, so when the new shift come rushing up to take on our men in the trench, this second unit can drop in
behind them as they pass and attack them from the rear. We can then
use the trench as cover and rush ahead to sabotage the new trench,
which'll be the real object of the sortie. The only point at which
we'll be fighting them on equal terms is here" – he pointed – "where
we'll need to send up a couple of platoons to hold them off while the
rest of us do as much damage as possible in the new trench. I'm
afraid this holding party probably won't be coming back.' (He looked
away as he said it.) "Still, the loss of two platoons will be a small price
to pay if we can stop them bringing up heavy machinery for a while."

It took a moment for the joint chiefs to realise that it was actually
rather a good plan; an excellent plan, in fact, and afterwards they
spent some time discussing among themselves where on earth the old
fool could possibly have found it. Not from any of the approved
texts, which several of them knew by heart; it must be that mysteri-
ous bloody book that he wouldn't let anybody else see. The thought
that Psellus had dreamed it up all by himself never occurred to them.
Even so, they said: a sortie. When will he get it into his head that we
aren't proper soldiers?

The point that the joint chiefs had overlooked, though it hadn't
escaped Secretary Psellus, was that the Vadani sappers weren't proper
soldiers either. When the sortie burst into the trench, they couldn't
understand what was happening. They'd been expressly told that
the Mezentines had no infantry; their mercenaries had all gone home,
and the citizens themselves were far too effete to fight. Who the men
in armour pouring into the trench could be, therefore, they had no

idea; nor had they any intention of staying around to find out. They dropped their picks and shovels and tried to scramble up the blind, unbanked side. Some of them made it.

To begin with, the Mezentines were, as one of them put it later, like a widow killing a chicken. They slashed wildly at the sappers' heads and arms, frantically trying to get the loathsome job over and done with, desperate not to touch or come into contact with the scrambling, wriggling bodies of their enemies. As a result, they killed few of the sappers but wounded all of them; long, slicing cuts to the scalp that sprayed blood like a cow pissing, chunks hacked out of shins and elbows – the pain revolted them, and made them flail even more furiously, their arms held out straight to maximise the distance (which meant more cuts were made with the tip than the edge; the wound the fencing books called a stramazone, designed to hurt and infuriate an enemy into making an error). Some Mezentines hit hard enough to sever hands or feet, others struck at too shallow an angle, so that the blade skipped off the scalp and sliced off an ear or a nose; results so grotesque that the Mezentines were sick with horror at what they'd done, and lashed out even more to put an end to the nightmare as quickly as possible.

All of which took time; rather longer than planned. Also, the relief shift (not being soldiers) failed to rush to their comrades' assistance, as they were supposed to do. Instead, as soon as they realised what was happening, they scampered back to the camp and called out the guard. The Mezentines waiting in ambush didn't know that, of course, and the ambush itself went flawlessly. Their attack (in rear, in the cramped trench) went home exactly as planned, but the Eremian and Aram Chantat infantry who'd answered the relief sappers' call were adequately armoured, though not as well as the Mezentines, and knew in a matter of seconds what was going on. They turned and fought back. The Mezentines, suddenly finding themselves facing line infantry instead of men in thin shirts with shovels, immediately tried to back away, but the sides of the trench were too steep for heavily armoured men to climb. After half a dozen had been cut down without making any effort to fight back, they rallied and launched a wild, completely unscientific counter attack. They did relatively little damage with their weapons, but their armour was too strong to be easily penetrated or smashed open, particularly in a crowded, narrow trench with no room for a really good swing. Accordingly, the allies jabbed and bashed at them but couldn't actually kill them, and they flailed and walloped back to more or less the same effect. Only when they were too tired to keep up their windmill assaults could the allies get close enough to find the weak joints and hinges in their armour; and by then, the Mezentines behind the fighting line had had the wit to pile up a few empty gabions into a makeshift stair, to get them out of the trench.

Because the guard was busy elsewhere, the two platoons sent to die nobly for their country got to the mouth of the trench and found nobody there to meet them. They stood about for a while, horribly afraid they'd messed up and gone to the wrong place. Then their nerve broke, and they ran back the way they'd just come, meeting up with the first gush of fugitives from the ambush party; who in turn assumed they must be reinforcements, and (bravely and with agonising reluctance) tried to climb back into the trench and continue the fighting. The result would have been very bad for them if a handful of men from the two platoons hadn't looked down on the helmeted heads milling around in the trench below them, and promptly started pelting them with rocks. Fortuitously (it could have gone either way), the heads they battered were Eremian and Aram Chantat rather than Mezentine, and the shock of the unexpected hail of missiles from a quarter they'd not expected trouble from prompted the allies to pull back out of the fighting, letting the surviving Mezentines in the trench get out safely.

None of which mattered, of course. The real objective of Psellus' plan was to let an assault party loose undisturbed in the new trench, which he correctly guessed was being built to take heavy machinery up to the ditch. Well aware that their time was limited, they set to with the ferocious determination of very frightened men. They smashed gabions, cut open fascines, scattered the brushwood in big heaps and set fire to them; they grabbed shovels or pulled off their helmets to scoop dirt with, and remarkably quickly managed to undermine the supports of the earth bank, so the spoil slid back into the trench and filled it. They even rolled back into the trench a huge boulder, which had taken two shifts of sappers a whole day to prise up and haul out of the way. As they were doing this, it occurred to them that they'd been rather longer than they'd anticipated. The two platoons should've been shredded and swept aside by now, and enemy soldiers should be pouring into the parallel, their cue to stop work and run. But no soldiers came, and they started to worry. Did the absence of the enemy mean that the plan had been wholly subverted; was there an enemy force waiting to intercept them on their way back, rather than engage them in the trench? By this point they'd done as much damage as they could without additional equipment. They had no idea what was happening, only a vague feeling that something had gone wrong and they were in a different danger than the one they'd been expecting to face. After a brief, slightly hysterical discussion, they decided that they couldn't trust their planned escape route any more, which meant they had no choice but to go back the way they'd come, down and along the approach trench . . .

By the time they ran into the enemy, the bombardment with rocks from outside the trench had stopped, and the allies were trying to make up their minds whether to press on and try and rescue the sappers, as they'd originally intended to do before the ambush hit them, or call it a day and go back. The sudden appearance of yet more Mezentines, coming *up* the trench, was rather more than they could cope with. The Eremian lieutenant who was now the ranking officer (the Aram Chantat captain had been one of the few allied casualties who'd actually died on the point of a Mezentine sword) ordered his men to pull back, intending to form a shield-wall at the point of the zigzag, where there was rather more room to deploy. But the surviving Aram Chantat officer took this for cowardice in the face of the enemy and ordered his own men to push the Eremians out of the way and attack the Mezentines at once. What happened next was never quite clear. The Eremian lieutenant maintained that a party of the Mezentines outside the trench, the ones who'd thrown the rocks, crept up along the bank while the two allied contingents were scuffling and contrived to undermine the gabions and loose spoil, bringing the bank down on the allies' heads. Other survivors maintained that in the course of the scuffle, the gabions at the base of the bank were dislodged, and that was what caused the bank to collapse. In any event, a good third of the allies were under the landslip, and when the dust settled, both sides found themselves separated from the enemy by a solid wall of earth.

All this time, the Mezentine detachment who'd started the sortie by attacking the allied forward shift were wondering what had become of the ambush party, who were supposed to come down the trench and join them after they'd finished dealing with the relief shift. The original detachment were in comparatively good spirits, once they'd got over the horrors of victory. They interpreted the ambush party's failure to arrive as evidence that they were in trouble and needed help; so they set off down the trench to find them.

Needless to say, they ran into the allies, taking them by surprise, in rear, while they were still effectively stunned by the disaster of the collapsing bank. As a result, the Mezentines caught them entirely unaware and began the engagement by killing half a dozen of them. This was, of course, the worst thing that could have happened for the Mezentines; it encouraged them to press home their advantage, so that when the allies realised they were being attacked again, by yet another separate enemy unit, they pulled themselves together and fought back with full professional savagery. It was only the speed with which the narrow trench clogged up with bodies that saved the third of the Mezentine detachment that made it out over the bank and escaped. The remaining two thirds never had the satisfaction of knowing they'd blocked the trench as effectively as the landslip.

Just over three fifths of the sortie made it back to the City embankment; rather fewer than planned, rather more than Psellus himself had dared to hope. For the allies, the aftermath was almost as chaotic as the action itself. The Mezentines, according to the report the Eremian lieutenant made to General Daurenja that evening, were unorthodox but nonetheless fearsome opponents. Their offensive and weapons skills were negligible, but their sheer grim determination, the way they kept on attacking, wave after wave of them, made them worthy of cautious respect. On the other edge of the camp, meanwhile, the advance-shift sappers who'd managed to get away were having their horrific wounds treated by the Vadani surgeons, and were telling anybody who'd listen that the Mezentines were vicious, sadistic savages who fought to inflict pain rather than kill, and if the general thought they were going back down in the trench again without proper infantry support, he was very much mistaken.

General Daurenja spent the night reflecting on what he'd been told, and called a full staff meeting at dawn. The situation, he told them, was not good. The approach trench for the heavy machinery was so badly damaged as to be useless; it'd be quicker and easier to start again. The main trench was blocked in three places. Casualties had been unexpectedly heavy – due mostly, admittedly, to the cave-in of the trench wall, but even so, it was clear that Duke Valens had underestimated the enemy's fighting spirit, if not their military competence. Sorties, contrary to what the duke had told them, were likely to pose a real danger to siege operations. Furthermore, the sappers were now deeply worried at the prospect of further attacks – understandably so, considering the horrific nature of the wounds their colleagues had suffered – and were refusing to go back to work until satisfactory arrangements for their defence had been made. Strictly speaking, this was mutiny; however, the sappers were civilian labourers rather than soldiers, and they had a genuine grievance, which no responsible general could afford to ignore. Accordingly, he had decided to advance the artillery to the point where it could lay down suppressing fire on the enemy embankment, and to station archers, sheltered by pavises, at the points of the zigzags, which would also be fortified with redoubts built of gabions and sandbags. Finally, each redoubt would be garrisoned with a platoon of heavy infantry to provide a rapid response in the event of future sorties. It was true, he conceded, that advancing the artillery would bring them in range of the enemy, quite possibly leading to an artillery duel, which Duke Valens had been anxious to avoid. But that, the general said, seemed to him to be ducking the issue. Victory would only be possible if the allies could establish clear artillery superiority. If that meant a protracted artillery duel, the loss of siege engines and trained crews, it was a price that had to be paid. As he saw it, they really had no choice in the matter.

"It was a mistake," someone was saying, and Psellus fought to restrain a smile. In the old days, when Boioannes sat in this chair, nobody would have dared to talk like that. Progress, he thought; I've given them freedom of speech to criticise me with. If we survive this, that really ought to be worth a statue, or my head on the two-dollar coin. But I don't suppose anybody except me has even noticed.

"You could well be right," he replied gently. "Some brave men lost their lives." And some cowards too, he added to himself; and I feel guiltier about them, because I conscripted them to fight. There's an argument for saying that brave men deserve what they get, but it's a serious business forcing cowards to stand in harm's way. "But you may recall, I said that the primary objective would be damaging the new trench, the one I feel sure is being built to shift heavy equipment. And on balance, we succeeded."

Someone else shook his head, rather dramatically. "Really, that's beside the point," he said. "That may be what you set out to do, and yes, you managed it. Congratulations. But the rather more important outcome is that they're moving their artillery up and fortifying the trench bends. Which means they're going to start bombarding the embankment very soon."

"True," Psellus said. "It's also true that if they can reach us, we can reach them. And they're in the open, and we're under cover."

"It's still an unlooked-for escalation," said the troublemaker (he chided himself for the instinctive characterisation; give them free speech, then brand them as troublemakers when they make use of it. Lucao Psellus, for shame!). "Furthermore, by prompting them to improve their defences, you've made launching further sorties much more difficult and dangerous."

This time, Psellus allowed his smile to show. "Actually, I wasn't planning any further sorties," he said. "We aren't very good at them, after all. The purpose of this one was to cause delay, because they only have a limited time in which to sack the City before their food runs out. Actually," he went on, "if you'll excuse the digression, I've been thinking about that, and doing a few simple sums, and I've reached the conclusion – I'll go through the figures afterwards with anyone who wants to see them – that they're rapidly approaching a point of no return in that regard, the point where they either have to capture the City and our food reserves, or else give up and go away before they starve. If they pass that point, whenever it comes, and fail to take the City within the critical time period, they will run out of food. Even if they win, if they leave it too long, there won't be enough food left in our stores to feed their army. Therefore, when that point in time comes, they'll have to make a decision – do we have a realistic chance of victory within the time limits imposed on us by the supply problem? – and if the answer is no, logically they should abandon the siege and go away." He paused, disengaging his mind from the train of thought these issues had set in motion. "As it happens," he went on, "and I can't claim credit for it, but it's extremely useful nonetheless, the sortie was far more successful in this regard than I expected. Now that they're guarding and fortifying the trench, their rate of progress will slow down significantly. If we can win the artillery battle – it doesn't matter if we lose half our trebuchets and mangonels in the process, we can easily build more – to the extent where we can silence their batteries and use our artillery to slow up their progress even further, we'll have done well for ourselves, very well indeed. We also have an advantage in the recent change of command, I believe. I know nothing about this General Daurenja, or at least nothing I'm prepared to believe without further and better evidence, but it seems to me that he is much more a soldier than the duke was. He thinks in strategies and tactics; models in sand-trays, if you like, or pieces on a chequerboard. He resents the losses we somehow managed to inflict on him, and has taken steps to stop us doing it again, because he's a good soldier. Duke Valens' instincts, on the other hand, would always be to make sure his people had enough to eat, regardless of the strictly military priorities. I think General Daurenja will be more likely to neglect the food deadline until it's almost on top of him, which will lead him to panic and overestimate the danger out of guilt. Or he may turn a blind eye to the problem and ignore it, in which case his allies the savages will depose him, and quite possibly end the alliance." He stopped talking and looked at their faces. They were watching him; listening, rather than planning out their next interruption. Remarkable. "I'm a firm believer in the merits of letting our opponents do themselves as much harm as possible, and in the situation we face, I feel sure that our enemies are our best allies."

He was glad to have reached the end of this impromptu speech. He found that sort of thing extremely draining: the physical effort of talking loudly for so long, the mental strain of intense concentration. Men like Boioannes had built up their stamina over a lifetime, but until very recently nobody had ever let Lucao Psellus get a word in edgeways, let alone talk uninterrupted for five minutes.

"This point of no return," somebody said eventually. "Just how long . . . ?"

Psellus shrugged. "Without knowing their precise numbers, the quantity of food that makes up their daily ration, the true extent of their supply reserves, I can't really put a date on it. My calculations are generalised; they tell me what's almost certain to happen, but the margin of error is such as to make any prediction unreliable, verging on misleading. I think, though, that a great deal will depend on how quickly and easily they manage to bypass the flooded ditch, and whether we are able to force a conclusive victory in the artillery battle. Those two actions, I feel, will decide the outcome of this siege; which is why I'm pleased to have postponed the first and brought forward the second."

They had to think about that, which suited Psellus very well; it gave him a few moments' grace in which to consider the issues, rather than keeping control of the debate. Of course, the flooded ditch and artillery supremacy were both side issues; he knew precisely what would win or lose the war, and it had precious little to do with sappers, siege engines or even food reserves Such a shame he couldn't share it with them; but it was altogether too private, too intimate for discussion in committee.

"I think we'll leave it there for today," he said accordingly. "Same time tomorrow, gentlemen, if you please, and we'll consider trebuchet shot stock levels and production targets. Thank you for your time."

Time was, as it happened, foremost in his mind. The meeting had over-run (because of those confounded interminable speeches he'd ended up having to make), and the two men sitting in the corridor outside his office had already been waiting half an hour, ten minutes longer than he'd anticipated. He wanted them apprehensive, not worried and stressed into a position of defence in depth. He quickened his pace – the chairman of Necessary Evil never runs in corridors, even if the building is on fire – and tried to clear his mind.

Of course, when you're in a hurry, you always meet someone. Psellus saw him approaching in good time, but there wasn't anywhere to hide in the narrow cloister.

"There you are." Livuo Barazus, permanent secretary of the accounts oversight commission. He'd been bombarding Psellus' clerks with urgent requests for a meeting for days, something to do with a discrepancy in the reconciliations of the grain purchasing budget. A vital and necessary issue, of course, but not now. "You're a hard man to find, Chairman. Now, in the provisional unaudited accounts for the week ending the seventh of—"

Psellus held up his hand. "Excuse me," he said, "but I'm late for a meeting. My chief clerk—"

"This won't take a moment, and then it's done and out of the way." Barazus smiled at him, all teeth. Magnificent teeth, they'd look splendid drilled and hung on a necklace. "There's an entry here, five hundred and seven dollars, paid out on the—"

"My chief clerk," Psellus repeated, slightly louder this time, "has the file and all the relevant papers. He can help you. I can't. I don't know any of the detail, and I'm late for a meeting."

"It's just this one entry here." Barazus was standing directly in front of him, a short, round roadblock. It'd only take the gentlest of shoves to move him out of the way, but that wasn't allowed, not for the chairman of Necessary Evil. A junior ledger clerk or a messenger would get away with it, but not the most powerful man in the City.

"Let me see that," Psellus said.

And there it was, curled up and cowering in among the great big numbers like a little nesting baby bird. He knew what it was the moment he saw it.

"Ah yes," he said. "Before my time, of course. Clearly some unlisted project of my predecessor's. It's such a shame he's not here to explain it for us. I don't suppose we'll ever know now." He shook his head sadly for a fact orphaned by time. "I suggest you annotate that as an unknown expenditure, reference Maris Boioannes. If you'd care to send me the finished account before it's presented, I'll sign the entry off, and that'll cover it for you."

Barazus looked at him in horror, as though he'd just been made an accessory to a murder. Which, in a sense, he had. "Very well," he said, in a quiet, subdued little voice. "Thank you for your time."

"That's perfectly all right," Psellus said, and walked away before Barazus' conscience woke up and started barking at him.

Well, he thought, as he walked. In a way, it was rather satisfying; like cleaning an old piece of silver and suddenly finding the mark of a famous silversmith lurking under the tarnish. And so neatly done; the amount just small enough not to be worth the effort of investigating, unless you happened to be an obsessive like poor Barazus. Presumably there were others just like it, tucked away in dark corners of other accounts, like truffles under the leaf-mould. You couldn't help admiring the cool assurance of the man who'd arranged it. Under other circumstances, it'd be a challenge and a pleasure to track them all down; a hunt, the sort of thing the Vadani duke was supposed to be so keen on, and he could see the attraction – knowing where to look, following the trail, flushing them out one by one and bringing them down with the hawks and hounds of scrupulous accountancy. But that would be an indulgence, and he didn't have the time. One was quite enough. He didn't even need to be able to quote the reference. The simple fact that he knew it existed was quite enough; and, of course, it couldn't conceivably have come to his attention at a better time. It was as though he was walking out into an arena to fight bare-handed for his life, and someone had just handed him a knife, hidden in a bunch of flowers.

They were sitting on a bench in the corridor. They looked up as he approached; he smiled at them, apologised for keeping them waiting, asked them to follow him into the office and sit down.

"I've just come from a meeting with Commissioner Barazus of the accounts department," he said – perfectly legitimate to say that, after all – "and he drew my attention to an anomalous, unexplained payment out of consolidated funds: five hundred dollars, made on the authority of my predecessor." He paused, taking a moment to observe the frozen look on their faces. "I won't ask you if you can shed any light on that. I know it's payment for your services – part of it, anyway – and I don't need to be able to trace it back to you and obtain proof that'll stand up in a court of law, because I don't intend to prosecute. In return," he went on, registering the tiny movements of their face muscles, "you will have to be completely honest with me, and then we can consider the matter closed."

Neither of them spoke, as expected. He went on: "You are both on record as being the investigating officers in the Ziani Vaatzes case. Your signatures were on the original indictment, your statements are listed in the index of pleadings and you both gave evidence at the trial. Now, as you know, I've been interested in the exact sequence of events for some time now. Before I was promoted to my present position, I wrote to you on a number of occasions asking if I could discuss the matter with you, but you never replied. When I approached your superiors, I was put off with vague promises of an interview, and nothing ever happened. When I came to find you, I discovered that you'd been relocated to new offices, and nobody seemed to know where you were. Then you were out of town on various assignments and couldn't be contacted. I was assured I'd be notified when you returned, but I wasn't. Meanwhile, all the files and records relating to the investigation seemed to have melted away; they'd been withdrawn to the archives, or they'd been taken out by someone else, or there'd be a brass tube on a shelf with nothing inside it. Of course, in a vast mechanism like the Guildhall, with its innumerable components constantly in motion, you come to expect a little slack and play here and there. Things go missing, people are inconveniently unavailable, people promise to do things and then forget, through pressure of work, the intervention of more important issues. At the time, of course, I was only a clerk and minor functionary, lacking the authority to make a nuisance of myself. I couldn't insist, I could only make representations in the strongest possible terms. It was safe to ignore me, in the hope that I'd give up and find something else to do."

They were watching him, perfectly still. It must be a very deep-rooted instinct, telling you that if you didn't move, the predator couldn't see you.

"Maris Boioannes, my predecessor," he went on, "personally recommended me for co-option to fill a vacancy in the defence committee. At the time I couldn't understand it: me, suddenly a member of Necessary Evil. I knew I had nothing to offer, and I was proved right, because they gave me nothing to do. It was a shrewd move, but based on a very rare misjudgement. Maris Boioannes assumed that I was an ambitious man – a safe enough assumption, because nearly everybody wants promotion, more money, more prestige. Men like me, who don't care at all about such things, are very rare. Boioannes wasn't to know that about me; why should he? To be honest, I didn't know it about myself until I got the promotion, the money, the prestige, and found they gave me no satisfaction at all. Instead, I felt hopelessly uncomfortable. I wanted to know why I'd been promoted, and I felt sure it was because something, somewhere was wrong. But, as I'm sure you're aware by now, I'm a very commonplace man, nothing at all remarkable about me. At that time, I'd never done anything noteworthy in my life. I thought it over, and reached the only possible conclusion. I was promoted because I'd been taking . . . well, an obsessive interest in Ziani Vaatzes, let's call it what it was. I'd been ordered to make a report on how he'd come to do what he did. They gave me the job precisely because I'd always been such an ineffectual little man, who could be relied on not to get under the skin of the matter. Nobody could have predicted that I'd become obsessed with the detail, the inconsistencies. When I started asking questions, asking to see you two, risking making a nuisance of myself, Boioannes thought the easiest way to get me off the case was to promote me; and besides, it suited him to have a nonentity filling the empty seat on Necessary Evil. You can hardly call it an error of judgement on his part. It was just bad luck, I suppose."

So much talking in one day; he felt physically exhausted, as though he'd been lifting rocks or loading hay. Still, not much further to go now, and then it'd be over.

"Now," he said, "look at me. Maris Boioannes is a wanted fugitive, and I'm sitting in his chair. Suddenly, quite unexpectedly, I'm in a position where all my questions have to be answered; and here you are, sitting across the desk from me, wondering if you're going to be able to get out of this in one piece. Well," he said pleasantly, "I don't see why not, assuming you tell me the whole truth, here and now. Boioannes will take all the blame. Now, I want you to tell me all about the Ziani Vaatzes case, everything you know, right from the beginning."

As he listened to them, he thought: how pleasant, above all, to hear voices other than my own, even if they're not telling me anything I don't already know. It's still a kind of silence; it's like reading only books you've read before, books you've written yourself. Before these people can be made to talk to me, I have to figure out for myself what they have to say, but at least hearing it from them confirms it. Otherwise, I could be forgiven for believing I'm the only human being left in the world –

At which point he smiled, to the bewilderment of the two witnesses. He was thinking: that's right, isn't it? I'm the only human left, and all these man-shaped things who exist only to listen to me speaking are lifesize mechanical dolls (aberrant mechanical dolls) made by Ziani Vaatzes. They can walk and sit and stand up and move their arms and legs, but they can only do what he's designed them to do, and they're all abominations anyhow; which presumably is why the City's got to be burned to the ground. Looked at that way, it all makes sense. Silly of me not to have realised before. The crowning joke, of course, would be if Ziani himself was also a construct, a subprocess in someone else's mechanism, a mechanical doll who makes other mechanical dolls. Now, wouldn't that be a triumph of engineering?

They told him everything. No surprises, though a few of the minor details were news to him. When they'd finished, he nodded, as if to say thank you, and then asked: "Do either of you happen to know why? Why he did it, I mean."

They looked at each other blankly, then shook their heads.

"Ah well." Psellus looked down at his interlaced fingers. "I imagine I should be able to work it out for myself." He lifted his head and smiled reassuringly at them. "You've been most helpful," he said. "In fact, it's probably no exaggeration to say that you've saved the City." He waited for them to ask him to explain what he meant by that. They didn't. "You can go now," he said. They stood up. "It goes without saying that if you tell anybody anything of what we've just been talking about, I'll see to it that you're assigned to one sortie after another until you're both killed." He said it so blandly that it took a moment for them to understand. Then they both looked very scared indeed. *I meant that*, Psellus suddenly realised. *It was a crude, horrible threat, and I was perfectly serious. How depressing.*

As they left the room he asked them to tell the back-office clerk to bring him a glass of milk.

It took an infantry division to move up the siege engines; Aram Chantat, because they were expendable. Some of them pushed, the rest hauled on ropes, while an advance squad with picks, shovels and long steel crowbars prised up and cleared away all the rocks, bushes and other obstructions. Moving the engines was like pulling teeth.

The Mezentines waited till they were on the move before opening up with all batteries. The result, seen from a distance, was spectacular and encouraging. Before the bombardment started, the artillery crews had tightened the mangonels' cord tensioner ratchets and topped up the trebuchets' counterweights to full capacity. Up till then, the machines had been downtuned, to shoot at less than their true maximum range, thereby misleading the enemy into believing that they were safely out of shot. The densely packed columns of men pulling on ropes provided fat, rewarding targets. From the embankment palisade, each shot as it landed looked like a flat stone skimmed across still water; on its first pitch, it splashed down, sending up spray. The it bounced, two, three, four times, each time splashing casualties into the air. The idea was that the fifth bounce should drop the shot on to the engine itself, wrecking it. The artillery crew commanders weren't expecting it to happen like that; the most they'd been hoping for was two, perhaps occasionally three splashes before the shot deflected and fell harmless. It was remarkable how often their expectations were exceeded.

At the other end of the trajectory, the stone at first appeared in the sky like a small, dark moon. To begin with it seemed to be hanging quite still in the air. Only as it dropped and the regularity of the curve of its descent began to decay did the men watching it suddenly realise how fast it was moving, and how impossible it was to predict accurately where it was going to fall. It was quite perverse how often a column of men decided, unanimous and unprompted, to move five yards to the right or left, only to realise (too late) that they'd put themselves directly under the falling stone. When it pitched, it scooped up a mess of torn and bruised turf, dirt, crushed and smashed bodies. A remarkable number of men were killed by splinters of rocks pulverised by the impact of the pitching shot; others had arms and legs broken when dead men fell on them. As the great stone balls bounced, they picked up extra spin from their contact with the ground. Some survivors spoke about the shot kicking up, darting inexplicably right or left, jumping up on the first bounce, then shooting low on the second. When a ball hit a siege engine, the result tended to be a shower of shattered beams, joists, iron fittings, along with blade-sharp chips of stone from the ball itself. The smaller flying debris struck with the force of a hard punch; at first the shock of the impact numbed you; it could be twenty or thirty seconds before you looked down and saw the blood, or tried to move a limb that wasn't there any more. Nearly all the survivors stressed the effect of the noise of the ball landing, saying that they'd never heard anything as loud before. Louder than thunder was a frequent comparison, followed by the qualification: so much louder, it wasn't really like thunder at all. It was a noise you felt rather than heard.

On the embankment, as soon as the sears were dropped, the crews stood still and watched the fall of shot. When they saw the first volley go home so beautifully true, they assumed it was all over; instead of bustling to span the windlasses for another shot, they were cheering, shouting congratulations to each other. It took a while for anybody to notice that, instead of scattering and running for their lives, the enemy (the surviving enemy) were still there, still grimly hauling on their ropes or heaving against their frames, as though nothing had happened. There were two or three seconds of complete silence; then the captains began yelling, and the crews jumped at windlass handles, frantically winding up for a shot they'd assumed they wouldn't have to take. That was perfectly understandable. From the embankment, they couldn't see individual men. The hauling parties merged into dense black shapes, so that you could imagine you were shooting at something like a huge beached jellyfish; and once you'd hit it fair and square, it was perfectly reasonable to assume you'd killed it, and that was that.

The second volley was a mess, as the captains themselves admitted afterwards. Mostly it was because they neglected to take up the elevation, to allow for the short but crucial distance each target had moved since the first volley. Most of them overshot; not by much, ten or fifteen yards. The few that hit something mostly scored direct hits on the engines themselves; extremely satisfying, to see an enemy trebuchet dissolve into a cloud of splinters, but a skidder splattering dead savages would've been better still. The third volley was better, although there were still more partial hits and outright misses than there'd been first time around. A good start, then, but spoilt somewhat by a failure to follow up.

The Mezentines were spanning for a fourth volley when the enemy started shooting back. They shouldn't have been able to do that. According to all the best estimates, the enemy line was still over a hundred yards out of range. They were, after all, supposed to be using copies of the obsolete and superseded Type Twenty-One heavy trebuchet, Type Seventeen light trebuchet and Type Twenty-Seven mangonel. It was only when the sky suddenly filled with small hanging moons that it occurred to anybody that Ziani Vaatzes may have made some improvements of his own.

Afterwards, the blame was placed squarely on the commissioners of the topographical and geological survey. They should have pointed out, it was held, that the enemy might be expected to have quarried stone for their shot from the limestone deposits at Veraiso, so conveniently adjacent to their predictable line of march. Given this important information, the ordnance and fortifications subcommittees would have known in advance that Vaatzes' engines would be likely to use smaller shot (because limestone was denser than the sandstone from the City quarries), which would fly faster, hit harder and – most important – shatter and disintegrate on impact into clouds of wide-dispersal shrapnel, liable to inflict serious casualties among closely packed groups of men. If only they'd known, the fortifications subcommittee could have specified more effective cover on the embankment – pavises, sidewalls of gabions and fascines, a half-roofed covered way. Casualties would still have been unavoidable, but the appalling carnage inflicted by the first and second allied volleys could certainly have been mitigated, possibly by up to forty per cent.

Night fell, and the artillery captains could no longer see to aim. Finished round shot was too precious to be wasted on random bombardment. By torchlight, the Mezentines counted forty-six of their engines wrecked beyond repair, including nine of the fifty heavy trebuchets. A further twenty-eight were taken apart and carried back to the factory to be rebuilt. It was hard to establish the number of the dead, let alone identify them; a preliminary estimate, based on responses to an emergency roll call, came to a hundred and sixty dead, as many again too badly injured to resume their duties. Around midnight, the bombardment started up again. The allies were launching unshaped rocks at random, to disrupt the salvage and repair operations, damage the embankment and stop the defenders getting even a few hours' sleep. Repeated impacts on the same spot had the effect of scooping out large holes in the embankment; when dawn came, it looked for all the world as though it was infested with giant rabbits. Nothing could be done to repair the breaches, or prevent further deterioration as the disturbed earth settled.

Chairman Psellus was awake when the messenger came. He received the news calmly, thanked the messenger and sent him away. As the door closed, the messenger saw him bend his head over a book, a little book which he shielded in his cupped hands, like a man cradling an injured bird.

As soon as the messenger had made his report, General Daurenja called a meeting of the full general staff, including the Aram Chantat liaison and his entourage. Losses, he announced, had been heavy: thirty-seven engines destroyed, nine others likely to be out of action for a day or more. He'd budgeted, he told them, for fifty or more engines lost, so the damage was less than he'd anticipated. On the other hand, he'd hoped to have won the artillery battle by now, and it was quite evident that he hadn't. The continuing bombardment was very much a fallback option, since it meant that each crew would have to work a full extra shift; as well as the machines themselves, they'd lost ninety-two trained artillerymen killed or put of out action, which meant he'd had to commit all the standby crews. That would inevitably lead to a loss of precision and efficiency when the battle resumed tomorrow, but he felt he had no choice but to take that risk. The advantages of keeping the enemy under pressure outweighed the drawbacks, and he firmly believed that the stress and loss of sleep the night bombardment would cause would more than make up for his own crews' likely inability to function at peak efficiency. The Aram Chantat liaison was quick to voice his support for the general's immediate tactical judgement and broader strategic vision. He would see to it that Aram Chantat volunteers were available at dawn to take over the unskilled tasks – shifting and loading missiles, spanning windlasses and so forth – thus reducing the load on the trained Eremians and Vadani. He also took the opportunity to commend the general for the vigour, energy and resourcefulness with which he was prosecuting the assault.

When the meeting broke up, the Aram Chantat went back to their tents; all but one of them, who took a horse and set off on the road to Civitas Vadanis. In spite of the danger, he took the border road, the same route Duke Valens had been following when he was attacked; the urgency of his mission outweighed the danger, and besides, there had been no reports of Cure Doce activity in the area ever since the ambush. He had memorised one message and carried another, written on a scrap of thin rawhide cut off the handle-wrapping of a broken bow. It read:

> Gace Daurenja to Ziani Vaatzes, greetings.
>   You need to upgrade the Type Three; it hasn't got the range. Can you modify all the pieces you still have at the city and send them _immediately_. Also send more finished shot. When will the worms be ready? Send prototypes as soon as they're serviceable. The horsehair you've been using for the mangonel springs hasn't got the strength for the top setting. Use four plies instead of three; also send spares, since they've been breaking. Most important: get the weapon ready to ship. Box it up so nobody can guess what's in there, and send it with at least 2 squadrons _Vadani_ cavalry escort. Things here are going well. GD.

The verbal message was duly delivered to the Aram Chantat privy council. It made them very angry for a while. Then they calmed down and composed a reply.

Chapter Fourteen

The artillery duel resumed next morning, but the situation had changed. During the night, while their engines kept up their blind pounding of the embankment, the allies had built a wall of gabions and fascines in front of their artillery line, to protect the working parties – every man who could be spared from other duties – who now set about digging a bank and ditch to shelter the engines from the Mezentines' incoming fire. They worked with a speed that astonished the observers on the City embankment, who immediately stopped trying to pick off the allied engines and began dropping their shot into the dense mass of diggers and earth-shifters. It was, as one artillery officer said later, practically impossible to miss. Each shot was sure of killing two or three workers, and the Mezentines quickly found out that if they managed to pitch a shot on the rapidly rising bank itself, there was a good chance it would skip and skim, cutting a bloody channel through the teams of men wheeling barrows of spoil or shovelling earth into gabions. As soon as Chairman Psellus heard about this, he ordered the artillery captains to stop it and go back to targeting the engines themselves. The captains were extremely reluctant to obey this order; the diggers were much easier to hit than the engines or their crews, and they felt they were achieving something. It was only when Psellus himself appeared on the embankment and gave the order in person that they eventually complied.

By mid-afternoon the bank was eight feet high, topped with a double line of gabions. It didn't provide a total defence, but it meant that the Mezentines now had to drop their stones directly on top of the engines in order to damage them, instead of being able to pitch short and either roll or skim their shot until it hit something. The allies, of course, had faced the same problem from the outset, but the fact that their shot tended to shatter on impact meant that although they rarely hit a machine, they were killing artillery crews at a rate which even the general expressed himself satisfied with. As he told the Aram Chantat liaison that evening, the Mezentines were manufacturers rather than soldiers; they could build new engines much faster than they could train men to use them, and so killing the trained men was a much more efficient course of action than merely smashing up equipment.

After his meeting with the liaison, Daurenja sent for Colonel Ducas of the Eremian contingent. The messenger found him, after a long search, leading a party of stretcher-bearers. They'd spent the afternoon collecting the wounded from the bank site, prising them out from under spent shot with beams ands crowbars. Miel himself had carried the axe and the saw, because a large number of them were pinned down by an arm or a leg; it wasn't a job he felt he could delegate. His knees were plastered with a putty of mud and blood, and he'd wrenched his back contorting himself as he tried to haul a paralysed man out from under a stone by his ankle and wrist. When the messenger found him, he said he was too busy to go; now that the bombardment had stopped, he said, they had to make full use of the time available to get as many wounded men out as possible. The messenger had to point out that it was a direct order from the commander-in-chief.

He found Daurenja sitting on an upturned bucket outside his tent. He was grinding something with a pestle and mortar.

"Colonel Leucas was killed in the bombardment," Daurenja said, looking earnestly into the mortar.

"Oh."

It wasn't what Miel would have chosen to say, but he was tired and frustrated at having to leave the work he knew he should be doing. Besides, Imbrota Leucas had been a pinhead, barely capable of blowing his nose.

"I expect you knew him," Daurenja said.

"Yes, of course. Actually, I never liked him much."

Daurenja shrugged. "Obviously, we need to replace him as commander of the Eremian contingent. You know your own people; they need a Leucas or a Phocas or a Ducas to lead them or they won't do as they're told."

Miel didn't grasp the implications of that straight away. Then he said, "I see."

Daurenja looked up. "I'd have thought you'd have been the natural choice instead of Leucas," he said, "only you weren't around when Valens made the original appointment; and besides, I seem to remember there's some kind of bad blood between the two of you. Anyhow, that's not important now. I suggest you use the existing staff, at least until you've had a chance to pick people you're more comfortable working with. I'm afraid I'll be asking a lot of you Eremians before this siege is over."

Miel looked at him, and thought: some kind of bad blood. "If I don't want the job, can I refuse?"

"Of course." Daurenja was staring into his mortar again. "But I don't imagine you will. You have a duty to your people, and that matters far more to you than any personal issues between you and me. I gather you've been rescuing the wounded."

"That's right."

Daurenja nodded. "Nobody told you to," he said. "In fact, you'd been assigned other duties, a nice safe job out of the line of fire. But you disobeyed orders and did what you felt had to be done. Well, that's fine. I know I can rely on you. Besides," he added with a yawn, "I owe you something for saving my life that time. I do try and pay my debts."

Miel frowned. "That's funny," he said. "The way I remember it, I tried to get Valens to have you hanged."

"That's right. But before that, you kept my ex-partner Framain from bashing my head in with a rock. If you hadn't done that, I'd be dead." He shrugged. "I tried to pay you back for that by assigning you to a job away from where the shot was falling, but I should've known better. The way to reward you is to give you a chance to do your duty. That's the sort of man you are. I understand you, you see. If you could stop hating me for a minute or so, you'd see we're not that different. Only, your duty's to your people and mine's to my work. Otherwise, we're basically the same. So," he added with a weary sigh, "you'll take the job, because you don't really have a choice. That's how I do things, you see. It's a basic premise of engineering. Components run in precisely cut keyways until they meet a stop. Everything does exactly what it's supposed to do, because it has no choice."

Miel thought about that for a moment. "Fine," he said. "Will it be all right if I get cleaned up first?"

Daurenja nodded. "And I'd grab some sleep while you can, if I were you. In the morning, I've got a job for your people. Nothing unpleasant," he added, with a faint smile, "but quite important." Then he turned his head and shifted his back a little, so that Miel no longer existed and he was free to concentrate absolutely on the contents of the pot on his knees.

The job turned out to be strenuous but simple: to collect, remove and pile up neatly all the finished round shot the enemy had fired at the allied line during the artillery duel. It was, the staff major explained, a marvellous windfall: thousands of rounds of precision-finished, Mezentine-made trebuchet and mangonel ammunition; hard, unlike the soft shit from the local quarries, and therefore exactly what they'd need for bashing down the City walls when the time came. The joy of it was (the major said) that the enemy couldn't reuse spent allied shot in the same way, since it smashed all to pieces when it pitched; every round, both outgoing and incoming, was a dead loss to them, whereas every shot that landed on or over the new bank was effectively profit.

The duel continued all through the next day, but the rate of fire on both sides gradually subsided. Because so many of their artillerymen had been killed or wounded, the Mezentines were having trouble finding fresh crews for the machines at the end of each shift. Increasing shift length from three to five hours kept the machines in action, but the men were exhausted, and the rate dropped from six to two shots per machine per hour, until Psellus ordered that the batteries should be rested in rotation, since fewer machines firing faster and more accurately put more shots on target than all the available machines shooting slowly and missing. He was also deeply worried about the rate at which the ammunition was being used up. The stone-cutting plant, working flat out, could just about keep up with the demands of the artillery so long as their supply of rough-cut stone blanks held out. Once they were all used up, however, the only way to get raw material was to pull down buildings, break up the stone blocks and cart them to the shot factory; Psellus told the supply commissioners to press as many men and carts as they needed, but the sheer volume of carts in the narrow streets around the factory led to horrendous jams, which in turn held up the supplies of finished shot being sent to the embankment.

The allies had similar problems. Daurenja was being careful with his finished shot, which was reserved for precision shooting at the enemy machines, since only perfectly round balls flew straight; the majority of his engines were throwing unshaped rocks and boulders, trying to batter down and collapse the parts of the embankment where the batteries were. This approach was proving successful, but he'd underestimated how much shot it took to dislodge enough earth to do any good. All the loose boulders and outcrop in the vicinity had been used up during the first night, and the quarrymen and carts that should have been making and shipping finished shot were busy with rough-hewn stuff; and even so, demand was outstripping supply. As a result, at sunset the bombardment stopped, giving the engineers a desperately needed opportunity to patch up the machines, which were starting to tear themselves apart under the stress of seventy-two hours' continuous use.

Not that Daurenja was unduly worried. As he told the Aram Chantat, the artillery battle was a sideshow compared with the serious business of repairing and extending the approach trenches. Work on these had continued at an entirely satisfactory rate of progress throughout the artillery battle, while the enemy's attention had successfully been drawn elsewhere. Most important of all, the machine trench had not only been repaired but was now half a day ahead of schedule, and with any luck should be finished and ready for use by the time the worms arrived from Civitas Vadanis.

Miel Ducas was woken up at dawn by the silence. He'd got used to the noise, and the way the ground shook every time a two-hundred-weight stone ball landed, and the smell of disturbed earth, which reminded him of flying falcons on newly ploughed fields, at the very end of the partridge season. He'd been dreaming about that, in fact, remembering a day when he was – what, sixteen? – when he'd been invited out for Closing Day with the Count Sirupat and his guests; and she'd been there, looking very nervous on a tall, slim chestnut mare that spooked every time the falcon on her wrist fretted and flapped its wings. His dream was mostly just memory, except that every time he looked in her direction, her face was turned away, and he could only see the edge of her cheek.

He woke up to find himself sitting upright, the blanket tangled; and he noticed that the little spindly-legged table they'd issued him with for writing his reports on was still standing upright. Yesterday and the day before, it had been knocked down by the vibrations.

He yawned, then winced, as he remembered that he'd hurt his back the previous day. Carefully he tried to turn his head: not good. That bothered him. Trivial aches and pains, that sort a civilian grins and bears; but anything that slows down a soldier or impedes his ability to move instinctively can easily prove more fatal than cholera.

But we aren't going to be fighting anybody today, he told himself. Instead, we're picking up stones and piling them neatly; our contribution to the war effort. Oh yes, and I've been appointed supreme commander of the Eremian army.

He looked at his armour, heaped up in the corner of the tent, and thought, the hell with it. There won't be any Mezentines roaming about on this side of the bank, and if I get hit by a mangonel ball, armour's not going to make any difference. For the sake of appearances he put on his padded aketon, but he left the ironmongery where it lay.

The young captain (he'd been told the man's name twice, forgotten it, was too embarrassed to ask a third time) met him in the trench, as he made his way out to the artillery positions.

"They've stopped the bombardment," Whatsisname said. "We won."

Miel smiled. "You may have noticed, we aren't shooting either. Doesn't that make it a draw?"

"Yes, but we're in possession of the field."

The field, he thought; well yes, that's what soldiers fight for. Not for a cause, truth, freedom, to save the lives of innocents, for countries or principles, trade routes, the resolution of disputes between nations. They fight for the field, thirty-odd acres of farmland ruined in the process, whose value lies only in the fact that the enemy have been forcibly excluded from it. Back on the home estate, there'd been a forty-acre pasture called Battle Moor; and from time to time, when it was ploughed and reseeded, they turned up bones, bits of rusty junk so badly corroded it was anybody's guess what they'd once been. Nobody knew who'd fought there, of course, or why.

The field. The Mezentines weren't farmers, and the plain in front of the City hadn't been cultivated for as long as they'd been there. Once a year, at midsummer, they hired foreigners to come and burn off the dried grass and the rubbish, to keep it from turning into a jungle. Apparently it was quite a sight to see, though the City people moaned about the smoke, and the flecks of soot on their clean washing for days afterwards. Other than that, they showed no interest in it whatsoever; until now, of course, when it had suddenly become the field, every last inch to be fought for to the last drop of blood. The deep strata of ash made it pleasantly light and easy to dig, according to the sappers, though once you got down underneath you hit flints, and a singularly bloody-minded type of clay.

Today, the field was different. The stones stood out like huge puffballs, the sort you can't resist kicking, because of how they disintegrate. There were also the dead bodies. Those killed on the second day were starting to swell, and there were flies everywhere. They soared up in a cloud as you walked past, and the soft hum was strangely soothing, like the sound of a river a quarter of a mile away. Miel Ducas knew all about battlefields, of course. The only thing that made this one different was the absence of the usual scavengers (he knew all about them now, of course; the useful function they performed in cleaning up and making good; like earthworms in a garden, or a graveyard).

"Organise a burial detail," he said to nobody in particular (because when the commander-in-chief speaks, there's always someone listening, with a notebook). "We've got enough problems without plague as well." Then it occurred to him to wonder: did the Aram Chantat bury their dead or burn them? It was the sort of thing that caused horrendous trouble if you got it wrong. "You'd better find out what the savages want done with theirs," he added quickly.

Not far away, ten yards or so, a man was trying to lift his arm. Most of his body was under a stone, and by the look of it his forearm was smashed as well; it flopped as he tried to wave. The kindest thing would be a dozen men with pollaxes, walking up and down and putting the hopeless cases out of their misery (he'd seen enough bullocks and pigs and sheep slaughtered; one peck between the eyes with the horn of the pollaxe. When you've done thirty in a morning, it's just a chore). Instead, he told whoever it was whose turn it was to be listening to get that man out of there, and organise some orderlies with stretchers, and let the surgeons know.

Men started bustling about; he assumed they were doing what he'd told them to do. He turned, slowly because of his cricked neck, and took a long, interested look at the bank, which so many men had died to build. It was just a mound of earth, with a row of those filled-basket things on top. Here and there it had been battered down, and men were working briskly to put it back straight again. It was, of course, a remarkable achievement, considered as the end product of human labour and effort. He tried to imagine how it'd look in two hundred years' time – a little bit lower and smoother, grassed over, with paths scratched deep in it here and there by the passage of sheep. Not the ruins of a city, not a road, or a levee, not even an aquifer or a drain; just an expedient scooped up in a hurry to keep the worst of the hailstones off, something that had briefly served a temporary purpose, but which would probably last for ever, long after the reason for its existence had been forgotten.

(Motives fade, he thought; actions endure. A thousand men died to win the field, and the lasting result is a grassy bank in the middle of a flat plain. But they didn't die to build a bank – that was just a trivial side-effect; they died – some immediately, some after three motionless days in the stink, trying to wave a broken arm – for the field, as all soldiers do.)

Collecting the spent shot was straightforward hard work. They let down the tailgate of the cart and laid the ends of two poles on the floorboards. Then two men rolled the stone ball up this improvised ramp, and a third man standing in the bed of the cart hauled it in so it wouldn't roll out again. So simple, Miel thought, even Eremians can do it. Presumably he was there to supervise, to make the men work as fast as possible. No need; they were going at it like lunatics, presumably because they expected the bombardment to start again at any moment. In which case, he wondered, what did they need him for? He could only suppose he was required as a witness, in case it should ever be necessary to prove that the artillery battle had actually taken place, and wasn't just an embellishment added to the story by an ambitious historian. Well, he was, after all, the nearest thing they had to a resident expert on the aftermath of battles, the sole representative of the corpse-robbers' profession. As such, he knew more about the field than any duke or general. Quite probably, he was the only one who really understood: that every battle is for the field, which is a place where dead men lie until the scavengers come to pick up, clean up and cart away the residues, both the useful and the useless. The war is a complex mechanism, whose escapement is the battle, whose function is to produce nothing but waste; as if you peeled apples to get the peel and the core, and threw the fruit away.

(He considered Daurenja, and wondered if the substantial enterprise of advancing the artillery and building the bank to protect it was simply a way of getting the Mezentines to supply him with ammunition. It was just the sort of thing he'd be capable of doing, if he needed finished round shot badly enough.)

They moved a stone, and under it was a man; an Eremian, who recognised him. The man was dying. The stone had crushed his ribs, and the sharp end of one of them had punctured his lung.

"I remember you," Miel said. "Only I can't quite . . ."

The man said he'd been a huntsman before the war, in the service of Jarnac Ducas. Then he remembered. This was the man who whipped the hounds off the deer as soon as it was dead, so they wouldn't tear it apart. He tried to think of something to say, but he couldn't find any words. Instead, the man asked him: was it true that Jarnac was dead? There were rumours, but . . .

Miel nodded. "Quite true, I'm afraid," he said. "He was with Duke Valens in the retreat, when they were making for the desert. He died very bravely."

The man nodded. "He used to worry, you know," he said. "About all the animals he killed. He said it was all right really, because we ate the meat, so actually it was no worse than farming. He used to give the meat away, most of it, to the people in the villages. But he hated it if an animal was badly pricked, like in bow and stable, and it got away and wasn't found. He said it must be the worst thing, dying slowly in pain."

Miel felt he should say something like: rest now, don't say any more, you need to lie still. But he knew the man was dying, beyond help, and he only wanted him to stop because he didn't want to hear any more. "I didn't know that," he said. "He never said anything like that to me."

The man tried to grin. "Well he wouldn't, not to his own kind. But he worried a lot about it, and I'd have liked him to know: actually, it's not so bad. You'd think you'd be scared, but you aren't. You just think, well, that's that, then, and then you just wait quietly." He let his neck and back relax, like a man settling into a soft bed with clean sheets. "It'd have been nice to have set his mind at rest, but I don't suppose it matters now."

Miel nodded; but he said: "I thought I was going to die, not long ago, and I was terrified."

The man smiled. "Ah well," he said. "You thought, you didn't know. When you know, it's really not so bad." And then he died, and as Miel watched he turned from a human being into an object, a dead weight for the burial detail; and with him faded all the other evidence he could have given. Miel looked down at his face for a while, but there was nothing there.

When it got too dark to see, he sent back to the camp for lanterns, picked on the first officer he could find, and delegated the conduct of the night shift to him. The poor young fool acted as though he'd been awarded a great honour.

On his way back to the camp, he thought about Jarnac, and Orsea.

As a matter of courtesy, Daurenja sent a note to Duke Valens to inform him that he'd appointed the Ducas to lead the Eremian contingent. He added that he had a high opinion of the Ducas' loyalty and sense of duty, and trusted that the appointment met with the duke's approval.

Nobody bothered to tell the messenger that the letter he was carrying was just a formality, so he rode through the night, taking the border road, changing horses twice at the military inns. Determined to make the best time he possibly could, he took a short cut through Stachia woods in the dark, rode into a low branch at the gallop and ripped the side of his face open. He had a scarf, which he wrapped round his head to stop the bleeding; it was sodden by the time he reached the Tolerance and Compassion, where he was lucky enough to find a fellow messenger heading for the city who undertook to take the general's letter the rest of the way.

The other letter he carried was to the Aram Chantat high council. It was read to them by a Vadani secretary, since the more traditional

Aram Chantat still tended to regard literacy as a weakness, liable to undermine the imagination and the memory. In it, the liaison reported on the conduct of the siege, commending General Daurenja for his diligence and resourcefulness. A motion was passed confirming the general as commander-in-chief for the duration of the siege. It was held that, although Duke Valens was a capable leader, he had not shown the same level of vision and commitment that the general had displayed; indeed, Valens' injury, though deplorable, could be seen as fortuitous. Naturally, once the war was over, the position would be reviewed. However, it was never too early to consider the future. The Aram Chantat nation faced the prospect of being ruled for the first time by a foreigner, since there was no male heir. As the widower of the heiress apparent, Valens was indisputably the legal heir. However, should he die before the king – unlikely, of course, unless he suffered complications to his wound; an infection, for example, all too real a possibility – the succession would pass through the king's great-niece, currently only twelve years old and therefore too young to marry, unless a special exemption from the law was made by, for instance, a regency committee appointed by the high council. In that event, it would be inviting internal dissent and possible civil war to permit her to marry an Aram Chantat, in which case a suitable foreigner would have to be selected; a man with proven leadership capability, strong-minded, dynamic, preferably someone held in high regard by the people on account of (say) his war service. All such speculation was, of course, entirely hypothetical, and simple loyalty required the council to hope that Duke Valens would make a quick and complete recovery. Nevertheless, the fact that the duke had married again, so soon after the death of the princess, and that his new wife had already conceived a child, meant that if Valens survived his present serious illness, the Aram Chantat could look forward to being ruled by an entirely foreign dynasty for the foreseeable future. It had not escaped the council's notice that this state of affairs had not escaped the notice of the people in general, and was not entirely to their liking. Voices of complaint (which the council naturally deplored, but could not afford to ignore) had been raised even before Valens was injured. The serious threat to his life posed by the wound and the drastic medical procedures that had been deemed necessary to attempt to heal it had inevitably led the people to reconsider the whole succession issue. Furthermore, there were unconfirmed reports that the king's own medical advisers were seriously concerned about the state of *his* health . . .

The Vadani secretary had been dismissed after he'd read the letter and taken down the brief formal acknowledgement to be sent in reply. But as reading aloud made him thirsty, he'd begged a drink from the chamberlains and sat quietly drinking it in the anteroom next to the chapterhouse where the meeting was being held; he had better than average hearing, and someone had neglected to close the connecting door properly.

"I shouldn't have told you," she said.

Valens frowned. "Yes you should," he said. "If they're really thinking about killing me . . ."

"We don't know that. It's much more likely that we're reading too much into this. After all, we don't really understand how their minds work, they were probably only discussing contingency plans, just in case you don't get better. And the doctors say you're healing up really fast now."

Very slowly and deliberately, like a team of engineers raising a tower, he hauled himself forward a few inches on his elbows and sat up. "It's what I'd do," he said. "Think about it. They've got to resign themselves to a foreign king, they've got no choice. They marry their princess to me, figuring it'll provoke war with the Mezentines so they can clear out everything our side of the mountains and have a new homeland to settle in. Turns out that wasn't necessary: when they get here, they find we're already at war, so that's all right. But then the princess gets killed. They've been reassuring themselves that it's all right really, the next dynasty will be only half-foreign, her and my children; but then she dies, I marry you and they're faced with being ruled by strangers for ever. What's more, by marrying you, I've shown them I'm not really interested in what's best for the Aram Chantat; otherwise I'd have waited till this twelve-year-old kid came of age and married her. Instead, I marry for love" – he paused on that word, frowned as much as the pain in his face would let him – "which probably doesn't carry much weight with them, I really couldn't say, I know so little about them. And to cap it all, they believe I've been lukewarm about the war. And now they've got an alternative, the brave, committed general, and he's neither Eremian nor Vadani, so he won't be likely to favour either race above the Aram Chantat if he becomes king. If you look at it rationally, they'd be failing in their duty if they didn't at least consider it."

She thought: he's talking to himself, not me. Which is fine; it's part of my job to be someone the duke can think aloud to, it's a very necessary function. "You make it sound like you sympathise with them," she said.

"I do," he replied. "They're in deep trouble. The other Cure Hardy nations have more or less driven them out of their own country. They've had to leave their home, cross the desert, come here and immediately start fighting a singularly vicious war; they know that even if they win, a lot of their people will die in it, and if they lose they're facing a famine. Added to that, their new king's going to be a foreigner who doesn't look like he really gives a damn about them." He shook his head. "And I happen to know that that's true: the heir apparent doesn't care about them, in fact he can't stand being in the same room with them for too long – something he's done his best to keep to himself, but he's a rotten actor and they're not stupid. And they're right about him being lukewarm about the war, too."

She looked at him again, noticing how lined and furrowed his face had become lately, as though it was under siege, deeply scored with trenches; and she thought, that's the face of a man who's only recently realised that love doesn't solve everything, that having each other isn't really enough. Poor man; he's lived his life thinking that the book closes at the first kiss, and being in love is like crossing a border, over which they can't follow you. Perhaps he thought love could be starved out with a blockade, or stormed with overwhelming force, once the defences had been undermined. Those are the sort of terms he'd tend to think in (Valens the problem-solver, the man who gets the job done, the good duke); and now they've taken away the command and given it to the freak, because of me.

But she said: "So what are you going to do about it?"; not because she wanted to know, but because he did, and if she couldn't be his soul, she could at least be that part of his mind that chafed him into action.

But he shrugged, as though they were talking about someone else, a friend of hers that he tolerated for her sake but had never really liked. "I'll have to go there," he said, "and take the war back from Daurenja."

It was the reply she'd been expecting, but it made her flinch. "You can't," she said. "You're not well enough."

"That's right," he said. "But it's not like I've got a choice." He wriggled his shoulders against the pillow. "First, because I don't want to be got rid of. Second, because Daurenja's getting it all wrong. He's doing exactly what they want him to, but he can't see that because he's convinced he's winning." He scowled, either at some thought that crossed his mind, or from the pain of moving. "Could you send someone to fetch Ziani Vaatzes?" he said. "I need to see him right away."

She didn't say *don't leave me*, because if she said it he'd have to obey. But she did say, "You're far too weak still to cope with running the war. If you go, you'll be playing into their hands. You'll make a mistake, and that'll give them all the excuse they need."

"That's possible," he said; and he was arguing against her now. She'd become yet another difficulty in his way. "But you never know, I might not. And if I stay here, I'm finished, and so are the Vadani. So . . ." He shrugged again. "There you have it," he said. "Look, do you think you could find someone to fetch Vaatzes? He'll be heading off to the camp any day now, and I'd like to hitch a ride."

"Will you take me with you?"

It wasn't the question she wanted to ask, but quite obviously it meant the same thing. It would, of course, have been better to have said nothing at all.

He paused, only for a short time, then said, "Yes, of course."

They always addressed him as "Engineer Vaatzes", and he wasn't quite sure how he felt about that. He assumed they meant it as a mark of respect, or they intended him to feel flattered by it; and it was, of course, an appropriate title. Somehow, though, it made him feel uncomfortable, maybe because it came from them. He didn't know for sure, since it wasn't the sort of thing he ever discussed with them, but he had an idea they disapproved of what he did on a very basic level, like vegetarians disapproving of eating meat.

Two of them he'd met before, though he couldn't remember their names or what they did; he knew they were fairly important but not very important, and so he had to be polite to them. The third one he'd never seen, and the other two didn't introduce him, which meant he was either some clerk or assistant who didn't matter at all, or someone very important indeed.

"We appreciate the exceptional effort you've been making," one of the familiar ones said, "and the quite remarkable achievement your results represent. Without your machines, the entire project would collapse; more than that, it could never have begun in the first place." He paused for a moment and touched the headstock casing of the Mezentine turret lathe, which was nominally what they'd come here to admire. He prodded it tentatively, as if expecting it to be dangerously hot. "However," he went on, "I have to tell you, the siege is rapidly approaching a critical stage. The general has instructed me that the design of the heavy trebuchet' (he didn't pronounce the word quite right) "needs to be modified, to give further range. He appreciates that this will cause delays, and you are therefore to ship all the completed pieces you presently have in hand without making the necessary modifications; the general will attend to that himself."

Oh really, Ziani thought, and smiled. "Sorry," he said. "It can't be done."

The Aram Chantat stared at him, as though Ziani had just spat in his face.

"It's quite simple," Ziani said cheerfully. "To increase the range, you need either a heavier counterweight or a longer throwing arm, or both. But we can't make the weight heavier or it'll crack the frame, and we can't make the arm longer, or it'll just snap as soon as you loose off a shot. I can beef up the frame and the arm, of course, but that'll add to the weight, which reduces the efficiency, and you won't actually get the shot to go further or faster; all it'll mean is the machine'll be harder to move about. Now, if I could use box-section steel instead of oak beams for the cradle assembly, like the Mezentines do, that'd be a different matter, but producing box-section would mean I'd have to build a special furnace and rolling-mill, which would take at least three months, even if I had enough skilled workers, which I don't." He paused, wondering why it was so satisfying to say no to these people. "Of course, if the general's found a way to get round the problem, I'll be only too happy to use it."

All three of them were looking at him; he could trace the workings of their minds, as if he was studying a mechanism. They believed him; in which case, they were thinking, the general's demand was unrealistic and unreasonable, and clearly he doesn't know as much about making these weapons as he thinks he does, which in turn is a fault in him which we weren't previously aware of. And yet, they were thinking, Engineer Vaatzes recommended him for the job . . .

"What I can do," he went on, " is forget about the trebuchets and concentrate on getting the worms ready to ship. After all," he added carefully, "they're what's going to win us the war, as you know as well as I do."

As quite obviously they didn't. "We were going to ask you about them," the third man said – he spoke, so that meant he had to be very important indeed. Ziani turned his head a little, towards the third man and away from the other two.

"Come and see for yourself," he said. "I can tell you how they work, if you like."

It annoyed him that they weren't interested in what he showed them and didn't even try to understand what he told them. Of course he appreciated that it was entirely alien to them, as remote as horse-breeding and cattle-herding were to him, but after all, it was their war and they should have made the effort.

Afterwards, he took them to see the small-arms line. They liked that. They were impressed by the drop-hammers churning out sword-blade blanks, and the four-foot-diameter wheels that ground in the bevels, though they made a point of telling him several times that they did it differently in their country, and their way was much better. The swages that formed complete arrowheads in one pass wiped the smirks off their faces.

"You made this machine?" the third man said.

Ziani nodded. "It's a copy of the plant in the City ordnance factory," he said, "except that I modified it. The original machine does it in two steps; it makes the socket, then it goes back in the fire to heat up again, and then it forms the blade. My version's almost twice as fast."

He could feel them wanting him. In fact, not having him would eat them slowly away. He considered pointing out that the swage blocks and the trip-hammer together weighed just over seven tons, so it'd be useless to them; even if they managed to build a wagon strong enough to carry it, the time and effort involved in loading and unloading it whenever they needed to make arrowheads made it completely impractical. But no, he thought, let them want me, by all means. "If you think that's impressive, just wait till you see how we turn and fletch the shafts," he said.

"And they have machines like this in the City?" the third man asked, when they'd done the full tour.

"Loads of them," Ziani replied. "But, as I'm sure you'll appreciate, the machines aren't any use without trained men to work them, and fix them when they break down. And it takes years to train someone."

"You could train them, couldn't you?"

He nodded briskly. "Yes," he said. "Me and General Daurenja. Apart from him and me, though, I don't think there's anybody outside the City."

The third man frowned, while the other two kept perfectly still and quiet. "And then there's the materials," he said. "I couldn't help noticing; all the iron and steel you use. The sheets perfectly flat, the same thickness all the way through; and the round and square bars we saw on the racks in your storeroom. Presumably you have other machines somewhere else . . ."

"That's right," Ziani said. "The furnace and the rolling-mill. Both of them are much bigger than this. There's well over a thousand people working there."

"All skilled men, presumably."

"That's right, yes. Far more difficult than this, in fact. But essential; before I built the furnace and the mill, we had to make do with hand-worked stuff, and you can't do precision work or mass production if your materials aren't exactly straight and true."

"But you trained all these men yourself," the third man said. "And in such a short space of time."

"Well, a great many of them are Eremians," Ziani replied, "skilled men, by local standards – blacksmiths, wheelwrights, coopers, joiners; they may not have been up to Guild standards when I started working with them, but at least they understood the value of a straight line. And the rest are Vadani from the mines, so they knew a bit about smelting ore. Mostly, though, it's a question of procedures: set up a properly designed production line, explain how each job is done – exactly, no margin for error – and there's not much that can go wrong, provided you have good supervisors." He allowed himself a faint grin. "What you're really asking is, could your people learn how to work like this? And the answer is, I don't see why not, if you're really determined. But I don't think you are. I got the Eremians and the Vadani to do as I told them because they realised they had no choice; without the stuff I was going to make for them, they didn't stand a chance. You're not in that position, so you haven't got the incentive. Simple as that, really."

The third man nodded slowly. "I believe you underestimate us," he said quietly, "but the point is entirely valid. If we need to change our whole way of life simply in order to make tools and weapons rather more efficiently, I don't think we'd be interested." Ziani noticed the intensity in his eyes, as he continued: "I believe that you are the sort of man who'd go to extraordinary lengths to do a relatively simple, ordinary thing, when other men would quite happily give up and go away. I believe that this tendency is evidence of exceptional strength, but it's debatable whether strength is always a virtue. A river in spate is strong; thunderstorms and earthquakes are strong, but to the best of my knowledge, nobody's ever found a use for them." He shrugged; he made the gesture elegant, somehow. "I don't think my people will want to stop being who they are just for the sake of *things*. I believe that that would be missing the point rather. I feel that if you change yourself in order to achieve something, you distort the objective. We have a story, a silly little story for children, about a dog who wanted to steal the meat from his master's table, but it was too high up for him to reach. If I were a bird, he thought, I could fly up there and get at it; and at that very moment, a sorcerer happened to pass by and heard his thoughts, and decided to teach him a lesson. He turned that dog into a bird, and the bird flew up on to the table, just as he'd wanted to do; but when he got there, he found his jaws had become a stupid little beak, and he couldn't open it wide enough to take the meat." He smiled. "I'm sorry," he said, "I shouldn't waste your time with such things. But as we were talking, it came into my mind."

Ziani frowned. "It's a charming story," he said, "but I don't see what it's got to do with what we've been talking about."

"Don't you?" The Aram Chantat raised his eyebrows. "Perhaps you think the bird was simply being feckless; he should have learned to use a knife, so he could cut the meat up into pieces small enough for him to eat."

"Not really," Ziani replied. "I can't imagine the dog wanting to be a bird. So it was the sorcerer's fault for interfering."

That made the Aram Chantat clap his hands and laugh. "Of course," he said. "Such a thing would never happen, and so the story is pointless. You would never wish to be anything other than what you are; I'd overlooked that point. In fact, you'd perch on the sorcerer's shoulder and peck his ears all day until he turned you back. I can see that, now I think about it."

It was three days since he'd last seen the duke, and he arrived outside the bedchamber door expecting to find evidence of progress; otherwise, why would he be up and about and demanding to see people?

He found Valens dressed and sitting in a chair; but the hole in his face, stuffed with wood-pith, was still as extraordinary as ever. For a moment, he thought he was looking at a mechanical object, a man-sized and shaped automaton with the faceplate partly removed and one of the screw-holes showing. Then he got a grip on himself and made the usual respectful enquiries.

"Actually, I feel terrible," Valens replied. "It hurts like hell, and every time I move I can feel this fucking plug, and all I want to do is get hold of a pair of tongs and pull it out, except I wouldn't have the strength." He stopped abruptly, as though he'd been punched hard in the pit of the stomach, then went on, "But I've got to get up and go to the front, because of your revolting friend Daurenja. Talking of which, what in God's name possessed you to recommend him for commander-in-chief? I thought you couldn't stand the man."

Ziani looked down at the floor. "He didn't leave me much choice," he said. "You know the position. If he told the Aram Chantat what he knows about me . . ."

"Fine." Valens scowled, and clearly that hurt. "I should have realised. Anyway, the savages are thinking about making the replacement permanent, so I've got to go down there and take the war back, assuming the journey doesn't kill me. I gather you're going there soon, with the new engines."

"They're ready," Ziani said. "There's a few bits and pieces still to do, but I can see to them once we get there."

Valens nodded. "In that case, we'll leave in the morning. Does that give you enough time?"

"I think so. I've got limbers and teams. But it'll take a while to get there, obviously."

"You won't be slowing me down," Valens replied. "Quite the opposite, in fact. The doctors say I've got to be carried in a litter at walking pace. Anything faster, and the wound might open up." He shuddered, a long, slight, convulsive movement that played up and down his body. When it stopped, he sighed. "I'm supposed to be brave," he said. "That's what they're telling everybody. Throughout, the duke has exhibited the utmost fortitude. Balls. The only reason I haven't screamed the place down is because it hurts too much to scream." He breathed in about halfway, then let the breath out slowly. "Really, I ought to thank you for making that horrible contraption the doctors used on me. They tell me it saved my life."

Ziani shrugged. "It was a job of work," he said. "I make machines. And it was a pleasant change to make something apart from weapons."

"That's beside the point," Valens said. "I got a really close look at it while they were using it. I'm no judge of these things, but it looked pretty impressive. Thank you." He pressed the tips of his fingers to his cheek, about an inch and a half below the swollen red mound surrounding the hole. "I guess I must be one of the very few people who's been on the receiving end of one of your inventions and survived."

"Like I said, it was just work," Ziani said; and he thought: one of the very few, and he's thanking me. "I'm sorry it had to be so painful."

Valens nodded. "Are you always sorry?" he asked. "No, you don't have to answer that. I believe you probably are, but you don't let it bother you too much. Anyway, I owe you my life. I take that sort of thing quite seriously."

"That's interesting," Ziani replied, looking past him at the wall. A heavy, slightly faded tapestry; the inevitable hunting scene, hounds pulling down a long, angular stag. No food without pain; no life without death. "You can see past the pain to the happy outcome."

"You have to, sometimes. I suppose it depends on what the outcome is. I mean, you can forgive someone who sticks a knife in you and cuts you open in cold blood if he happens to be a surgeon; he chops your leg off at the knee and you don't just forgive him, you pay him handsomely." He fell silent for a while, presumably gathering his strength. Then he said: "You say Daurenja forced you to nominate him; blackmail, this terrible secret you told me about."

Ziani said: "That's right."

"You said it was something I'd never be able to forgive."

"Yes."

Valens looked thoughtful for a moment. "This secret of yours has already caused me a lot of trouble," he said. "Let's do a trade. That instrument of torture you made saved my life. I'll trade you the debt in return for a complete free pardon, for whatever it is you did, provided you tell me about it. No going back on my word, no repercussions, no consequences. Well?"

"If you like," Ziani said. "Though I warn you . . ."

"Don't. Just tell me."

So Ziani told him: how he'd opened the gates of Civitas Eremiae to the Mezentines, allowing them to slaughter the people and burn the city. He kept it short and concise; Valens had bought the confession, but he hadn't paid enough for details. When he'd finished, he made himself turn his head a little and look at Valens' face; pale as milk, apart from the angry red around the wound.

"Why?" Valens asked.

"There were a number of reasons," Ziani replied. "The city was bound to fall sooner or later, so the people inside it were as good as dead already. I was sick to death of watching the scorpions I'd built shooting their soldiers down by the thousand. I thought that if they took the city, it'd end the war." He paused, then said, "And then I thought I could go home."

Valens nodded very slightly. "That was the deal, was it?"

"Yes. They cheated me, of course. There was supposed to be a safe conduct to get me out of there, we'd arranged it all beforehand. But when the time came, the men who were supposed to be meeting me didn't show up, and I knew they weren't going to keep their side of the bargain. So I made my own way out, and luckily—"

"You rescued Veatriz," Valens said quietly.

"That's right, yes. I figured that if I could get both of us out of the city and across the border into your country, you'd let me stay as a reward for saving her. Of course, you turned up and spared us both a long and unpleasant walk."

For a moment or so, he wondered if Valens had forgotten how to breathe. "You're right," he said eventually, "it's not something I could ever have forgiven. But I gave you my word, and so we'll forget all about it." He winced as he said that. "Partly because you made that thing for the doctors; but that wouldn't have been enough, on its own. Mostly it's because I've been profiting from your crime: if you hadn't done it, Veatriz would probably have been killed when they eventually took the city; as it was, I brought her here, and now she's my wife, and that's the only thing I ever wanted. It practically makes me your accomplice." He shook his head, like a horse refusing the bridle. "All right," he said, "those are the reasons why you did it. I still can't see *how* you could bring yourself to do it, though. It was . . ." He paused, scowling because the right word wouldn't come. "It was inhuman," he said. "So utterly callous . . ."

"Tell me," Ziani said. "If you'd been me, and opening the gates would've given you the woman you love, would you have done it?"

Valens nodded, once.

Chapter Fifteen

To punish the Cure Doce for the cowardly and unprovoked attack on Duke Valens, General Daurenja sent six thousand cavalry into their territory with instructions to do as much damage as possible in the course of a week. The expeditionary force was made up about equally of Eremians and Vadani, under the command of Colonel Miel Ducas.

As soon as he crossed the border, the Ducas divided his army up into three squadrons. Two of these he entrusted to seasoned Vadani officers; the third he led himself. He had a reliable map of the border country, with all the principal farmsteads marked. His orders to the two subordinate commands were to kill everybody they found, secure any stocks of food they might encounter, and burn the buildings. He set a schedule and arranged a rendezvous where the three squadrons would meet up before returning to allied territory.

The first farm on his itinerary was tucked away in the seam of a river valley. He attacked at dawn, aiming to catch the enemy at morning milking; that way, the herd would have been brought in to the main sheds, saving his men the trouble of rounding them up, and the farm workers would likewise be conveniently assembled in one place: the men and boys in the sheds, the women in the kitchens, fixing the men's breakfast.

Two thousand men were far too many for such a straightforward operation, and excessive numbers would simply get in the way. Accordingly, he drew up eighteen hundred of his men in a tight

cordon around the perimeter of the home meadows, to pick up strag-
glers, and divided the remaining two hundred into five units of forty.
The best available intelligence put the number of people living on the
farm at sixty. Time was of the essence – as the Ducas put it, they had
a lot of work to do in just seven days – as was thoroughness; given
their tight schedule (six farms a day for seven days), it was imperative
that no survivors escape to raise the alarm at the neighbouring farmsteads.

Everything went well. All five units were able to approach without
being seen, thanks to the cover of the farm buildings. Squads one,
two and three surrounded the sheds, burst in and killed all the men
in just over three minutes. Simultaneously, squad five barred the
doors of the main house and set it on fire, while squad four secured
the herd. Squads two and three broke into the barns and loaded as
much grain and hay as they could fit on the farm carts, while squad
one skirmished the rest of the buildings, picking out half a dozen
Cure Doce who happened to be there. The buildings were set alight,
a prize party was detailed to take the cattle, grain and fodder back to
the main camp as quickly as possible, and the squadron re-formed to
move on to the next target. The whole operation was completed in
just under the hour.

As he repeated the procedure at six more farms on the first day –
he was so far ahead of schedule that he found he had time to fit in an
extra raid – he rotated the duty assignments so that nobody had to
take part in more than one attack. He himself was the only exception;
in all seven raids, he insisted on leading the main strike force himself.
By the time they camped for the night, carefully hidden away in a
wood on the slopes of a deep combe an hour's ride from the last
farmstead, the Ducas had personally killed seventeen men, nine
women and seven children.

That night, he dreamt that she was standing over him as he slept; he
was standing off to one side, looking at her as she stared down at
him, lying huddled on the ground, his head under the blanket.

She said: Why?

You wouldn't understand, he said. It's all to do with duty.

Don't give me that, she said. All your life, you've protected the
weak and the defenceless: your tenants, the people of Civitas Eremiae,

the refugees after the city fell, when you led the resistance. Now you've turned into the enemy you spent your life fighting. Why?

Duty, he said. I'm an officer of the Alliance. I have my orders. And I can't tell anybody else to do something horrible and evil if I'm not prepared to do it myself.

She said: that's not the real reason.

No, he admitted. It's a valid reason, or at any rate a valid defence to a charge of monstrous inhumanity. But it's not the real reason.

She repeated the question: why?

Because I want to, he said. Because each time I carve into a neck tendon or chop open a skull, it gives me pleasure, and it's permitted by the proper authorities, I'm allowed to do it. I've fought so long on the opposite side and I've always lost; it's a pleasure to be on the winning side for a change.

She said: you can't lie to me, Miel, we've known each other too long. Is that the real reason?

He thought before he answered: I don't know. I think it might be, but I'm not sure. It could be that I hate myself so much, and this is the most effective way of hurting myself I can find; to become the thing I hate the most.

She said: that seems more likely. But is it the real reason?

He thought some more, and said: it's the duty of the Ducas to help his friends and hurt his enemies. These people are my enemies, because my orders say so.

She said: your orders came from that freak Daurenja. He sees nothing wrong in rape and murder. Your duty is to protect the weak and the defenceless.

He saw himself stir in his sleep; a movement of the arm, as if trying to push something away. He said: my duty is to the Eremian people, who are part of the anti-Mezentine Alliance, whose leader was attacked and nearly killed by these people. It is essential that such a grave crime should be punished.

She said: that's not the real reason.

True, he conceded. All right, then: when I was with the scavengers, and then later, when I was killing and robbing soldiers just to feed myself and you . . .

(She frowned, but didn't interrupt.)

. . . when I was doing all that, it wasn't for duty or politics or in a just cause in a just war. I was a predator, killing to live. Now, you know what happens when a fox gets inside a henhouse. He can't help it, it's his nature.

She said: you know you can't lie to me, not after all these years. Is that the real reason?

He said: I'm not sure, but I think it might be.

As he woke up, he saw a man standing over him, looking worried. He recognised him as the sergeant of the troop he'd led on the last raid. "Are you all right?" the sergeant asked.

"Of course," Miel replied. "Why shouldn't I be?"

"You were screaming," the sergeant replied.

The next day they destroyed eight farms; the day after that, seven more. There would have been time for an eighth, but during the killing, a man managed to stab the Ducas in the thigh with a hayfork. The wound was deep but clean, missing the major blood vessels, and the Ducas tried to make light of it, but his senior staff insisted that he should rest and let the surgeon clean it up and dress it.

"It should heal just fine," the surgeon told him. "Unless you insist on exerting yourself and opening it up again; in which case, you'll lose blood, and that'll make you weak, and you won't be able to do your job. What you need," he added firmly, "is rest and sleep."

That made the Ducas laugh. "Actually," he said, "I've been having trouble sleeping."

"I can give you something for that," the surgeon said.

Whatever it was (he didn't like to ask), it worked; and when she came and stood over him that night, he could see her but wasn't able to make out what she was saying, and after a while she went away. That was good, except it meant he was left alone with Orsea.

How long have you been here? Miel asked.

I've been here all the time, Orsea replied. I go with her wherever she goes. Actually, it's embarrassing, now she's married Duke Valens.

It must be distressing for you, he said, watching them together.

Yes, Orsea said. But he has a better right than me. She loves him, you know. She never loved either of us.

Orsea turned to walk away, then hesitated. He asked: why?

Because I want to, Miel said. Because Jarnac hunted wolves and foxes and all the scavengers and predators in the forest, but now he's dead, so there's nobody to stop me. And they always gave me duties I was never able to perform, because I was too weak or too stupid, but this is something I can do really well.

You're screaming again, Orsea said. You'd better wake up, before you disturb the whole camp.

So he woke up and looked round, and Orsea was nowhere to be seen; but for several minutes he felt sure that he was there somewhere, behind the armour stand or under the bed, like the adulterer in a farce. Then he told himself: get a grip, Orsea's dead, Valens had him killed, and that wasn't your fault, either. Even so, when he breathed on the polished steel of his breastplate, which he used as a shaving mirror, he had the strangest feeling that the face he could see was not his own but Orsea's, toad-belly white where the blood had drained from the severed neck veins; and he thought, yes, but why Orsea? Why not one of the hundred or so innocent civilians I've murdered over the past few days, or one of the soldiers I killed for his boots, or even some Mezentine I dispatched in the war?

They let him ride, because they couldn't stop him, but they wouldn't allow him to go with the raiding parties. He had to stay behind with the main cordon, watching for the first plume of black smoke; it made him feel like he was a small boy, being punished for something.

He gave up taking the sleeping medicine, and that stopped Orsea from following him around. He still had dreams, but instead of talking to him, she just looked at him and shook her head sadly, as if to say, I knew you'd end up like this.

It had become the fashion for the artillerymen's wives to bring them their lunch up on the embankment, and to sit with them watching the enemy sappers digging the approach trenches. They were getting closer, and occasionally a man who wanted to show off would string his bow and shoot an arrow or two at the lead sapper as he poked his head and chest up out of the trench to move the shield trolley and place the front gabions. Some of the artillerymen were getting quite good – there was plenty of time to practise, now that they'd given up on the bombardment, and precious little else to do – and once or even twice a day, an arrow would hit the target; the head would slump forward, until the dying man's wriggles dislodged him and he slid back down into the trench. The lucky archer got free drinks all evening. The enemy never shot back. But when the trench came close enough for the artillerymen to catch the occasional word of what the enemy were saying, the lead sappers took to wearing monstrous full-face close helmets and breastplates, which the arrows couldn't penetrate. The scorpion crews were under strict orders not to shoot at them (nobody knew why), so the lunchtime sniping stopped and they started playing backgammon instead. Even then, the wives used to say that the enemy were getting worryingly close, and shouldn't Chairman Psellus be doing something about it? To which their husbands replied, explaining patiently, as men do to women, that it really didn't matter, since there was no way on earth they'd be able to get past the flooded ditch, and that was all there was to it.

Scouts told General Daurenja that the worms were coming two days before they actually arrived. He'd sent observers out to keep watch for them; as soon as anybody spotted the dust from their wheels, they were to flash a mirror to the rear observation post on top of the ridge, who'd light a beacon. When the tiny orange glow eventually appeared, Daurenja went in person to inspect the progress of the machine trench. He wasn't satisfied, and issued an ultimatum; he also added another shift to the rotation. By the time the worms came into view from the ridge top, the trench was no more than seventy yards from the edge of the flooded ditch, which the general said was close enough. He then tripled all the work parties assigned to it, and set them to deepen and widen it, and to dig a number of spur trenches down on to the flat. To cover them, he ordered the general bombardment to resume. When the Mezentines returned fire, he noted with satisfaction that they were now shooting baskets filled with broken bricks, instead of finished shot. When they told him that the bricks made extremely effective missiles and casualties in the digging parties were high, he didn't seem particularly interested. Nor did he seem concerned when they told him that Duke Valens had come with the worms, though it was held to be significant that he sent for all the senior Aram Chantat officers, and met them in his tent for over an hour.

There was no point in worrying about it, they kept telling him. They'd considered the matter very carefully. They'd consulted all the available literature on the subject, and questioned representatives of the Architects', Cabinetmakers' and Stonemasons' Guilds. Having examined the evidence, they'd taken a vote on it and found by an overwhelming majority that the flooded ditch couldn't be crossed in the time available to the enemy.

Psellus raised his eyebrows. "You *voted* on it," he repeated.

Dorazus of the military engineering subcommittee nodded gravely. "Seventeen to two," he said, "with one abstention. So you see . . ."

Psellus rubbed the corners of his mouth with forefinger and thumb. "You voted on it. Thank you, that certainly puts my mind at rest. Please tell the subcommittee that I'm greatly obliged to them for their efforts."

Dorazus went away, taking his papers and his diagrams with him, though he left the exquisitely detailed scale model behind. Psellus sat staring at it for several minutes after he'd gone; then, quite tentatively, he reached out his hand and scratched gently at the edge of the miniature embankment. A few flakes of green-painted plaster fell away, leaving a white scar.

He sighed, and opened the book. He'd marked the page with a scrap of paper torn off the corner of some report.

To cross a flooded ditch, he reminded himself, the usual method is to construct a siege mound directly overlooking the ditch at its narrowest point, or, where more expedient, at the point at which it is most advantageous to cross. Sappers then undermine the base of the mound, causing it to subside into the ditch, filling it. Where necessary, firm standing can be provided to cross the filled section by nailing planks to long ropes, which are then rolled up. A special machine (see Appendix Twenty-Six) is used to roll them out again.

A siege mound. He did some calculations, using brass counters on a chequerboard. No, they wouldn't have time for that; and besides, if that was what they had in mind, why hadn't they started it already? Instead, as far as he could make out from the reports, they were deepening the wide, broad trenches, which suggested an attempt to drain the ditch and carry the water away into the slight dip at the base of the ridge. That, however, would be impossible; it would take the sappers far too long, they'd be vulnerable to mangonel and scorpion fire, and even if they succeeded, they'd be swept away and drowned when the water broke through; surely even the savages weren't fanatical enough for that. So, Dorazus and his subcommittee were quite right. There was no way it could be done. If he'd been at the meeting, he'd have had no choice but to vote in support of the motion.

He picked up his pen, dipped it in ink and wrote on a piece of scrap paper:

Allow three days for breaching/crossing/ filling in the flooded ditch.

Because he knew they'd do it, somehow; and then they'd face the embankment itself; which they'd sap and undermine. *Allow   days for sapping the embankment.* He frowned at the space he'd left blank, then turned back through the pages of the book.

There wouldn't be *time.* Surely they understood that. Undoubtedly they had some plan for coping with the flooded ditch; their preparations told him that, even though he couldn't figure out what they were planning to do. But once they were past the ditch, they had to get through, or over, or under the embankment before they could get at the walls, and there was no way they could achieve that in the time available to them . . .

A thought occurred to him, and he made way for it politely. Reports said that the allies were plundering farms in the Cure Doce country, on the pretext of punishing them for the attack on Duke Valens. Wagons loaded with food and hay had been seen coming down the border road. Would these extra supplies extend the time available to them to any significant degree? His fingers paddled the brass counters across the chequerboard, and he frowned. Answer: no. The simple fact remained that the allied army presently camped on and behind the ridge consumed in a single week more than the three adjoining Cure Doce counties were capable of producing in a year.

Assault, he said to himself; a straightforward, brutal attack, with scaling ladders, siege towers, similar primitive equipment. Suppose they sent a hundred thousand men (he couldn't visualise that many people all in one place) to carry the embankment by storm. He found the place in the book where the author set out a clearly tabulated ready-reckoner. To carry a defended position by storm. (His finger traced along the line.) Light or heavy defences; well, say light, for the sake of argument. That gave him a multiplication factor of forty, reduced by thirty per cent (untrained or poorly trained defending army). He did the calculation. No, not possible. According to the tables, twenty thousand defenders entrenched on the embankment, poorly trained but equipped with short- and medium-range artillery, should be able to resist an assault by up to two hundred and thirty thousand attackers; projected casualties for an army of a hundred thousand, assuming the assault wasn't abandoned until the losses reached the point of critical perceived failure (there was a complicated equation to find this, but as a basic rule of thumb, say fifteen per cent losses in eight hours or less), between twenty and twenty-six thousand for the attackers, no more than fifteen hundred for the defence . . .

Psellus closed his eyes. He didn't for one moment doubt the accuracy of the tables, but how on earth did the book's author know these things? It could only be that, at some time in the past, so long ago that nobody remembered them any more, there had been sieges of great cities; so frequent and so commonplace that scholarly investigators had been able to collate the data – troop numbers, casualty figures – and work out these ratios, qualified by variables, verified by controls. The cities, the men who'd lived in them, had been forgotten for so long that nobody even suspected they'd ever existed. The only mark they'd left behind was the implication of their existence, to be inferred from the statistical analyses in a manual of best city-killing practice. Extraordinary thought. There were people who held that certain kinds of stone weren't stone at all, but the compressed bones of innumerable billions of fish, crushed into solid blocks by the weight of the sea. He didn't actually believe that; but suppose the book was the only residue left by the death of thousands of cities, each one of them as huge and arrogant in its day as the Perpetual Republic – the Eternal City of this, the Everlasting Kingdom of that, squashed down by time and oblivion into a set of mathematical constants for predicting the deaths of men in battle.

So what, he thought; all that told him was that the real enemy wasn't General Daurenja or the Aram Chantat, but war itself, a truth so profound as to be completely useless. Even so, something had snagged in his mind, like a bramble on a sleeve, and he wondered what it could be. Curious, he glanced over the tables once more, until suddenly he saw it, and was immediately paralysed by its implications.

Light and medium artillery; and in the earlier chapters of the book there were detailed descriptions of each class of engine – the light field engines, such as scorpions, springalls and torsion rock-throwers; the medium engines, mangonels, onagers, the heavy springalls and lithobales; the heavy engines, such as the trebuchet. When he'd first read it, he'd been pleased and impressed – the engines in the book are just like the ones we use now, he'd told himself, so the data in the book is still useful and relevant. Now, it stunned him that he could have missed such a devastating point so completely; because the engines described in the book weren't just similar to the Guilds' approved types. Apart from a few inconsequential details, they were the same. But the book *wasn't Mezentine*; it had been translated by a Mezentine, two hundred years ago, from a very old manuscript, written by some foreigner belonging to a city and a race that had completely disappeared. In which case, the designs, the specifications, were hundreds of years old, quite possibly thousands; in which case, the Guilds hadn't created them, they'd simply copied them from somewhere else. True, there was a special dispensation for military equipment; but that wasn't enough to prop up the gaping sap that suddenly threatened to undermine his entire world. *The Guilds hadn't created these specifications*; they were the work of foreigners, savages, who'd achieved perfection at some point in the obscure past, long before the Mezentines had even left the Old Country. In which case . . .

He was having trouble breathing. In which case, we aren't the authors of Specification. We're just thieves, like Ziani Vaatzes, who stole designs from our betters, which is the greatest sin. In which case . . .

Before he realised what he was doing, he was on his feet and running: down the passageway, recklessly fast down the worn steps of the back stair, into the middle quadrangle, across the lawn where Necessary Evil used to meet, up more stairs, along more passages, to the door of the records office; through that into the entrance lobby, where there was a wall with a niche in it about four feet up from the floor, and in the niche . . .

"Chairman Psellus." He recognised the voice (alarmed; shocked; well, understandable. Not every day the ruler of the City bursts into your office like a madman). "Is there anything I can help you with?"

"Yes." He was short of breath, and the word came out creased. "This thing here."

As he lifted it out of the niche in the wall, he couldn't bring himself to call it by its name. A name, a common noun, carries deadly implications of identity. Call it what it is – a padlock – and it's identified; a padlock is a specific identified object, which means it must conform to Specification. Or . . .

"Ah, yes." The chief archivist relaxed very slightly. "That."

Psellus forced himself to breathe. "It was dug up in the flowerbed outside, wasn't it? When the drains were laid."

The archivist smiled, a little awkwardly. "That's right," he said. "Just before my time, actually, but my predecessor was there when it was found. It was knocking about in a drawer for ages, but I thought it'd be nice to put it up somewhere on display. There are so few old things from before the City was built, it's a shame to—"

"From before the City was built," Psellus repeated, laying down each word like a blow. "You're sure about that."

"Oh yes." The archivist nodded enthusiastically. "We can tell, because it was found under the thick seam of ash about three feet down; and we know the ash was left over from the destruction of the earlier city that was built on this site; we aren't certain how long—"

"Thank you," Psellus said. "Please go away."

When he was alone, he sat down on the edge of a table, the thing resting on the palm of his hand. The touch of it disgusted him; not because the thing itself was repulsive, but because of the guilt that came with it, like an infection. It was a padlock; corroded, rusted shut, the rivets and plates welded into a solid lump (pressure of time, like the weight of the sea). He knew it was a padlock, because there was the loop, and there was the casing that housed the mechanism; but the shape and the size were different from any type approved by the Guilds. In which case . . .

(He shuddered, and it seemed to hop off his hand like a frog on to the floor.)

In which case. This was the original specification, and the padlocks the Cutlers' Guild made nowadays were different, and the difference was abomination; the deadliest sin. We came here (the thought ploughed up his mind) and we found a city of men, where they made things, and we burnt the city and we changed the specifications, just like Ziani Vaatzes, and so everything we've done and said ever since must, logically, have been *evil* . . .

He didn't know how long he sat there, staring at the thing on the floor; it had him pinned down, he daren't move because of it. He thought: perhaps there's a pattern, a type, a specification for the death of cities. Perhaps all cities are a mechanism, of which Ziani

Vaatzes and his equivalents throughout time are the escapement, transmitting the energy of the motive components to the delivery system – engines, sappers, fire – to complete the task for which the mechanism was designed, namely its own destruction. Perhaps that's what cities and societies are for, to destroy themselves; just as a tree sheds leaves that rot into mould to nourish the roots. In which case, the fall of Mezentia is the necessary evil. Perhaps (he didn't like the conclusion, but he really had no choice) all evil is necessary.

But evil ought to be opposed, which is why we have laws and specifications and Compliance and war engines and armies. So perhaps it's necessary that we should oppose evil, and equally necessary that we should always lose.

Perhaps the only way to win the war is to lose it.

Ziani Vaatzes.

He stood up, laughed aloud and kicked the padlock across the floor. It skittered, hit a chair leg and vanished under a cabinet. The idea taking shape in his mind was so monstrous that he could scarcely believe he was allowing himself to consider it. But it made sense, when nothing else did, and it was all there in two words, so familiar he'd long since stopped asking himself what they actually meant: necessary evil.

For the first time in many years, he felt inspired, bursting with energy. Naturally, having found the answer, he wanted to dash out and start putting it into practice, straight away, before he lost his nerve. But he forced himself to stay calm. Just because it was the right thing to do, it didn't necessarily follow that it'd be easy. He could still fail, and that would be disastrous. He felt the passion inside him sublimate, into a kind of serene determination. It could be done. He could do it. But it had to be done right. First rule of all the craft and artisan Guilds: the easiest way to do anything is *properly*.

So he walked slowly back to his office, the long way round, pausing to admire the Founders' Monument in the centre quadrangle. It too was so familiar that he'd stopped seeing it years ago; he remembered that when he first set eyes on it, as a young trainee clerk just starting in Clerical Support, he'd thought it was crude and ugly, and the head of the allegorical figure of Perfection in the centre of the group was too big for her body – but, needless to say, he'd never dared say it to anybody. Now he looked at it again, and yes, he'd been quite right. The head was much too big. The Artists' had established the true ratio two hundred years ago. The head should be precisely one-eighth of the length of the body. Perfection, on the other hand, had a head like an oversized watermelon, and the expression on her face was little short of idiotic. It was so perfect, he could almost believe it was deliberate.

But it wasn't, of course, so he went back to his office, closed the door, took a clean, new sheet of Type Sixteen paper, and wrote on it: *Lucao Psellus to Ziani Vaatzes, greetings.*

While he was doing that, an Aram Chantat working party was unloading the wagons that had arrived from Civitas Vadanis.

They had to use the crane to lift the worms off. The crane had been General Daurenja's idea; he'd designed it and supervised its construction, and it worked extremely well. The frame, counterweight and bearings were salvaged from a wrecked trebuchet, to which he'd fitted a new, reinforced arm with a chain and hook in place of the throwing net. Once it had been hauled into position, and the arm was directly over the thing that needed to be lifted, the counterweight was wound up to its maximum height, bringing the arm down low enough for the hook to reach the transfer straps or carrying ring. Once it had been secured and the chain ratchet locked, the weight was released, lifting the arm and the cargo up into the air. All that remained after that was to drive the unloaded wagon out of the way and slowly feed out the chain until the cargo was resting on the ground.

As well as the worms themselves, the wagons carried a number of stout oak posts, thick as a man's waist, nine feet long, fitted at the top with pulleys, cogs and a ratchet. Once they'd been craned off the wagons, they were lowered on to flat wheeled trolleys, to which teams of a dozen mules were harnessed. They were pit mules taken from the silver mines, where they were used to haul the ore carts up the shafts to the bulk elevators. Even so, the sappers had a hard time trying to get them down into the machine trench. They dug their heels in and started up a long, exasperating chorus of brays, creaks and whines, until someone hit on the idea of walking in front of them with a bucket of crushed oats. After that, the only difficulty was the very real threat to the bucket-carrier, who didn't dare stumble and fall as he walked backwards down the trench holding out the bucket, for fear he'd be trodden on and squashed to death under the trolley wheels. A team of sappers marched behind; they were wearing the heavy-duty helmets and breastplates that caused so much frustration to the lunchtime snipers on the embankment, and in addition to their usual gear, they were carrying crowbars, sledgehammers and sacks.

The observers on the embankment had been wondering why the sappers had widened the trench about ten yards from the end nearest to them. The answer was quite prosaic. It was nothing more than a lay-by, somewhere to turn the trolleys once the posts had been unloaded. The mules were sent back, and the sappers dragged the posts the rest of the way. Something about the manner in which they set about the job must have bothered the artillerymen; in spite of their earlier discouragements, they got out their bows and started shooting, though now they weren't calling out bets and nominating their targets. They managed to hit one sapper in the hollow of the elbow joint and another in the thigh, but nobody claimed the shots or yelled out congratulations. Meanwhile, the sappers were digging out post-holes, five feet deep, through the topsoil and down into the dense red Mezentine clay. Behind them, other men were emptying the sacks, which turned out to contain sand and cement, and mixing up concrete.

A captain of artillery (Lucuo Dozonas of the Clockmakers' Guild, only recently promoted) ordered his crew to span and load their scorpion. Several people pointed out that this was directly against orders, but he didn't even reply. Since he was still quite new to all this, he had to get out his book of elevation and windage tables before he could wind in the settings. Fortunately, since the head of the trench was so close to the edge of the flooded ditch, he knew roughly what the range was. He gave the order to loose, and watched the bolt lift into the air. At first he thought he'd overshot, but the trajectory decayed and the bolt dropped, the sun flashing briefly on its point, glanced off one of the gabions and hit a man bringing up a pail of water. He was wearing one of those breastplates, but the bolt went through as though it was just a shirt.

Dozonas hesitated, well aware that everybody was looking at him. "Fine," he snapped, in a rather shaky voice. "Span and reload."

Before his scorpion could loose again, four or five others had beaten him to it. Then the short-range mangonels opened up, throwing bricks and rubble. Before too long, they'd killed half a dozen sappers and wounded twice as many again, but the working parties hardly seemed to have noticed. They'd finished digging the holes; they were scooping in the concrete and manhandling the posts upright, with the machinery at the top. One scorpion bolt – pure luck – hit one of the posts dead centre, splitting it neatly up the middle. That seemed to bother the sappers far more than their dead and dying. They piled up more gabions and moved the shield trolley a few inches.

To get the posts into the holes, the sappers had to stand upright, giving the Archery Club something to aim at. Most of the arrows that connected with the target skittered off the heavy helmets (someone had consulted a dictionary; the proper technical term was *cabassets*), but eight kills were later confirmed, another three claimed but disputed. The posts reared up and dropped into the holes, with guy-ropes to hold them up straight. One scorpion crew managed to shoot the winch-and-ratchet arrangement off one of them; it took sixteen shots, and they were officially reprimanded for wasting ammunition. The next morning, they saw that the mechanism had been replaced during the night.

"It was a wonderful bonus when they started shooting at us," said General Daurenja, sharpening a pen with a little blue-bladed knife. "I thought they had more sense, but apparently not. Now we know exactly how many scorpions and mangonels they've got up there, and precisely where they are." He tested the point of the pen with his finger; just right, apparently. "It doesn't matter for the next stage, of course, but it'll be a great help when we come to take the embankment."

The Aram Chantat liaison nodded gravely. "Most satisfactory," he said. He was trying not to stare, but he couldn't help watching Daurenja fiddling with the pen. Such small, delicate movements, such precision in such a trivial cause; and (he wasn't at all sure what to make of it, though it made him feel slightly queasy) such complete confidence each time he cut. He wondered if surgery was yet another of the general's accomplishments. "However, I didn't come here to talk about that."

"No." Daurenja looked up at him; his eyes were pale, almost

empty. "You want to know what I'm going to do now that Valens has come back."

"Yes."

Daurenja dipped his head in acknowledgement. "Surely that's up to you," he said. "You make the decisions, after all. If you feel Duke Valens is better at this than I am, naturally you'll want the best man for the job. If you want me to stay on, I'll stay on."

The liaison kept his face straight and blank. "If I decide otherwise?" he said.

"Then I hope you'll let me carry on making myself useful," Daurenja replied. "That's all I ask."

"That's all," the liaison said.

"Well, yes, of course." The glow of sincerity in his eyes was as perfect as his cutting. "If you're interested in what motivates me, it's quite simple. I'm a man of various talents, and my aim is to use them as advantageously as possible. After years of wandering around indulging my intellectual curiosity, I want to make something of myself. I flatter myself that I have a certain amount to offer, and I'm prepared to work hard to earn whatever I'm given. That's it, essentially. Please don't think I'm complicated, because I'm not."

The liaison found that he didn't want to look at the general's face. "I was led to believe that you're rather more than what you say," he said quietly. "I have it on good authority that you have developed a new weapon, and it was this weapon that Engineer Vaatzes had in mind when he recommended you to us so vehemently. I gather he believes it's crucial to the success of the entire venture. Is that true?"

"Absolutely," Daurenja replied. "But I don't need to be in command to deploy it. In fact, doing this job means I haven't been able to spend as much time as I'd have liked getting it ready. But I was asked to do this job, and I accepted, so . . ." The liaison heard the creak of a chair but didn't look round. "Like I said, it's entirely up to you whether I carry on here or not. Whatever you want me to do, I'll do it."

The liaison stood up. He really didn't want to be in a confined space with this man any more. "We would be grateful if you would continue to lead the army for the time being," he said. "We feel that Duke Valens is still weak from his injury, and should not be required to exert himself unduly until his recovery is complete. However, we will require further information about this weapon, so that we can decide how best to use it. You will be so good as to arrange a demonstration as soon as reasonably possible."

"With respect." There was an edge to his voice now; no, not quite that. It put the liaison in mind of the way the fine feather of a cutting edge curls over on itself when it's inadvertently struck against something hard; still sharp, but distorted. "I've avoided conducting tests so far because I want to make sure the enemy don't find out anything about the weapon until we actually use it against them in earnest. With the best will in the world, if we test it, they'll find out. The same goes – no offence – for telling you any more about it. I know you wouldn't tell anybody, but you can't control the information once you've passed it on to your superiors. I'm sorry, but I really must insist. At the moment, the only people besides myself who know what it is or what it does are the duke and Ziani Vaatzes. And if it means you don't want me to stay on as general, well, like I just told you, I could use the extra time."

"I understand." The urge to leave was too strong. He stumbled towards the tent-flap, like a diver trying to reach the surface before he lost control of his breath. "I need to confer with my superiors. I'll let you know what they decide."

Outside in the fresh air, he took a moment to pull himself together. Try as he might, he couldn't account for the panic (no other word for it) he'd just experienced. He knew there were people who went to pieces in closed spaces. He wasn't one of them, but now he reckoned he could understand how they felt.. Quite ridiculous, of course, and he was properly ashamed of himself, but the feeling had been too strong to ignore. As he walked away (and each step he took eased the pressure in his mind), he tried to analyse it. Not anger; not fear. The nearest he could get to it was disgust, but there wasn't anything about the general that could have provoked him so violently. He knew Daurenja had an unsavoury reputation: he was violent and licentious, like so many of these city-dwellers; there was talk of murders and violence towards women. Not that; he was certain of it. He disapproved of such conduct, naturally, but he knew he was capable of putting it out of his mind when he was dealing with foreign leaders. Consider Duke Valens, for example. He'd killed Duke Orsea just so he could take his wife. Even if what they said about Daurenja was true, it could hardly be worse than that.

About a hundred yards away to his left, they were dragging tarpaulins over the machines the duke had brought with him from Civitas Vadanis, which he assumed were the famous worms (strange name) he'd heard so much about. Partly from curiosity and duty, partly to help clear his head, he changed direction and headed towards them.

Heavy carriages, made of big square oak beams, fitted with solid wheels; the sides boarded in to head height with oak planks two inches thick. As a result he couldn't see inside to examine the mechanism. Ten yards away, the machines looked like ordinary conventional battering rams, except that the ram wasn't tipped with a spike or a beak. Instead, he saw four rounded steel blades sticking out of a central boss like the petals of a flower. Their shape made him think of windmills, except that the blades were twisted, and reminded him of the claws of a bird.

He had no idea what they were supposed to do.

Neither (small consolation) did the general, if he'd been telling the truth; at least, the general said he'd never seen one, since they were Engineer Vaatzes' invention, completely new, and that they'd been designed specifically to breach the banks of the flooded ditch, so the water could drain away along the trenches. All well and good; but, quite apart from how they worked, he couldn't see how they were going to get them into position. They were big – smaller than a trebuchet but bigger than a mangonel or an onager – and it'd take a team of twelve oxen to draw them. You'd never get oxen down in the trench; and besides, he couldn't see any fixings to attach booms and yokes to, just one massive steel ring riveted to the front at axle height. Surely Vaatzes wasn't expecting the sappers to haul it down there with ropes?

He reminded himself that the engineer was an inventive, resourceful man with an eye for detail. It was inconceivable that he could have overlooked something as crudely fundamental as how the machines were to be moved about. He considered Engineer Vaatzes for a moment, taking the machines he'd designed and built as a model. On the outside, plain and closed; on the inside, systems so complex that he would never be able to understand them properly, let alone aspire to emulate them. Admirable; but it should nevertheless be borne in mind that the purpose for which they'd been created was violence – in his case, violence directed against his own kind for the benefit of strangers, which was something the liaison was very glad he couldn't begin to understand. A mind that could create something like that must be so utterly hateful that looking into it would surely damage you for ever.

As he approached his own tent, he saw a crowd of people standing about outside it. Their clothes told him they were Vadani soldiers (cavalrymen, to be precise, wearing the thick, comical-looking horse-hair-stuffed jerkins that went under the heavy Vadani armour); there was also a woman with them, and a man in what looked like a night-gown, sitting in a chair. They stopped talking before he could get close enough to hear what they were saying, and stared at him. But it was the woman who spoke.

"Are you the Aram Chantat liaison officer?" she asked.

He nodded. "I'm afraid I don't—"

"My name is Veatriz Sirupati," the woman said. "I'd have thought you'd have recognised my husband."

The man in the chair turned his head, and he saw the wound, which he'd heard and read so much about. The man behind the wound – it was the only possible way to think of him – smiled bleakly and said, "I need to see General Daurenja."

"That's not possible right now," he heard himself reply. "If I'd known—"

"That's what the duty officer said," the duke interrupted. "And the guard captain, and the sentries. Not possible. I find that hard to believe."

The liaison was suddenly aware that the Vadani soldiers had moved. They were standing round him, closing in a step at a time when he wasn't looking, like inquisitive bullocks mobbing a stranger. "I'll tell the general you'd like to see him," he said. "Perhaps tomorrow, if there's—"

"I think I'd rather see him straight away," the duke said quietly. "You'll come with us, and then there won't be any fuss."

Well, he thought; the general wants to be useful, so he can start with sorting out this situation before there's any bloodshed. But he couldn't put his duty out of his mind, so he said: "I think you should know that we have decided to retain the general as commander-in-chief until the end of the present campaign. We feel that in the interests of continuity and . . ."

He tailed off. The silence was far worse than any shouting would have been. Duty done, he told himself. Now it's up to the general. "I'll take you to him straight away," he said, his voice strained but brisk. "If you'd care to follow me."

"We know the way," said one of the soldiers.

They'd folded in on him; he had to be careful where he put his feet to avoid treading on the heels of the man walking in front of him, and all he could see was shoulders and necks. Then they stopped, and he was gently squeezed through the group until he emerged to find himself back outside the general's tent, face to face with two extremely worried guards.

"It's all right," he said (clearly it was very far from all right, but the truth was the last thing any of them needed right now). "These gentlemen have urgent business with the general, so if you'd just step aside . . ."

"Very sorry, sir." The guard's voice was so high it was almost funny. "The general's not to be disturbed right now. Direct orders."

"I'm relieving the general of command." Valens: he moved through the group like the prow of a ship. "It's only polite to tell him, don't you think?"

The guards had had enough. They looked at each other, and then they simply weren't there any more. Valens' hand attached itself to the liaison's wrist, and he felt himself being drawn forward, into the tent.

Daurenja was sitting in his chair with his feet up on the small charcoal stove. He had a cup in one hand and a book in the other. Spharizus' *Eclogues*, Valens couldn't help noticing; typical Mannerist pastoral poetry, the amorous shepherd to his love. He'd been told to read it when he was fifteen, but had never managed to get further than the author's preface. Without thinking, he said, "You read Spharizus?"

"Yes." Daurenja frowned at him. "I maintain you can't begin to appreciate the later Mannerist movement unless you're fully grounded in its neo-classical origins. What the hell do you mean, you're relieving me of command?" He turned his head very slightly, like an artilleryman adjusting for windage, and stared at the liaison. "I assume he's brought you here by force," he said. "I take it you'd like him restrained and placed under arrest."

Valens grinned. "Well?" he said, relaxing his grip. "Is that what you'd like?"

"I have no authority," the liaison said. It came out as somewhere between a bark and a whimper. Daurenja frowned, and Valens laughed. "I need to consult the war council and get their instructions. This is not—"

"Let's not bother them right now." Daurenja stood up; it was like watching liquid being poured into a glass vessel. He's got no joints, Valens thought, he just extends, like a worm crawling. He remembered a legend he'd heard many years ago, about the fox demons: country people believed that once they left their bodies, they took on whatever shape the person looking at them expected to see. "I have a commission from the Aram Chantat high council to conduct this war on their behalf. As I understand it, that commission was confirmed a short while ago by this officer here." (Maybe the liaison was a fox demon too; he was trying very hard to look like someone who wasn't even there.) "But you're the Vadani duke, and you're going to tell me you don't recognise the high council's authority, because you're the leader of this alliance. Well?"

"Yes," Valens said.

"You realise what'll happen?" Daurenja was growing taller before his very eyes, he was sure of it. Not broader; if anything, he was losing breadth as he gained height. "The Aram Chantat will stand by their appointment, because to back down would shame them. Your people, who don't like the savages – that's what you call them, isn't it? – they'll back you, and pretty soon we'll be treating the Mezentines to the pretty spectacle of their enemies fighting each other; it'll confuse them half to death, but I'm sure they'll enjoy it, even so. Is that what you want?"

Valens shook his head. "I don't see any need for that," he said. Veatriz was beside him, tugging at his sleeve. He ignored her. "The way I see it, I got myself shot, and you very kindly took over running the siege while I was sick. I'm better now, and I'm relieving you of command. I'm sure you'll be happier without the responsibility. You'll be able to get back to your pet project, which Vaatzes tells me is very important to the war effort. After all, you're not a soldier, are you? In fact, I'm not really sure what you are."

For a moment, Daurenja stared at him, his face white with anger. Then he smiled. "I'm a gentleman," he said. "I'm a man of good birth and breeding, a scholar, a soldier and a scientist. I flatter myself that everything I do, I do extremely well. I imagine you'd describe yourself in the same terms, so really, there's not a great deal to choose between us, as far as qualifications go. Wouldn't you agree?"

I know what he's going to do, Valens thought suddenly; I know what he is. He's a fox demon with a mirror. "Not really," he replied pleasantly. "I think you're a sinister, dangerous creature who lives in a world of his own and believes that none of the rules applies to him. Everywhere you go, you hurt people and make trouble; you'd have been put down years ago, except you're cunning and talented enough to escape." (This is what he wants me to say, Valens realised, but I have no choice.) "I think it's high time you were put in your place, and I suppose it's up to me to do it. I wish it didn't have to be now, but that's my own stupid fault for letting you burrow your way in deep, like a maggot."

Daurenja's smile told him everything he needed to know. "I have to disagree," Daurenja said. "And really, you've gone too far, saying all that in front of these people. It's ridiculous, but you brought it on both of us. You do see, don't you, there's only one way we can resolve this. Otherwise . . ." He looked round, and the liaison seemed to reappear, like a genie summoned by a charm. "I'm very sorry," he said. "You must be wondering what sort of people you've allied yourselves with. But this gentleman and I have got to fight each other now. He's insulted me, so either I challenge him or else I insult him right back, which means he'll have to challenge me." He frowned. "No, wait, I'm forgetting. He's a duke, and you aren't supposed to challenge your social inferiors, you've got to make them challenge you." He looked back at Valens; the smile on his face was practically friendly. "Isn't that right?" he said. "You're the expert, of course, but . . ."

"You do what you like," Valens replied.

As Daurenja's smile split open into a grin, Veatriz pushed in front of Valens, so he couldn't see past her. "This is stupid," she said, angry and pleading at the same time. "For a start, you're in no fit state—"

"I'm the best fencer in the duchy." It was a weary statement of fact, practically an admission of a shameful and inconvenient truth. "He thinks he's being clever and manipulating me, but he's made a mistake. I'd be stupid not to take advantage of it." He reached out and, gently but very firmly, moved her out of the way. She stared at him in horror, then looked away.

"Splendid," Daurenja said. "And another insult for good measure."

He cleared his throat; brisk, businesslike, calling the meeting to order. "As the challenged party, you have the choice of weapons. Of course we're limited by what's available, but I do happen to have a case of rather fine rapiers – Mezentine, first export quality . . ."

Valens smiled. "I bet you do."

"That's settled, then." He dropped on to his hands and knees, a remarkable movement, like putting away a folding chair, and fished out a long rosewood box from under his camp bed. "The man I bought them from said they're plunder from Civitas Eremiae. There's a monogram on the escutcheon on the lid – look, there, you can just make it out. That's the Phocas, isn't it?"

Valens reached out his foot and gently kicked the lid open. "Buying plunder," he said. "That's just about your level. And that's the Erylas, not the Phocas."

"Of course, you're quite right," Daurenja replied smoothly. He picked the two swords out of the box and presented Valens with the hilts. Valens snatched the nearest one, not bothering to look at it. "That's the splendid thing about Mezentine rapiers," Daurenja said. "Since they're all identical, you don't have to worry about finding one with the right balance. I see you favour placing the middle finger in front of the cross. Unfashionable these days, but if it was good enough for Ferro . . ."

Valens sighed, an oh-for-pity's-sake noise, and left the tent. As Daurenja started to follow him, Veatriz moved quickly to block his way. "If you hurt him . . ."

Daurenja smiled. "I wasn't planning to," he said mildly. "But really, it's up to him. I'm afraid I can't undertake to let myself get killed for your sake. Let's both of us hope his injuries have slowed him down."

(She thought: if he really loved me . . .)

She said: "You manipulated him. You've been planning this. You want—"

"You can have absolutely no idea what I want", and it was as if someone totally different had spoken, a man standing behind him she hadn't seen before. "Listen," he added gently, so very gently; you could imagine the owner of that voice tapping a cranefly in his hands, so careful not to break its fragile wings. "The Alliance needs its best general, and unfortunately, that happens to be me. Your husband is the duke, and of course he has my loyalty and my service, but right now I can only do my duty, to him and the Alliance, by replacing him, until the siege is over and the war has been won. After that, I'll go away, I promise you. I won't be needed here any more and I have other things to do. But until then . . ." He smiled, and she had to fight not to trust him. "I'll do my very best not to hurt him," he said kindly. "You have my word of honour."

She looked at him, and saw something completely artificial, something like Ziani Vaatzes' mechanical doll, except that this one, this unique type, had built itself. She understood, then. Daurenja was the better general, the best the Alliance had. He would take the City, succeeding where Valens would most likely fail, because he needed to, in order to move on to the next stage of his development. Therefore the monster had to be stopped, right now, before he could grow and spread. At the same time, she recognised that Valens had left her, putting his duty ahead of her, as a good duke should. When he came back from the fight with the monster's blood on his hands, he'd try and make her believe he still loved her exactly the same way, that nothing had changed, but neither of them would ever believe it. It would be as if he hadn't ridden to Civitas Eremiae to save her and drag his people into the war; he'd be absolved of that by renunciation and sacrifice, which was of course the right path for the duke to follow. But the man who'd loved her would never come back from the duel.

"I hope he kills you," she said calmly.

"Of course you do," he replied. "Nobody can blame you for that. And now you'll have to excuse me. I mustn't keep them all waiting any longer."

He left the tent. She stayed where she was. It was her duty to be there, watching the fight; Valens needed his witness, regardless of the outcome. But she stayed where she was.

"There you are," Valens said, as the tent-flap parted. "I was starting to wonder where you'd got to."

Daurenja took a few steps forward, the crowd of bewildered onlookers shrinking away from him as he moved. Then he stopped, like a ship dropping anchor. Valens noticed he'd shifted his grip on the rapier: two fingers in front of the cross now, instead of just one. He wants to be me, he thought, right down to the smallest detail.

"I suppose we'd better get started," Daurenja said. "Do you want to bother with seconds and marshals? Strictly speaking—"

Valens lunged. As he committed his body to the movement, he knew he'd got it wrong; he could hear the sergeant click his tongue, *too much left shoulder*, but of course he was out of time. Daurenja raised an eyebrow as he sidestepped, not bothering to raise his sword, though Valens had left himself open to a lethal riposte. He recovered to the back guard as quickly as he could, but it was a scramble, open and shameful.

"No seconds, then," Daurenja said pleasantly. "That's fine."

Immediately, he changed shape; there was no perceptible movement. Now he was straight-backed, his feet just under a shoulders' width apart, right foot pointing at Valens, left foot behind and at ninety degrees; his sword-arm held out at shoulder height, very slightly bent at the elbow. He was a fencing-manual illustration of the circular fight, unbreachable defence, every attack countered in time, with two dimensions of distance.. The sergeant hadn't even tried to teach him the circular fight; it was far too difficult to learn, unless the student was really committed. Instead, he'd been taught the linear fight – low right hand, all major developments in double time, a debate rather than a conflict of inflexible assertions. Suddenly, without fear but with depressing certainty, Valens realised he'd made a very bad misjudgement. The only way you could win against the circular fight was if your enemy made a mistake.

Daurenja smiled at him, and he felt a furious urge to lunge again. That, of course, was what Daurenja wanted him to do. As he lunged, pursuing the straight line, Daurenja would take a small step, not back but sideways, his feet following the invisible circle, and as he stepped and Valens' sword punctured the empty air where he'd just been, all he'd need to do was poke gently, and Valens' own momentum would drive him on to the sword-point, a plank hammering itself against a nail. So, he couldn't attack, and Daurenja wouldn't attack, because the circular fight is all defence and reaction; all he could do was stand in the back guard (which you can't do for very long before cramp sets in, and a fencer with cramp is as good as dead), hesitating, unable to do anything, ridiculous, a joke . . .

He felt his back twinge. Weeks lying in bed; even when he was in the peak of condition, he couldn't have held this contorted stance for very long. He knew what he had to do: relax his hand, let the sword drop from it like an apple from a tree, then take two steps back and apologise, because there was no way he could carry on with the fight, let alone win it. The only other choice was to lunge, keep on lunging until Daurenja stuck him and he died, and that was no choice at all. He scrabbled through the archives of his mind, every exhibition bout he'd ever seen, every stupid book he'd ever read, for some ploy or trick that could beat the circular fight: all the special plays, for the advanced class only, the volte, the pass in single time, the boar's thrust. Absolutely nothing.

Oh well, he thought; and he leaned forward a little, bending his right knee, extending his arm, edging himself forward into distance, until the needle tip of Daurenja's sword was so close to his face that it blurred. It was ridiculous, but it was the only thing he could come up with: tempt him beyond endurance until he attacked, and then, in the thousandth of a second available, try and think of something. He saw his face, reflected, distorted, in the polished cup guard of Daurenja's sword. So much distortion, he could barely see the grotesque red swelling around the wound: lies that rectify, two wrongs making a right, necessary—

Daurenja moved his hand. It was just a little twitch. The proper name for it was the stramazone; using the tip of the rapier to scratch a cut. No force; but the pain of the sharp point in the inflamed mound around the wound stunned him. He heard his sword clatter on the ground – his eyes were closed – and a fraction of a second later, the ground hit him. The other noise was someone screaming. He had a pretty good idea who that was; but he didn't associate the sound with himself particularly. His brain seemed to clench tight, and that was forcing the air out of him, a simple mechanical process.

"Get the doctor," a voice said; a calm, safe voice, a sensible friend not yielding to panic. He thought: I've lost. That's Daurenja's voice, and I'm grateful to him for making them get the doctor. Then the pain flooded out that thought too, and there was no space left in his head for anything.

"I'm sorry," Daurenja was saying. "I really didn't want to cause him so much pain, but you'll appreciate, I had to stop it somehow." He smiled. It was almost charming. "My fault," he said. "I overestimated him, as a fencer."

She heard herself thank him; and later, she thought: a compassionate man, resourceful, he stopped the fight without doing any lasting damage. I owe him my husband's life. A good man; he turned pain to his advantage, but he used it to save the life of his enemy. What was the phrase? Necessary evil.

She didn't go back to the tent. She told herself it was because she didn't want to get under the feet of the doctors while they were treating him, but that was nonsense, of course. It was just a scratch, by all accounts, all it needed was cleaning and a light dressing. She told herself: I don't want to be there, he won't want me to see him lying there, beaten. That was a good reason, but not the true one.

Instead, she wandered through the camp, not bothering to notice how people stared at her, got out of her way. The truth was – it was stupid, she could hardly believe it, but she had to accept it; the truth was, she couldn't love him any more, not now that he'd been beaten, by that creature. He'd chosen, as he had to do, between her and his duty; he'd made the right choice, even though it meant breaking the wings of their love, but on the strict understanding that he'd *win*, that the victory over evil would justify the betrayal. She thought about that. Suppose you did a bad, terrible thing, for the right reason, the end amply justifying the means, but then you failed. The good evaporates, leaving the evil behind. He'd risked death, risked her only chance of happiness, their unborn child's future, everything, in order to stop the monster, but he hadn't stopped the monster, if anything he'd made it stronger. The intention was good enough, but the outcome was disastrous, and so . . .

So, instead, she'd thanked the monster for sparing him, but what he'd given back to her was spoiled, unacceptable; and Daurenja had done the right, the noble thing, but he'd turned it into waste and evil. It was ridiculous, but it had happened.

She went back to the tent. The doctor was just leaving. "He's asleep," he said. "Try not to wake him up. God only knows what possessed him to go fighting a duel in his condition."

"So it was the wound, then," she said. "Why he lost, I mean."

The doctor looked blank. "I really couldn't say," he said. "It can't have helped, anyway. The main thing is, there's no real harm done, it's just a—"

"Thank you."

The doctor flinched, as though she'd hit him. "I'll come back tomorrow," he said cautiously. "Meanwhile, if there's any problems, send for me."

She stepped aside to let him pass, but when he'd gone she turned away. The last place she wanted to be was in the tent, with him.

Chapter Sixteen

His authority confirmed, General Daurenja held a briefing for the sappers and miners. It was dark by the time it finished, which fitted the schedule perfectly.

While the meeting was going on, the quartermasters' division went round the camp gathering up every lantern they could find, filling them with fresh oil and trimming the wicks. Another detail reported to the foot of the machine trench, where the carpenters had spent the day putting up a large holding pen. At dusk, the stockmen drove in four hundred draught oxen. A rumour quickly spread that the oxen were going to be slaughtered, butchered and salted down to supplement the dwindling meat ration, and a crowd gathered, firmly convinced they'd be giving away offal and tripe. Instead, they were pressed into service yoking the oxen into one enormous team. It soon turned out that nobody knew how this was to be done; the general had given the order, presumably in the belief that someone had the knowledge and the necessary equipment, and it was only when the animals had been paired up and driven under their individual yokes that the full depth of the problem became apparent. The drovers pointed out, loudly and often, that oxen had to be yoked to a rigid beam, such as a cart-pole. The staff major who'd just discovered, much to his annoyance, that he was apparently in charge of this stage of the operation pointed out that he didn't have a pole or a beam or a tree-trunk long enough to yoke two hundred pair to, because it was impossible that such a thing should exist. The drovers asserted that that wasn't their fault; if someone had asked them earlier, they'd have told them it couldn't be done. The major replied that it could be done, because it had to be done, because the general had given an order; then, rather more calmly, he said that he was sure he'd heard somewhere about huge teams of oxen being used to drag enormous stone blocks on sledges, so it *was* possible, and presumably a stonemason would know about that sort of thing. Consulted on the point, the stonemasons said that they'd heard of such a thing, but none of them had done it themselves or talked to anybody who'd ever seen it done. One mason, dissenting, said that he'd heard that six hundred oxen had been used to drag the lintel stones when they built the municipal flour-mill in Mezentia; if the major wanted advice, all he had to do was take a walk down the trench, swim the ditch, climb the embankment, knock on the City gates and ask to speak to the clerk of works.

The discussion was interrupted by the arrival of a colonel of engineers from the general's staff, who wanted to know what the hold-up was. On being told the reason, he ordered the major to think of something, and left quickly.

At this point, someone remembered the chain.

Nobody knew what it was or what it had once been used for. They'd found it in the ruins of a burnt-out transport depot beside the Lonazep road, and the most popular theory was that the Mezentines had made it for their customers in the Old Country, part of the payment for the services of the mercenaries they'd hired for the attack on Civitas Eremiae. For some reason it had never got to Lonazep; instead, it had been left in a shed, as often happens to awkward consignments, until the war overtook it and deprived it of significance and purpose. General Daurenja had read about it in some report and ordered that it should be sent to Civitas Vadanis to be broken up for scrap; it was four hundred yards long, each link weighing fifty pounds, all steel, so hard a file could scarcely cut it. The problem of shifting it had been passed around the transport executive like a hot coal until the commander of an Aram Chantat infantry division, with a point to prove in some long-forgotten argument, undertook to see to it. He sent two regiments to the depot site, where his men struggled for five days with rollers and levers to lay the chain out in a straight line. Then the regiments lined up beside the chain, and on the word of command, each man bent down and lifted up one link. It took them two days to get the chain back to the camp, at which point the commander, who'd forgotten about his undertaking, reassigned the regiments to other duties.

The major wasn't keen on the idea. For one thing, there was the obvious problem of shifting the thing. Furthermore, there was the matter of the weight, which he anticipated would burden the oxen so much that they wouldn't be able to do the job they'd been brought there for. Also, how were the yokes to be attached to the chain, and who was going to lift it up while it was being attached? In any case, the chain was, by definition, not a rigid beam; if a flexible beam would suffice, they might as well use rope and have done with it.

By now, however, the idea of the chain had taken hold in the minds of the senior engineers, who started suggesting solutions to the problems he'd raised, disagreeing with each other and all shouting at once. Why not a flexible beam, they wanted to know; and the drovers, when this question was put to them, replied that they'd specified rigid beams because that was all they'd ever used, but for all they knew a flexible beam might work, though they wouldn't be held responsible if it didn't. The stockmen disagreed fundamentally among themselves on the weight issue, one faction maintaining that an extra hundredweight or so was nothing to a good ox, the other asserting that it'd take six hundred oxen just to pull the chain. Bringing the chain and lifting it was dismissed as a trivial concern, especially by the Vadani miners. The camp was overflowing with Aram Chantat, they said, who sat around all day doing nothing while brave Vadani dug in the trenches and got shot at. Let them do it, and make themselves useful for a change.

Faced with this difference of opinion, the major referred the matter to General Daurenja, who expressed deep concern that the issue hadn't been addressed earlier, deplored the fact that they were now severely behind schedule, and ordered the major to use the chain. Taking this order as his authority, the major sent for three regiments of the Aram Chantat and an additional hundred oxen.

It was now pitch dark, and every third man in the Aram Chantat contingent was issued with a lantern, so he could walk beside the chain-carriers and light the way. The shortest, straightest route was right through the middle of the camp, and the Mezentine observers on the embankment reported that the enemy were holding some kind of festival, involving a torchlight procession. This was taken as an indication that it would be a quiet night, and four of the five artillery batteries were allowed to stand down and go home.

Shortly after midnight, when the chain was finally in place and lashed securely to the yokes with requisitioned cart-reins, a small party of sappers slipped quietly into the trench, dragging behind them trolleys mounted with large spools for paying out rope. The Mezentines' attention, what there was of it, was concentrated on the lights of the presumed festival, so they weren't observed as they fed the rope ends through the pulleys attached to the stakes they'd planted and cemented in a few days earlier. They checked the pulleys were greased and running smoothly, then led the ropes back up the trench. One end they tied to the last link of the chain. The other went round the towing hitches bolted to the fronts of the worms.

There was a young Mezentine artilleryman, Lucazo Boerzes, a member in good standing of the Wiremakers', and for some reason (his motivation has not been recorded) he decided to climb down the embankment and creep up behind the trench bank to get a closer look at the enemy festival. Anticipating trouble, or maybe simply because he was the sort of young man who made the most of any opportunity to carry a weapon, he took with him his bow, a quiver of arrows and a sword. It was later remembered that he'd been an enthusiastic member of the lunchtime archery club, and had twice scored a verified hit. Crawling most of the way, he eventually reached the head of the trench, where he'd seen a large concentration of moving lights. He was bewildered to see a long column of cattle, and his first thought was that these animals were being driven off to be slaughtered, either as part of some Aram Chantat religious ceremony or to feed the festival-goers. As he came closer, however, he couldn't help noticing that the cows (he'd never left the City before in his life, and didn't appreciate the difference between an ox and a cow) were wearing collars, which were somehow attached to what he recognised as a naval blockading chain, designed to be stretched across the mouth of a harbour to prevent ships from entering. It was, in fact, the chain he himself had worked on – his shift had drawn the bar stock from which the links had been formed – and he was entirely at a loss as to how to account for it being there, when it should have been spanning a harbour mouth somewhere in the Old Country. Fortunately, there was plenty of light, although he himself was safely outside it and therefore to all intents and purposes invisible; he carefully worked himself in closer, and saw that the chain was connected to a series of ropes lying in the trench. He couldn't help noticing too a number of large and completely unfamiliar-looking machines, also with ropes attached to them.

It was at this point that Boerzes came to the conclusion that what he was looking at probably wasn't a festival at all, but something rather more sinister. He therefore crawled in closer still (according to the report; some commentators have found it hard to credit much of what follows), and actually climbed up the blind side of the nearest machine and looked inside for some clue as to its function and purpose.

He saw (if the report is to be believed) a mechanism by which the weight of a heavy lead block suspended from a rope wound around a spindle turned a driveshaft connected to a gear train, which in turn drove a headstock to which were fixed four curved and twisted blades. From the shape and profile of these blades, he deduced in a sudden flash of insight that they were designed to cut and scoop earth. Furthermore, the sear that released the weight, allowing it to descend and thereby drive the mechanism, was connected to an elaborate system of wires and levers leading to a pressure point on the front of the machine, just above the tow-hitch; the implication being that when the machine crashed into a solid obstacle, such as a bank of earth, the weight would be tripped and the blades would start to turn, without the need of a human operator.

At this point (so the report states) Boerzes found himself torn between his perceived duty and his personal desire to engage the enemy and single-handedly thwart what he recognised as an entirely viable plan to breach the bank of the flooded ditch and thereby drain it. Again, his true motivation can only be guessed at; the report records that he settled himself on the top of the machine, nocked an arrow on his bowstring and started shooting.

If this is indeed what happened, it's easy to imagine the bewilderment and panic it caused. It's entirely plausible that the drovers and sappers believed they were being attacked by a sortie in force from the embankment. Allied accounts of the incident confirm the Mezentine report's assertion that at least one of Boerzes' arrows hit an ox, which shied, broke its traces and plunged into the crowd of sappers and lantern-bearers. Many of them understandably sought the nearest cover, some of them crowding behind the worms; Boerzes asserted that, having by this time run out of arrows, he killed two of them with his sword before making his escape back to the Mezentine lines. In any event, the allies halted their operations, and Boerzes, having made a frantic report to the watch captain, urged him to start an artillery bombardment at once, to smash down the posts cemented in at the foot of the trench.

The watch captain pointed out that most of the artillery crews had been sent home, and the only men available were partially trained general infantry, incapable of working the engines, let alone aiming with sufficient precision to take out the posts. Instead, having sent a message to Chairman Psellus, he took the decision to launch a sortie with the forces at his command.

Psellus' reply, forbidding him to leave his position under any circumstances, came too late, and the sortie, no more than sixty men strong, scrambled down the embankment into the flooded ditch. Since none of them had been trained to swim in armour, it was inevitable that a number of them soon got into difficulties and were drowned; others were saved by their fellows or managed somehow to get across, but the commotion they made soon drew the attention of the allied sappers, who by now had realised that they were no longer under attack and were hurrying to get the operation back on schedule.

The surviving members of the sortie, meanwhile, had reached the trench; but they were leaderless, the captain having drowned in the flooded ditch, and most of them had only a very vague idea of what the purpose of the sortie was supposed to be. Instead of breaking down the posts or cutting the ropes, they advanced slowly and warily up the trench, apparently expecting to meet a raiding party of allied infantry.

Instead, they met the worms. General Daurenja, directing this stage of the operation in person, had given the order for the oxen to be led forward, pulling on the ropes fed through the pulleys at the far end of the trench and thereby drawing the worms on their wheeled carriages down the trench towards the already weakened wall of the flooded ditch. The sortie took them for some kind of siege tower and, displaying a remarkable degree of courage in the circumstances, charged them and clambered aboard. Instead of finding them full of armed men, however, they quickly realised they were unmanned, and moving at a slow but steady rate towards the ditch. The sortie's nerve finally broke; they jumped down behind the worms, still not having the wit to cut the ropes, and tried to climb out of the trench over the gabion wall. In the dark, however, they had no idea how tall it was; they appeared to have concluded that it was too high to scale without ladders, and dropped back into the trench; for some reason, it didn't seem to have occurred to them to try the other side, where there was no wall and they could have scrambled out relatively easily. As a result, they were still in the trench when the worms hit the bank and set off their blade-spinning mechanisms.

Ziani Vaatzes had of course tested a prototype before shipping the worms to the camp; it helped, as well, that the weight of the ditch-water was pressing in from the other side. Even so, the speed and efficiency with which they bored through the bank surprised everybody, including the general. The bank collapsed and the water flooded out into the trench, sweeping before it a tumbled mess of gabions, shield trolleys, fascines and other equipment. Most probably it was the debris, rather than the floodwater, that accounted for the Mezentines in the trench; only six of them escaped to report back to Psellus on the embankment. The worms, on the other hand, remained firmly tethered to the posts, cemented into the trench floor, and when the water had drained away and the first allied troops arrived at the foot of the trench, they found them substantially intact, ready for use in the next stage of the operation.

Psellus' head was still full of sleep as they bundled him, in his frayed nightgown and slippers, into the Guildhall yard, where a covered sedan chair was waiting. He protested: he hated being carried around in those things, he'd far rather walk. They ignored him as though he hadn't spoken, which put him in his place.

He particularly hated it when one of the four chairmen was a few inches taller than the others. It meant that one corner of the chair was always higher, while the man diagonally opposite was taking more than his fair share of the weight, which meant he stumbled on cobbles.

As a result, Psellus found it impossible to concentrate on what he'd been told, as the chair lurched and wobbled through the back alleys, heading for the Ridgeway gate. That was unfortunate; he needed time to clear his mind, before people started talking at him in loud voices. All he'd managed to grasp while they were waking him up and putting his slippers on his feet was that the enemy had somehow managed to burst the banks of the flooded ditch; there was also some ridiculous talk about a sortie – he'd sent a runner ahead to forestall that – and other stuff about monstrous unmanned digging machines. He'd let it flow over him; he'd have to deal with it when he got there, and the world stopped swaying.

The first face he saw as the chair stopped and he yanked back the curtains was Dilao Zosoter, colonel-in-chief of the artillery; a pompous, braying man who'd bounced his way up the hierarchy of the Pipemakers'; but when he saw him, Psellus couldn't help feeling sorry for him. He looked empty, as though someone had tapped his ear and siphoned out his personality.

"Dilao." He felt gingerly with his foot for the folding step, and scrambled out of the chair on to blessed motionless earth. "What's all this about draining the ditch? What's going on?"

Zosoter told him. To do him credit, he was clear and concise, an indication of how badly shaken he must be. He ended his narration with the admission that he'd told the artillery crews to go home. "I've sent runners to fetch them back," he added wretchedly, "but it's got to take time. I can't understand, actually, why the enemy haven't started bombarding us. If they're going to press home an attack tonight . . ."

Tempting providence. While Zosoter was speaking, Psellus felt the ground shake under his feet, and heard the dull, soft thump of a round shot landing. There was silence for one second, before everybody on the embankment started shouting at once. Typical Mezentines, Psellus thought; they're telling everybody else to take cover while standing perfectly still themselves.

Which reminded him. He dropped to his knees – mercifully, the earth where his troublesome left knee landed was soft and free of stones – as another shot passed by, close enough for him to feel the slipstream and hear the unmistakable swish-swish-swish noise of the spinning stone ball. The thump shook him up like a coughing fit.

Zosoter had been knocked off balance by the shaking of the ground under his feet, but he scrambled up again straight away. He was screaming orders, but Psellus couldn't make out a word of what he was saying over the background noise. Psellus looked past him, to the edge of the circle of light thrown by the palisade lanterns. He saw four men frantically spanning the windlass of a scorpion, as a round shot dipped out of the sky and landed no more than five yards away from them, lashing them with a hail of dirt and smashed brick. Another shot skimmed overhead and crashed into the wall behind him, and Psellus suddenly thought: that's not possible, they can't reach the wall, it's outside their maximum range. So they must have advanced their batteries, quietly, while all the commotion was going on. In which case, we'd better drop our sights, or when we get going again we'll all overshoot . . .

Another groundquake and thump, further away this time; and then a thought hit him, unexpected as shrapnel. They couldn't have advanced their batteries, or else the hero who'd raised the alarm, Boerzes, would've noticed them as he came back to the Mezentine lines. In which case . . .

He scrabbled himself upright and grabbed Zosoter by the shoulder. "Listen," he shouted (shouting always made him hoarse, very quickly), "whatever you do, when you return fire, don't lower your sights. Got that? Keep the solutions exactly as they are now."

Zosoter was shaking his head. "We've got to drop our aim," he said. "Their shot's hitting the wall, which is seventy yards further than they were able to reach last time. They must've moved up, which means—"

"They haven't moved," Psellus croaked back. "Trust me, I know exactly what they've done. Don't change the solutions, do you understand?"

It was beautiful, in its way: simple, patient, the perfect moment so perfectly chosen. In all the previous artillery exchanges, the enemy had been dropping short deliberately, to give the Mezentines the impression that their engines were less powerful than they actually were. Maybe they'd lowered their elevation, they may even have slackened off the torsion springs, and lightened the counterweights of the trebuchets; however they'd done it, their motive was suddenly and blindingly clear: to fool the Mezentine batteries into thinking they'd moved up, at this crucial moment in the assault, and make them alter their solutions and so drop short.

Briefly, he considered trying to explain that to Zosoter, at the top of his voice, with huge rocks falling out of the sky. Instead, he grabbed the nearest part of him he could reach, his knee, and shook him, bawling, "Do you understand?" Zosoter gave him a look of terrified fury, and nodded. If we're still alive in the morning, Psellus vowed to himself, I'll explain it to him. But not now.

"All right," Zosoter was yelling. "So what do you want us to do? Can we return fire?"

"Yes, of course."

"You're sure?"

Psellus had often wondered about violence: why some men chose to initiate it when they didn't have to. Now he could cheerfully have smashed Zosoter's face in. "Yes. Get on with it. Please," he added, on the off chance that politeness might succeed where a succession of direct orders had apparently failed. Zosoter gave him a last resentful look, and darted away to talk to the engine crews.

With only a fifth of the engines manned and operational, it wasn't much of a return volley; but the enemy weren't expecting it. The bombardment stopped for two minutes, almost but not quite long enough for the Mezentines to span and loose again. Instead, the allies' next shot fell just as the crews were loading their projectiles into their slings and sliders, an operation that could only be done standing up. This time, the allies had loaded with junk instead of finished shot – bricks, rocks, chunks of smashed shot, bits of broken timber, gabions filled with flints and small stones which burst on landing and shredded anybody within ten square yards down to the bone. They learned that from us, Psellus thought, staring at a dead body a few feet away. Chips of flint had torn away one side completely, and a tangled mess of guts hung out, spoiled with patches of dust. He thought about the hundreds of cartloads of broken masonry his side's engines had hurled at the allied lines over the past few weeks. He thought: war is a curious sort of reciprocal mirror. We never see the slaughter and injury our shot causes, only the results of the inevitable retaliation. Hardly any wonder, therefore, that we fall into the error of believing that it's the enemy who are to blame, rather than ourselves . . .

"The ditch is empty," someone was shouting in his ear. He vaguely recognised the voice, but couldn't put a name or a job description to it. "All the water's drained away down their big trench. What do you want us to do?"

What did he want them to do? What a very challenging, complex question. He wanted to say: stay here, defend the embankment against the attack in force which should be along at any moment, die (but keeping within the parameters of politically acceptable losses) and give me a few hours while I save the city by doing something so terrible, you wouldn't believe me if I told you about it. That's all.

Instead, he replied, "Keep up the bombardment and get as many armed men up here as you can." Then, as he noticed blood on his ridiculous nightgown, and realised (he felt surprised, bemused even, because he hadn't felt anything when it happened, and it wasn't hurting at all) that his left leg had been sliced open just above the knee, he added, "And find my sedan chair and get it over here as quickly as possible. I'm going back to the Guildhall."

The look in the man's eyes hurt him. "If you're leaving, who's in command up here?"

Psellus smiled. "My dear fellow, you are. Now, please hurry up and find my chair."

They were shooting round shot rather than scatter, which meant they were trying to take out the engines rather than simply kill artillerymen. The general wasn't happy about that, coming as it did on top of the failure of the carefully planned undershooting ploy. He'd been banking on getting artillery superiority before sending the sappers up to start work on the embankment. By now, the scorpion batteries should have given up or been pounded into the dirt. Instead, they were maintaining a slow but steady fire – shooting blind in the dark, true enough, but they were still able to blanket a significant area. That left him with a choice between moving forward and thereby betraying his numerical strength, and staying where he was and taking thirty per cent more casualties than he'd budgeted for. He had no option but to choose the latter course, and he was quite obviously annoyed about it. Needless to say, it couldn't possibly affect the outcome, but it was sure to spoil his projected casualty ratio; and all for nothing.

He joined the sappers, and went up the trench with them,. It was hard going. The floodwater from the ditch had turned the loose soil in the bottom of the trench into thick glue which tugged at their boots, like scavengers after a battle stripping the dead. There were no lanterns to spare, so they followed the gleam of faint moonlight reflected in puddles. Enemy shot whistled and twittered overhead, urging them to hurry, trip and sprawl. Occasionally they trod on dead men partially buried in mud and silt. As they approached the ditch, the lights on the embankment seemed almost welcoming – the friendly inn at the end of a long night ride – but they could hear the sharp clack of the scorpion sliders hammering against their stops: not friendly at all.

Crossing the ditch was a problem nobody had considered. The mud was knee-deep and aggressively sticky. The only way to get through it, once both your legs had sunk in and there was nothing firm to push against, was to lay your shovel sideways on the surface and lean over it, pushing against it with your arms until you'd levered one leg out of the mud; get a knee on the shovel handle and drag up the other leg; half crawl and half swim a yard ahead, then repeat the process. It was easier once your boots had been sucked off your feet, but the sheer effort was exhausting, harder work than anything the sappers had ever done in the trenches or the mines.

When the general arrived and saw the problem, he sent some men back to pull fascines off the trench wall. The first fifty or so sank into the mud without a trace, but gradually they were able to build a sloppy, dangerous causeway that could be crossed on hands and knees; and someone had the wit to fetch a rope, which was stretched across the ditch for a handrail.

By now, however, the Mezentines had seen what was happening, and they were shooting arrows down into the ditch. It was too dark to aim, but that scarcely mattered. A wound was as good as an out-right kill, if it was enough to hinder the use of an arm or a leg. The effect, however, wasn't what the Mezentines would've wanted; bodies, shot or drowned in mud, made better duckboards than bundles of brushwood, and once the ditch bottom was nicely clogged with dead men, crossing was much easier.

Once they were across the ditch, the sappers were safe from the Mezentine arrows. They had no choice but to rest for twenty minutes or so; then they started to work. It was perfectly straightforward: dig out the base of the embankment, throwing the spoil back into the ditch, until they'd undermined it enough to cave it in. The earth was relatively soft and loose, and they propped as they went with spars and planks. The Mezentines were rolling masonry blocks down the embankment at them, but all that achieved was to help fill in the ditch and make it easier to bring up timber and fresh digging crews. The Aram Chantat had brought archers to shoot at the helpfully backlit defenders; the palisade took most of the arrows, but that hardly mattered; the intention was to make the enemy keep their heads down, and it worked well. The bombardment continued, of course, and observers at the ditch were able to send more accurate solutions back to the artillery captains; the priority now was to smash up the palisade and loosen the embankment directly above the sap, to make the job of undermining easier. The Mezentines were still shooting blindly into the dark, trying to find the allied artillery. They were doing a good job of it, but it really didn't matter: for every mangonel and trebuchet Daurenja had deployed in the artillery park, he had two more in reserve, to be brought up for the final assault. The machines the Mezentines were shooting at were really nothing more than bait.

Vadani observers out in the plain noticed a concentration of lights moving about on the embankment. They took this to mean that the enemy had brought up as many men as could be crowded in, to defend against an assault in force. When he was told about it, the general didn't seem unduly bothered; in fact, he said, that would make the job easier rather than more difficult. He then sent an order back to the quartermasters, who queried it. He sent it again, ordering them to do as they'd been told.

As it happened, Ziani Vaatzes was in the quartermasters' store when the confirmation came through. He grinned when he heard it.

"Flour," the quartermaster repeated. "Twelve tons of flour. What's he planning to do with it, feed the buggers to death?"

"Is it in sacks or barrels?" Ziani asked.

"Both," the quartermaster replied. "We've got fifty tons in barrels and a hundred and seventy-five tons in sacks. What's that got to do with anything?"

"Send the barrels," Ziani said. "And they'll want lamp oil, say thirty gallons. Did they ask for that?"

"No."

"Ah." Ziani looked smug. "Just as well I'm here."

The quartermaster looked at him blankly. "You know what he's up to, then?"

"Yes," Ziani said.

"It makes no sense," Psellus repeated furiously, dismissing the bearers who'd brought him back from the Guildhall. They were glad to go, pushing a way through the crowd of soldiers and artillerymen crowding towards the line of craters where the palisade had once been. "It'd take them a week to dig in far enough to undermine this position effectively. And he must know that as soon as the sun comes up and we can see to aim . . ."

He realised he was shouting, and he didn't even recognise the man he was shouting at: some junior infantry officer, reporting the arrival of his unit. But he *wanted* to shout; because his whole view of the assault was founded on the assumption that General Daurenja was a good commander who'd do the right thing, sensibly and predictably; and yet here he was, making an obvious mistake. If you can't trust your enemy . . .

"Ignore me," he said calmly, and that seemed to alarm the poor young man more than the yelling. "I'm just thinking aloud. You go ahead and get your men in position. But be prepared for a long wait. I really can't see what he thinks he's playing at."

The young man bounded away, clearly relieved to have escaped from the leader of his people, who'd finally broken his spring and was raving. Not, Psellus had to admit, an entirely inaccurate assessment. I'm doing no good at all up here, he realised, I'm just getting in the way and upsetting people. I'm being self-indulgent, playing at being a king or a duke. And not making a very good job of it, he added. A king or a duke wouldn't be crouched in a shot-crater in a muddy nightgown and slippers.

Besides, he knew what was going to happen here, sooner or later. Nothing he could do about it; and he had a war to win, in his office at the Guildhall.

A slab of rock about the size of a horse's head had turned the hated sedan chair into kindling. Not to worry, he thought cheerfully, I'll walk back. People I pass in the street can stare at me, it'll take their minds off the war.

On his way down, he stopped a half-platoon of soldiers en route to the front. "Excuse me," he said, "do you know who I am?"

Embarrassed horror; I've done it again, he thought. "What I mean is," he went on, "do you recognise me?"

"Of course. You're Chairman Psellus."

He smiled. "Excellent," he said. "I'm sorry, I'm still not used to being able to order people about. I keep expecting them to ask me who the hell I am, issuing orders. Very well. Come with me." He wiped the smirk off his face and added, "This is very important, do you understand me?"

He was relieved to find that the streets were empty. He'd sent someone to issue a proclamation that everybody not on active service should go home and stay there, but he hadn't really expected it to be obeyed. He made it as far as the Guildhall gates, but then his knee gave way and he couldn't walk any further.

"I'm very sorry," he said, "but you'll have to carry me."

He'd been quietly dreading something like this, but the soldiers didn't seem at all put out. Two of them held a spear at approximately knee height, and he sat on it like a child on a swing, his arms round their shoulders to stop him falling off backwards.

The stairs were rather tricky, but eventually they got him to his office and into his chair. The familiar feel of it revived him to a remarkable extent, and he gave them the names and locations of the people he wanted them to go and fetch. "And do please be quick," he added. "I know it seems unlikely, but this is the most important thing in the City right now."

They left; and for five minutes or so he leaned back in his chair and closed his eyes. He'd never thought of himself as an old man, as so many of his colleagues and contemporaries did, as soon as they passed fifty. In fact, he realised with a jolt, he had no real idea of himself at all. If he was anything, he was simply an observer, a point of view drifting through events great or trivial, hardly able to distinguish between them from his off-centre, ill-informed standpoint.

Until now, he thought. If it's true that you're as old as you feel, I'm well over ninety.

The soldiers must have believed him, because they assembled the prisoners (he called them that in his mind for want of a better word; "witnesses" wasn't quite right, "guests" was absurd) in no time at all. Psellus couldn't resist opening the door a crack and peering at them, sitting in a row on a bench in the corridor. She was in her nightdress; the two investigators were wearing the heavy padded jerkins that went under armour (he could never remember the technical term), so they must have been pulled in from the embankment. The politicians were still in their formal daywear, as if reluctant to get undressed just in case someone came by in the middle of the night wanting them to form a government. He closed the door carefully, so as not to make a noise.

Now he was waiting for just one more . . . witness? He felt comfortable with the word in this context. The delay chafed him, of course, but it was only to be expected: the witness would inevitably be hard to find. Until then, it'd do the rest of them no harm to sit in a draught on a cold bench.

A messenger burst in about half an hour later. He'd come from the embankment. As far as anybody could tell, the enemy were still digging. All the surviving siege engines were now manned and operational, shooting round shot at the last known position of the enemy artillery, whose rate and quantity of fire was materially though not substantially (Psellus liked that distinction) reduced. There were now seven divisions of general infantry in place on the embankment to resist an assault in force. It was still too dark to see what the enemy were doing, but there were no reports of the movement of lights except in the main trench; however, the machines that had breached the ditch had been moved up, and so presumably were back in service undermining the embankment. There was, the messenger concluded reluctantly, no other news.

"Thank you," Psellus replied gravely. "How long till it gets light?" He smiled, and added, "There aren't any windows here, as you can see."

"Three hours, more or less," the messenger replied.

"Three hours," Psellus repeated. "That's about right. You couldn't just ask my chief clerk to come in for a moment, could you?"

He sent the clerk to chivvy the men who were searching for the witness; then, since he had nothing else to do that really mattered very much, he picked up the book he'd been reading – how long ago, exactly? He found it hard to remember. He'd been immersed in Stamnus' *Lives of the Great Administrators*, an old favourite, and someone had interrupted him with some important business; he'd marked the place with a scrap of paper and put it down, expecting to pick it up again in a moment or so. Three days ago, he realised; and yet it felt as though it was only minutes, and he could remember the last line he'd read. I don't actually believe in any of this, he suddenly thought. I don't really believe I'm the head of state of the Perpetual Republic, or that there's a war going on twelve minutes' walk away, or that the savages are about to burst through the defences we all thought were impenetrable. He frowned. Not the right attitude, he told himself. But it didn't matter. Any minute now, as soon as the missing witness was brought in, he'd do the only thing he could to save the City; and if it failed, everything would then be out of his control, and in any case, he'd be dead. He found that thought almost comforting.

*

"You came," Daurenja said.

He's pleased to see me, Ziani thought, genuinely pleased that I'm here. "That's all right, isn't it?" he asked. "Only I've finished my work now, there's nothing left for me to do. So I thought I'd come and watch."

Daurenja smiled, nodded enthusiastically. He was covered in mud from head to foot; in the lanternlight he looked like some curious mythical creature, shaped like a man but with a cracked grey skin, unfinished face and strange pink eyes. He'd been digging when Ziani found him, kicking the blade of a shovel into the fine dirt of the embankment like a man cutting up a whale. There'd been something about him that made Ziani stare for a long time, trying to figure out what it might be: the energy, the purpose, but it wasn't a hero in battle or a great king leading his people to victory. Daurenja reminded him, he realised with astonishment, of a small boy playing in a sandpit, and the strange aura that surrounded him, incongruous and bizarre, was happiness.

"Delighted that you're here," Daurenja said. "After all, this is your victory, not mine."

True, Ziani thought; but you don't know that. You're just trying to be *nice*. "They're bringing up the flour," he said. "Should be here any minute. And you forgot the lamp oil."

Daurenja winced, then grinned. "But you didn't."

"No."

"Thanks." Such warmth in his voice. How often do you meet someone who's truly, sublimely happy? "I knew I could rely on you. I want to say it right now, before we go any further, how grateful I am. I couldn't have done it without you."

"Don't say that till it's over," Ziani replied. "We aren't home yet."

"Doesn't matter. If we fail, it'll be my fault, because I've got something wrong. Everything you've done has been perfect."

"But it wasn't me," Ziani said, smiling. "All along, ever since you first came sniffing round me asking for a job. You've been using me, like you use everybody who could conceivably be useful."

Daurenja laughed. "Well, of course," he said. "You're trying to make it sound negative for some reason, but that's exactly right. I see the potential in people, just like I see it in things. I bring together, I plan ahead, I *expedite* – that's a good word, don't you think? – but that doesn't make the individual components' contributions any less valuable. Really, Ziani, I'm very, very grateful for everything you've done for me. For the cause. And I know you didn't do it for my reasons, but who cares about motives, really? Who'll care a hundred years from now, when every army in the world will be using my invention, and all this stuff, all the digging and mining and hand-to-hand fighting's a thing of the past? And it's not just war that's going to change." His eyes were glowing like coals. "That's what's so special about it. *Everything's* going to change, that's why it's so important. There'll be no more walled cities, so no more great city states, no more empires, no more *war*. Hadn't you worked that out for yourself? If you can't defend a secure place, you can't fight a war, not the way we think of it. And pitched battles – impossible. My weapon will sweep all those massed armies, all the pikemen and cavalry and infantry formations right off the field; who'd be crazy enough to stand out in the open and be smashed to a pulp by rocks thrown from a mile away? No more war, Ziani; and no war, no nations, no governments, because all authority relies ultimately on force of arms; we'll do away with all the evil, corrupt systems that crush people like you and me, people who just want to be different. My weapon will do all that. Oh Ziani, I thought you understood, I was sure of it. I was convinced you must've seen it for yourself, when you got them to give me the command." He looked sad, but only for a moment. "It doesn't matter," he said. "We're here now, and everything's going well, it won't be much longer now. They'll bring it up as soon as we've dealt with the embankment. You will promise me, though; you'll be there when we use it the first time."

Ziani had to make an effort to speak. "Of course," he said. "After all, it's going to get us into the City, isn't it?" A man pushed past him, rolling a barrel. "And that's all I've ever wanted."

She looked at him.

He'd thought he understood her; the argument being, if you know everything that's inside someone, nothing that looks out through the eyes can surprise you. Not so, apparently.

"I know what you're thinking," he said. "Haven't I got anything better to do? The City's being attacked, they've drained the ditch, they're digging under the embankment like rats in a corn bin, shouldn't I be out there leading something, instead of harassing poor harmless civilians. Well?"

Shrug, nod. Well, her words had always been precious, bought at great cost.

"Listen to me." He leaned forward across the desk. "The enemy are coming. They're savages. We don't understand them; we *think* they want to kill us all and burn down the City so they can turn this country into pasture for their animals, but we don't even know that. But I'm fairly certain that if I don't do something very soon, hundreds, thousands, hundreds of thousands of people will die in pain and fear. Do you understand me?"

Her eyes were defences; too high to scale, too hard to batter down, too deep to undermine. She said, "What can you do?"

"Me? Not a great deal. I can't fight, and I'm not clever enough to come up with a brilliant strategy. And we're none of us soldiers. So," he added with a faint smile, "that just leaves me with you."

She sighed. "What's that supposed to mean?"

He thought: even this is too difficult for me, I simply don't have the strength. But he said, "We think the enemy has a secret weapon, something that can tear down walls or smash through gates. Most likely it's something your husband made for them, he seems to have a flair for that sort of thing. But I'm not too worried about that, because I know for a fact that I've got an even better secret weapon. I've got you."

Another sigh, and she looked away.

"Listen to me," he said again. "I know what you did. Outside in the corridor are the investigators, the men Falier reported the abomination to. They've told me how he told them what to look for. I've also got Falier. He's told me about your agreement, how you both decided Ziani had to go. He says you told him about what Ziani was doing – indirectly, of course, but you put the idea into his head. It was your plan, the whole thing."

"That's stupid," she said. "I couldn't have done anything like that. I'm not an engineer."

"No." He nodded. "But you asked Ziani to build the doll, for Moritsa. You told him it had to be the kind that could move its arms. And you knew that if you asked him to do something, he'd do it. He'd have no choice, no matter how terrible it was, because he loved you."

"Rubbish," she said. "How would I know about types and mechanisms and stuff?"

He smiled. "Thank you," he said. "For giving me my cue. You wouldn't know, unless somebody told you. Somebody who also wanted to get Ziani out of the way. Someone you were in love with – you never cared anything for Falier – and who, for a time at least, was infatuated with you."

"You're a very strange man," she said. "You're sitting here telling me all this garbage when the savages—"

He held up his hand. "But that wasn't the only reason," he went on. "He loved you – I suppose you could call it that, though I should imagine it was more of an obsession on his part; the usual thing with a middle-aged upper-class man and a young low-class woman: the thrill, the sin, the exhilaration of breaking the rules and getting away with it. And I'm assuming the physical side was at least adequate. After all, he chose you, and a man like that could've had practically any woman in the City."

She said nothing.

"Although," he went on, "from what I can gather, he wasn't like that. Usually, as I understand it, when a man of Boioannes' stature and position gets obsessed with sex, a large part of the pleasure is the number and variety of conquests. Curiously, all my researches have only turned up six verifiable liaisons, all of them brief and fairly low-key. The rest of the time, he seems to have been a contentedly married man, until he found you. Now, looking at you, I really don't see—"

She yawned. "What was that name you said?"

"Maris Boioannes." He steepled his fingers. "Your lover. It was Boioannes who came up with the idea of tricking Ziani into breaking the law. He told you to nag and wheedle Ziani into making the doll with arms that moved; he'll have said it was so Ziani could be got out of the way, and then you'd pair off with a nonentity – Falier, who happened to be smitten with you anyhow – and after a decent interval he'd find a way of getting rid of Falier as well, and then you could be together. I wonder," he went on, "how he explained how Falier fitted into the plan, why he was needed. My guess is that if anybody came snooping round – me, for instance – they'd assume it was all Falier's idea; that Ziani started building the doll off his own bat, Falier noticed the abomination and turned him in to Compliance to get you for himself. Something like that? I'll take that as a yes. I expect the way he explained it made a whole lot of sense. Whatever else he was, Boioannes was a wonderfully persuasive man."

"Maris Boioannes," she repeated. "I've heard of him. Isn't he some grand politician?"

Psellus smiled. "You're forgetting something," he said. "I don't need to prove a word of this to anybody else. I just need to know it, and make you do what I want you to."

She was still for a long time; then she nodded, a tiny movement. "All right," she said. "What's that?"

"Barrels?" the colonel repeated.

"That's right." The staff major shrugged. "Beats me, too. But that's what they've been doing. According to my best observers, all those lights we've been watching come up the trench are men rolling barrels."

The colonel sat down on a smashed beam and rubbed his cheeks with his palms. "What do you make of it?" he said. "I guess they could be using them to prop up the roof of the sap, but it seems like a lot of effort to go to."

A thump, and the ground shook. Neither man seemed to notice. After four hours of the bombardment, they were getting used to it. "We ought to dig a countersap," the major said. "If we dig under their sap and undermine it—"

"I suggested that two hours ago," the colonel replied. "He didn't even answer my note."

"He's not a soldier."

The colonel grinned. "Neither are we. So, no countersap. There's probably a very good reason," he added wearily. "Probably it'd damage the embankment even more than what they're doing."

"Not if we shored it properly."

"You know how to do that?" The major shook his head. "I don't, either. Their sappers are mineworkers, they know what they're doing. If we go digging bloody great big holes in the ground, we'll probably bring down the City walls. No, leave well alone, sit tight and do as we're told. And no sorties," he added quickly. "Leave it all up to Chairman Psellus and whoever does his thinking for him. Then, whatever happens, at least it's not our bloody fault."

The major drew in a deep breath and let it go slowly. "As you say," he said. "Actually," he went on, "you didn't let me finish. What I was going to say was, they were bringing in barrels, but now they've stopped. In fact, there's nothing going on in the trench at all, as far as we can see."

The colonel frowned. "But the sappers are still there," he said. "They haven't gone back down the trench."

"We don't know that. They might have gone back, it's still too dark to see."

Now the colonel was rubbing his temples with the tips of his fingers. "Chairman Psellus himself told one of my junior officers it'd take them a week to dig in deep enough to bring down this embankment. It'll be daylight soon, and then we'll be able to see what's going on, and presumably the chairman and his advisers will have a plan of action. Meanwhile, we stand to, as ordered, and resist the temptation to think for ourselves. As I understand it," he added, "that's what being a soldier's all about."

The major left to report back to whoever he reported back to, and the colonel sat still for a while, watching the red stains seeping through the crack between the horizon and the sky. Daylight, he thought; soon it'll be daylight, we'll be able to see what's going on, and everything will be just that little bit easier. He closed his eyes, and he could still see red streaks. Bad omen, he thought, so he made a conscious decision to think about something else. For example: what could the enemy possibly want with several hundred seventy-gallon barrels?

That, however, was too much for him; he managed to come up with several explanations, but they were all equally improbable, with nothing much to choose between them, and none of them was he inclined to accept. His mind drifted away, slipping through tunnels of memory to the time when his grandfather had taken him to see where he worked, in the varnish factory (that was the connection, because the cellars of the factory had been crammed with barrels full of varnish waiting to be shipped, and he'd got into the most terrible trouble because he hadn't left the lamp outside the door as he'd been told; one mistake with a lit lamp in here, Grandad had told him, and they'd have to redraw all the maps) . . .

He jumped up, his mouth open, barely aware that he was yelling. A round shot landed a few yards away, and he felt the spray of dirt it kicked up hit him like a slap across the face. Someone was screaming, but that didn't matter. He listened to himself; he was howling, "Clear the embankment, evacuate," but nobody was listening; there were men scrambling round a collapsed redoubt, trying to pull some poor devil out from under the heaps of shattered brick. He ran up to the nearest man and started tugging at his arm; he was shouting, "No, no," at the top of his voice, but the man didn't seem to *understand*, which was ridiculous, because there just wasn't time to explain; but he had to try, so he bawled, "If that lot goes up, they'll have to redraw all the maps." But the man still didn't seem to have understood, and now there were at least two other men he couldn't see, grabbing his elbows from behind, pulling him back. But that was ridiculous, because they had to listen to him and get away from the embankment, quickly, now, before whatever was in those barrels blew up . . .

"Have you thought," Ziani said suddenly, "how you're going to light it?"

Daurenja grinned. The mud had dried on his face and was beginning to crack and peel, like flaking skin. "Actually, yes," he said, and he slipped his hand down the front of his breastplate, fished about for a moment and pulled out a cloth bag about the size of a shoe. "I think it's only fair that you should be the first man to see it in action, so to speak. I think you deserve that."

He untied the cord round the neck of the bag, and started sprinkling some kind of coarse black powder. It reminded Ziani of the dust left behind in a cellar after all the coal had been used up.

"Is that it?" he asked. "Your magic powder?"

"Hardly magic," Daurenja replied, not looking up. "Just plain science. And also, incidentally, my life's work and my gift to all mankind. When I say the word, get ready to run like buggery."

He'd used up the last of the powder, and shook out the bag. He'd made a line about two yards long, starting under the nearest oil-soaked barrel. "It looks like ordinary soot," Ziani said. "Is that what it's made from?"

Daurenja turned his head and smiled at him. "No," he said. "Ready?"

Ziani nodded, and Daurenja picked up the lantern and threw it on the floor where the powder line ended. "Run!" he heard Daurenja shout, but he ignored him; the sight of the burning powder was too interesting. That little trail of dust wasn't just burning. It was like watching a blossom unfurl; he simply couldn't believe that so much fire could come out of a little trail of powder, and the noise it made, and what was that smell?

Daurenja must have grabbed his arm and yanked him; he felt himself stagger, then found his feet and scrambled to keep from falling over. Then the force of the oil catching fire hit him in the back like a door, and a stripe of burning pain licked across his shoulderblades. So that's why he said run, he thought, and ran.

He had no idea how far he'd gone, but Daurenja stopped suddenly and he stopped too. They'd reached the first zigzag, where the trench folded like an elbow. He felt himself being pushed to the ground, but he took no notice; he was staring at the huge orange rose of flames bursting out of the side of the embankment. It was an extraordinary sight, flames at least twelve feet high reaching out like a trapped man's waving arms, but he thought, That's not enough, surely. It's got to get really hot to make the flour—

Then the noise came. It slammed into him, and suddenly there was dead silence as his ears overloaded; but he didn't really notice that, either. He was watching the embankment, as much of it as he could see, *move* – as though it had been lying down and was now standing up, yawning and stretching, taking its time, until it filled the sky. And then it came down again.

Stones, timbers, whole machines and bits of machines, and so very many people. He saw them scrabble in the air as they fell, and when they hit the ground they crumpled, as the force of the fall squashed them against the ground. Then the dirt and the dust came down, dropping over the tumbling mess like a veil. Out of nowhere, a chunk of brick hit him on the point of the elbow. He yelped with pain, and debris fell on him, hard enough to push him down on his face. His eyes were clogged with dirt and grit. He closed them, rubbing furiously at his eyelids. He tried to congratulate himself, to feel pleased; after all, he'd been the one who remembered what happened to the shed full of flour back at the camp, when the Cure Doce set fire to it. His idea, his fault; but it didn't seem to want to fit. Might as well try and claim the credit for a volcano or an earthquake.

"Shit," he heard Daurenja say, and the way he said it was almost comical: awed, afraid and very deeply impressed, the tone of voice men use when making lewd remarks about women. He tried to peer through the dust, but it was too thick in the air.

"Right," Daurenja said shakily, "that worked pretty well. Now we'd better get moving."

Ziani remembered: the next stage in the plan. Any moment now, the flower of the Aram Chantat would break cover and advance at the double across the plain, to swarm up through the breach and start clearing the defenders off what was left of the embankment. That wouldn't take very long . He thought about the people he knew, the men he'd worked with in the factory, trying to be soldiers and fight hand to hand with sharp weapons: ludicrous. He could picture them in his mind, lying on the ground like things spilt from a broken crate, skin sliced open, skulls crushed – he remembered a bad accident in the machine shop, some fool letting his hand get too close to a spinning chuck; flesh ripped open (like an impatient man opening a package), a glimpse of white bone before the blood oozed up to cover it; he thought of the blank horror that emptied the minds of the bystanders, how they shrank away, as though physical damage on that scale was somehow contagious. Since he'd escaped from the City, he'd seen more violence and injury than all the rest of them put together: he'd seen men gutted in fighting, Jarnac Ducas paunching and skinning deer, all the conventional horrors that only doctors and savages saw. Now, if he applied his mind to it, he could look at skin, blood and intestines and see only casings, hydraulics and components, and to him all human beings were simply mechanisms, subassemblies of his design. That was a better perspective, he'd come to believe. After all, whoever heard of a mechanic who got squeamish at the sight of a box of gears?

He looked up at Daurenja. The rising sun was behind him, so that he looked like a man wearing a burning hat; his eyes were wide open, fixed on something nobody else would ever see, and the dried mud was peeling off his skin in small, square patches. Let him have his moment of joy, he thought. One moment is all we need, and generally all we deserve.

It was a messy sunrise, like a wound clogged with mud, and as the light soaked into the plain, men started to appear, stumbling forward out of pools of shadow. They were the Aram Chantat, and they were on their way to slaughter the Mezentines.

A man he'd never seen before burst in through the door. His face was bleeding, and he'd wrapped his left hand in a bit of rag.

"They've got in," he said. "They did something with fire, and the embankment just flew up in the air. They're killing people everywhere, and—"

Psellus held up his hand, palm facing outwards. "Are the City gates shut?" he asked.

The man nodded. "We've got to open them and let our people get in," he said. "Otherwise the savages'll kill them all. There's nowhere they can go."

"No." The word came out in a voice he didn't recognise. "On no account are the gates to be opened, is that perfectly clear? On no account." He paused, just to catch his breath (and he remembered signing the report that started the Eremian war; just one man doing one little thing). "Our soldiers on the embankment will just have to look after themselves. We can't risk opening the gates. Do you understand?"

The man was staring at him, as if he couldn't believe what he was hearing. "They sent me to ask you—"

"Yes," Psellus said, "and now I'm giving you an answer. The gates must stay closed. Tell the City wardens to get as many men as possible on to the walls and man the tower batteries. They're to target the enemy artillery, only the artillery. Have you got that?"

A little nod, but he was still staring wildly. As well he might.

"Thank you," Psellus said gravely. "Report back to me once the message has been delivered. And tell my clerks, no more interruptions, no matter what happens. That's very important. Do you understand?"

When the man had gone, she looked at him. "They're going to take the City," she said, "and you're not doing anything about it."

He closed his eyes, just for a moment. "Wrong," he said. "I will do something about it very soon, and as a result, they will not take the City. We have an ally who will save us, just as Duke Valens saved Duke Orsea and his wife at Civitas Eremiae."

The look she gave him made him want to laugh, or to smash her face in. "Really?" she said. "Who's that, then?" He kept his face still and straight, but under the table he clenched his fists till they hurt. "Ziani," he replied.

Chapter Seventeen

He was right. It took no time at all.

Later, it was estimated that a third of the Mezentine dead were killed when Daurenja exploded his mine, either by the force of the blast, or by injuries caused by being thrown into the air, or by falling debris. The Aram Chantat disposed of the rest. An Eremian officer who arrived with unnecessary reinforcements halfway through the operation said it reminded him of killing rats in a barn: you lifted up a trough or a feed bin, then clubbed or stamped on them as they scurried frantically past. They hardly fought at all, he said, like it simply didn't occur to them to try using their weapons.

In fact it was an Eremian officer, Major General Miel Ducas, who co-ordinated the reduction and elimination of Mezentine forces on the embankment after the breach had been made. His approach was simple but effective. Having used flying wedges to split up the mass of the enemy, he pressed them back against the City wall, surrounded each segment in detail and let the Aram Chantat get on with the job. In spite of their enthusiasm for the work, even the Aram Chantat eventually grew tired from the sheer effort of cutting bone and hammering metal, so he organised them into shifts, a fresh unit coming in to relieve the executioners when they grew too weary to continue. The number of Mezentines killed on the embankment was never reliably established, since a great many bodies were buried under the spoil and rubble; Chairman Psellus later put the figure at twelve thousand, but this was generally held to be an excessively conservative estimate.

Because the chairman was otherwise engaged when the embankment was breached, and all his superiors in the chain of command were killed or severely injured, or disappeared and couldn't be found, Colonel Zosoter of the artillery took charge of the defence of the forward positions and the evacuation of the survivors. He had precious little to work with. The enemy's flying wedge tactics meant that his forces were fragmented into isolated segments, and he was unable to communicate with them given the risk – practically a certainty – that any message he sent would be intercepted by the enemy. He was confident that the gates would be opened to let the survivors back in, and acted on that assumption, falling back on the gatehouses as the enemy pressed home their assault.

The gates stayed shut.

When it became apparent that Chairman Psellus had abandoned him, Colonel Zosoter ordered his men to lay down their weapons and surrender, on the entirely reasonable assumption that the enemy took prisoners. He was wrong about that, too.

He had her escorted to the top of the Chandlers' bell-tower, whose window overlooked the main gate. She didn't want to look, insisting that it was none of her business, and she'd done nothing wrong.

Psellus had always taken refuge in the fact that he wasn't a violent man. He hadn't even tried to hurt anybody physically since he was eight years old. He reached out as if to pat her comfortingly on the shoulder, wound his fingers in her hair and tugged till she gasped. Then he twisted her head to face the open window.

"In that case," he said, "there's no reason why you shouldn't look."

She swore at him, but struggling made it hurt more. "Let me go," she said. "I've got my eyes shut."

"If you don't open them," Psellus said gently, "I'll push you out of the window."

She called him some names he didn't actually understand, though he got the general idea. He leant against her gently, and she screamed.

"Look," he said.

(Afterwards, he felt very badly about it; partly because he thought he'd let himself down, partly because if she hadn't opened her eyes, he was sure he would have pushed her out, and killing her would have meant the end of any hope of saving the City. He was also deeply disturbed by how thrilling he found the texture of her hair and the softness of her body as he pressed against it. Just as well, in fact, that she gave in when she did, and opened her eyes.)

She said nothing; and after thirty seconds or so, he relaxed his grip on her hair and let her pull away. She glared at him, as though he'd trodden on her foot.

"I agree," he said. "You've done nothing wrong. You just wanted to be happy. But now you can see why you've got to help me. Otherwise, they will break in here, and they will kill you. Ziani won't be able to stop them."

She frowned. "I never thought we'd lose," she said. "I thought we'd win. We always win, don't we? We're better than everybody else."

He shook his head. "We're better at everyone else at some things," he replied. "The things that matter, naturally. But they're stronger than us, just as I'm stronger than you. One thing this has taught me, you can't win against brute force if you're weaker."

Her frown deepened; it was as if he was insisting that two and two made five. "But they're savages," she said.

"Yes. And savages are better at fighting than we are. We've always tended to see that as evidence that we're superior to them. I'd like to believe that's true, but I'm beginning to have my doubts. Now, will you do what I asked you?"

She nodded. "I don't have a choice, do I?"

"Not really," he said.

When it was all over, the Ducas reported to General Daurenja, who nodded and smiled at him. "Thank you," he said. "You've done well."

The Ducas made some formal gesture, which the general assumed was an Eremian military salute. "Just doing my duty," he said.

"Carry on," the general replied.

Miel left him and walked slowly back towards the ditch. The Mezentine dead were piled up like grain sacks waiting to be loaded, a great wealth of commodities. He paused, stooped and turned over a body at random. Then he searched it, taking a bronze cloak-pin, a finger-ring, a linen handkerchief and twelve dollars cash.

An Eremian soldier was watching him. He straightened up, dropping the goods he'd taken into his pocket, and nodded affably. The soldier saluted.

"We made them pay for what they did to us, didn't we, sir?" the soldier said.

Miel raised his eyebrows. "I suppose so, yes," he replied.

He walked down the steep slope formed by the collapse of the embankment, concentrating to keep his balance. Around him he was aware of men calling out (the wounded, too badly hurt to move; it reminded him of the bleating of sheep), and thought of the expression the scavengers used: *live one here*. Of course, they made a point of salvaging any wounded men who could be expected to recover, and putting the others out of their misery. He envied them their humanity, but reflected that it had done them no good in the long run. If they hadn't spared him, they'd probably still be alive now.

The ditch was easy to cross now; they'd brought up planks and laid them on top of the rubble and dead bodies, making a road wide enough to drive a cart over. He noticed the silence, and realised that the Mezentines had given up shooting from the wall batteries. It made sense, of course, to conserve their ammunition. He thought about the hail of scorpion bolts that had wiped out Orsea's wretched attempt at an invasion. Now it was the other way around, like a reflection in a mirror; a different angle, but the same thing.

He remembered saving Daurenja's life, when Framain and his daughter had wanted to kill him. It had been the act of a humane man. He couldn't imagine those circumstances arising now. He wouldn't have got involved in the first place.

He crossed the ditch and walked slowly up the trench, labouring through the mud, working out in his mind how to approach the task of clearing up the mess. Burial details: first, of course, the dead would have to be stripped, the recovered goods sorted into piles: military equipment in one heap, personal items in another. Carts to haul away the armour, weapons, bales of clothing, footwear; sacks for the rest. As he understood it, the correct procedure was to appoint a factor to take charge of the salvage, notify the principal dealers and organise a series of auctions. The proceeds of sale of the military equipment went back into consolidated funds, while the private property of the dead went into a separate fund, to be divided up between the soldiers who'd taken part in the relevant action. The important thing was to make sure that everything was visibly fair and equitable. The factor, if he remembered correctly, took five per cent of the gross. He was sure the general would give him the job, if he asked politely.

He stepped aside to let a wagon go by. The carter leaned down and called to him. "What's it like up ahead?"

"Not so bad," he replied. "The trench is a bit sticky still, but the slope's pretty gentle. You'll get across the ditch all right, but you won't get much further. Too steep."

The carter nodded. "You know where I can find whoever's in charge?" he said. "Sounds like I'll need men to haul this lot up to the wall."

"You've found him," Miel replied pleasantly. "I'll send a couple of platoons, if you think that'll be enough."

The carter thanked him. "Special delivery for the general," he explained. "Top priority, is what I was told."

"Ah, well then," Miel said. "I won't hold you up any longer."

True to his word, he sent on the two platoons before he started rostering the burial and recovery details – he was, after all, still first and foremost a soldier, and his duty must take precedence. The men he'd dispatched squelched up the trench at the double, anxious not to keep the general waiting. So far they'd had nothing to do, and it looked as though the preliminary assault was now as good as over. If they were lucky, they'd be on the spot for the attack on the City itself, and first in meant the best pickings. Everybody knew the general had a special trick up his sleeve for busting down the gates, so that wouldn't be any problem.

They overtook the cart just as it was about to cross the ditch. The sergeant went ahead, to make sure the planks were firmly seated, and shouted back that it was all as firm as a rock. Later he told anybody who'd listen that it was the carter's fault, for not driving straight. Also, the boards were slippery with mud, and he hadn't realised the load was so heavy. The offside back wheel slid off the boards and went over, cracking the axle, and the shifting of the cart's weight skewed it sideways. The boom twisted and snapped, and the cart turned over, rolling its cargo off the improvised road and into the deep, wet mud.

The general was furious. He came scrambling down from the gate as soon as he heard what had happened, screaming at the carter and the soldiers, threatening them with court martial, torment and eventual death, and plunged into the mud up to his knees, wading like some rare marshland bird towards the tarpaulin-wrapped bundle half sunk into the mud. He yelled for ropes and long poles, attached the ropes himself, got behind the lump with a lever to work it loose from the grip of the suction. The heavy cylinder came out without too much trouble, considering its weight, and likewise the oak barrel; but two of the stone shot sank without trace in the mud and had to be abandoned.

"It's all right," he panted at Ziani, "we can get by with three. In fact, we can get by with one. Don't worry," he added with a brilliant smile, "it's going to be fine. It'll take more than a bit of mud to stop me now."

"I believe you," Ziani said.

With the ropes and levers, they dragged the cylinder up the bank, ploughing furrows in the loose dirt with their feet. Glancing up, Ziani saw movement behind the gatehouse rampart; he shouted for pavises, a shield trolley, archers to cover them and keep the enemy's heads down. But nothing happened, and he saw that Daurenja was gently shaking his head. "Don't worry," he was saying, "it'll be just fine, we don't need them. We'll be under the lee of the wall soon, where they can't reach us." He doesn't want witnesses, Ziani realised; he wants to keep the secret to himself, right up to the very last moment; and he knew intuitively that the soldiers hauling so energetically on the ropes wouldn't be living much longer. They'd be right at the front in the next action, or there'd be some horrible accident. Not for him, though. Daurenja would never do anything to harm him, because he trusted him implicitly.

(The good leader, he thought; he's got all the qualities of the good duke, everything Orsea tried so hard to copy and failed. Certainly, he couldn't think of anybody else who'd be able to hold the alliance together, or who'd have got this far . . .)

A few arrows pitched around him, but they were harmless, out of shot, and he ignored them. The only effect they had was to encourage the men to pull harder. They were a good three yards under the overhang of the wall by now. A man would have to lean right out over the parapet to see them, and then he'd be too cramped up to draw a bow. But they were still far enough away from the foot of the wall to be safe from bricks and rubble dropped on them. In which case . . .

"Here," Daurenja said, his voice low and choking. "This'll do. Right, let's get the wraps off and set it up."

Four men were struggling with the barrel; another four were laboriously rolling a round of shot up the slope, bracing their backs and thighs against it to stop it from slipping and rolling back down. Daurenja was fumbling with the knots of the cords that bound the tarpaulin round the cylinder. He scrabbled, tore a fingernail, swore, frowned and pulled a jack knife from his pocket. It took him quite some time to open out the blade. Ziani had never seen him be clumsy before. In a way, it was almost touching.

In the end, he cut the cords and slit the tarpaulin, like a hunter paunching the game. Inside the cut cloth lay the black tube, a horrible fruit inside its split shell. Daurenja reached in and touched it for a moment, laying his palm flat on it, the way Ziani had seen ostlers calm fractious horses. Then he turned his head and shouted to the men to go back to the cart; they'd find wooden blocks and timber sections, some wedges, a hammer and something that looked like a glue-boiler's iron pot.

"It's in two sections," Daurenja was telling him. "There's the tube proper, and a sort of reservoir that slides into the back end, to hold the charge of blasting dust. The two together sit in a wooden cradle, and the reservoir's held tight in the tube by a wedge bearing against the back member of the frame. It's not wonderful, but I didn't want to risk trying to close the tube at one end, welding in a bung or anything like that. The reservoir's just a pot, turned out of solid, so it'll be plenty strong enough. Of course, it's got to be practically an interference fit, where the reservoir joins the tube . . ."

Crude, Ziani thought. You'd do better with a screw thread or a couple of locking lugs. He's perfectly capable of thinking of that, but he's in too much of a hurry. Not that it mattered. The wedge arrangement would be good enough for one firing, and that was all it'd take.

While the men were fitting the timbers together (Daurenja had cut mortices in them beforehand, a beautiful job; all the men had to do was slot them into each other and tap in a few dowels), Ziani straightened his back and looked thoughtfully at the gate. The proper nomenclature was a Type One; a six-inch thickness of quarter-inch plies, the lie of the grain pointing alternately up and down, side to side. No battering ram yet made would be capable of splintering that. And of course it'd be wedged shut from the other side, and there'd be bars across it, and reinforcing struts jammed into the ground, and behind that a portcullis, which they'd already have lowered. They'd tested a Type One in the factory once by shooting at it with scorpions and onagers at point-blank range, but the plies had flexed and bounced back the shot. No weapon known to the Republic had been able to smash up a Type One. It was Daurenja's tube, then, or nothing.

They were lifting it on a stretcher of spars and lowering it gingerly into the assembled frame – as simple as a box without a top or a bottom, with a semicircle cut out of the front for the tube to rest in. Daurenja was talking to it.

Not, Ziani insisted to himself, that it mattered. It'd be over soon, and before long he'd be inside the City. He focused on that. Nothing else was important, after all.

One of the men was prising the lid off the barrel. Daurenja left the tube and elbowed him gently out of the way. In one hand he held the iron bowl that fitted into the end of the tube, and in the other was a plain tin cup from a soldier's mess kit. He dipped the cup into the barrel and brought it up again full of a shiny black compound that looked like charcoal dust. He ladled seven cupfuls into the bowl, then nodded to the man to put the lid back on the barrel.

"Well," he said, in a shaky voice, "here goes nothing."

He knelt to fit the bowl into the tube; then he held it in place with the fingertips of his left hand while he scrabbled for the hammer and the wedge with his right. Five smart taps, precise as a woodpecker, and then he laid the hammer down and stood up. Three men heaved a round of shot up to the mouth of the tube and rolled it in, snatching their hands away to keep their fingers from getting trapped. With a nod of his head, Daurenja gestured them out of the way. He was kneeling again, his head directly over the back end of the tube. He wasn't sighting down it, the way the Mezentine engineers peered along the groove of a springal. Instead, he was looking at the gate as though he was the weapon, training and aiming himself at it. Appropriate, Ziani couldn't help thinking. At some time or other, everybody turns himself into a weapon for some purpose or other.

Someone was messing about with a tinderbox, frantically cranking the handle and puffing air through the hole in the side. Without looking round, Daurenja extended his arm, his hand palm up to receive the box. His eyes still fixed on the gate, he stuffed the end of a short piece of cord into the hole and blew gently. He's completely forgotten about us, Ziani thought. This is the crucial moment of his life, and there simply isn't room for anybody else.

As he took the cord out of the box, Ziani could see the little orange tip. It glowed bright as Daurenja breathed on it, his breath as soft and urgent as a kiss. He saw Daurenja's lips begin to move (it could have been prayers or endearments, or a mixture of the two) as he guided the bright orange spot towards the hole drilled in the top of the pot. Quickly, Ziani stepped back; something obstructed his heel, and he turned round and saw a gabion, lying on its side. He ducked down behind it, but couldn't resist peering round it.

"Get back, all of you," Daurenja muttered (and it wasn't concern for their safety; he just wanted to be alone with the weapon when the moment came). "Any moment now, there's going to be a very loud noise, but that'll be just fine." He sighed on the burning cord, and it glowed back at him: true love. "It's going to be wonderful, just you wait and see."

Tender as a bridegroom, he touched the cord to the hole in the pot; and Ziani, his eyes open, could see only the cold spot in the heart of the welding fire, plain as a gate in a wall, a gate about to open. I warned him, he told himself, but he wouldn't listen.

For a fraction of a second, Ziani was sure he saw the tube swell, like a puffed-out cheek. Then it tore open, from the point where he remembered seeing the cold spot up to the muzzle. The noise and the heat slammed him back like a punch, and he felt something clip the side of his head. The sound rolled, echoed back off the city wall, washed over him and dissipated, leaving his head buzzing. He felt the warm lick of blood trickling down his cheek, and his burnt skin started to pulse.

He scrambled to his knees. The gabion he'd been hiding behind had turned into a mess of smashed osiers; there was a chunk of twisted steel buried in the dirt where it had been. He thought: it must have worked, nothing could've been so close to that and survived. He stood up, then stumbled and sat down in the loose earth.

Daurenja was lying on his back, about ten feet from where he'd been standing. His chest and half his stomach had been sliced away, and a tangle of wet tubes and pipes had been slopped out into the dirt. There was a steel splinter lodged in his cheekbone; the force of its entry had popped out his left eye. One arm had been torn off and was nowhere to be seen; the other was shredded. He was still breathing.

Ziani crawled closer. "Daurenja?" he said.

A tiny movement, as he tried to turn his head, and a horrible bubbling noise.

"I just wanted to thank you," Ziani said. "When I was at a loss for an escapement, I found you, you and your stupid bloody invention." He grinned, and the one eye blinked. "It didn't work," he said. "Well, I guess you know that. It was the cold spot. I warned you, but you didn't want to know. The gate's still there, and just look at you. Can you hear me? I want you to hear what I'm saying. I want you to know you failed. I succeeded, and you . . ."

Dust, drifting down from the air, settled on the surface of Daurenja's eye, but the lid didn't twitch. Drawing a deep breath, Ziani crawled a little closer, sucked and spat on the shattered face. No movement. He breathed out slowly. I'll miss him, he thought.

There wasn't much left of the weapon: one large fragment of the tube, concave, like an empty walnut shell, and a few splinters of the wooden frame. The rest of the tube and the powder pot had gone. Well, Ziani thought, so much for love. The trouble is, there's always a cold spot, and when it gives way, something like this is bound to happen.

He brushed blood out of his eye with the side of his hand. Blood would have to do instead of tears; he couldn't find any of those for Daurenja, the scholar, the inventor, the arch-abominator, the best engineer he'd ever known. Better than me, he added, surprised at the conclusion, but love was his undoing.

"Is he . . . ?" Someone behind him, talking in a very small, quiet voice.

"Yes," Ziani replied without looking round. "His gadget didn't work after all. Give me a hand up," he added, and he felt himself lifted to his feet. "Let's get away from here, before the Mezentines start shooting at us."

The other survivors of the carrying party joined them as they scrambled down the bank to the ditch. As they crossed it, a scorpion bolt missed them by no great margin. After that, they made good time to the cover of the trench.

The man who'd helped him to his feet confirmed his account of the death of the general and the failure of his device. The war council listened in dead silence, and Ziani nodded to him to leave.

"Which means," he said, his voice clear and steady (because the worst was over now, and the hardest part successfully concluded), "we're in a pretty bad way. In fact," he added, looking round the ring of blank, unhappy faces, "it's hard to see how it could be worse. Sure, we got past the ditch and took the embankment, and we killed a lot of men. But the walls and the gates are still there, our secret weapon didn't work, we can't build another one even if we wanted to, and the general's dead. Talking of which," he added forcefully (and nobody looked interested in interrupting him), "someone's got to take his place. I don't see Duke Valens here. Didn't anybody tell him about the meeting?"

One of the Aram Chantat cleared his throat; a small, dry man. "The duke was told about what happened," he said, "but he was not disposed to attend. We take this to mean that he is no longer concerned with the conduct of the war, which is fortuitous. We have no confidence in him."

Ziani nodded. "In that case," he said, "who do you want to . . . ?"

The dry man looked at him; and even though he'd prevailed and nothing could stop him now, the intensity of the stare made him uncomfortable. "We feel there is only one possible choice," he said. "You are the senior engineer, and you alone have the expertise. We are in your hands."

Yes, Ziani thought; but he said, "That's true as far as the technical side goes, but surely one of you . . ."

The dry man shook his head. "We have already decided," he said. "Short of an outright refusal, you have no choice."

He'd never lost the feeling of wonder that came from the soft, firm click of a component fitting perfectly into place: the snick of a ratchet, of a locking bolt feeling its way exactly into its appointed place. A machine works because each part of the mechanism goes where it's designed to go, entirely constrained in its movement by the other pieces. The precise fit is because there's nowhere else it can go; because it has no choice. "I suppose you're right," Ziani mumbled. "And I suppose I'd better accept." He paused for a moment, trying to look as though the whole weight of the world had come to settle on his shoulders, though of course the reverse was true. "But if you want me to do this, you're going to have to trust me. Really trust me, I mean. Otherwise, you'll all have to go and be extremely polite to Duke Valens, because I won't be able to help you."

The dry man was still looking at him, but the stare no longer bothered him. There were no more choices for anyone. "Of course," the dry man said. "You have our unequivocal support in everything, General Vaatzes."

He allowed himself a grin. "Not that word, please," he said. "Just engineer, if you've got to call me something, and on the whole I'd rather you didn't." He settled himself in his chair, like a man who had just come home. "Now, the first thing I need to do is arrange a parley with Chairman Psellus."

He came back from the meeting two hours later, and reconvened the war council. "They won't surrender," he said. "I didn't really imagine that they would, but it was worth trying."

An Aram Chantat said: "But we don't want their surrender. We want to sack the City and burn it to the ground."

Ziani grinned. "That's what I told them," he said. "I guess that's why they weren't keen. I told them that if they opened the gates, we'd march them to the edge of the desert. They could go to where you've just come from, and take their chances with your cousins whose names I can never remember. No skin off your noses, since you're going to be settling here permanently. But Psellus didn't like the idea. He said that if they were all going to die, they might as well save themselves the long walk. That's my people for you. We never did like walking much."

A silence, rather awkward. "And now we continue with the assault," someone said.

"Yes." Ziani closed his eyes for a moment. "Yes, we continue with the assault. Which means," he went on, sitting up a little straighter, and opening the file of papers he'd brought with him, "an artillery barrage to neutralise the batteries on the wall, and a new advance trench. This is what I'd been hoping to avoid, gentlemen, but we don't seem to have an alternative, and of course we're dangerously short of time. We have to undermine the main gate, which means digging a sap under it. That involves cutting a chamber at least three hundred yards long through the bedrock, which means our Vadani miners are going to be working very hard indeed for the cause. You can more or less guarantee that the Mezentines will try and countermine us, so we can expect to have to fight underground.

If we had plenty of time, I'd say leave the work to the specialists, the Vadani, but my best guess would be three or four months before we got under the gate. With strict rationing, we can supply ourselves for three weeks; after that, we need to get at the Mezentine food reserves, or we starve. So that means we have to approach the job the other way: everybody in the army, apart from the artillery crews and the Vadani specialists – I want to save them for the final break-through – is going to have to get a spade or a pick and start digging." He looked up at the ring of faces around him. "I need to know right now if that's acceptable. If not, I can't help you."

"We will do what you tell us to do," an Aram Chantat said. Presumably he had the authority. "Tell us your requirements and we'll see to it."

Ziani nodded, and picked up a sheet of paper. "These are just rough estimates," he said. "I propose five shifts – that's one fifth of the available manpower, working a four-hour shift, with fifteen-minute changeovers. Here" – he stabbed at a map with his finger –" is where we start digging. You'll see it's out in the open, well within range of the walls, but we haven't got time to start further back, we'll have to rely on the artillery to cover us. That means I want all the Eremians and Vadani back at the artillery park; no disrespect, but the Aram Chantat don't make good bombardiers; as well as working the machines, they'll be gathering and shifting rock and rubble for ammunition, fixing broken machines, building new ones to replace the ones we can't salvage. It's essential that we keep the bombardment going, day and night; it's not just a question of keeping their heads down, we need to make them believe we're trying to bash a hole in the wall, so they'll expect an assault with ladders and towers and divide their resources." He paused for breath, and for effect. "Is all that acceptable?" he asked briskly. "If it's not, you should say so now. We simply don't have time to change our minds once we've started; we decide what we're going to do here and now, and then we stick to it. Is that agreed?"

When the meeting ended, Ziani left the Aram Chantat to organise their own people into shifts, and went to brief the artillery. He sent the Vadani out to gather stones and rubble, and assigned the Eremians to patching up the machines. Then he called in the battery captains. They told him how many machines were still working, how many could be fixed, how many trained crew were available, how much finished ammunition they still had. He was particularly interested in the onagers and the scorpions, and when they pointed out that there were more usable machines than trained men to work them, he told them to take men off the long-range weapons, the trebuchets and mangonels, to ensure that all the short-range engines were fully manned. Then he dismissed his staff and went to talk to Duke Valens; just a courtesy call, he said, to put him in the picture and make sure he didn't intend to interfere with the arrangements.

Observers he'd sent forward directly after the war council closed came back with the news that the Mezentine batteries were now fully manned; they were winching huge quantities of ammunition up to the wall with giant cranes, as well as brand-new machines, presumably straight off the production lines. The estimates they gave him suggested that the Mezentines had the edge in numbers of engines, though their long-range capacity was significantly less: two thirds of their machines were scorpions, while most of their trebuchets had been smashed up in earlier engagements and didn't appear to have been replaced. Ziani received the news with a distracted nod of the head, and went back to examining ammunition inventories.

Two hours after the war council, Aram Chantat staff officers reported that the first shift was ready, with the other four shifts standing by. As ordered, every man had a spade, a pick or a shovel instead of his usual equipment, they'd taken off their armour and they were ready to go.

"All right," Ziani said. "Get them moving. You know where to go."

An officer frowned at him. "With respect," he said, "shouldn't you start the bombardment first? Otherwise—"

"We start shooting when they start," Ziani snapped back. "Not before."

He watched as the first shift marched out into the empty plain: seventy-five thousand men, according to the roster. Five shifts of seventy-five thousand men, shifting five square feet of dirt each; you could change a country out of all recognition in a week. He shook his head. So much effort, so great an effect, all to accomplish such a simple objective. But it was too late to change anything now. The escapement was running, and very soon it'd all be over. He beckoned to one of his aides (didn't know the man's name; didn't care).

"Take this letter to Duke Valens," he said.

*

Valens read the letter, screwed it up into a ball and threw it on to the little charcoal brazier. "I'm just going out for a while," he said.

She looked at him. "Where are you going?" she asked.

"It's all right," he said. He was looking round for something. "You haven't seen that hanger, have you?"

"I don't know," she replied. "What's a hanger?"

"Shortish sword, with a sort of curved bit on the hilt. I put it down somewhere, but . . ."

"What do you need a sword for?"

He shrugged. "Not properly dressed without one," he replied. "Ah, here it is. It's lucky," he added, smiling bleakly. "At least, that's the theory. Hasn't actually brought me much luck so far, but there's still time."

She caught her breath. "Is something going on?" she said. "I thought you said you were out of it now."

"I am," he replied, not looking at her. "That bastard Vaatzes is in charge now, and welcome."

"What did he want to talk to you about?"

"Oh, nothing much." He was having trouble with the buckle of his sword-belt; not like him at all. Usually, all his movements were so precise.

"Was it about the war?" she asked.

"Everything's about the war," he said; and she thought, he doesn't really mean that.

The tent-flap opened, and she saw Miel Ducas standing in the light. "Are you ready?" he asked. He didn't seem to have noticed she was there.

"As I'll ever be," Valens replied. "All set?"

"Yes."

Valens took a step forward, then turned back to face her. "I won't be long," he said. "And then there'll be some things we'll need to talk about."

She shrugged. "I'll be here," she replied. "Sewing something, probably," she added.

He nodded, no expression at all on his face. Then he left and the flap dropped back, shuttering out the daylight.

Miel had brought a horse for him, and held his stirrup as he mounted. "Are you all right?" he asked.

"Of course," he answered irritably. "I'm not a cripple or anything."

"You heard about Daurenja."

"Yes." Valens picked up the reins. "You know," he said, "I've been in charge of everything around me practically all my life. It's nice to have someone else running things for a change."

Miel shrugged. "You say that now," he said.

Valens laughed. "Hardly matters what I say," he said. "And what about you? Are you going to use the title? Only, Duke Ducas is a bit of a mouthful."

"People can call me what they like," Miel replied.

They rode together in silence for a while; then Miel said, "Are you really going to accept this?"

"Yes," Valens said. "For now, anyway. Things may change later, of course. But right now, it's the only realistic course open to me."

Miel nodded; but he said, "I really don't want to do this."

"It's no big deal," Valens replied.

Then they discussed technical matters: positions, tactics, co-ordination of movements, concealment of intentions and the element of surprise. As they rode over the top of the ridge and looked down, Valens reined in his horse and sat still for a moment.

"There aren't enough of us," he said.

"No," Miel agreed. "But that's all there is, so it'll have to do."

But he hadn't meant it; because the sight of the Vadani cavalry, twenty thousand men-at-arms, standing in formation with lances at rest, was a glorious illusion, and he wanted to enjoy it for as long as he could. It made him think of his father, who believed in all this sort of thing, just as he believed in the hunt, and the concept of the good duke and the contract between ruler and people. Besides, he told himself, as they rode down to take their places at the head of the formation, Ziani Vaatzes thinks there's enough of us, and he knows best.

"He'll send a rider," Miel was saying. "Till then, we just stay here still and quiet."

There was a mild stir, a gentle buzz, as the artillerymen realised that Chairman Psellus had come up on to the wall. It hadn't escaped anybody's notice that he hadn't been there when the enemy blew up the embankment and slaughtered all those people. It was curious: nobody really believed he'd gone away because he was afraid, or anything like that. He'd gone, they knew, because he'd been called away to deal with something more important; so if he was here now, it meant that whatever happened next mattered . . .

"We think it's a work party," someone was telling him. "We sent a few scouts down; apparently they're not armed, they've got digging tools. We put the number at somewhere between eighty and a hundred—"

"Yes, thank you," Psellus said mildly. "I believe I know what's happening." Someone brought up a chair, and he sat down. "Their artillery."

"A lot of activity," whoever it was replied. "All the signs are, they're getting ready to launch a massive bombardment, though oddly enough they've taken men off the trebuchets and put them on the—"

"Indeed." Psellus wiped his nose, which was running. "Our artillery is ready, I take it?"

"As ordered," the man replied briskly; a slight, anxious hesitation, then: "I take it you do know we've stood down the long-range engines and—"

"Yes, thank you." He was looking straight ahead, at the huge square shape moving toward the city, and beyond it, to the enemy artillery. "You've done very well. Please make sure we're ready to start shooting as soon as I give the order. Not before, under any circumstances. Is that quite clear?"

Whoever it was nodded. "Of course," he said. Another pause, and then, "But you haven't given us the targets yet," he said, tactfully. "You did say to stand by and you'd give the targets when you were ready, but . . ."

Psellus sighed, like a man being chivvied into a task he'd have preferred to avoid. "Not quite yet," he said. "Let's all just stay still and quiet for now."

Still and quiet, as though the world was holding its breath; until, some time later, whoever it was said, "Chairman, they're practically within scorpion range now, surely we should be *doing* something . . ."

Psellus sighed again. "You're quite right," he said. "Tell the captains to target the main body of the enemy – is that the right expression? I mean that great big square of them coming towards us."

Whoever it was hesitated just for a split second. "With respect, shouldn't we take out their artillery first? Otherwise—"

"Please," Psellus said, very quietly. "Do as I say."

Orders were passed down; it amused him, the way one officer passed them on to another, who went and told someone else, who went and told someone else . . . The chain of command, presumably, and it was admirably military. But absurd, nevertheless. "All ready, Chairman," the nonentity was saying. "At your command."

"Thank you," he said firmly. "Please wait."

They all think I'm mad, he thought. They're trying to make up their minds to push me out of the way and do what needs to be done; but they won't do it. Which is just as well. Even so, we're a pathetic excuse for a nation . . .

Then a flash of light caught his eye, and he looked at the top of the ridge, where he'd been told to look when the moment came. "Tell me," he said urgently. "My eyesight's so poor these days. Is there a large body of horsemen on top of the ridge?"

Slight pause. "Yes," whoever it was said. "But . . ."

Deep breath. "In that case," Psellus said mildly, "kindly open fire."

Miel Ducas galloped down the slope, terrified in case his horse should stumble and throw him, and keep him from his duty. But the Ducas is, of course, a supremely accomplished horseman, and his mount is the finest money can buy.

Ten yards short of the artillery line, he reined in and looked round for someone to talk to. An artillery captain (an Eremian, thank God) turned round and stared at him.

"Hey, you," Miel shouted at him. "Do you know who I am?"

The captain nodded.

"Good. New orders. You need to bring down your elevation fourteen minutes, all of you."

The captain was doing mental arithmetic. "That can't be right," he said. "If we do that, we'll be shooting straight at—"

"Fourteen minutes," the Ducas repeated. "*Now.*"

The parts of a machine fulfil their various functions because they have no choice. A lever pivots a sear, which slips out of the notch cut in the underside of a roller. Unsupported, the roller gives way, releasing the slider, which shoots forward under the pressure of two springs along a close-sided keyway, driving the arrow shaft along its channel and away through the air. The arrow has no choice but to fly until it hits the target. Or a lever pivots a sear, which slips out of its notch in the roller, which releases the swinging arm, which rushes through ninety degrees, pivoting around its axis pin, until it slams into the crossbar, launching a net full of bricks, broken masonry, flints and potsherds into the air. Then the hook goes on the slider or the arm and the winch begins to turn. The tongue dances over the teeth of the ratchet as each turn drags back the slider or the arm against the furious resistance of the springs, until the sear drops into the notch on the underside of the roller, and a new arrow or a new consignment of lethal junk lands in the slot, and the lever drops, and the sear falls out. Between the spanning of the spring and the release there is only the sear, the trigger, the escapement, and once it lets go, the force is committed beyond recall.

Then the scorpion bolts lift, like a flock of rooks disturbed while feeding; they climb into the air on a lifting curve that reaches a high point, hesitates for a tiny moment, then (as though a sear has been tripped) falls in a decaying trajectory, accelerating as it slants down out of the sky. Or the hundredweight of jumbled, ballistically inefficient rubbish soars in a dissipating pattern, hangs, decays and drops, each lump spinning and twisting in the air like a falling man treading emptiness, powered by its own height and the furious pull of the ground, until it pitches . . .

Miel Ducas had seen it all before, of course. Once upon a time, he'd watched the Mezentine artillery beat flat the Eremian army, the way the wind lays a field of corn. Once you've seen one wipeout, there's a case for saying you've seen them all. So it didn't bother him that he couldn't see what happened after the cloud of bolts lifted up into the sky. He could picture it in his mind easily enough.

Instead, he watched the Vadani cavalry pouring down over the ridge, parting into two wings as it reached the plain and surging up to surround the remaining four fifths of the Aram Chantat as they waited still and quiet for their shifts to begin. Of course, they couldn't see what was happening on the other side of the bank that shielded the artillery from the city batteries. They wouldn't have the faintest idea, until the scorpions swung round on their traverses to point straight at them.

Even so, he thought, it'd probably be a good idea to get out of the way. He walked his horse through the gap between the head-high stacks of scorpion bolts, dismounted, handed the reins to someone or other and scrambled up on to the wall, at a place where a Mezentine shot had punched a hole. What he saw was quite familiar.

"One more shot," he called out, "then a new setting."

This time, nobody questioned the order.

The war council was still sitting, of course. There had been issues they wanted to discuss without General Vaatzes there. But the general came in anyway, and he had a platoon of Eremian soldiers with him.

"Your attention, please," he said.

No choice at all, as he explained to them. A fifth of their men were already dead, shot or squashed by the combined fire of the Eremians and the Mezentines. The remainder were unarmed, packed close together, surrounded on three sides by the Vadani cavalry and faced on the fourth side by the allied scorpion batteries. As Ziani pointed out, if they chose to fight, there was a chance they might prevail by sheer force of numbers, eventually, but their losses would be something of the order of seventy per cent; and then they'd still have the Mezentines to contend with.

"I arranged it with Duke Valens and Chairman Psellus," he went on. He was almost too tired to speak, but the impetus of the final stage swept him along. "We all agreed that, compared with the threat you represent, our differences are relatively trivial; the sort of things we can always sort out later on, we decided, once we've got rid of you."

They were staring at him, but he really couldn't care less about that. His mind was a long way away, preoccupied with far more important issues.

"At any rate," he went on, "we've solved the supply problem – which," he added with a grin, "I created when I told Daurenja how to blow up the embankment. It was my gesture of good faith to Chairman Psellus; by using up a third of our flour reserve, I guaranteed to him that the City couldn't be taken by conventional siege and assault, because there simply wouldn't be time before our supplies ran out. He had to take my word for it that General Daurenja's secret weapon wouldn't work, but that was a foregone conclusion. I was there when it was made, and I knew it would fail. Now, of course, the supply problem's been solved, simply by virtue of the fact that there's eighty thousand less of you and twenty thousand fewer Mezentines. It was a brutal solution, but rather less so than the alternative, which was to slaughter all the Mezentines. And if you discounted that, there really wasn't any choice."

He paused for breath. He'd been talking quickly, to get it over with so he could move on. He slowed down a little as he continued:

"My deal with Psellus is as follows. We – I mean the Vadani and the Eremians – will disarm you and escort you over the mountains to the edge of the desert. Once you've crossed back to where you came from, Mezentine engineers will destroy the string of oases, so no one will ever be able to bring an army across there again." He shrugged. "I have no idea how you go about wrecking a large pool of water, but my people have the expertise, not to mention the incentive. Then, apart from the inevitable small raiding parties every so often, we'll never see or hear from you again, which is how it should be. The Mezentines will break down the City walls and undertake never to raise a standing army; and there'll be a trade agreement, we haven't worked out any details yet, but it'll mean the Mezentines will sell their goods for a fair price, and pay a substantial war indemnity; there'll also be a lot of changes in the way the Republic's run, but that's an internal matter, nothing to do with you. In return, the Vadani and the Eremians will be responsible for the City's defence." He frowned. "It's not a very good deal for any of us, and I expect it'll break down sooner or later and we'll all be back at each other's throats again before very long, but at least we'll be rid of you. It took this war to make us all realise that you're the one problem none of us can accommodate. You're a different kind of threat; you change everything."

One of the Aram Chantat said: "You realised it, though. Before the wedding, even. That's why you made it happen."

Ziani gave him a blank stare. "I'm not important," he said. "What possible relevance could one man's concerns have to the fate of nations? What I've done is end the war with the minimum of bloodshed and damage, and given the people of three countries some kind of chance of living in peace. Surely that's a leader's duty, and if it isn't, it should be."

"We misjudged you," said another. "We assumed you wanted revenge."

"I'm not a savage," Ziani replied calmly. "Only savages think like that."

He was about to dismiss them, but one of the Aram Chantat caught his eye and said, "Will you go back to your wife and daughter, and your work in the factory? Isn't that what you wanted?"

Ziani looked back at him, like someone looking into a mirror. "The meeting is closed," he said.

Chapter Eighteen

There was a man called Cuno Abazes; a Mezentine, about thirty-two years old, a bachelor in a city where nearly everybody over the age of twenty was married. He didn't belong to a Guild, having failed the trade test for the Carpenters'. Instead, he'd earned a sparse living as a porter, drover and general labourer, loading and unloading, holding horses and collecting nightsoil for the Fullers.'' The war had been remarkably kind to him: he'd joined the army on the first day of recruitment, realising it was his one and only chance of making good, and had done so well that within a matter of weeks he'd been made an officer, a captain of general infantry. He'd been assigned to guard duty on the embankment on the day of the assault, but a splinter of rock from an allied round shot had hit him on the side of the head as he went to report for the start of his shift, and when the embankment was blown up he was lying in bed in the hospital. His injuries proved to be superficial, and next morning he was passed fit for active service and told to report to the Guildhall for sentry duty. There he heard the news that the war was over.

"That's terrible," he blurted out. "What's going to happen to the army?"

"Being disbanded," they told him. "Express term of the peace treaty. You'll be able to go back to your old life, pick up where you left off. Isn't that good news?"

Cuno Abazes didn't reply to that. Instead, he asked, "So who won?" and they said, "You know, that's a very good question."

*

Later that day, Captain Abazes was on duty in the main hall when Chairman Psellus himself passed through, on his way to the small conference suite. Since hearing the bad news about the end of the war, Abazes had had time to calm down and think it over, and he'd reached the conclusion that even if they were doing away with the army as such, they were still going to need guards, sentries, security officers, and this was exactly the time when they'd be choosing who to keep and who to let go. Accordingly, as Psellus went by, he snapped to attention like the swinging arm of an onager slamming against the stop. Abazes had always been good at drill, and he put everything he'd got into it, with the result that the crack of his heels coming together made Psellus shy like a horse and stare at him for a moment. That disconcerted him; he'd assumed the commander-in-chief of the armed forces of the Republic would be a connoisseur of fine drill, but Psellus had reacted as if he'd stuck his tongue out at him and blown a raspberry.

"Very good, Captain," said the other man (shorter than the chairman, somewhere between thirty and forty-five, oddly dressed but otherwise completely unmemorable). "Carry on."

Instinctively, Abazes saluted, but neither the unmemorable man nor the chairman were watching. They were walking away from him, chatting in low, comfortable voices; old friends, he could tell. Well, he thought, obviously the other man had to be something to do with the military; at least, he sounded right, and he'd known what to say. Cuno Abazes muttered a silent prayer, and went back to doing his imitation of a statue, or one of those lifesize mechanical people that used to be in fashion, many years ago.

"You've got them saluting already," Ziani said. "I'm impressed."

Psellus shrugged. "Did he do it right? I don't know about these things."

"He wouldn't have gone down well with a Vadani drill sergeant," Ziani replied. "Slouching, gut sticking out, hand wobbling around like he was trying to swat flies. You'd never have made soldiers out of them, not if the war had dragged on for twenty years. It's not in our nature."

"I'm delighted to hear you say so," Psellus said. "War is neither a craft nor a trade, and I'm pleased we have an excuse not to meddle with it any more. By all means let's leave it to your precious Vadani. Let them get from it what pleasure they can."

Ziani laughed. "You still don't understand them," he said. "Not that there's any reason why you should. There's rather more to them than you think, but compared to us they're still just savages."

They walked on together in silence as far as the foot of the grand staircase; and Psellus thought: I've come here every day for as long as I can remember, but I've never seen it before, there's always been too many people in the way – my colleagues, my fellow clerks, hurtling up and down the stairs with files and ledgers. It's almost as though they were there to distract attention from the building itself; because we didn't build it, did we? The people who came before us did that, the people who made the padlock. And then he thought: I saved the Republic, but I don't want it any more; even looking at it makes me feel sick. And then he said: "You're really a patriot, aren't you, Ziani?"

Ziani nodded. "Always have been," he said.

"A true believer?"

"Always."

Psellus accepted the statement with a slight movement of head and shoulders. "You never intended to destroy us," he said.

"Of course not." Ziani wasn't looking at him. He was gazing at the staircase, the vaulted ceiling, the carved balustrades, the allegorical frescoes on the walls (Perfection illuminating the assembled crafts and trades; Perfection being a tall, big-bosomed woman in flowing red robes, and each craft and trade represented by a grey-haired man carrying the archetypal tool or instrument of his calling; but why, he couldn't help wondering, had they all been painted with white skins, like they were savages?). "Only a lunatic would burn down his own house; he'd have nothing to come home to."

"And that's really all it was," Psellus said, hesitating, as though he couldn't set foot on the first tread of the stair until he'd had an answer. "You just wanted to come home."

"Of course." Ziani traced the edge of a carved border with the tip of his finger; it was smooth, the sharp edge worn down by a million clerks brushing against it as they made way for each other on the stairs. "If I'd wanted to be rich and powerful, I'd have gone far away, the Old Country or somewhere like that; I'd have settled down and started a factory. Probably I'd have founded a new Mezentia, just like this one only better. That's what big men do, heroic types, idealists, rebels." He shook his head. "I just did what I had to, to put things right. No choice, really."

Psellus climbed the first step. "The death toll . . ."

"I can't help that," Ziani said briskly. "I can't be held responsible. Nor can you." He turned his face, and Psellus couldn't meet his eyes. "I don't know all the ins and outs of administrative procedure, but if you were chief clerk of Compliance, it was you who gave the order that started the war. Yes?"

"Yes."

"Not me," Ziani said. "Sure, I planned the whole thing. I worked out every step, while I was dying of thirst out on the plain, before Duke Orsea's people found me. By the time they picked me up, I'd planned as far as turning the scorpions on the Aram Chantat – I didn't know they were called that, of course, I just knew there were millions of savages out there beyond the desert, and they were the only force on earth that could bring down the Republic; so of course they were part of the plan from the beginning; like a mainspring, if you like. Orsea and Valens were the gear train – I was lucky there, I admit it. I knew that if I could persuade the Eremian duke to let me build a factory, the Republic would have to declare war. I wanted to bring in the Vadani, to keep the war going, and I knew I'd have to find some mechanism to get the Vadani to bring in the savages beyond the desert. That was quite easy, once I found out the Vadani duke was unmarried, and the stupid courtly-love triangle with Orsea, Valens and the duchess gave me that whole assembly practically complete, I just had to make a few connections. The chain of oases across the desert was a stroke of luck, but I was pretty well sure there had to be something like that once I heard about the raiding parties. If I hadn't had those strokes of luck, I'd have had to manufacture something myself to do the job; it'd have taken longer and needed a lot more effort, but I'd have got there in the end. The real luck was finding Daurenja."

"Oh." Psellus raised his eyebrows. "You surprise me. I'd have thought he was more of an unforeseen difficulty."

"He was, at times." Ziani smiled. "But I knew from quite early on that I'd make him the commander-in-chief of the Alliance. I assumed I'd have to find a way of disgracing him when the moment came, to get him out of the way when it was time for me to take command. But he blew himself up instead, which was far better."

"You knew his weapon wouldn't work?"

"Not at all." Ziani shook his head. "It works perfectly, if you make a tube without a flaw in the weld. But there was a cold spot – I actually did try and warn him about it, but only because I knew he wouldn't listen. And then I saw it all quite clearly, in my mind, exactly the way it eventually happened."

They paused on the landing, and Ziani looked down over the banister at the entrance hall below. "My father always wished he'd been a clerk," he said. "He thought it must be the grandest thing, to work with clean hands all day, in a place like this. Of course, he never saw the inside of this place, but he'd heard stories. He used to tell me about it; got it completely wrong, of course. He said there were gold statues, twice lifesize . . ."

"There were, once," Psellus said. "About a hundred years ago. But they moved them into the main chapterhouse one time when the roof cracked and the rain got in. They should have gone back after the repairs were completed, but nobody ever got around to it. Actually, I think the council rather liked having them all to themselves."

Ziani nodded. "Get them put back," he said. "Dad would've liked that."

"Very well."

Ziani said: "I'd appreciate that." And then: "I gather you're taking orders from me. I wasn't quite sure where we stood."

Psellus shrugged. "It's my impression that you still command the allied army. And the gates of the City are open, as you insisted. If you want the furniture moved about, I'm hardly going to argue."

Ziani smiled. "Very soon, though," he said, "the army's going to go away, escorting the savages to the border. Then what?"

Psellus walked on, and Ziani took a long stride to keep up with him. "The question doesn't arise," he said. "You don't want to give orders or rule the City. You just wanted to come home. And here you are."

"That's right," Ziani said. "But will you let me?"

"No," Psellus said gently. "After everything you've done, naturally you can't stay here. In due course you'll be declared a public enemy and sentenced to death – in your absence, I sincerely hope; but by then you'll be far away where we can't reach you. I think you mentioned the Old Country just now; I think that would be a very good idea. After what happened in the war, I don't suppose we'll be very popular over there for a great many years. Your idea of starting a factory sounds eminently sensible. You do seem to have a flair for it. And perhaps," he added, with a faint smile, "you'll find another Daurenja to help you. I don't really believe you'll ever be complete without someone like that at your side."

Ziani was silent for a moment. "What exactly do you think of me?" he said.

"Now there's a question." Psellus stopped, frowned, thought for a long time. "I believe you were the victim of the most atrocious cruelty," he said, "from the person you loved most in all the world. I believe the City you love treated you shamefully, that you suffered a monstrous injustice, and that the system that so abused you is worthless, being founded on a lie."

Ziani shook his head, but said, "Go on."

"When I was investigating your case," Psellus continued, "I asked myself from time to time, what would I have done in your position? And the answer, of which I am ashamed, was that I'd have submitted to my fate, furiously angry but far too weak to resist. But you resisted; and since then I've watched you with a sort of horrified fascination, because what you've done has been evil – there's a word whose meaning I don't know any more – and it's what I'd have done if I'd had the strength."

"Would you?" Ziani grinned. "I don't think so."

"Curiously, I do. You gave back evil for evil; well, perhaps. Your callous indifference to the deaths of thousands; that must be evil, surely. Or perhaps you simply used the fundamental evil inside all of us to achieve something that nobody could reasonably object to: the setting right of an injustice, the overthrow of a bad system of government, the breaking of a lie." He sighed, as though he was disappointed with himself. "I can't find it in myself to blame you for anything you've done to the Republic," he said. "I imagine the Eremians and the Vadani would see things differently; but they've been fighting each other for generations, and the peace between them was founded on that poor, weak man Duke Orsea. I don't imagine it'd have lasted very long after Duke Valens' death, or even until then. And then they'd have brought themselves to more or less the state they're in now, or worse. As for the savages, they came here to take the entire country for themselves; they'd have wiped us out, and presumably the Vadani and the Eremians as well, in due course. No," he went on, his voice firmer, "you didn't make the evil, you only used it, and your motives and objectives were understandable, good even; which leads me to the unpleasant conclusion that there is no such thing as good or evil, or else that they're mixed together so completely that you can't have one without the other – like an alloy, I suppose you could say, like bronze is copper and tin, but in order to extract the tin you have to destroy the bronze. I think that what you've done is so horrible that I can't really get my mind around the true scope of it, and it'd have been far better for the world if you'd never been born. But I can't *blame* you for it."

Ziani shrugged. "Most of that's too deep for me," he said. "And I'm not proud of what I did. But the Republic took my life away and I had to get it back; I did it as little harm as I could to get what I needed; and as for the others, the Eremians and the rest of them, they're only savages anyway; like you said, they'd have slaughtered each other sooner or later, so no harm done."

For some reason, Psellus laughed. "You know," he said, "the way you put it makes my gorge rise, but it's not very different from what I just said. I suppose that proves my point. No, the difference is basically the difference between you and Daurenja."

"Daurenja? What's he got to do with it?"

"Only that he was an evil man who kept trying to do good things, and you were a good man doing evil. As I understand it, Duke Orsea spent his life trying to do the right thing, and by any objective criteria he caused just as much harm as you did. And Duke Valens; I see him as a man made up equally of good and evil who chose the good side believing that you can part copper and tin and still have bronze; and so he did more damage than anybody, in the end. And as for myself . . . Well," he said, "I can't have you arrested and put to death as long as your army's camped outside the City, which spares me from forcing myself to acknowledge that I wouldn't want to do it if I could. There are times when it's a great relief not to be able to do the right thing, or your duty, or whatever you want to call it."

Ziani was silent for a while. Then he said: "That was a good speech, for something you just made up on the spur of the moment."

Psellus smiled. "I used to read a lot of books," he said, "on days when work was quiet and there wasn't a lot to do. Dizanes on forensic and political oratory. Six fat volumes, I found them wedged under the legs of a wobbly table in the Coopers' library." He stopped; they were standing outside a door. "You think that just because I made it into a speech, I can't really mean it."

"If it was what you really thought, you wouldn't have needed to dress it up."

They were standing outside a door.

"What I think doesn't matter," Psellus said abruptly. "I'm not important. We're here."

Ziani nodded; then he said: "I can't stay here, then?"

"No."

"That's a pity, considering what I've been through to get back here."

"Yes," Psellus said. "But if you really want to stay, you'll have to kill us all. I believe you'd be capable of it, but there'd be no point; it wouldn't be your home any more. And besides, it's not what you really want, is it?"

"I want it to be how it was," Ziani replied angrily. "What the hell is so difficult about that?"

"Accept the compromise," Psellus said gently. "You had to come this far to get it; you could never have trusted any deal we made with you, especially while Boioannes was still in power. Take what you came for and go, while you still can."

Ziani breathed out; it was as though he'd been holding that breath for a very long time. "No choice, then," he said.

"No."

"Oh well, then," Ziani said, and he put his hand to the latch.

She said: "So what are you going to do now?"

Valens leaned back in his chair, as though he was melting into it. "I'd like to go home," he said, "to Civitas Vadanis. I'd like to look after my people, try to be a good duke. I'd like to hunt twice a week in the season, business and weather permitting. I'd like to be a good father to our child. I'd like to spend as much time as I can with my wife, though I don't suppose it'll ever be enough." He closed his eyes. "Is that really so unrealistic?"

She looked at him. The wound was healing fast, in spite of what Daurenja had done, though there'd always be the second scar; and the third, on the inside. "Do you love me?" she asked.

"Yes," he replied. "As much as I always have, ever since I first saw you. I've never stopped loving you, and I've never loved anyone else." He opened his eyes and looked at her. "Is that enough?"

"It's all anyone could ask," she replied.

He nodded. "When did I lose you?" he asked.

She hesitated, then said, "When you let that man beat you."

"Oh." He thought about that for a moment, then said: "Was that all? You can't love a man unless he always wins?"

But she shook her head. "It's not that," she said. "I loved Orsea, and he never won anything."

"I see." Valens was massaging the swollen place under the scar. It had become a habit; he probably didn't know he was doing it. "So you can't love *me* unless I always win, is that it?"

She sighed. "It's a very stupid reason," she said.

"I don't know," he replied. "I don't think there's good or bad reasons for loving someone, or stopping loving them. But it's a little bit hard to understand."

She stood up, turned her back on him. "I think it's because . . ." She didn't speak for a while. "I think it's because my life kept going wrong, and each time you came and rescued me. From Civitas Eremiae; and before that, when I was stuck in that awful excuse for a life with Orsea, and your letters gave it some kind of meaning." She kept her voice level; it took some doing. "I loved the man who wrote the letters. I loved the man who rode into the battle, just for me, even though it meant the end of everything he cared about. I loved the man who fought the Mezentines to save his people. The thing is, though," she added, "I think that man's only one part of you, and I think Daurenja killed him. The man who's left is the awkward boy who kept staring at me when I was sixteen, and I never really loved him. Not like I loved Orsea."

Valens nodded. "And if I'd won the duel and killed Daurenja? Then it'd all have been all right."

"I did try and stop you, remember."

He grinned. "I thought it was because you were afraid he'd kill me."

"That's right." She couldn't help letting just a little bit of the bitterness through. "One way or another, I thought he'd kill you, and I was right. If you'd listened to me, if you'd put me first instead of doing the right bloody thing, there'd have been no fight and you'd still be . . ." She shook her head. "You can't expect me to explain something I don't understand myself."

"Oh, I understand," he replied gently. "The man you thought you loved never really existed. I wrote him, like a character in a book; I made him up when I wrote you those letters. It was so hard, it took me a whole day to write one. I guess I always knew you'd never love the man I really am. He'd never have ridden to Civitas Eremiae, and screwed up everything for his people, just to save one woman. I had to invent him, too; just like I invented my father's perfect son, who never really existed. There was a real Valens Valentinianus once; he was a stroppy boy who hated hunting and fencing and hated his father, and loved a girl he saw once. When my father died he had to go, because there was a country to be governed; and I suppose I must've thought, if I can't be me, I might as well be someone perfect – the good duke, the world's best huntsman, the ideal of pure courtly love; and after that, the great leader in adversity, and then the avenger, though I was never really comfortable with him." He laughed again, and went on: "The strange thing is, I've been the imaginary man so long, I don't know how to be anything else. And, as you say, Daurenja killed him, just because he was better at swordfighting. It's a hell of a thing, for your entire conception of good and evil to depend on the outcome of a fencing match. If I won, my ideas of right and wrong are vindicated. If I lose, I must've been wrong all along. And I lost." He closed his eyes again. "So what are you planning to do now?"

"Nothing," she said, as she sat down and picked up her embroidery. "Nothing of any importance. What I've been doing my whole life."

A courier rode to Civitas Vadanis with the news that the war was over. No, the City hadn't fallen; in fact, the Mezentines were now friends and trusted allies against the Aram Chantat, who'd turned out to be the real enemy all along. After a certain initial surprise, the news proved to be popular, because the war was over, and surely that was all that mattered. Besides, the duke was very wise, and had their best interests at heart. If that was what he'd decided, it had to be the right thing to do.

After he'd delivered the message, the courier gave another letter to the captain of the citadel guard. He wasn't happy about it. He tried to get out of it on the grounds that he didn't take orders from Engineer Vaatzes. But the courier told him that General Vaatzes was the commander-in-chief now, and they all had to respect the chain of command.

So the captain took six men and went down to the cells, where the

Mezentine prisoner Boioannes was being held. First, they gave him a letter. He thanked them and said he'd read it later. No, they said, read it now. So he read it; and when he'd done that, before he could say anything, they threw him down on the floor and the captain stabbed his eyes out with a saddler's needle. Then (carefully following the instructions in the letter; they were very specific) he used the needle to puncture Boioannes' eardrums. That was all he felt he could do, so he left the rest of the orders to his men; they cut off the prisoner's hands, being careful to cauterise the wounds with a hot iron afterwards, and then his tongue.

The rest of Vaatzes' letter said:

> *After you've done that, you will give him food and water every day for the rest of his life, which I trust will be very long. I won't be there to enforce this, but you'll have no choice, since he'll be incapable of doing anything for himself, and you won't be able to bring yourself to let a helpless man starve to death. You should bear in mind the fact that he was the sole cause of the war; he started it to further his political ambitions, and he is directly responsible for everything your people have suffered. Keep him safe and well. By the time you read this, I will have promised my wife to spare his life and see to it that he wants for nothing.*

There was an announcement: by joint declaration of the commander-in-chief and Duke Valens, with the concurrence and goodwill of Chairman Psellus, Miel Ducas had been appointed Duke of Eremia, with immediate effect.

While the announcement was being read out, Duke Miel married some woman nobody had ever heard of, in a perfunctory ceremony conducted by a clerk, promoted to the rank of chief registrar of Eremia for the occasion. The few people who witnessed the ceremony said afterwards that they found the whole business too bizarre to understand. The bride was neither young nor beautiful; in fact, her face was quite hideous because of a scar and a broken nose and jaw that hadn't been properly set. As for her rank and birth, she was nobody at all, the widow of some provincial squire. Afterwards there was no reception, no speeches, no scattering of coins or conspicuous donations of food to the poor (true, there weren't any poor to be found, unless you counted soldiers and camp followers, but it was the look of the thing), and the happy couple walked away unescorted, not even holding hands. It was unworthy of the Ducas, they said, and an insult to the Eremian people, who deserved a little pageantry and splendour to raise their morale after the misery of the war and the occupation.

The new duke's first official act was widely regarded as equally ill-omened. Instead of announcing measures to alleviate conditions for the refugees, or plans to rebuild Civitas Eremiae, or any of the things that were expected of him, Duke Miel chose to inaugurate his reign by granting a monopoly in perpetuity for the manufacture and sale of fine porcelain, along with a grant of land in the mountains somewhere, to some minor nobleman called Framain. No explanation was given, a further proof of arrogance. People with long memories seemed to recall rumours of some kind of liaison between the duke and Framain's daughter. Later it emerged that Framain had been General Daurenja's business partner, and this went some way towards reconciling popular opinion; Daurenja, already much admired by the Eremian people during his lifetime, had won a lasting place in their hearts by his heroic death (if only he'd survived, they said, we'd have taken the City and lived like princes on the spoils for the rest of our lives). Even so, as many influential figures pointed out, it was a most unhealthy precedent. None of the duke's predecessors had ever granted monopolies. Power had clearly gone to his head; hardly surprising, given his family history, and what had the Ducas ever done for the ordinary people?

"They're in there," Psellus said.

"Thank you," Ziani replied. He'd known, without having to be told.

Psellus hesitated. "I imagine you'd like me to go now."

"Yes."

"Of course. Will you see me again before you leave?"

Ziani shook his head. "I don't think so," he said. "I was planning to slip away as quietly as possible. I don't suppose it'll take them long to realise their commander-in-chief has gone absent without leave, and in the circumstances I'd be grateful for as much of a head start as I can get."

Psellus nodded, but he seemed reluctant to move. "What about money?" he said. "You'll need some for your journey, and—"

"Taken care of." Ziani cut him off short. "They can add embezzlement of public funds to the list of charges at my court martial. Now, if you'll excuse me."

Psellus took a step away, and saw Ziani put his hand to the latch again; he reached out and caught his wrist. "Are you sure this is a good idea?" he said. "You know what she did to you . . ."

Ziani took his fingers and prised them gently apart. "My daughter hasn't done anything to anybody," he said, "and I love her very much. And she loves her mother. That's a good enough reason on its own."

Psellus nodded. "That's an eminently reasonable justification," he said. "But it's only half the truth. Less than half, quite possibly."

"Goodbye, Chairman," Ziani said. "And thank you. You're a good man."

"No," Psellus said, and walked away.

Well, Ziani thought, and he pressed the thumbplate of the latch. Then he turned round quickly and called out, "Psellus."

Psellus turned slowly. "Yes?"

"Down there, in the main hall," Ziani said. "Those paintings on the wall. They're . . ." He struggled for the word. "Allegories," he said. "For the ideals of the Guilds, Specification and things like that."

"That's right," Psellus said.

Ziani nodded. "Then why have they all got white faces?"

Psellus smiled. "It's an old artistic convention," he said. "Many years ago, the walls of public buildings were decorated with carved marble reliefs. Fashions changed, or it was too expensive. But the painters made everybody white to look like marble carvings."

"I see." Ziani dipped his head in acknowledgement. "Thanks. I don't know why, but it seemed important. It'd have bothered me to death if I'd gone away without knowing."

Psellus walked away, and this time no voice called him back, which was just as well. He respected Ziani's intelligence, at least, and it wouldn't be long before it occurred to him to wonder why, if the faces and skins were white to represent marble, the clothes and the objects they held were in colour.

*

He pressed the latch and pushed the door open.

They were sitting by the window. Moritsa was holding a book, and she was leaning over her shoulder, pointing at the page. She was teaching her to read.

"Hello," Ziani said.

She looked up; and Moritsa dropped the book, screamed, looked at him, and ran across the room to hug him. He stayed still for a few seconds, letting her hold him, then gently moved her away. He walked past her to the window, picked the book up and gave it to her.

"Just go outside and look at your book for a minute, honey," he said. "I need to talk to Mummy."

Moritsa looked up at him, then went through the door. He heard the latch snick.

"Is she my daughter?" he asked.

"No," she replied.

"His?"

"You mean Boioannes? No. That was much later."

Ziani nodded. "It doesn't matter," he said.

"Falier," she said. "I'd been seeing him for a long time before Maris came along."

"I see." Her eyes were fixed on him. "Falier's dead, by the way," he said. "He was killed on the embankment."

"Oh," she said.

"I've taken care of Boioannes," he went on (and he watched how she reacted to the ambiguity; just a flicker of the eyes). "I had him sent away. He'll be safe there now, and well provided for." He waited, then smiled. "You were worried for him," he said. "You thought I'd have him killed."

"Yes."

He shook his head. "I'm not a savage," he said. "You don't know me very well if you think I'd do something like that."

"I'm sorry," she said.

"It's all right."

"It was all his fault," she said. "Boioannes. He—"

Ziani raised his hand. "I know," he said. "He fell in love with you, or got obsessed with you, and you didn't dare send him away because he was so powerful. Then it all got out of hand; he forced you to help him get rid of me, with the mechanical doll. That's right, isn't it?"

Her eyes were wide, round, wary, closed, like a fencer watching his opponent, trying to read his next move. "That's right," she said. "He made me do it all, and I was so scared. He said he'd hurt Moritsa if I didn't do as I was told."

He admired her for that, even though he was pretty sure it was a lie. It was strong enough to be the foundation for a reconciliation, and Boioannes could never deny it, not now. "He used you, you know," he said. "He didn't really love you; or if he did, it wasn't the real reason he wanted you. I found out the truth – well, Chairman Psellus . . ."

"Oh," she said. "Him."

He couldn't allow himself to smile, but that brief cold glare was priceless. "He investigated the whole thing," he said, "which is how I know you're telling the truth." (She hadn't expected *that*; but she hid it well.) "Boioannes wanted power; he was the chairman of Necessary Evil, but in peacetime it isn't the same. It's only when there's a war on that the chairman has the power to run the City all by himself. Boioannes wanted a war that'd last a long time. It nearly went wrong when the Eremians attacked us and we wiped out their army in a few minutes; he knew that'd happen, which is why he had to go to such extreme lengths. He wanted the sort of war where we'd have to attack them, rather than just defending ourselves; he figured that the only way he'd get that was if someone broke the most sacred rule and defected to another country with Guild secrets. I was the perfect choice. I knew enough to do what I eventually did, but I was unimportant enough not to be able to defend myself or fight back when he framed me. Falier must've been in on it too. They fixed it so I'd have an opportunity to escape – I nearly screwed it up – and after that, it all worked out just how he wanted it to, except he never imagined I'd find a way to bring the savages into the war. But you can't really fault him there. He had no reason to believe I'd be so resourceful. But of course, he was never really in love with you, not the way I was. That meant he couldn't hope to understand me. Anyway," Ziani went on, moving a little nearer, like a fencer closing the distance (coming close enough to hit and be hit; you can never attack without making yourself vulnerable), "let's forget all about him now. I've sorted him out and put everything right, so we can start all over again, just the three of us." He paused, then added, "If that's what you want."

"Of course," she said immediately. "That's all I've ever wanted."

He nodded gently, his movements slow and even, like those of a hunter stalking a deer or a wolf. "We'll have to go away, I'm afraid," he said. "Psellus has made it clear we can't stay in the City. But that's all right," he added, still watching her closely; he'd read all about it in *King Fashion* while he was staying at Orsea's court. Keep eye contact, and the quarry won't bolt. "We'll go across the sea to the Old Country. I've got money. I'll start a factory there, we'll be rich in no time, far better off than we could ever have been here. And it won't be like it was for me in Eremia and those places" (he let himself speak faster and more urgently), "where everybody could see I was a stranger just by looking at me. It'll all be different there, which means we can start again completely fresh." He paused to pull in a deep breath (the bombardier spanning the mainspring). "All I've ever wanted to do was look after the two of you, make it so you can have a better life, the sort you deserve. It was all my fault really, after all. I was working so hard, we never saw each other, never talked, never made love. No wonder you started seeing Falier, and Boioannes; you must've thought I didn't love you any more."

As if he'd made a mistake and left his guard open. "You were never there. I was so lonely."

"Of course," he said. "So really, I've only got myself to blame. I was trying to do the right thing, but it made everything go wrong. You'd be surprised how often it works out like that. If only I hadn't been so stupid, I'd have seen I was letting you down, losing you. But I didn't, and now it's taken so much pain and trouble to get back to you, and I'll never make that mistake again, I promise you. Just so long . . ." He felt the mechanism drop into place. "Just so long as we love each other. You do still love me, don't you?"

She looked at him, and her eyes were as cold as stone; and he thought of the carvings that were really paint, and the lies; and he told himself, a lie will be good enough, because I love her, because I have no choice.

Author's Note

Readers may find the medical content of chapter eleven a trifle far-fetched. Understandably. But King Henry V suffered the same injury at the battle of Shrewsbury, was cured by more or less the same treatment, and made a full recovery.

KJP

About the Author

Having worked in the law, journalism and numismatics, **K.J. Parker** now writes and makes things out of wood and metal. Parker is married to a solicitor and lives in southern England. For more information visit www.kjparker.com

Find out more about K.J. Parker and other Orbit authors by registering for the free monthly newsletter at www.orbitbooks.net